Praise for the Novels of Peter S. Beagle . . .

The Last Unicorn

"The book is rich, not only in comic bits but also in passages of uncommon beauty. Beagle is a true magician with words, a master of prose, and a deft practitioner in verse."
—*The Saturday Review*

"Almost as if it were the last fairy tale, come out of lonely hiding in the forests of childhood, *The Last Unicorn* is as full of enchantment as any of the favorite tales readers may choose to recall."
—*St. Louis Post-Dispatch*

"[Peter S. Beagle] is an artist writing about matters of consequence. . . . His is the very special magic of the poet and storyteller whose only desire is to bring forth beauty and enjoyment for his readers. . . . Peter Beagle is a writer of the first order. His charm, wit and stylistic brilliance have gone into a work to which I will return often and with great pleasure."
—*Chicago News*

continued on next page . . .

The Innkeeper's Song

"An unaffected eloquence that we recognize as the voice of the natural storyteller. . . . In [Peter S. Beagle's] capable hands, even the most timeworn material shines again."
—*New York Times*

"Its true strength lies in Beagle's treatment of his characters. They are eminently authentic, worlds away from the cookie-cutter heroes and heroines of so many lesser fantasies. *The Innkeeper's Song* is a fine and complex novel by a popular author working at the top of his form."
—*San Francisco Chronicle*

"Peter Beagle's famous lyricism from the days of *The Last Unicorn* . . . has matured like the finest of wines, growing drier, subtler, more complex with time."
—*Locus*

Tamsin

Peter S. Beagle

A ROC BOOK

ROC
Published by New American Library, a division of
Penguin Putnam Inc., 375 Hudson Street,
New York, New York 10014, U.S.A.
Penguin Books Ltd, 27 Wrights Lane,
London W8 5TZ, England
Penguin Books Australia Ltd, Ringwood,
Victoria, Australia
Penguin Books Canada Ltd, 10 Alcorn Avenue,
Toronto, Ontario, Canada M4V 3B2
Penguin Books (N.Z.) Ltd, 182–190 Wairau Road,
Auckland 10, New Zealand

Penguin Books Ltd, Registered Offices:
Harmondsworth, Middlesex, England

First published by Roc, an imprint of New American Library,
a division of Penguin Putnam Inc.

First Printing, October 1999
10 9 8 7 6 5 4 3 2

RoC REGISTERED TRADEMARK—MARCA REGISTRADA

LIBRARY OF CONGRESS CATALOGING-IN-PUBLICATION DATA:

Beagle, Peter S.
    Tamsin / Peter S. Beagle.
        p.   cm.
    ISBN 0-451-45763-3 (alk. paper)
    I. Title.
    PS3552.E13T36   1999
    813'.54—dc21   99-30695
                                                            CIP

Printed in the United States of America

BOOKS ARE AVAILABLE AT QUANTITY DISCOUNTS WHEN USED TO PROMOTE PRODUCTS OR SERVICES. FOR
INFORMATION PLEASE WRITE TO PREMIUM MARKETING DIVISION, PENGUIN PUTNAM INC., 375 HUDSON
STREET, NEW YORK, NEW YORK 10014.

*To the memory of Simon Beagle,
my father.
I can still hear you singing, Pop,
quietly, to yourself,
shaving.*

One

When I was really young, if there was one thing I wanted in the world, it was to be invisible. I used to sit in class and daydream about it, the way the other kids were daydreaming about being a movie star, being a big basketball player. The good part was, if I *was* invisible, Mister Cat—my cat—Mister Cat would always be able to see me, because invisible doesn't mean anything to a cat. As I know better than anyone, but that comes later.

I used to let Sally see me, too—Sally's my mother—in the daydream. Not *all* the time, not when I was mad at her, but mostly, because she'd have worried. But I really liked it best when it was just me and Mister Cat drifting along, just going wherever we felt like going, and nobody able to tell if my butt was too fat or if my skin had turned to molten lava that morning. And if I got my period in P.E., which I always used to, or if I said something dumb in class, nobody'd even notice. I used to sit there and imagine how great it would be, not ever to be noticed.

It's different now. I'm different. I'm not that furious little girl daydreaming in class anymore. I don't live on West Eighty-third Street, just off Columbus, in New York City—I live at Stourhead Farm in Dorset, England, with my mother and my stepfather, and I'm going to be nineteen in a couple of months. That's how old my friend Tamsin was when she died, three hundred and thirteen years ago.

And I'm writing this book, or whatever it turns out to be, about what happened to all of us—Tamsin Willoughby and Sally and me, and Evan and the boys, too, and the cats.

It happened six years ago, when Sally and I first got here, but it seems a lot longer, because in a way it happened to someone else. I don't really speak that person's language anymore, and when I think about her, she embarrasses me sometimes, but I don't want to forget her, I don't ever want to pretend she never existed. So before I start forgetting, I have to get down exactly who she was, and exactly how she felt about everything. She was me a lot longer than I've been me so far.

We have the same name, Jennifer Gluckstein, but she hated that, too, and I don't mind it so much. Not the Gluckstein—what she hated was the damn stupid, boring Jennifer. My father named me. He used to say that when he was a boy, nobody was called Jennifer except in a few books, and Jennifer Jones. He'd say, "But *I* always thought it was a really beautiful name, and it actually means Guenevere, like in King Arthur, and why should you care if everybody in the world today is named Jennifer, when they aren't named Courtney or Ashleigh or Brittany?" *His* name is Nathan Gluckstein, but his stage name is Norris Groves, and everyone calls him that except Sally and me and his mother, my Grandma Paula. He's an opera singer, a baritone. Not great, I always knew that, but pretty good—semifamous if you know baritones, which most people don't. He's always off working somewhere, and he's on a couple of albums, and he gives recitals, too. He's sung at Carnegie a couple of times. With other people, but still.

Meena says—Meena's my best friend here in England—Meena says that if I'm really going to write a book, then I have to start at the beginning, go straight through to the end, and not ramble all over everywhere, the way I usually do. But where does anything begin? How far back do you have to go? For all I know, maybe everything starts with me rescuing Mister Cat, when I was eight and he was just a kitten, from a bunch of boys who were going to throw him off the roof of our building to see if he'd land on his feet. Maybe it really starts with Sally and Norris getting married, or meeting each other, or getting *born*. Or maybe I ought to go back three hundred years ago, back to Tamsin and Edric Davies . . . and *him*.

Well, it's my book, so let's say it all starts on the April afternoon when I came home from Gaynor Junior High and found Sally in the kitchen, which was strange right away, because it was a Tuesday. Sally's a vocal coach and piano teacher—back in New York she worked with people who wanted to sing opera. A couple of her voice students were in the chorus at the Met, and I think there was one doing small parts with City Opera. She's never had anyone famous, so she always had to teach piano, too, which she didn't like nearly as much. The singers mostly lived downtown, and she went to their homes on different days, but all the piano people came to our place, and they always came on Thursday, the whole gang, one after another; she scheduled it like that on purpose, to get it over with. But *Tuesdays* Sally never got home until six at the earliest, so it was a little weird seeing her sitting at the kitchen table with her shoes off and one foot up on the step stool. She was eating a carrot, and she looked about eleven years old.

We don't look anything alike, by the way. She's tall, and she's got this absolutely devastating combination of dark hair and blue eyes, and I don't know if she's actually *beautiful,* but she's *graceful,* which I will never be in my life, that's just something I know. In the last couple of years my skin's gotten some better—because of the English climate, Sally says—and Meena's taught me stuff to do with my hair, and I'm actually developing something that's practically a shape. So there's hope for me yet, but that's not like being graceful. It doesn't bother me. I can live with it.

"They fired you," I said. "All of them, all at once. A detriment to their careers. We're going to be selling T-shirts in Columbus Circle."

Sally gave me that sideways look she never gave anyone else. She said, "Jenny. Have you been—you know—smoking that stuff?" She never would call boom or any drugs by their right names, it was always *that stuff,* and it used to drive me mad. I said, "No, I haven't," which happened to be true that afternoon. I said, "I was making a *joke,* for God's sake. I don't have to be booted to make jokes. Give me a break, all right?"

On any other day, we'd probably have gotten into a whole big fight over it, a dumb thing like that, and wound up with both of us hiding out in our rooms, too pissed and upset to eat dinner. We used to have a joke about the Gluckstein Diet—stay on it for two months and lose twenty pounds and your family. But this time Sally just put her head on one side and smiled at me, and then suddenly her eyes got huge and filled up, and she said, "Jenny, Jenny, Evan's asked me to marry him."

Well, it wasn't as if I hadn't been practicing for it. I can still close my eyes and see myself, lying in bed every night that whole year, holding Mister Cat and visualizing how she'd be when she told me, and how she'd expect *me* to be. Sometimes I'd see myself being so *sweet* and so happy for her, I'd never have gotten through it without puking; other times I thought I'd probably cry a little, and hug her, and ask if I could still call Norris "Daddy," which I haven't called him since I was three. And on the bad nights I'd plan to say something like, well, that's cool, only it doesn't matter to me one way or the other, because I'm off to Los Angeles to be a homeless person. Or a movie director, or a really famous call girl. I varied that one a lot.

But when it actually happened, I just looked at her and said, "Oh." I didn't even *say* it, exactly, it just came out—it wasn't a word, it wasn't anything, but it was what came out, after all that imagining. "Oh." The story of my life.

Sally was actually shaking. I could tell, because the table had one leg shorter than the others, and it was sort of buzzing against the floor as she sat there. She said, "I told him I'd have to check it out with you." I could barely hear her.

"It's okay," I said. "It's fine." Sally got up and came around the table and she hugged me, and now I couldn't tell which one of us was trembling. She whispered into my hair, "Jenny, he's a good, good man—he *is*, baby, you'd know it if you ever just *talked* to him for five minutes. He's kind, and he's funny, and I feel like *myself* when I'm with him. I've never felt that way with anybody, never, I never have." Then she grinned at me, looking like a little kid again, and said, "Well, present company excepted, natch." Which was a nice thing to say, but silly, too, because she knew better. We got on well enough most days, but not the way she was talking about. I only felt really like myself with Mister Cat, back then. Back before Tamsin.

Anyway, Sally kept hugging me and going on about Evan, and I just kept standing there, waiting to feel something besides numb. My breath was sort of hardening in my chest, like the asthma attacks I used to get when I was little. But I wasn't wheezing or anything—it was more like things inside me pushing up all close together, huddling together. When I did finally manage to speak, it sounded like somebody else, somebody far away, nobody I knew. I said, "Are you going to have to go to England? With him?"

The way Sally looked at me was like that moment in a cartoon where the fox or the coyote runs straight off the cliff and doesn't know it right away, but just keeps on running in the air. She said slowly, like a question, "Well, honey, sure, of course we are," and then her eyes got all wet again, so now of course *she* couldn't talk for a bit. I gave her my wad of Kleenex, because to this day she absolutely *never* has one—I don't know how she manages. She blew her nose and grabbed hold of my shoulders and shook me a little. "Baby," she said. "Baby, did you think I was just going to walk off and leave you? Don't you know I wouldn't go anywhere without you, not for Evan McHugh, not for anybody? Don't you know that?" Her voice sounded weird, too, like a cartoon voice.

"Why can't he just move *here?*" I mumbled it, the way I still do when I can't not say something, but I don't really want people to hear me, especially the one I'm saying it to. Meena says I've practically quit doing that, but I know I haven't.

"Honey, that's where his work is," Sally said. God, I remember it used to drive me wild that she'd never talk about Evan's *job*, it always had to be his *work*. "I can do what I do anywhere, but Evan's got to be in England, in London. Besides, the boys are there, Tony and Julian, they're in *school—*"

"Well, I'm in school, too," I said. "In case you didn't notice." Mister Cat jumped down from the top of the refrigerator and stalked across the table to me with his legs all stiff, doing his Frankenstein-cat number. I hadn't seen him on the refrigerator, but Mister Cat's always *there* or *gone*, he's never anywhere in between. That's how I wanted to be, that's what I mean about being invisible. Most black cats are really a kind of red-brown underneath, if you see them in the right light, but Mister Cat's black right through, even though he's half-Siamese. "Black to the bone," my friend Marta Velez used to say. He stood up and put his paws around my neck, and I could feel him purring without a sound, the way he always does. He smelled like warm toast—dark, dark toast, when you get it out just right, just before it burns.

"You could take him with you," Sally said, really quickly, as though I didn't know it. "He'd have to wait out quarantine, but that's just a month, I think." She looked at me sideways again. She said, "You know, I had this crazy idea you might actually be glad to start a whole different life somewhere else—another country, new school, new people, new friends, new ways of doing things. I mean, let's face it, it's not as though you've been having such a great time this last year or two—"

And I just lost it right there, I have to write it exactly like that, I just went up in smoke. I didn't know it was going to happen until I heard that faraway voice screaming at her, "Yeah, well, maybe I don't have the greatest life in the world right now, but I'm *used* to it, you ever think about that? And I know I've only got a couple of friends, and they're even weirder than I am, but I *know* them, and I don't *want* to start everything all over in some shitty, snobby place where it rains all the damn time and they make you wear uniforms." Sally was trying to interrupt, and Mister Cat was looking at me and flicking his tail, the way he still does when I'm not being cool like him. I just kept going, "It's fine, it's okay, I'll move in with Marta, or Norris or somebody, I'll call Norris right now." And I grabbed up the phone, and the receiver slipped right out of my hands, they were so shaky and sweaty. It just made me crazier. I told her, "Don't worry about me. You go to England, that's fine, have a nice life. Say hello to the *boys*, okay?"

And I banged the phone back down, and then I *did* head for my room, and the door was already slamming while she was still yelling something about finally getting me away from my damn druggy friends. Mister Cat ran in right after me—someday he's going to get *nailed*, I keep telling him—and jumped up on the bed, and we just lay there for I don't know how long, hours. The Gluckstein Diet.

I guess I must have cried a little bit, but not very much. I'm really not a big crier. Mainly I lay there with Mister Cat on my chest and started reviewing my options. That's something Norris used to say all the time—how when you're in a bad place and confused and not sure which way to turn, the best thing is to get yourself quiet and think really coldly about your options, your choices, even if they're all shitty, until you can figure out which one's the *least* shitty of the bunch. Of course, when Norris talks about options, he mostly means a better contract, or a bigger dressing room, or a first-class ticket instead of flying business class. Whoever thought artists were a lot of dreamy twits with no clue about money never met my father.

My options narrowed down in a hurry. Marta would have been great, but I knew she didn't even have enough room for herself, with five other kids in the family. Unlike Sally, who's an only child, and Norris, who's got the one sister way up in Riverdale, Aunt Marcella. *She's* got a daughter, too, my cousin Barbara, and we were always supposed to be lifelong buddies, but the first time we met, when we were maybe two years old, we tried to beat each other to death with our toy fire engines, and it's been downhill from there. I *still* can't believe we're cousins. Somebody's lying.

So in about a minute and a half it was Norris or nobody. Something I should put in here is that I like my father. Sally always says, "That's because you weren't married to him," but what's funny is that I know Norris a lot better than she ever did. As much time as she's spent with show people, she's never understood, they're *real*, they're just not real all the *time*. Norris really likes having a daughter, he likes telling people about me, or calling me up—the way he still does now, when he's singing in London—and saying, "Hey, kid, it's your old man, you want to come down to the wicked city and hang out?" Only he'd be a lot happier if I were electric or electronic, something with a cord he could plug in or a remote he could turn on and off. It's just Norris, that's how he is with everybody. Maybe he'd have been different with me if we lived together, I don't know. He left when I was eight.

I must have fallen asleep for a while, because suddenly it was dark and Mister Cat's girlfriend, the Siamese Hussy, had started calling from across the street. Mister Cat yawned and stretched and was over at the window, giving me that look: *It's my job, what can I tell you?* I opened the window and he vanished, nothing left but his warm-toast smell on my blouse. There were a couple of dogs barking, but it didn't worry me. Mister Cat never has to bother about dogs, not in New York, not in Dorset. It's the way he looks at them, it's magic. If I knew how to look at people like that, I'd be fine.

I was thinking Sally might come in—she does sometimes after we've had a fight. But she was on the phone in her bedroom. I couldn't make out any words, but I knew she'd be talking to Evan half the night, same as practically every night, buzzing and giggling and cooing just like all the damn Tiffanys and Courtneys in the halls, in all the stairwells, with their Jasons and their Joshuas and their Seans. So I flopped back in bed, and started thinking hard about what I'd say to Norris tomorrow, to keep my mind off what Sally and Evan were probably saying about me right now. And I suddenly thought how Norris used to sing me a bedtime song, a long, long time ago. The way we did, he'd sing one line and I'd have to sing the same line right after him, and each time faster, until the two of us were just cracking up, falling all over each other, yelling this gibberish, until Sally'd have to come in to see what was going on. I was still trying to remember how the song actually went when I fell asleep.

Two

Mister Cat wasn't back when I got up. Sally was already up and dressed and running, because Wednesdays she had to be at the Brooklyn Academy of Music by eight to teach a class in accompaniment, and after that she had four voice students and a part-time job playing rehearsal piano for some friend's dance company. We slid around each other in the kitchen, nobody saying much, until Sally asked me if I wanted to meet her and Evan for a late dinner downtown. I said thanks, but I thought I'd go over to see Norris after school, and we'd probably be eating out ourselves. I don't *think* I was nasty about it, just casual.

Sally was casual, too. She said, "Maybe you ought to call him tomorrow. He just got in from Chicago last night, so he's likely to be pretty beat today." She and Norris don't see each other much, but they talk on the phone a lot, partly because of me, partly because in the music world everybody knows everybody anyway, and everybody's going to have to work with everybody sooner or later. They get along all right.

"I just have some stuff I want to ask him," I said. "Like could I keep on going to the same school if I was living with him? Just stuff." Okay, I was being deliberately nasty, I know, I can't lie in my own book. And yes, I still do things like that, only not so much now, not since Tamsin. I honestly don't think I do it so much anymore.

Sally turned and faced me. She drew in her breath to say something, and then she caught it and said something really else, you could tell. She said, "If you change your mind about dinner, we'll be at the Cuban place on Houston, Casa Pepe. Probably around eight-thirty."

"Well, we might float by," I said. "You never know." Sally just nodded, and reminded me to lock up, which she *always* did and I *always* did, and then she took off. I hung around as long as I could, hoping Mister Cat would show up before I had to catch the bus, but he didn't. So I finally had to close the window, which I always hated, because then he'd have to be out all day. Mister Cat didn't mind. Mister Cat's too cool to mind.

I wanted to call Norris early, because you have to give him time to get used to new things, like seeing me when it wasn't his idea. And I wanted to line up dinner, because if there's one thing my dad can do it's eat out. So during homeroom break, I ran across the street to a laundromat and got him on their pay phone. He said, "Jennifer, how nice," in that deep, slow, just-waking-up voice that probably drives women crazy. He is the only person in the world who calls me Jennifer—never once Jenny, even when I wouldn't answer to Jennifer, not for months. Norris is incredible at getting people to be the way he wants, wearing them down just by being the way he is. It works with everybody except Sally, as far as I know.

"I was hoping I could come over after school," I said. I still hate the way I get when I talk to my father. As well as I know him, as much as I keep thinking I've changed, and if he called right this minute, while I'm writing, I'd sound like a *fan*, for God's sake— even my *voice* would get sweaty. Norris must have been expecting me, though, because he hardly hesitated at all before he said, "Absolutely. I've been wild for you to see the new place. There's even a guest room for weird daughters, if you know any."

"I'll check around," I said. "See you about four. Somebody wants the phone, I have to go." There wasn't anybody waiting, but I didn't want Norris to pick up my anxiety vibes. He's really, really quick about that—he knows when you want something, almost before you know. But I remember I felt hopeful all the same, because of the guest room. Because of him mentioning the guest room.

At lunch I sat with Jake Walkowitz and Marta, like always, since third grade. You couldn't miss our table—Jake's tall and freckled and white as a boiled egg, and unless he's changed a whole lot in six years he probably still looks like he goes maybe eighty-five pounds. Marta's tiny, and she's very dark, and she's got something genetic with one shoulder, or maybe it's her back, I never was sure, so she walks just a little lopsided. Then you add in me, looking like a fire hydrant with acne, and you figure out why the three of us always ate lunch together. But we liked each other. Not that it matters much when you're stuck with each other like that, but we did.

I don't make friends easily. I never did, and I don't now, but it doesn't matter anywhere near the way it mattered in junior high school. New York City or Dorset, when you're thirteen, you're not even yourself, you're a reflection of your friends, there's nothing *to* you but your friends. That's one of the things most people forget—what it was like being *out* there every day, thirteen. I guess you have to, the same way women forget how much it hurts to have a baby. I used to swear I'd never forget thirteen, but you do. You have to.

Anyway, when I told about Sally and Evan, Jake shook his head so his huge mop of curly red hair flew around everywhere. He said, "Oh boy, oh boy, Evan McDork." I felt a little guilty when he said it, because I knew that far back that Evan wasn't any kind of a dork, even if he *was* wrecking my entire life. But that's what I called him then, so that's what Jake and Marta called him, too. Jake said, "So your mom'll be Mrs. McDork, and you'll have to be Jenny McDork. We won't even recognize the name when you write to us."

"And you'll have two instant brothers," Marta put in. "Lucky you." She and Jake kept looking two tables down, where one of *her* brothers—I think it was Paco—was glaring at Jake as though he was about to start ripping Marta's clothes off. Marta's got four older brothers, and every time you turned your head, in school or anywhere, there'd be some sabertooth Velez keeping a mean eye on her. I don't know how she stood it. They never used to be like that, not until we started junior high.

"I'm not changing my name, I'll tell you *that* much," I said. "And I'm not going to England either." I told them how I was going to see Norris right after school and get him to let me move in with him. Jake sneaked another look at Paco and scooted right away from Marta until he was hanging on to the bench with about half his skinny butt. He asked me, "Suppose it doesn't work out with your father? I mean, let's just consider the possibility."

"Ward of the court," Marta said right away. "My cousin Vicky did that. Mother beating on her, her dad was hitting on her, the judge put her in a foster home, and then later she got a place by herself. That's *it*, I love it!" Jake was already shaking his head, but Marta slapped her hand on the table and raised her voice, looking over at her brother. "That's *it*, Jenny! You get your own place, and I'll come and live with you, and we don't tell my damn family where we are."

"My mom doesn't beat on me," I said. "She wouldn't know how." That made me feel funny, I remember, thinking about Sally and how she wouldn't know how to hit anybody. I said, "Anyway, I mostly don't mind living with her. I just don't want to live with her in England, that's all."

Jake said, "You want to avoid stepfathers. Just on principle." He was on his second then, and his mother was already lining up Number Three. I said, "Count on it."

"Ward of the court," Marta said again. "I'm telling you, Jenny."

We bussed our trays, and then we went off to our special place, where they keep the trash cans, because Jake had one small joint, about the size of a bobby pin. Marta got giggly, but it didn't do much for Jake or me. Jake said it was a question of body mass.

After lunch, Marta and I had Introduction to Drama together. Jake got off early because he and his parents went to family counseling on Wednesdays. Usually I liked Introduction to Drama, but lately I'd been having a problem with the teacher, Mr. Hammell. Anyway, I *thought* it was a problem, but I wasn't sure then, and I guess I'm still not, all these years later. Mr. Hammell had beautiful one-piece walnut hair, and he had sort of ravines in his cheeks, and half the girls at Gaynor were writing stuff they'd like to do to him on the walls of the john. Some of it was funny, and some of it made me feel strange, not knowing which way to look when Marta showed me. But some of it was really funny.

Anyway, for the last month or so Mr. Hammell had been maybe not exactly coming on to me. Not that I'd have known if he was, because nobody in the *world* had ever actually come on to me, except Mark Rinzler one time, at a Christmas party. At first it was okay, fun even, and then it just turned gross—no, that's not the word, it turned stupid and scary, and I made Mark quit, and he never spoke to me again. But Mr. Hammell used to stand right beside me while he was talking, and he'd let his long fingers trail over my desk, and now and then he'd look at me, as though I was the only one in the class who could ever *possibly* understand what he was saying. Which was *not* true. And after class, or if we met in the hall, he'd stop me and ask what I thought about Antigone or poor dumb Desdemona, whichever, while I stood there getting redder and redder and sweatier and sweatier. He even gave me his home phone number, in case I ever had any questions about the homework assignment. I didn't throw it away for a couple of days.

Meena keeps saying I should have complained about sexual harassment. Only Meena's pretty, and there's a lot of stuff pretty people don't know. Pretty people like Stacy Altieri and Vanessa Whitfield and Morgan Baskin, they'd come drifting up to me at my locker and they'd ask, "So. What's it like with him?" And they'd *look* at me, the way people do when they're waiting for some kind of right answer from you, some kind of password. And all I had to do was say it, the word, and there I'd be, I'd be with them. But I didn't *know* any password, I never do. So they'd go on looking at me for a while, and then they'd drift off again, back to their cool boyfriends, back to *pretty*. And I'm standing there, still pink sweaty me, and I'm going to know what's sexual harassment and what isn't? Right, Meena.

Anyway. We had Introduction to Drama, and it went okay, except for Stacy Altieri and Kevin Bell making their usual dumb jokes about "TB or not TB." Mr. Hammell stood right by my desk, the same as always, and I could smell his aftershave, like fresh snow, and see that he had a couple of broken black fingernails on one hand, as though he'd caught them in a door or something. Funny to remember that, when I can't remember my own damn name half the time.

After class, Mr. Hammell was sort of beckoning to me, trying to catch my eye, but I pretended I didn't see him and just ducked out of there in time to grab a quick hit with Marta in the girls' john before I caught the bus to go see Norris. Probably I shouldn't have done that, because all it did was make me jittery, instead of easy and relaxed, the way I wanted to be. I put my head back and breathed huge deep breaths, in and out, and tried really hard to feel that I already lived at Norris's apartment and was just going home, like always. It helped a little.

He'd moved into a new place just last month, way over east, right on the corner of Third Avenue. An old building, but cleaned up, with a new awning and the number written out in letters, and a doorman wearing a uniform like one of Sally's tenors in an opera. When I told him I was here to see my father, Mr. Norris Groves, he looked at me for the longest time, just *knowing* I was actually some sort of damp, squirrelly groupie with an autograph book in one coat pocket and a gun in the other. Then he went to the switchboard and I guess he called Norris in the apartment, because I heard him talking, and then he came back looking like he'd swallowed his cab whistle. But he told me which floor Norris lived on, and which way to turn when I got off the elevator. And he watched me all the way *to* the elevator, in case I stole the skinny little carpet or something. I remember, I thought, *Boy, when I come to live here, I'm going to do something evil to you every day. It'll be my hobby.*

Meena, when you read this, I already told you I'm no good at *all* at describing where people live, and telling what color the bedroom was painted and how many bathrooms they had, and what they had hanging on the walls. I hated doing it in Creative Writing class, and there is no way I'm about to do it in my own book. So the only thing I'm going to say about Norris's apartment is that it was old, but *sunny* old, not smelly old, with a lot of big windows with curly iron grates on the outside. Not much furniture, no paintings or anything, just some framed opera posters and some pictures of Norris with famous people. I think they were famous, anyway. They were all in costume.

Norris gave me a huge hug when I came in. That's his specialty, a hug that makes you feel all wrapped up and totally safe—I never knew anybody else who could do it just like that. He held me away from him and looked at me, and grinned, and then he hugged me again and said, "Look what *I* got!" like a little kid. And he stepped back, and I saw the piano.

Okay. I may not know anything about *decor*, but I can't *help* knowing about pianos. This one was a baby grand—I didn't see a manufacturer's name anywhere. It was a dark red-brown, the color I said most black cats really are, and it looked as though it was full of sunlight, just breathing and rippling with it. I never in my life saw a piano like that one.

Norris stood beside me, grinning all over himself. He's not really handsome, not like Mr. Hammell, but he's bigger, and he's got thick, curly gray hair and big features that really stand out—nose, chin, eyes, forehead—which is great if you're going to be onstage in makeup a lot. I don't look anything like *him* either. He said, "Go ahead, kick the tires. Take it for a test run."

One thing about Sally, she never made me take any kind of piano or voice lessons, even though that's what she teaches all day. (I can't sing a note, by the way: Two parents who do it professionally, and it's all I can manage to stay on pitch. They could probably take the hospital for *millions*.) But I teach myself stuff sometimes, just for fun, banging it out for myself, stuff like "Mack the Knife" and "Piano Man," and "When I'm Sixty-four." I was nervous about playing for Norris, so I made a big thing out of it, sitting down and rubbing my hands and cracking my knuckles, until Norris said, "Enough already, kid, go," and I finally went into "The Entertainer."

I had to stop. I got maybe ten or twelve bars into the piece, and I just had to quit. The sound was so beautiful I was just about to get sick, or have hysterics, or I don't know, wet myself—*something* was going to happen, anyway, that's for sure. Some people get that way when they see flowers or sunsets, or read poems, whatever. I don't, I never have, but that damn piano. I stopped playing, and I looked up at Norris, and I couldn't talk. He laid his arm around my shoulders. He said, "Yeah, me, too. I *know* I don't deserve it, I'm embarrassed every time I use it just to sing scales, but I keep telling myself it's a present for what I'm *going* to do. You have to believe that stuff, Jennifer, in our business."

Norris always talks to me as though I were a real musician, the way he is, and the way Sally is. Sometimes I like it, sometimes I really don't, because it's not true and he knows it. He wanted me to play some more, but I got up from the piano and went over to him. I said, "Sally's getting married."

"I know," Norris said. "Nice guy, too, Evan what's-his-name. You like him all right, don't you?"

I shrugged and nodded, that mumbly nod I do. Norris was watching me really closely. "She says you're a bit antsy about the move to London."

Sometimes I really wish I had the kind of parents who got divorced and never ever spoke to each other again to the day they died. "I'm not *antsy* about it," I said. "I'm just not going."

Norris laughed. "What are you talking about? Babe, listen, you'll love London. I'm crazy about it, I'd sing there for nothing—hell, I practically do. Jennifer, you will adore England, you'll have the time of your life. I promise you." He was holding my shoulders, smiling down at me with those confident eyes that really do flash all the way to the balcony when he's being Rigoletto or Iago. Show people feel things, like I said—they just can't help knowing a good scene when they see one. Like Mister Cat, it's their job.

If I was ever going to do it, now was it. I took a deep breath, and I said, "I was wondering if I could maybe stay with you." Norris didn't drop his teeth, or anything like that. He stroked my hair and looked straight into my eyes, and sort of chanted, "Jennifer-JenniferJenniferJennifer." It's an old joke—he used to tell me that that was my real name, that he only called me Jennifer for short. That was long ago, when I was little, when the name hadn't yet started to bug me so much.

"I could take care of things," I said. "I could do the shopping, the laundry, keep things clean, forward your mail. Water the plants." I don't know why I threw *that* in, because he never *has* any plants. "You wouldn't have to pay a housekeeper. Or a secretary." It doesn't look right on the page, because it all came out in one frantic *whoosh*, but that's about what I said.

Norris said, "Jennifer. Honey. Come and sit down." And I knew it was all out the window right there. He pulled me over to the sofa and sat next to me, never taking his eyes from mine. He said, "Honey, it wouldn't work. We couldn't do that to Sally—you know she'd be devastated, and so would I, and so would you. Believe me."

"I'd get over it," I said. "So would Sally. New husband, new country, two new kids—she wouldn't have *time* to be devastated about *anybody*. Norris, I could go visit her once in a while, that'd be fine, I'd love it. But I can't live there, Norris, I just can't, why can't I stay with you in the guest room?" I'm writing it all down, just the way it was, as fast as I can, so maybe I won't be too ashamed. But I might just cut it out later on.

Norris ran a hand through his own hair and then squeezed his hands together. He said, "Jennifer, I don't know how to say this. I'm not in a very good place right now for having anybody living with me. It's not just you, it's anybody. I'm coming off a bad relationship—you remember Mandy?—and I guess I need some privacy, time to be by myself, time to think through a lot of stuff—"

I interrupted him. "I'd be in school most of the time, you wouldn't even know I was *there*." I wasn't going to beg anymore, I wasn't going to say another word, but it came out anyway. Norris didn't hear me. He went right on. "Besides, going to England would be the best thing in the world for you. Trust me on this one, kid. I know how incredibly dumb this sounds, but someday you really will thank me. Really."

Well, that was pretty much it, there's no point in writing anything else about it. Norris said it was my turn to choose a restaurant, so just out of spite I picked a Russian place, way down in the

Village and so fancy it looked like a crack house from outside. Before we went, Norris asked me, very shy and sweet, if I'd mind if somebody joined us for dinner, because if I *would* mind, that'd be fine. Her name was Suzanne, and I think she did something on the public radio. Actually, she was nice. My father's women mostly are. She paid more attention to me during dinner than she did to Norris, asking all kinds of questions about school and my friends, and what kind of music I liked, and she pretty much listened to the answers. Afterward they took me home in a cab. Both of them got out and hugged me good-bye, and Norris told me he'd give me all kinds of addresses in London, and they both waved back to me as the cab drove away.

Three

We were supposed to leave in August. Sally wanted me to finish the school year at Gaynor, and meanwhile she had so much stuff to do before we'd be ready to go, I hardly ever *saw* her anymore. Besides the whole business of plane tickets and passports and clothes, and what to take and what to store, and what to do about the apartment, she had to keep on with her teaching and at the same time be looking around for somebody to take over for her. *That* was a thing, by the way. I don't know how the singers were, but every one of the piano students went into major shock when she told them she was getting married and leaving the country. I'd never actually thought much about whether my mother was a good teacher or not—she was just Sally, it was what she did. Now, watching these grown people coming absolutely unglued at the idea of not being able to study with her anymore, as though she was the only piano teacher in the whole world, it suddenly made me look at her like someone else, a stranger. Practically *everything* was making me look at her that way, anyway, those days.

Like watching her with Evan. I haven't put anything in about Evan so far, and I know I should have, I just kept feeling a little strange about it, even now. He's about Sally's age—which was middle forties then—and he's not big, and he's not good looking. He's not *bad looking*; it's just that you wouldn't look at him twice on the street. A longish face, sort of diamond shaped, lumpy where the jaws hinge. He's got hazelish-gray eyes that go down at the outside corners, and hair more or less the same rainy color, pretty thick except in the front, and it's always a mess. Nice wide mouth, *ugly* nose. A horse broke his nose when he was a kid, thrashing its head around or something, and it never got set right. And later it got broken again, but I can't remember how. Small ears, more like a woman's ears than a man's. And he's thin—not *skinny*, but definitely bony. Sally couldn't have picked anybody who looked less like Norris.

He came home with her a couple of days after she told me, and I grabbed an apple and three raisin cookies and headed for my room, the way I was used to doing when he was there. But this time he said, "Don't vanish just yet, Jenny. I'd like to talk to you for half a minute."

I already knew he didn't talk like any English people I'd ever seen on TV. Like he said, "Half a minute," not " 'Arf a mo', ducks"—six years, and I haven't heard *anybody* say anything like that—but he didn't exactly talk *Masterpiece Theatre* English either. It's a husky voice, deeper than you'd expect to look at him, and at least his mouth moves when he talks. I mostly understand English women now, but the men can drive you crazy.

I didn't say anything. I just turned and waited. Evan said, "Jenny, this must all be crazy and frightening for you, I'm sorry. You've not even had a chance to get used to the idea of your mother and me getting married, and right on top of it you're having to deal with packing up your whole life and going to a strange place where nothing's familiar. I'm truly sorry."

Sally came to stand beside him, and Evan put his arm around her. That made me feel funny—not so much *him*, but the way she flowed against him like water, which I'd never ever seen her do with anybody. Evan went on, "Look, I can't tell you everything's going to work out, that you'll be instantly, totally happy in England. I can't promise to be the perfect stepfather for you, or that you won't hate Tony and Julian on sight. But Sally and I will do our best to make a home for us all, and if you'll give us the benefit of the doubt, that'll help a great deal. Do you think you can manage that, Jenny?"

I know, I know, writing it down now it looks like a reasonable, really *friendly* thing to say to somebody who hadn't been the least bit friendly to him since the day Sally introduced us. And I know it makes *me* look totally pathetic to say that I just sort of nodded and mumbled, "I guess," and made a lightning get-away to my room and Mister Cat and my favorite radio station that I wasn't going to be able to get in London. But the thing is, I didn't *want* him to be reasonable, I wanted him to be cold and mean, or anyway at least stupid, so I wouldn't have to worry about his feelings, or about liking him better than Norris. He was probably a better person than Norris in a lot of ways, I already knew that. So a lot of people are, so what? It didn't make any difference to me.

Back then, I didn't even know what Evan did for a living. I didn't want to know. Sally told me he was an agricultural biologist, doing stuff for the English government on and off, but I didn't have any idea what that meant, except that she said he talked to farmers a lot. He'd been in Iowa or Illinois, someplace like that, going to seminars and conventions, and then he'd come on to New York, I don't remember why, and that's how he became definitely my mother's only pickup *ever.* They met at a concert—I think she wanted me to go with her, but I went over to Marta's instead—and Sally came floating home that night, late as Mister Cat, bouncing into my room to tell me she'd met this sweet, funny English person, and they'd gotten thrown out of the West End, not for being drunk, but for sitting and laughing for hours without drinking at all. When she went off to bed, I heard her for the longest time, still laughing to herself.

I didn't think much about it then. I only realized I was in trouble when they started playing music together. Sally spends so much time at the piano every day, working or practicing, that she just about never touches it for fun. She used to, sometimes, with Norris, when he lived with us—I remember they used to do old stuff, Beatles, or rhythm and blues, clowning around together to crack me up. But once they split up, she quit all that, never again—that fast, that flat. And now here was Evan coming over with somebody's beat-up classical guitar, and the two of them waking me up at night singing English and I guess Irish folk songs. He was all right, nothing much, about like me on piano. But they were having a great time, you could tell. I could tell, lying there listening in the dark.

Of course he was over practically every day after they got engaged. They'd order pizza and sit in the kitchen talking about finding a place in London, because Evan's old flat wouldn't be nearly big enough, and about where I'd go to school, and where Sally might teach regularly, instead of freelancing the way she did here. I didn't talk if I could avoid it, and I really tried not to even listen. I think I felt that if I ignored everything that was going on, maybe none of it would actually happen. Mister Cat is terrific at that. All the same, I still couldn't help picking up a few things, whether I wanted to or not, and some of them didn't sound *that* terrible. London, for instance. London sounded pretty much like New York, give or take, with all kinds of crazies wandering around, and all kinds of at least interesting stuff going on everywhere. And I even started to think, well, okay, just maybe I could handle London. If I absolutely had to.

Sally told me Evan had custody of his two boys, the way she did of me—they were staying with his sister while he was over here—so I knew they'd be living with us, and that was about all I knew. He showed us four million Polaroids, of course, a whole suitcase full. One of the boys was just a baby, nine or ten—that was Julian—but the other one, Tony, was a couple of years older than me, and Evan said he was a dancer, been a dancer practically since the day he was born. Wonderful. I love him already.

Evan never spent the night at our place. I knew that was because of me. I also knew that Sally stayed over with him every now and then, but she always came slipping back in at five or six in the morning, shoes in her hand, trying like mad not to wake me. They never even went away together overnight, not one time. The whole business was incredibly stupid—who *cared*, after all?—but I'm trying really hard to be honest, so I have to say I enjoyed every minute of it. Because *I* cared, I *liked* making that much hard for them, it was the only thing I *could* make hard for them. And I also have to say that my mother never once ran me out of the house, never once even suggested wouldn't it be nice if I spent the weekend up in Riverdale with my disgusting cousin Barbara. Not that it would have worked, but *I'd* have tried, if it was me.

So I got used to having Evan around most of the time. I didn't talk to him much, but he didn't seem to care—he just went right on including me in the conversation, whether I said anything or not. What I didn't *want* to get used to was the way Sally and he were together, which was just . . . I can't find the word, and I don't know how to say this so I don't look too childish, too immature. I was thirteen years old, and I didn't *want* to see my own mother giggling and whispering in corners, and getting all dazy eyed and heavy mouthed like some girl backed up practically into her boyfriend's locker. It made me feel weird, off-balance, and I hated it. When I saw them staring at each other, not saying a word, my skin turned cold, and my whole stomach started to tremble. I wouldn't talk to *anybody* then; I'd go into my room and be with

Mister Cat. They never noticed; they'd gone away with each other while I stood there. Nothing I could do about it.

But Evan went back to England in May, and was gone for more than a month. Sally said he had some kind of a job offer, and besides, he needed to be with his boys for a while. He'd been telling them about her and me on the phone for months—Sally'd even talked to them a couple of times—but he still had a whole lot of explaining waiting for him back home. Meanwhile, she wanted *us* to spend some time by ourselves, just us girls, getting reacquainted and all set for the big adventure. We were going to see movies about England and read books about England together, and watch every damn Merchant and Ivory video we could find. "It'll be fun," she told me. "It'll be like going into training."

I said, "Training for what? Life among the limeys?" Sally went absolutely into orbit. I wasn't *ever* to say that, it was as bad as calling the French "frogs" or calling Germans "krauts," or people calling *us* what they do. It trailed off right there—I told you, Sally has trouble saying the real names of some things. Anyway, for once I actually kept my mouth shut as she kept going on and on. "We're going to be living there, Jenny. Not visiting, *living*. We're going to be limeys ourselves." I didn't say anything.

Well, us girls didn't get to spend all that much quality time together, as it turned out. We did some clothes shopping, which I *know* women are supposed to love, and I *know* it's a big mother-daughter buddy thing, but I've hated it all my life, and I always will, I know that, too. Except part of the bonding is having a long, chatty lunch afterward, and that's all right. And we applied for our passports, which was definitely an adventure, because Sally found *my* birth certificate but not *hers*, so we turned the whole apartment totally upside down until it finally showed up in the piano bench, which figures. Then we had to get our pictures taken, and I came out looking like a pink smudge, the way I always do—and *then* we had to go downtown to the passport office, and that took all day just by itself. But it was exciting, if you didn't think about what it really meant, which I'm good at. And we did go to an English movie that night, and Sally fell asleep with her head on my shoulder.

But she was mostly frantically busy, the way I've said, and when we were home together she didn't like to go out much, because Evan might call. When she had any free time, she made lists, millions of *lists*. I'd find them all over the house—stuff to pick up, stuff to get rid of, people to call, people to make sure to say good-bye to, questions about cleaning the apartment, about which way to ship stuff, questions to ask Evan about London schools—even a list just of things she knew about Evan's boys, Tony and Julian. That's my main memory of her in that time, sitting at the kitchen table, entirely surrounded by little boxes of Chinese food, leaning on her elbows with one hand in her hair. Making lists.

A couple of her friends practically lived with us, helping her with the packing and cleaning and running errands. Louise Docherty, who's a composer, and Sally's best bud, and laughs like a car alarm—anyway, there was Louise, and there was Cleon Ferris, black *and* gay *and* shorter than I am, who did lighting for concerts and musicals, and used to baby-sit me all the time. Norris brought me home one night—I was still working on Norris, trying to—and we walked in on the three of them, sitting on the floor, wrapping and taping up one box after another. Norris said, "Well, don't you look like the Weird Sisters?" and Louise turned and looked at us, Norris and me, and said, "*You* look like *Death and the Maiden.*" And went back to wrapping boxes.

I didn't help pack. I didn't do a thing Sally didn't yell at me to do. I got some of my own stuff into boxes—clothes and books and albums and things—but I didn't close up the boxes, or label them, or anything like that. Like I said, I kept figuring I could maybe make all this craziness not be happening by *acting* as though none of it was happening. So I mainly hung with Jake and Marta, getting lifted, and watching game shows on TV. My grades went straight to hell that last term, and Sally got on me about it, but you could see she was always thinking about a million other things—she wasn't even there when she was yelling at me. It was very weird. I actually found myself almost wishing Evan would come back.

Also I got sick a lot that summer. I don't mean anything big or dramatic, just colds and stomach stuff, and the strep throat I usually get in May every year. Then I'd get into bed and curl around Mister Cat, and find a classic rock station because he can't *stand* heavy metal, and I'd mostly sleep for a couple of days. One time Cleon Ferris came in to look at me, and he sat down on the edge of my bed and said, "Jenny. Little sugar." He always called me that, since I can remember. He said, "Give it up, Jens. Short of terminal mogo on the gogo, there is no way you are not going to England with your mother. The deal's down, cookie."

I didn't even turn around. I said, "I'm *not* faking it. And it wouldn't be anybody's damn business if I was."

"That's *were*," Cleon said. "If I *were*. They get on you in England about stuff like that." He reached over my shoulder and scratched the little soft place under Mister Cat's jaw. Then he said, "I lived in London for a while. Long ago, in another world. I liked it pretty much, most of the time." His face was sort of like an acorn, and there was a space between his front teeth, so when he smiled, he looked about seven. He said, "But what I really liked, little sugar, you go to a new place where nobody knows you, and you get to be someone else, anyone you want to be. Even black dwarfs, you'd be amazed. I recommend it."

I didn't say anything, just pretended to be falling asleep, and Cleon finally said, "Yeah, well, keep it in mind," and left. He died a couple of years ago, from bone cancer. I think he had it then, when he was sitting on my bed talking to me.

A couple of weeks before school was out, Mr. Hammell called me into his office and asked me if it was true about us going to England. When I told him yes, his face changed—the lines down his cheeks sort of smoothed out, and his eyes were so sad and puzzled. Although they were mostly like that anyway. "Oh," he said. "Oh, that's a pity, Jenny. I was certainly anticipating having you in Advanced next year."

"Me, too," I said. "I'm sorry."

Mr. Hammell stood there in front of me, looking younger every minute. He asked me, "Jenny, are you happy about this? Is this what you want? You're important to me—to the class. I really want to know."

I didn't know what to say. I just nodded finally. Mr. Hammell said, "Well. Well, that's good, then. That's good. Good for you, Jenny."

Then he did a strange thing. He reached out, awkward and slow, and put his hand on my cheek. It felt cold and shaky, like my Grandma Paula's hand.

Mr. Hammell drew his hand down my cheek. He said, "Jenny, you take care of yourself over there in London. Go see a lot of plays, and remember us, because we'll be thinking about you. I'll be thinking about you." He pushed my hair back a little and his voice got so low I could hardly hear him. "You're going to be so pretty," he said. "You remember I told you."

I don't know if that counts like sexual harassment; and I'll never know if Mr. Hammell was really trying to hit on me or what. But I remember what he said, to this day, and I always will, because he was the first person who wasn't family who ever said that to me. Whatever was going on in Mr. Hammell's head about me, it must have been *strange*, and Meena's probably right, maybe I should have reported him. But I'm not sorry I didn't.

Another definitely weird thing that happened was that Mister Cat started staying really close to home, following me from room to room and miaowing every minute, which he never does unless he's just starving or completely pissed. He wouldn't let me out of his sight, no matter how much the Siamese Hussy yowled in the street. It was scary, actually, because he's not *like* that. I should have known he knew something.

I found out what it was the same day Evan came back. Sally went to the airport to meet him, but I was at a Mets game with Norris. Not that either of us is that crazy about baseball—I just didn't want to be there for the big reunion scene, and Norris wanted to aggravate Sally about all the family-tradition stuff I'd be pining for in England. And each of us *knew* what the other was doing, so it was fun in a way, although we didn't *say* anything. Anyway, I made sure I didn't get home until pretty late, but Sally and Evan still weren't in yet. So I talked on the phone with Marta for a while, and watched some TV, and then I went to bed with Mister Cat tucked about as close under my armpit as he could get. He hadn't slept like that since he was a kitten.

I must have drifted off myself, because all of a sudden Sally was sitting beside me, asking me if I was awake. I sat up fast and said, "I'm awake, I'm awake, is there a fire?" Because there *was* a fire once, a bad one, when I was little and we were living on West Eleventh, and Norris was still with us. I dreamed about that fire again just a couple of nights ago.

Sally laughed. She said, "No, baby, no fire, it's all right. But Evan and I have something we wanted to share with you right away, we couldn't even wait till morning."

Evan was standing in the doorway, looking really uncomfortable. He said, "Jenny, it's a bit of a good-news, bad-news joke. The good news is that I've been offered a fine job at home—I'm quite surprised and excited about it. The bad news is that it's not in London. It's rather west, I'm afraid, a place called Stourhead

Farm, down in Dorset. That is, it used to be a farm, very long ago, and the family who own it now, the Lovells, they want me to get it running properly again for them. And to go on managing it afterward."

I was too groggy to be disappointed right then. All I could manage was something like, "Oh. Where's Dorset?"

"I'll show you on the map tomorrow," Sally said. "It's Thomas Hardy country, Evan says it's utterly beautiful, you'll love it. And there's the Cerne Abbas Giant, and we can go to Salisbury Plain and see Stonehenge—and we'll be living on a big old estate, a real *manor*, Jenny. I know you had your face fixed for London, but we can get to London anytime we want. This is special, baby, this is *better* than London, believe me."

Mister Cat got up and walked across my legs to say hello to Sally. He always ignored Norris completely, from day one, but he likes Sally okay. She rubbed her knuckles against his head, the way he loves, and I could feel him purring in the bed. She said, "Yes, you old street guy you, yes, you'll love it, too, yes, you will, you'll go wild. All the turf in the world to pee on and patrol, all kinds of new little creatures to chase, dozens of English lady cats looking for a fling with a hip Yank like you. Just a few weeks in nasty quarantine and you'll be back in business, we'll have to call you *Sir* Cat." She was pushing it, even sliding back down into sleep I could tell that, wanting me so much to love the idea of living on some farm in the west whatever of England. Sally just gets to me sometimes, like nobody else ever. Even Tamsin.

And I'd probably have mumbled, "Oh, okay, sure," and been asleep halfway through, except that Evan said something that woke me up faster than ice cubes down my back, which is how Sally used to do it on desperate Mondays. He said to her, "I'm afraid it'll be more than a few weeks, love. It's a full six months he'll have to stay there."

This next part is hard to get down, because no matter how I write it, it keeps coming out really embarrassing, like a lot of things in this book already, it seems to me. I'm hardly even *started*, and if it's going to be like this all the way through, with me looking like a supreme idiot every ten seconds, I may just quit the whole thing, never mind what I promised Meena. I'll keep at it a while longer, I guess, but I'm just warning everybody now.

Anyway. What happened was that something I hadn't even

known was ready to go just *snapped*. I screamed and I yelled, and I was shaking, and I grabbed Mister Cat away from Sally and jumped out of bed and kept on yelling. "I'm not going without him! That's *it*, forget it, I'm not *going* to England if he has to be in a cage for six months! The one thing I've got in the *world*, and I'm not leaving him in any damn cage, he'll think I've abandoned him! Forget it, no chance, no way, I'm calling Norris, I'll find someplace to stay, but I am not going to *fucking* England without my *cat*!" There was a whole lot more of it, but that's all that's getting into my book.

Sally didn't yell back at me. She just sat there, looking as though she'd been punched in the stomach. Once she said, real low, "Jenny, I didn't know, I really thought it was just for a month," and I knew it was the truth, but I screamed at her anyway. And that part is *not* going in, I don't care.

Evan stopped me. He just finally looked at me and said, "Jenny, that's enough. Don't talk like that to your mother." He never raised his voice, but I stopped. Evan can do that. He said, "Let's get this silly crap out of the way, Jenny. Like it or not, you're coming to England, because that's where Sally's going, and she's in charge of you until you're eighteen years old. And yes, your cat *will* have to spend a full six months in quarantine, I'm very sorry. But he'll be at a kennel as close to us as possible, and he'll be treated well, and I promise you can go and see him there whenever you like. I'll take you myself." He grinned at me, and that was the first time I noticed that his eyes turn practically blue when he smiles, not gray or hazel at all. Evan said, "Come on, girl, this is England we're talking about. Don't you know they let animals vote in England?"

I didn't laugh or smile back. I'd about have died first just then. But I didn't yell anymore. My throat and the back of my mouth hurt so I couldn't even swallow. Mister Cat stretched low against my ankle and dug in his claws very lightly. He doesn't ever scratch me, but that's what he does when he's mad at me. Then he jumped down off the bed and left. I told Sally I was sorry, and she hugged me, and Evan got me some orange juice for my throat, then they went away. I left the door a little way open, but Mister Cat didn't come back in, not all night.

He was there in the morning, though, lying on his back between my feet with one leg sticking straight up in the air. When you're as cool as he is, you can look as stupid as you want, and it doesn't matter.

Four

Probably it was getting the visas that made it real. You need a visa to go to England if you're staying longer than six months, and Sally made a big point of us making sure we got them right away, because we were going to be residents, not just tourists. "We'll still be there when they've all gone home," was what she said, and my stomach turned right over and froze solid, because I could *see* it. The sky getting darker and darker, and everybody but us gone home.

Or maybe it was Mister Cat's red label finally arriving. Sally was going to handle all the quarantine stuff, but I told her I'd do it. I didn't want to, but he was my cat. So I wrote off to England, to MAFF (that's the Ministry of Agriculture, Fisheries and Food), and they sent me an import license application to fill out, and another thing for Customs, and a whole long list of specially approved kennels and vets and what they call "carrying agents"—people who could pick up Mister Cat at Heathrow Airport and take him to wherever he was going to spend the next six miserable months. Meena says she had to do the same thing when her family came to England, and all *she* had was a white mouse named Karthik. If I'm spelling it right.

So then I wrote to every one of the kennels in Dorset, and they all sent me their fancy brochures with color pictures of where they kept their animals, and actual menus of what they fed them, and how the runs and cages were heated, and what days the vet would come for checkups, and what days they did worming and grooming and all. (I crossed out that last part, because you don't *groom* Mister Cat—you could lose an arm trying. He does that himself.)

Evan wanted to help me pick a place, but I wasn't talking to Evan then. I chose one myself, called Goshawk Farm Cattery, because they said you could come and visit anytime without calling ahead, and Sally said not to worry about the cost, because she was feeling guilty, which was fine with me. I picked a carrying agent myself, too, and I hunted all over to find the right kind of travel cage, with enough ventilation and *two* water bottles. And I filled everything out and sent it off, and after a long time MAFF sent back what's called a "boarding document" and a red label to stick on the cage. When I put it on and just stood there looking at the big number and the small print—I don't know, maybe that was it. When I knew we were really going.

No, the piano, I think the piano's what finally did it. Because everywhere we've lived, everything's always been centered around Sally's piano. Always. First you figure exactly where the piano wants to be, then you worry about how you get into the bathroom. Everything took second place to the piano being happy, I can't remember when I didn't know that. And the day I got home and the piano was gone, shipped out, out the window, the way it came in, it felt like a steam shovel had crashed in and scooped out our apartment—like a lot more had vanished than just the piano. And I knew that piano was on its way to some English farm somewhere, and I edged around the space where it had been and got to my room and started packing for real. Because we always followed my mother's piano, that's *one* thing I understood.

And after that the boxes started going, all the stuff Sally, Louise and Cleon had been taping up, day by day, faster and faster, like it was all getting sucked out through the hole the piano had left. I guess it was worse because I'd put such a lot of effort into not noticing what was being packed. I got up one morning and every book in the house had disappeared in the night, along with most of the towels and bedsheets. Or I came home late another time, and there were three chairs left, and *no* silverware. My footsteps actually echoed in the living room, because all the paintings by Sally's friends were gone, and the big rug Grandma Paula gave her and Norris when they got married. Dinner was Sally and Evan and me at the kitchen table, eating Italian takeout with plastic knives and forks. Then the table went, and we sat on the floor to eat, because the last chairs were gone too. I remember the weather was really hot that summer, but that poor scooped-out apartment just kept getting colder and colder.

But Sally loved it. The emptier the place got, the brighter and livelier *she* got. She said it reminded her of how things looked when we moved in, and she kept telling me, "Jenny, it's an *adventure*. Everybody needs to start from scratch once in a while. Just to scrap all your security, all the things you're sure of, and step right off the cliff. Look, here we are, right now, falling through space, and all we've got to trust is each other and Evan. Isn't that exciting?"

"Wild," I said. "Mister Cat can't sleep at night because of all the noise, and he's going bananas because his dish and his box aren't in the same place two days in a row. And he *hates* that travel cage, I can't get him to go in—he just braces his legs and pees on it. He knows what it is."

Sally looked straight at me. She said, "Well, that's tough. He'll survive just fine. We'll all survive." She'd never have said it like that once, that was Evan, no, that was her *with* Evan. It was really confusing, watching my mother leaving me, flowing into some other shape, the way they do it in movies. Sometimes, watching her, I felt like I was the only person in the world who couldn't move, couldn't change shape. Everywhere I looked, everything was being dragged away and not one damn thing put back. I'd have peed on *my* travel cage, too, if I could have gotten hold of it.

I remember Marta and I were in Central Park one afternoon, watching people dancing to a salsa band, and both of us were sort of semi-lifted on some Hawaiian she'd found in her brother Paco's coat pocket. It was a hot, clear, sunny day, with little kids and their dogs chasing each other around, and Frisbees slicing overhead, and people on rollerblades zipping past you like bullets everywhere you looked. I was saying, "Something's going to happen. I don't know what, but *something*."

Marta shook her head. She can look really wise when she's high, because her face is so small and her eyes get so big and black. She said, "I'll write every week. I promise. Jake, too."

"I'm scared about going to school there," I said. "It's just the pits, I've been reading about it. They beat up everybody who isn't English. I'm going to get killed."

Marta laughed. "Come on, people think like that about this country. Just wear your grungy leather jacket, they'll think you're a big gangster." She did a kind of Benny Hill English voice. "Ooo, ooo, nono, I don't wanna mess with her, she's from *Noo Yahk*." She got to giggling then, and couldn't stop, so that got *me* doing it, and we just sat there in the sun, looking at each other and *giggling*. The salsa band quit, and a couple of skinny tattooed guys started juggling torches and moonwalking at the same time. I said, "I'm really scared, Marta. I really am."

"It'll be okay," Marta said. She put her arm around me, which was awkward because of her being smaller than me, and we sort of snuggled, just for a little bit. It didn't exactly help, but it was nice.

And then it was three weeks to go, and then two weeks, and then like *that*, two *days*. I couldn't believe it. Sally's students were giving all kinds of good-bye parties for her and Evan, and she asked me to come with them every time, but I never did. Norris and his girlfriend Suzanne took me out to a fancy dinner at a French place on the East Side, and Norris gave me a genuine Burberry secret-agent trench coat, waterproof, for wearing in England. It was too big, but Norris said I'd grow into it. I actually have.

Jake and Marta wanted to give me a farewell party of my own, which was when I realized that I didn't want one. I just wanted to do exactly what we always did, so we settled for picking up gyros at the Greek's on Amsterdam, and then just walking, going absolutely nowhere, eating and talking like nothing was different, just the three of us messing along the same as always on one more summer night, like being inside some kind of warm, sweet, sticky pastry. When we got to my place, we just stood there under the awning and looked at each other. They didn't want to leave, and *I* didn't want to go upstairs, and everybody knew everything, and there wasn't anything to say. So finally Marta just said, "You take care, *vata*," and she hugged me, and Jake hugged me, too. He was crying a little. He said, "Man, when you've only *got* a couple of real friends . . ." and I said, "Yeah, yeah, yeah, I know already, get out of here, Walkowitz, go on." So then they left.

Mister Cat was home. I turned on all the lights, and we sat on a box by the window in my room. There were people working outside, tearing up West Eighty-third, same as they'd been doing for the last couple of years, day and night, except Sundays. They're probably still at it. I listened to the jackhammers, and I thought about how noisy New York is all the time, everywhere, and how you get so used to it you never even notice. Maybe I was so used to it I wouldn't be able to *breathe* someplace quiet, the way I already felt I couldn't breathe in this empty apartment. I'd probably just die of quiet, over there on some farm in Dorset, and nobody'd ever figure out why. I started to cry myself, thinking about it. It felt great, but Mister Cat got annoyed at me sniffling and honking into his fur, so I quit, and we just sat there at the window together until Sally and Evan got home.

The whole trip to London is one miserable blur, and I don't want to write much about it. Evan tried to put Mister Cat in his travel cage while I was still asleep, but he quit while he still had everything he was born with. So I had to get up way early and spend an hour talking Mister Cat off the ceiling and into my lap, and *then* finally into that little tiny box. He gave me a *look*, just one long yellow look, and then he walked in by himself and lay down facing the back, facing away from me. He was so mad at me. I can get depressed right over again when I think about that time, even now.

It was four in the morning, something like that, and I was so out of it I never actually got to say good-bye to anything. Maybe that's just as well, but I don't know. I remember the limo sliding up to the curb like a submarine, and a couple of street people staring at Sally and me crawling into the back with suitcases stacked around us, because the trunk was so full. Evan got up front with the driver, and Sally put her arm around me. I had Mister Cat on my lap, and every now and then I'd bend down and whisper to him, "It's all right, I'm here, it'll be okay." I could see his eyes in the darkness, but he wouldn't talk to me.

And that was all, that's how we left New York. Nobody to wave to, no tears—no *feelings* even, exactly. Four in the morning, and it's all just *gone*, nothing left to take with you except suitcases.

I'd been on a plane one time before, when Norris was doing something with the San Francisco Opera, but I don't remember any of the details because I was five years old, maybe six. They gave me a coloring book on the plane, and I loved the food in the little plastic trays. Not a lot of training for flying across the ocean to your wild new life, especially when you have to hand your cat over at the ticket counter like a damn garment bag. I saw other cats and one dog in cages like his, and that helped a little, because I knew at least he'd have some company in the baggage compartment. All the same, when I held the cage up for the last time and looked at him through the mesh, and he stared back at me and let out one single ice-cold miaow, it just went right through me, it was really awful. I said, "I'm sorry, I'm sorry." Sally put her arm on my shoulder, and it was all I could do not to slap it away.

The clerk put the cage on the conveyor belt. It bumped slowly away, with suitcases and packages piling up behind it until I couldn't see it anymore. The clerk tried to be nice. He said, "Your kitty'll be fine, honey. They'll take him off the belt and put him in a special safe place with all the other animals. Everything but the in-flight movie." He winked at Sally and Evan over my head. I can still *see* it, that fucking stupid wink.

The only thing I really remember about the flight is taking off, because we flew in a long circle over the city, and I'm still sure I saw old messed-up Eighty-third Street, even though I probably couldn't have. But I *know* I saw the Park, I know that much, so for just one second it was all right down there under us—Jake and Marta, and William Jay Gaynor Junior High School, and the crystals-and-auras place on our corner, and the tiny Jamaican market on Amsterdam where Sally used to buy mangoes and papayas, and I'd get my reggae tapes. The woman in the Navy pea jacket, walking up and down Eighty-first all day, jerking her thumb at the cabs, yelling at them, trying to get one of them to stop and take her *out* of here. The big blind guy with the nose rings, who liked to scare the people having their dinner outside the Columbus Cafe, and the two old men I've seen on Broadway all my life, shuffling along arm in arm, yelling at each other. The black woman who runs the newsstand, who saved piano magazines for Sally, and kept telling me how I should do my hair. And the Siamese Hussy, wondering and wondering where Mister Cat could have gone. All down there, my life under our wings.

And after that it was all clouds, all the way to London. Nothing to see, no ocean, no sky, about as romantic as the IRT. I couldn't sleep, but I wasn't exactly awake either—I got one of those tiny pillows and crammed it up against the window and leaned my head on it, trying to get halfway comfortable. I tried to let my mind just float off, like it does in class half the time, but it kept seeing Mister Cat in the baggage compartment, lonely and crowded and being jolted around, not knowing what was happening to him, *scared* for the first time since he was a kitten and those boys were dangling him off the roof. I couldn't stand to think of Mister Cat being scared, but I couldn't think about anything else.

Meena says I have to describe landing at Heathrow, but it's hard to remember what's really that first miserable gray evening, and what's from other times we've been there. Tunnel after echoey, endless tunnel, and the three of us pushing four luggage carts.

Sally nudging me every minute, pointing to the people going through Customs with us, whispering, "Jenny, look at them, those are real *monks*, from Tibet!" and "Jenny, *look*, see what that lady's wearing, that's called a sari!" Evan helping a tall old black man in red and yellow robes and a red hat like a flowerpot to carry his duffel bag . . . like I said, things blur. And I didn't want to look, or notice, or remember anything—not then.

We didn't have any trouble at Customs, except for having to stand in line forever, and all that time Sally and Evan were waving to Evan's sons, Tony and Julian, who were waving back from behind a big high window, along with a red-haired woman, Evan's sister Charlotte, whom they'd been living with while he was gone. Everybody in the world was waving like mad, except me, even when Sally grabbed my arm and pointed up toward the window. I just kept looking somewhere else, all that time.

You can imagine all the hugging and gushing and carrying on when we got out of Customs. I'm not going to write about it, mostly because I still feel bad about the way I was with Sally then. Here she was, just off the plane and meeting an entire new family—stepchildren, sister-in-law, the works, and more coming—and nobody but me from the bride's side, and I wasn't about to deal with any of it. I saw a young guy holding up a sign saying GOSHAWK FARM CATTERY, and I was over there like a shot, because it gave me an excuse to duck out on all the at-long-last stuff, and I took it. I'd be different today, but that doesn't do yesterday any good.

The Goshawk Farm guy's name was Martin. He'd already picked up Mister Cat, and just needed someone to sign all the blue and yellow forms on his clipboard. So I did that, and then I kneeled down to say good-bye to Mister Cat and tell him I'd be seeing him really soon. And not to forget me.

He was crouched in his cage, scrunched down as far back as he could get. All I could see at first were his eyes, which aren't green or yellow, like most cats'—they're a kind of really deep orange, with a few little gold specks in them, too. Now they were glaring at me and he made a sound like a rusty old creaking door. He makes it at strange dogs and children he doesn't know—Mister Cat really hates most children, which you can't blame him for. But he never, *ever* made it at me, no matter how mad he got. I kept trying to say, "It's me, you dumb old cat, it's me," only my throat hurt so much

I couldn't get the words out. And I wasn't going to cry, either, not right in Heathrow Airport, in front of a stranger in a country I didn't want to be in. So I just kept kneeling there by the cage.

Then this really funny voice, like a seal barking at the zoo, said over my shoulder, "I say, is that your cat?" I looked around and almost fell over backward, because there stood this small boy wearing a blue school coat, with a sort of Cub Scout cap, and absolutely *huge* gray eyes in this little pointy-chinned face. It took me a while to figure out why he looked familiar, until it hit me that his face was shaped just almost exactly like Mister Cat's face.

I knew who he was, of course—God knows I'd seen enough snapshots of him and his brother, *and* their dog, *and* their school, *and* their mother. Julian. Not the dancer, the younger one.

"Yeah, he's my cat," I said. "Mess with him, you'll never pick your nose again," because Julian was wiggling his fingers through the mesh, trying to get Mister Cat to rub up against them. He pulled them back, but slowly, so I wouldn't think he was scared. The next thing he said to me was, "I'm a whiz at maths. Are you any good at maths?" They call it that here.

"Actually, I'm terrible," I said—which is still true—and Julian's face just lit up. He said, "Oh, splendid, I'll help you." I couldn't get over his deep, froggy voice, sounding like it had broken years before they're supposed to. He's always had it, practically since he started talking, I found that out later.

Martin, the Goshawk Farm guy, said politely that he guessed he'd be off with Mister Cat, then; but I was looking past him at Sally and Evan and Charlotte coming toward us, laughing, with their arms around each other—and past *them* at an older boy who had to be Tony, Julian's brother. He wasn't actually handsome, any more than Evan was handsome—his hair was all bushy and messy, and his skin wasn't even all the way cleared up yet—but you couldn't not look at him. It's like that with some people—they don't just catch your eye, they *grab* it so it hurts sometimes. I don't know how it works. I just wish I was one of them.

So I got introduced to Charlotte again—she's red-haired, I said that, and short, and everyone calls her Charlie, and she looked as though she'd been minding other people's children all her life. And I shook hands with Tony, and I noticed he had sort of brownish-greenish eyes and was trying to grow a mustache, and I remember thinking—and Meena says I should absolutely *not* put this in—all I could think was, "Well, is it incest if he's your *step-* brother?" That's the truth, and it goes in, and I'll worry some other time about what Tony might think if he reads this. Dancers don't read a lot, that's one good thing.

That's it for Heathrow, because it all starts getting hazy around this point. I was really tired, and really upset about Mister Cat, and maybe that's why I just sort of sleepwalked the rest of the way. Because the next thing I remember is waking up in the London hotel bed, with Sally bending over me asking if I'd like some tea to start our new life with. She *knows* I hate tea—I still do, after six years in England—but that's exactly Sally for you, she *never* gives up, she never quits on anything. I just went back to sleep. Sometimes that's the best thing you can do with my mother.

Five

We stayed in London five days, with Sally and me sharing a room in a bed-and-breakfast place off Russell Square, and Evan bunking in at Charlie's with Tony and Julian. I liked that part, once I got over being tired, and as long as I could make myself believe that we were just being tourists, summer people, people who go home. But all I had to do was see real tourists—sometimes all it took was a plane going overhead—and everybody says I'd turn between one minute and the next into a sullen little hemorrhoid with feet. And I know I did. I meant to.

Julian took me over from day one. It didn't matter how I acted—he was going to show me everything in London that *he* liked—later for the National Theatre and the Tate Gallery and the changing of the guard at Buckingham Palace. And practically everything Julian liked was American-style stuff—the Pizza Pie Factory in Mayfair, the video arcades around Earl's Court, the Taco Bell in Soho (you can't buy Julian for Mexican food, but you can definitely rent him). Which was all fine with me, you couldn't make anything too American for me. I kept trying to make England not *be* there all around me, and Julian, ten years old, was the only one who seemed to understand, even though he didn't really. Maybe that's why we're still *vatos*, as Marta would say—still buddies—even though he's sixteen now, and completely impossible.

I liked London right off, though I wasn't going to admit it for one minute. It did feel like New York—tense and crazy, but in a slower sort of way—and it looked just familiar enough to be exciting. (You don't realize how many movies you've seen about a city until you're actually in it, recognizing all kinds of places you haven't been to.) The only thing I didn't like was the driving on the left—it made my stomach feel weird when Charlie was zipping us around London. One time, crossing the street, I almost got totally creamed by a bus I never saw. Tony snatched me back at the last minute, and Julian told him that now he'd have to be responsible for me forever, the way the Chinese or someone believe. Poor Tony.

Sally kept asking me every night, after the others had gone back to Charlie's flat, if I liked England any better now. And every night I'd say, "I like *London*. I really wish we could stay in London, if we have to be here." And then Sally'd get tears in her eyes and say something like, "Baby, I know, but you'll love Dorset, I promise. If you'll just give it a little time, just not make up your mind before we even get there. Can you do that, darling?" I didn't want to lie to her, but I didn't really want her to be miserable—only at the same time I really *did*—so I'd usually mumble something about wanting to see Mister Cat. Which wasn't lying, and at least that way we'd both get to sleep.

I'm going to skip over where we went and what we saw. Anything you can see in London in five days, just figure we looked at it. Probably had lunch there, too—it seemed like we were always eating, that first time in London. When we weren't running to catch the tour bus.

Julian mostly stayed with Charlie those days, unless Evan swore on a Bible we'd hit Taco Bell, but Tony came along with us now and then, especially if it was anything to do with dance, or seeing a play, or anything with music. We had that much in common anyway, but we didn't get to talk about it a lot, what with Sally and Evan both working so hard at being stepparents. Sally kept asking Tony about his school and his grades, and about his studying dance, and how he thought he'd like living in Dorset. I got the feeling early on that he felt more or less the same as I did, but I was trying not to look straight at him, because my damn skin, that Sally had told me the English air would be great for, started acting up as soon as we arrived. Tony answered all the questions, talking softly and not volunteering a thing. He's really shy, even now—Julian's the least shy person in the whole world, but Tony definitely makes up for him.

But he got me alone once, when we were wandering around the rose garden in Regent's Park and Evan and Sally had gotten a little way ahead. He took my arm and pulled me over to a rosebush, so we'd seem to be talking about it, and he said, "Look here, Jennifer, I do wish you'd try to remember, this is every bit as hard and—and *strange*—for Julian and me as it is for you." He didn't have Julian's cute croaky baritone, but his voice was so intense you could have struck a match on it. He said, "We never asked to have our dad and mum split up and her marry a Frenchman and go off to live with him and his kids in Bordeaux. And we didn't exactly ask to have *him* run off to the States and come back with your mother and you, and just whisk everybody right out of London to some bloody farm in Dorset." He was trying to keep cool, but he doesn't do cool much better than I do, and I could feel his hand trembling on my arm. He asked, "Do you understand me, Jennifer?"

"Don't call me Jennifer," I said. "I'm Jenny. And yeah, I know it's all really tough for you, and I'm really sorry, but at least you're still in your own damn country. You didn't have to leave everything that ever meant anything to you and start your whole life all over in someplace where you don't belong and never wanted to be in the first place. And I want my *cat*," and with that I just started crying. I told you I'm not a big crier, but when it does happen it's always like that, without warning.

Tony did a nice thing then. He moved around me so Evan and Sally couldn't see me, and he gave me his big blue, perfectly folded handkerchief to bawl into. I never cry long, but I make it up in volume. That handkerchief was absolutely soaked by the time he got it back.

He never said anything dumb like "Don't cry." He waited until I'd finished, and then he just said, "They're waving, we'd better be walking on." And that's what we did, with him talking away to me about however many kinds of football they play in Great Britain as we came up with Sally and Evan. Sally stared hard at me for a moment, but I'd been having allergies, and my nose and eyes were red half the time anyway. So we all walked on through Regent's Park, and Tony explained to me what a googly is in cricket. Cricket is the only game duller than baseball, because it lasts longer, but that was another nice thing.

Sally and Evan got married the day before we left for Dorset. It was a civil ceremony in a judge's chambers, over in ten minutes, with just Charlie and a court clerk for the witnesses. Bang-bang-bang, kiss the bride, sign here, best wishes, long and happy life, off to dinner, absolutely painless—and that fast I had a stepfather and two stepbrothers. I didn't speak to anybody all day, but nobody noticed *that*, not even Sally.

And the next day, way too bright and early, we were packed into Evan's little car—a gray Escort, matched the overcast perfectly—luggage in our laps stacked up so high Evan could hardly see out the back window, and the whole car sagging until I swear I felt my butt bounce on the road whenever we went over a bump, and we're actually off for Dorset, wherever it is. I knew it was somewhere south, that's all. And sort of west.

We were in the backseat, Tony, Julian, and me. Julian grabbed one window right off, and Tony let me have the other, treating me exactly like Julian, and letting me know it. I just lay back and tried to get comfortable under a suitcase and a box of kitchen stuff, and closed my eyes.

I actually dozed a little bit on the drive out of London, and maybe a bit more than that, because I only woke up when Julian started to sing "One Hundred Bottles of Beer on the Wall," which I had no idea they sang in England. We were still in the suburbs, which look just about the same there as they do in New York—malls and McDonald's and cineplexes and garages and TV antennas sticking up from so many red roofs your eyes go funny. I don't know why they're all red, even today.

Evan told Julian he might want to reconsider his repertoire if he had any plans for his eleventh birthday, so Julian sang "I Am the Walrus," all of it, straight through, and then he was going to sing "Come Together," but Tony got a headlock on him. Julian loves the Beatles the way he loves enchiladas and pizza. It still takes a headlock to stop him.

Sally wanted me to sing with her, some of the old stuff we used to do together, like "The Water Is Wide," or "*Plaisir d'amour*," or "Diamonds Are a Girl's Best Friend," but I wasn't about to, not in front of these people, no chance. That hurt her feelings, and I felt a little bad about that, but I was also starting to feel sick, because of the car wallowing so much, and because we kept hitting one roundabout after another just going in circles and circles until I had to shut my eyes again and think about nothing. Sometimes I thought about Mister Cat, and sometimes about Jake and Marta, but thinking about nothing's better for your stomach. I guess I slept some more.

What woke me this time was Evan singing by himself. It was a long, slow, really sad song about a fisherman and a mermaid, and his accent was funny, different from how he usually sounded. I listened to him, trying not to, and now and then Sally would come in, harmonizing in a couple of places where she knew the words, and my eyes would start to fill up, and you're just going to have to imagine how much I hated that. Because it wasn't the damn song that was making me cry—it was something in Evan's voice that wasn't sad at all, but *peaceful*, and it was me having to face the idea that he and my mother had been making this other world for themselves that didn't include me for one minute. Oh, it did, in a way—I knew that, Sally's my *mother*—but now there were places in it where only they went, places where I just *wasn't* and Norris wasn't, and there wasn't any history but theirs together. And that's what I hated, and that's why I didn't talk to anybody or sing a damn note on that whole absolutely endless drive to Dorset.

It's a pretty drive, too, now that I know it. We took the freeway from London, and once we were out of the red roofs and round-abouts, the country started becoming *country*, with cows and a lot of sheep, and stuff growing in the fields, which I can mostly iden-tify now, but I couldn't then, so there's no point pretending. The land turned rolling after a while, but in a nice rocking-chair sort of way, and the sun even came out, practically.

This first part of the trip was Hampshire—that I *did* know, but only because of Sally. She kept turning around in the front seat every other minute to tell me something like, "Jenny, look, we're coming up on Winchester—you remember, 'Winchester Cathe-dral . . .' " and she sang a lick from that dorky song. "It's really old—it was the Saxons' capital, and then King Alfred was crowned here, and William the Conqueror built the cathedral." And a mo-ment later it'd be, "Jenny, *quick*, over there, Evan says that's a Roman camp!" She was like a damn tour guide—"Baby, look, *look*, on the horizon, that's *Salisbury*, doesn't it look like the Constable painting we saw?" And Tony and Julian would look at each other, and Evan would sort of murmur, "That's Southampton, love, we're a good bit south of Salisbury." And Sally would just laugh and say, "Shows you what *I* know," and I didn't know who I was madder at—her for sounding like such a total idiot, Evan for being right and gentle, both, or the boys for having good manners and look-ing so embarrassed for my mother and me. Boy, Meena's right—you start writing something down, and it *all* comes back.

After Southampton, we went through the New Forest, which didn't look anything like the way I'd thought a real forest would look. There weren't even that many trees along the road—it just seemed like more of the cows-and-sheep country we'd been driving through forever. Sally was just starting to talk about the Knightwood Oak—how it was practically the biggest, oldest tree in England, and how oaks were always supposed to be magic—when all of a sudden Julian grabbed my arm and said, "There! There's one!"

I pulled away from him, hard, because he was hurting my arm, and I said, "Quit it!", and then I saw what he was pointing at, just up ahead. There were two of them, actually—a couple of shaggy little ponies standing right by the road, almost *in* it, one of them eating grass, the other just looking at things. Evan slowed down to go around them, and the one who wasn't eating lifted his head and stared right at me, looking me over with his big, *wild* black eyes. And I can't explain it, but I think that was maybe the first time I knew I was really in England, and not going home.

Tony said, "They're supposed to be descended from the Armada horses." I guess I blinked, because then he said, "The Spanish Armada. Some of the ships broke up in a storm, and the horses swam ashore. In 1588."

"I know about the Spanish Armada," I said. Tony nodded and didn't say anything more. Evan caught my eye in the rearview mirror. He winked at me, but I didn't wink back. He said, "Jenny, you want to be very careful if you see a black one—all black, like your cat, without a white hair on him anywhere. It might be a pooka."

I wasn't going to say a *word*, but I couldn't help it. I said, "A *pooka?*"

Evan grinned at me. "Very magical creature. The country people say it can change into almost anything—an eagle, a fox, even a man, if it wants to. But mostly you meet it as a fine black pony, absolutely black, inviting you to get on its back and take a ride. Don't you do it."

And he didn't say one thing more, just to make me ask. Evan does that. I held out all the way through the New Forest, before I mumbled, "Okay, why shouldn't I?" And when he just raised his eyebrows and waited, I said, "Why shouldn't I go for a ride on a pooka?"

"Because it'll toss you right into a river, or into a bramble patch. That's a pooka's idea of a good joke. They aren't as dangerous as Black Annis or Peg Powler or the Oakmen, but you don't ever want to trust one. *Very* warped sense of humor, pookas have."

Julian giggled. He said, "Maybe our house'll have a boggart, wouldn't that be splendid?"

Tony punched his shoulder lightly. "We've already got one, thanks very much."

Julian got really pissed then. You couldn't ever tell what'd get to him in those days. He hit Tony back, *hard*—he could get in a good shot because there was a lot less stuff piled on him than on either of us—and he started yelling, "I'm *not* a boggart, I'm *not* a boggart, don't you call me a boggart!" He's a lot better now, but you still have to be a little careful with Julian. Don't ever tell him he's got curly hair, for instance. He *hates* having curly hair.

Sally handled it pretty neatly, considering she was just learning how to be a stepmother. She leaned into the backseat and caught both of Julian's hands, very gently, but really quickly. Sally's got big hands for a woman—she can reach tenths on the piano, and she can do card tricks and shuffle a deck like Maverick or somebody. She asked him, "Tell me about boggarts. What's a boggart?"

Tony answered her. "It's a sort of brownie. Lives in your house and plays stupid tricks." Julian lunged for him again, but Sally had him. "Julian," she said. "I'm a Yank, I don't know anything, you tell me. Why is it so terrible if someone calls you a boggart?"

Julian wasn't exactly crying, but his nose was running and he had to swallow a couple of times before he could talk. He said, "Boggarts are ugly—that's why *he*'s always calling me that. They're small, and they've got warts and bumples and all, and they like to live in the cupboards and under the floor. But they're not always mean—you can make friends with a boggart if you're really nice to him. You leave milk out for them, and things. I just thought it would be funny if we had one."

Tony started to say something, but Evan caught *his* eye, and he shut right up. Evan said, "Well, if it's not a boggart, it'll be something else, likely enough. Dorset's full of ghosts and hobs and bogles, and things that go *boomp* i' the nicht. And Stourhead Farm's been around long enough that we've probably got a grand mob of them already settled in. Some of them probably knew Thomas Hardy and William Barnes."

(This is probably going to come up again, so I have to put in that I didn't know who he was talking about then. I do now, because Meena's made me read all her Thomas Hardy books. He's all right. I can't *stand* William Barnes.)

Evan told us stories the rest of the way down, as the land got steeper and greener and the poor little Escort kept overheating. I can't remember all of them, but he talked about bullbeggars and Jack-in-Irons, and the Wild Hunt, which was scary, and about the Black Dog, and a weird thing called the Hedley Kow. With a *k*. He was good, better than Norris even—he did the different accents, depending on where the stories came from, so Julian kept sniffling and giggling all the time, and Tony forgot to be superior and just sat there *glued*, I could tell. That's the thing about Tony. He really thinks nobody can read what he's feeling—he really works on it—but everyone always knows.

I dozed off a third time in the middle of a story about someone called The Old Lady of the Elder Tree. I was actually trying to stay awake, because it was interesting, but I fell asleep and dreamed about Mister Cat. In the dream the quarantine was over, and I was coming to get him out of his cage, and he stood up and put his paws on my face, the way he does. It was so real and sweet that I woke up, but it was just Julian asleep on my shoulder with his hair brushing my cheek, and we were at Stourhead Farm.

Six

So far, the hard part about writing a book isn't telling what happened, even if it happened a long time ago—it's trying to call back, not just the way you felt about the thing that happened, but the entire person who felt that way. Writing about the early days at Stourhead Farm is like that.

After six years, Stourhead's just *ordinary*, I guess that's the only word. When I'm here I can wake up in the morning and look out my bedroom window, and if there's an old floppy cow named Lady Caroline Lamb looking back in at me, that's as ordinary as the sound of Evan's old floppy Jeep on the far side of Spaniards Hill, or the way the air around the kitchen well sort of trembles, because of the electricity from the pump. As usual as Tony dancing between the cabbage rows, when he's not off touring somewhere, practicing his *entrechats* or whatever in the South Barn with Mister Cat and a bunch of chickens for an audience. Natural as hearing Julian, who's the only one of us home now, bugging Ellie John or William or Seth to let him drive the baler. Ordinary as not feeling Tamsin anywhere in the house, ever again, when I wake.

But I can't get to Tamsin yet, although that's really all I want to write about. Meena says I absolutely have to describe what Stourhead Farm was like when Evan and Sally took it over, and the trouble they had bringing it back to being a working farm, the way it is now, and especially how everything was for me back then, being snatched right out of New York and plopped down on this raggedy ruin of a Dorset estate. And she's right, I know that—that's what you *do* when you're writing a book. But it's hard.

First off, it *was* a ruin, Stourhead—even a West Eighty-third Street child could see that. Not that I knew what a real farm was supposed to look like, except you had to have cows. But I didn't need to notice that half the fences were caved in like old people's mouths, or that the two barns and all the little sheds and coops and pens were dark and soft looking, as though they'd been rained on for years, and that what wasn't rotting was rusting, from the plows and harrows and stuff like that to the well casings and even the wheelbarrows. All I had to do was watch Evan's face, seeing his eyes going back and forth between Sally and those crumbly barns, between the boys and the scrawny chickens scratching around their feet, between me—still sitting in the car when everyone else had gotten out—and the house, "the Manor," people around here still call it. I just looked at his face, and I knew he was feeling like pure pounded shit, and I was glad.

You see, he hadn't really thought about anything but the soil. Evan's like that. He can scoop up a handful of earth and sniff at it, even taste it, and tell you what it'll grow and what it won't, and what it just *might* grow if you add this or that or something else to it. And he's always right, always—the same way some people can tell you where to dig for water or what the weather's going to be tomorrow, that's how Evan is with dirt. But it hadn't ever occurred to him how it would be for his boys, for Sally and me, to be living right *on* that dirt, in a falling-down house at the end of the world. All that planning and dreaming with Sally, and it just hadn't come up.

Sally was good. I didn't know to be proud of her then, but I am now, when I think of her standing and staring across a rutty dirt road and a stretch of baby-barf-colored dead grass at the house that had looked so great in the Polaroids. I couldn't see her face, but she said in this perfectly *daily* voice, "Come on, Jenny, let's go. We're home."

Everybody carried a couple of suitcases or boxes, because you couldn't drive right up to the house back then. You can now, of course—it took Evan a year to find the original carriageway about two feet down, under three centuries' worth of guck—but I'll always remember the lot of us, heads down, nobody saying a word, just schlepping our stuff across that dirt road toward that old, *old* house that didn't want us. I remember Sally shifting a duffel bag to carry it under her right arm, so that she could reach out with her left hand to take hold of Evan's arm. The way he looked down at her . . . I'm really not a *total* idiot. I knew damn well, even then, that Norris hadn't ever looked at her like that.

And I remember the windows. There were so many of them—

round and long and square and pointy—and because the sun was slanting down behind us, all those windows were blazing up as though the house was full of fire, you couldn't look straight at it. There was one small, sharp window on the third floor that didn't reflect the sun at all. It looked absolutely black, surrounded by all those others, like a hole in the sky, with the darkness of space showing through.

Julian was walking really slowly, hanging back more and more, until Sally looked around for him and let Evan go on ahead so she could take Julian's hand. Then I wished *I* was a scared little English kid wearing a dumb school cap whom she didn't even know a week ago, and then I got mad at myself for feeling like that. So I grabbed his other hand and just marched on up to the house. To the Manor.

For a farmhouse, it's enormous, the biggest house I'm ever likely to live in, the biggest house in this part of Dorset, and when it was built in 1671, was the biggest in the whole county. But Dorset's never run to mansions, even in the towns—it's always been farms and villages, like in Hardy's books, and Stourhead was always a farm, from the beginning. So compared with some of those humongous old piles they run tour buses out to, the Manor is a studio apartment. But compared to *it,* my cousin Barbara's house in Riverdale, that she was so snotty-proud about, is a broom closet in a Motel Six. I hope she reads this.

I've already said I don't know how to describe rooms and interior decoration, and the same definitely goes for houses. The Manor has been built and rebuilt and burned down once—I *think* only once—and then it was rebuilt again and added to and added to, until nothing exactly fits with anything, which is just how the English like it. Anyway, the house has three floors, with a sort of east wing and a sort of west wing, and then there's what everybody still calls the Arctic Circle, the central section, where you come in. Tony was the one who started calling it that, the Arctic Circle, because that part of the house is on the original stone foundation, and you can't ever get it really warm, even today. But when we moved in, that was the only part of the house that *worked*, with running water and some electricity, and a cooking range the size of a pool table. I can still see us all clumped together there, hanging on to our bags and stuff, everybody trying to think of something cheery to say. Everybody except me, I mean.

Sally finally managed it. She said, "Well, a gas range, that's great! I'd much rather cook over gas." And Evan gave her this incredibly, unbelievabiy mournful look and said, "Actually, love, it's a wood stove. I'll show you how to work it, it's not that hard." And after that, nobody said anything for the next year and a half.

Finally Julian announced in that creaky little voice of his, "Well, I don't know about anybody else, but *I'm* going exploring." And before anybody could grab him, he was out of there, his clunky new school shoes rattling on the oak floors. (That's one thing about the Manor, it's got fantastic floors—they're so old and hard, even the termites break their teeth on them. When this house *dissolves,* those floors will still be hanging in the air.)

Tony said, "I'll get him," and Evan said tiredly, "No, he's right, let's look around this museum. There's supposed to be a caretaker here somewhere, but I think the boggarts got him." So we all went trooping after Julian, with *our* footsteps echoing up stairs and down corridors, in and out of one room after another, with the boys already fussing over who was going to sleep where. They'd always had to share a bedroom; there was no way in the world they could deal with that kind of abundance. Nice word.

I couldn't take any of it in myself. I'd never in my life been in a house like this one. Farm or no, you could have dropped our old apartment into some of those rooms without raising dust or knocking over a plant stand. And then there were some no bigger than bathrooms, narrow as coffins, which is what they really looked like. Evan said those were for the servants. First useful thing I learned about the seventeenth century.

What else is important to put in about the first time I saw the Manor? The smell, of course, I should have done that right at the start. Not just because the house was so old, but because of the way the different families running the farm had been letting it go to hell for the last hundred years or so. So you had the *old* smell, which is one thing, and you also had that dark, dead-cold mousey smell of the layers of neglect, no getting away from either of them wherever you went. Six years of cleaning, six years of repairing and replacing, scraping and painting, digging away at those layers, and some days I can still *taste* them, both of those smells.

We didn't get above the second floor that day because the third was closed off then, which everybody thought was just as well. It was, too, and not just because we were all absolutely worn out by that time. But all I'm going to say about the third floor right now is when Julian was home on his last holiday, he found a whole new room we'd never seen, a little tiny chamber like a lady's dressing room, tucked away behind a door about as wide as an ironing board. There were a couple of semisecret passages, too, but they didn't go anywhere. The third floor's like that.

It made me think of Tamsin, when Julian found that room, because that was how

No, I'm scratching that out, that *has* to wait. I'm still talking about that first day. We brought all the other stuff in from the car and dumped it in the front parlor, which Sally's got looking great now, but which was just bare and gray then, with nothing on the floor but a dirty rag rug and a beat-up harmonium in a far corner. Evan broke up a junky old table and got a fire going, but it didn't help much, because the ceiling's way too high. He stood up from the fireplace with his back to us, and and took a really long breath before he turned around. "Well, my legions," he said. "Doesn't look much of a bargain, does it?"

Tony said, "It's not so bad," and Julian said, "It's *big*" at the same time. Sally just laughed. She said, "Darling, it needs work, I knew that. I've never lived anywhere that *didn't* need work."

"The farm doesn't," Evan said, "not so much." Then he laughed himself and said, "Well, yes, it does, it needs a deal of work, but I can handle that. It's this house. I knew it was going to be hard for a bit, but I didn't quite realize *how* hard. I want to say I'm sorry, everybody." Then he looked straight at me and added, "Especially to you, Jenny. You didn't need this on top of all the rest of it. I'm very sorry."

So, of course, now *everybody* was looking at me. I could have killed Evan, and at the same time I felt guilty and horrible, because he was really trying to be nice. Sally put her arm around me and she said, "Jenny's all right."

Tony said, "We're all all right. We none of us thought it was going to be a dizzy round of pleasure." And Julian growled, "It'll be like camping out. I love camping out." So now I *had* to say something, but the best I could manage was, "Well, I don't care, I wasn't expecting . . ." and I just let it trail off there. The absolute best I could do then.

"All right, then," Evan said. "What's for dinner?"

Because there wasn't any Chinese fast-food place around the

corner—there wasn't any *corner*—and the nearest grocery would have been back in Sherborne, which is the nearest real town, which we'd passed through when I was asleep. But we did all right with the leftovers from the car, and after that we worked out who'd sleep where for now, and which bathrooms were usable—Evan got the boiler going, so there was hot water anyway, even if it was exactly the color of New York sidewalks. And then everybody went to bed early. Because there wasn't anything else to do.

Tony and Julian were downstairs, trading rooms every five minutes. I was on the second floor, in the room right next to Sally and Evan's. The way I was feeling, I was really hoping they'd put me in one of those mean little servant garrets, so I could catch TB or something. This one smelled major mildewy, like all the others, and the lightbulbs were so dusty you could tell they'd been dead for *years*. But it had ceilings so high I couldn't see them in the darkness, and big windows for Mister Cat to come and go by—once we finally got them open—and the bed was all right, once I got some West Eighty-third Street sheets on it. It was a brass four-poster, but the canopy was just rags, and I pulled them all off.

I could hear Sally and Evan talking softly, even though I was really trying not to, I really didn't *want* to hear them being private. Evan was saying, "I don't think money's going to be the problem. The Lovells are in this for the long haul—they'll lay out whatever it takes to bring the farm back to life. I'm not at all bothered about that."

"But it's all going to take twice as long as you thought," Sally said. "Because of the house. That's the bother, isn't it?"

I couldn't get used to the way she sounded, talking to him—not like my goofy New York single-mom Sally, more like an older person, so thoughtful and *mature* it always made me feel strange. Evan laughed a little and said, "Well, it's my fault, I should have stashed you lot back in London with Charlie, and come down here alone, until I got things put shipshape. I *knew* that, damn it. I just wanted you with me."

I heard them kissing then, and I curled up tight and pulled that cold, floppy pillow over my ears. I didn't expect to sleep at all, but I did, straight through, and I had one weird dream after another, all of them full of people I didn't know. Sometime in the night Sally sat by me on the bed for a while, unless that was a dream, too.

I should have asked her then, but I wasn't about to, and now she can't remember. But I think she did.

Okay. The first months were solid nightmare, and it's no good my pretending they weren't. And I was a big part of the nightmare, maybe the biggest, I know that. I'm not going to go on and on about it, I'm just going to say that I was absolutely miserable, and I spread it around, and if everybody else at Stourhead wasn't absolutely miserable, too, it wasn't my fault. I did the very best I could.

But I had help. There was the house itself, to begin with. If I ever knew a house that truly did not want to be lived in, it was the Manor back when we arrived. I don't just mean stuff like that sidewalk-colored water coming out in smelly burps, or the wood stove smoking up the kitchen every time Sally tried to cook something, or the weird way the electricity was hooked up, so you could turn on the light in my bathroom and blow every fuse in the west wing. Or the Horror Of The Septic Tank, which I am not going to describe, ever. That's not what I mean.

Since that last sentence, I've been sitting here for half an hour, figuring how to explain how all of us were always tripping and falling over *nothing* at least once a day, as though those beautiful old floors absolutely hated the feet that walked on them. I'm talking about the way you could hear ugly little murmurs in the two chimneys, even when there wasn't any wind, and the way some corners just ate up light, just stayed cold and shadowy forever, never mind how many lamps you plugged in. And I'm talking about the quick, scratchy footsteps everybody heard right above the Arctic Circle, one time or another, and nobody wanted to mention; and about that east-wing window that wouldn't reflect the sunlight. We couldn't even find the room it belonged to, that's how the Manor was.

Julian was wildly excited about all this at the beginning. He ran around saying, "It's a haunted house, how splendid—I'll be the only boy at school living in a real haunted house!" But there were a couple of rooms on the second floor that Julian absolutely would not go into, from the first day. Everybody else did—there didn't seem anything weird or scary about these two at least—but Julian just stopped right at the door, like I've seen Mister Cat do sometimes, and nobody could get him to take another step. He kept mumbling, "It feels *funny*, I don't like it." When Evan tried to talk him into going in, he cried. When Tony teased him about it, Julian hit him. Of course he says he doesn't remember any of that now.

Oh, there *was* a caretaker, by the way—I forgot to put that in. His name was Wilf, he looked exactly like the Pillsbury Doughboy in weird rubber overalls and hip boots, and he wandered up from the cellar the first morning we were there, totally and permanently hungover. He had a shuffly, wincing style of walking, as though his head were made of glass, just about to roll off his shoulders and shatter into a million bits. He was supposed to be there just for a couple of weeks, to show Evan where things were around the house and the farm, but he hung on after that, and you couldn't ever quite get rid of him. Evan fired him once or twice a week, but he didn't pay any attention.

Evan and Sally worked like crazy people. Evan got rid of the wood stove as soon as he could find someone to haul it away, and we actually did sort of live on pizza and takeout from Sherborne until the Lovells—the family who own Stourhead Farm—put in a new electric range. Which meant replacing all the wiring in the whole Arctic Circle, but they never hassled Evan about that. Besides the electricity, they paid to have the plumbing redone—so between one thing and another the house was a total ruin for months, with tools and torn-out boards all over everywhere, and nests of wires hanging out of the walls, and the men Evan hired to help him tramping around growling at each other, scattering pipe ashes on the floors and taking tea breaks every ten minutes. They mostly had ponytails and big thick yellow mustaches, and I never could tell them apart.

They also quit a lot. Most of the time it was over ordinary stuff like the pay or the hours or the tea breaks, but not always. One guy quit because his tools kept disappearing on him, and I think he tried to sue the Lovells about it. And there was one who just didn't show up for work one morning, and *he* never did come back for his tools. Later on, he wrote Evan and Sally a letter, trying to explain, but it was mixed up and misspelled, and full of ramblings about sad voices, and music he couldn't hear, and about "pudles of cold air," and something like invisible fur brushing his neck all the time. There were a couple of others who talked about the voices and the cold air, too, and a man who said he kept smelling vanilla the whole time he was rewiring the Arctic Circle, and it made him so nervous he had to stop. Evan said most of them drank, and just kept hiring new ones.

Tony said, "Maybe we really do have a boggart," but he said it out of range of Julian's feet. The two of them are going to hate this, because it makes them seem as though they were fighting all the time, but back then they *were.* Julian was always the person who started hitting and kicking and crying, but Tony usually had it coming, one way or the other. That's the way I remember it, anyhow.

"Well, it just might be," Evan said. The weirder the question, the more seriously he answers it; that's another way Evan is. "There's certainly something playing tricks in the kitchen lately, and if it isn't you two—"

"It's not, it's not!" Julian rumbled, and Tony said quickly, "Well, I just took a *couple* of the chocolate biscuits, but I didn't knock all those bottles down—"

"And I didn't, didn't, *didn't* draw those pictures in the flour!" Julian was shaking his head so hard it actually made me dizzy to look at him. "And I didn't throw the eggs around, and I didn't make the horrible mess under the sink, and the fridge wasn't my fault—"

Evan sighed. "I wish I *could* blame that on a boggart." We'd already had two different refrigerators put in by then, and neither one could keep stuff cold for more than a day. There wasn't a thing wrong with them—each time all the food went bad, Evan had an old man come down from Salisbury, but all he could ever figure was that the electricity was screwed up some way. Which didn't make any sense, with the new wiring; but the last time he came, the Salisbury man rubbed a finger alongside his nose and closed one eye (I'd read about people doing that, but I'd never actually *seen* it), and told Evan, "There's some houses, ones that was here before the electric, they don't *like* the electric. They'll be fighting it, squeezing at it, trying to choke it off all the time. It's fighting the electric, this house, that's what's happening." Evan called somebody else the next time, but it didn't make much difference.

Me, I was flat out hoping for a dozen boggarts, and fifty pookas, and a whole herd of Hedley Kows, and all those other creatures Evan had told us about on the drive down. Anything that would make it absolutely impossible for us to stay on at Stourhead, anything that would force us at least back to London, even if we couldn't go home to New York—was for it all the way, no matter how messy or how scary. Anyway, I *was* for it until the *thing* that happened in my bathroom.

Sally used to tell me that the English air would do wonders for my skin and, besides, my skin wasn't nearly as horrible as I thought it was. All I knew was I'd been sprouting torrid new English zits from Heathrow on, and I was developing a hunchy slouch, the way tall girls get, from sneaking past mirrors. Except one, the mirror in my bathroom, where every night and every morning I'd face off with my face one more time. Try any damn thing anybody said might work—all kinds of ointments and soaps and masks, stuff that made my skin tight and flaky, stuff that smelled like rotten eggs, other stuff that was supposed to soothe your skin, only when it dried on you it *hurt*. . . . I don't like talking about that time. It was years ago, but it comes right back.

Anyway. I was leaning in close to the mirror, doing exactly what Sally always said not to do, which was squeezing a thing on my forehead which was forever boiling up in the exact same place. (Meena says that it was probably my third eye trying to get me to pay attention, but what it *looked* like was a zit about the size of an M&M. A bright red one.) Once I got it open, I was going to clean it out with alcohol, and I didn't care if it burned. I hoped it *would* burn—then maybe the damn thing would get the idea and leave me alone. And then I heard the voices.

Not words, mind you. I didn't hear real words, just two voices, one of them squeaky as a Munchkin, the other one a bit deeper, definitely slower—still shrill, mind you, but with an explaining sort of tone, like Tony whispering to Julian about what was happening in a movie. He was really patient with Julian that way, even in those days when he was calling him a boggart.

I swung around, but I couldn't see anything. It was a small bathroom, no shower even, and no hiding place except in the shadows behind the old lion-foot tub. That's where the voices were coming from.

I took just a step toward the tub, and I said, "Who are you?" And if that sounds brave or anything, you can hang that notion up right now. I wasn't afraid of anyone who spoke in tiny squeaks and could hide behind a bathtub. What I was afraid of was that if I wasn't really careful I was going to start understanding them, because I was almost making words out already. And that was the last thing I wanted, to understand squeaky voices behind the tub.

They went silent for a minute when I spoke, and then they

started up again, both of them, sounding excited now. I could have screamed—I *felt* a scream working its way up through my chest—but that would have brought everybody in, and I didn't want Sally to know I'd been digging at zits. Probably sounds incredibly dumb, but there you are, that was me. I took another couple of steps, and I stamped my foot down really hard, so my toothbrush rattled in the glass. "I can see you," I said. "You might as well come out of there. Come on, I'm not going to hurt you." I threw that in because my voice was shaky, and I didn't want them to think I was scared.

What that got me was a flood of giggles. Not squeaks, not talk, and not real giggles, either. Nasty little titters, the kind you're supposed to hear off to one side when you're walking down the hall. I know those. In school I never let it get me, but then—in that old bathroom, in that strange, smelly old house, with *them*, whoever they were, spying on me picking my face, and snickering about it, I just lost it, that's all. I ran at the tub, stamping and kicking out like Julian when Tony'd been teasing him one time too many. It's a good thing there wasn't anybody there, or I'd have trampled them flat, I didn't care if they were Santa's elves. But they were gone. I heard feet skittering off somewhere in a corner, but no voices, except for Sally in the hall, calling to know if I was all right. I said I was.

That night I lay awake for hours, wishing more than ever that Mister Cat was with me, snoring on my stomach, and I tried to stay cool and decide whether I was going crazy, which I'd always almost expected, or whether there really were boggarts running around in my bathroom. Crazy was comforting, in a way—if you're crazy, then nothing's your fault, which was just how I wanted to feel right then. Boggarts were scary, because if they were possible, and possible right here in this house, then all kinds of other stuff was possible, and most of it I didn't much want to think about. But it was *interesting*, at least, and crazy isn't interesting. Handy, I could see that, but not interesting.

When I did fall asleep, I didn't dream about boggarts exactly. I dreamed that Julian and I had shrunk down to the size of boggarts, and that big people were chasing us with sticks. I don't know why sticks, but that's not important, that wasn't the frightening part. There was something else in the dream, too, something or someone with big yellow eyes, such a raw, wild yellow they were practically golden. Big, big eyes, with a slitty sideways pupil, filling up the dream. We couldn't get away from them until I woke, all tangled in my sweaty sheets and listening for voices. But I never did hear them again, not those.

Seven

Meena keeps saying this is where I should put in all the stuff about Stourhead Farm, but it's hard to know where to start. First off, it's in the country—not that *country* means much when you're twenty miles from Julian's Taco Bell pretty much wherever you are. But when you've lived your entire life in downtown Manhattan, waking up to hear cows wondering when they're going to be milked instead of police sirens, and hearing wild geese yelling overhead instead of jackhammers tearing up West Eighty-third and Columbus, and hearing the plumbing burping like mad because there's some kind of air pocket in the well instead of drunks puking and crying right under your window . . . well, that's it, that's country. Maybe not to Willie Nelson or Thomas Hardy, but to West Eighty-third and Columbus, it's country.

Okay, Meena. You can trace Stourhead Farm back to 1671, when Roger Willoughby bought a big piece of a rundown manor—freehold, that's outright, not like being a tenant farmer. He *wasn't* a farmer, he made his money selling supplies to the Royal Navy, but he had all kinds of ideas about farming in his head, and he couldn't wait to try them out. He wrote letters to the newspapers, he wrote pamphlets on how you could get double yields by rotating the crops just so, and how to breed bigger Dorset sheep, and why everybody in west Dorset should quit growing wheat and raise millet instead. Evan says everybody in west Dorset sat back and waited to see him go under. That's when they took to calling his big new house "the Manor," to make fun of him. Roger Willoughby was from Bristol, and in those days he might just as well have been from Madras, like Meena. It's different now, like everywhere, but not *that* different. Dorset doesn't change as fast as some other places.

Well, he didn't go under, Roger Willoughby. He couldn't do

anything about the sheep—they're still pretty small—but he must have had *some* sense about farming, because Stourhead stayed in his family for almost three hundred years. They weren't gentry, and they weren't absentee landlords, buying up farms they never saw. They lived on the land, and they always seemed to have their fingers in it, messing around with some new notion. Roger Willoughby planted barley and oats at first, and then peas—and he did try to plant millet, but when it just wouldn't take, he went back to wheat, like everybody else. Because he might have been a Prodigious Romantic—that's what Tamsin called him—but he wasn't crazy.

It's not a big farm, maybe seven hundred acres. In the States, that's like a playpen, a backyard, you can't even make it pay for itself. But it was big enough for this part of Dorset in Roger Willoughby's time. It used to be bigger—I don't know how much—but the Willoughbys sold off some corners and slices over the years. Especially in the nineteenth century, when there was a long run of terrible weather, and a bad slump in farm prices. Stourhead just went straight downhill from about 1900 and never really recovered. The last of the Willoughbys sold out after World War II—I think there were four or five owners after them, each one more clueless than the one before. When the Lovells took over, the place was probably the exact same wilderness it was when old Roger Willoughby moved in.

The Lovells were always business people, just like the Willoughbys were farmers. (In England, people always know what your family's always been.) The ones who own Stourhead actually live near Oxford—Evan mostly goes there to meet with them these days, because they don't come down here nearly as often as they used to when we were first at Stourhead. Back then they practically lived with us, showing up in red-faced coveys to hold big conferences with Evan about their plans to have Stourhead at least breaking even in a couple of years, and maybe making a profit after that. Evan thought they were as prodigiously romantic as old Roger Willoughby, and I used to hear him telling them so, over and over.

"You can't turn a farm as exhausted as Stourhead all the way around that fast," he kept saying. "I'm not talking only about the physical aspect—the barns and the outbuildings and that—I mean the land itself. Your topsoil's a disaster area—it's starved for nitrogen, it's been fertilized for years by the criminally insane, and whatever thief put in your irrigation system ought to be flogged through the fleet." One Lovell or another usually started spluttering right about this point, but Evan would just go straight on over him. "You need a fourth well, and very likely a fifth—that's simply not negotiable. Three wells were just fine in good King Charles's golden days, but nothing's what it was back then, including your water table. That's why the corn's not growing—that, and the fact that it's the wrong strain for this acid soil and this climate. And where you *do* have enough water, in the upper meadows, you've got yourselves a proper little marsh bubbling along. The only malaria swamp in England, I shouldn't wonder."

The Lovells would always wind up asking Evan if he thought it was possible to salvage the farm at all. And he'd tell them what he always told them: "Yes, but you can't do it overnight, and you can't do it on the cheap. It's going to cost you money and a great deal of time, and if you're not willing to invest both of those, you might just as well chuck it in and sell the place for a Christmas-tree farm." Those are really big in Dorset, by the way. I don't have any idea why.

Watching him with those people day after day was like seeing a whole different Evan, in a way. I mean, he still talked quietly, and his hair was always still messy, and he sometimes actually wouldn't remember to come in when it rained, because he'd be thinking about something. But he knew what he was talking about—that was the big difference—and all those Lovells knew he knew, and that he didn't care what they thought, this was the way it was. You can't fake being like that. I've tried.

The Lovells had to be impressed, but I didn't, not if I put my mind to it. I didn't see a whole lot of Evan during those early months at Stourhead, except at dinner in the Arctic Circle, because he'd be out all day every day, and I'd mostly be with Sally, trying to deal with the Manor, which kept being torn up and put back together and torn up again—more or less how I was feeling then. I wasn't a lot of fun for Sally, but I was some use anyway, I'll say that for myself. I helped clean up after the wiring and plumbing finally got done, and Tony and I swept and dusted and scoured out all the rooms on the first floor and most of the ones on the second. We didn't say ten words to each other all that time, but we worked well together. I even thought for a hot minute about telling him about the voices in my bathroom, but I didn't. Today I would, Tony, if you ever read this far.

And if I wasn't working, I was being dragged all over the farm by Julian—half the time I'd wake up with him tugging at my foot, going, "Oh, come *on*, Jenny, *do*, let's go exploring!" Only *exploring*, to Julian, could mean climbing around on some old rusty hulk of farm machinery, trying to figure out how it must have worked, or it could just as easily mean getting me to chase him through this dark little hillside oak forest that he started right away calling the Hundred-Acre Wood, like the one in Winnie-the-Pooh. We all call it that now. And sometimes he'd want to search for the room with that dark third-floor window. He bugged Evan so much about it that Evan finally dug out the oldest plans of the house—they have to be kept vacuum-sealed behind plastic, because they'll crumble right away if they're exposed to air. Julian and I counted the windows in those drawings over and over again, but there was always one missing. Evan said it happened.

Sometimes we'd hike up and down across the fields—Dorset is *all* up and down—to the stretch of heathland that I guess was always too bumpy for even Roger Willoughby to plough up. I'm glad nobody ever farmed it, because it feels good to look at, rolling away softly toward the skinny two-lane road that's the north boundary of Stourhead Farm. Julian would run off to check out the flock of sheep that the Lovells still kept on the downs, and try to play with Albert, the collie, and I'd flop onto the turf and stare up at fluffy clouds like glops of whipped butter, and not think about anything. Except maybe the butterflies. I never in my life saw so many different kinds of butterflies as they have on the downs. They'll land on your face if you lie very quiet.

I still don't know why Julian took to me from the beginning, at Heathrow. He's the only person in my life who's ever walked right up to me like that. I mean, even Jake and Marta took awhile, and Meena wasn't sure she'd ever like me, that first term. But that ten-year-old English kid in his school uniform coat . . . Day One. There was one time, exploring, when he just *had* to jump from rock to rock across a stream we found running through a sort of little hollow—what they call a *coombe* here—because that's in Winnie-the-Pooh, too, and of course he fell in and I had to get him out. Not that it was so deep—he could have waded across—but he caught his foot under something, and he twisted it trying to get loose, and

I got soaked through hauling him to the bank. He went around for days telling everyone how I'd saved him from a watery grave. First I thought he was doing it to get up Tony's nose, but then I realized he meant it. He was so proud of me, and so proud of himself for being saved. Julian.

He did something for me once, something he'll forget way before I do. It was the day Sally and I went to Goshawk Farm Cattery to see Mister Cat for the first time. I'd been agitating about it from the moment we hit Stourhead, but there was too much to do right away, and Evan needed the car every day. Finally Sally and the wheels were free at the same time, and she drove me to Dorchester, which is where Goshawk Farm is, right on the outskirts. It was a really nasty, windy day, raining on and off, the beginning of Dorset autumn.

Mister Cat wouldn't speak to me. He knew me, all right, but he wouldn't look at me. I'd expected him to be in a wire cage, like the one he'd traveled in, only bigger, but it was more like a cat motel room, with things to scratch and climb on, and dangling things to jump at for exercise, with its own outdoor run for good weather. And he wasn't going hungry—his coat was the glossiest I'd ever seen it, and he'd put on a little weight. But he couldn't even be bothered to make that evil warning noise at me again. He just turned his back and curled around himself, and closed his eyes.

Sally tried to help. All the way back to the farm she told me one story after another about people she knew who'd had to put their pets in quarantine, and how some of the animals felt so lonely and angry that they wouldn't come to their owners when it was time to pick them up. But of course they all forgave them in time, and Mister Cat would forgive me, too. Fairy tales, like the ones she told me when I was little, and all her stories had happy endings.

When we got back, it was near dark. Evan had dinner waiting, but I just went to my room and lay on my bed. I didn't cry—I told you, I don't do that much. It wasn't like being mad at Sally on West Eighty-third Street, which you could sort of enjoy all the time you were feeling miserable. This *hurt*, it hurt my stomach, and no matter which way I turned, it kept on hurting. My throat got so swollen and tight, I might as well have *been* crying, only I couldn't. I just lay there.

I wasn't asleep when Julian came into the room—by then I was sure I'd never want to eat or sleep or talk to anybody again. He pushed the door open very slowly—I could feel the hall light on my eyes, but I kept them shut tight. It doesn't matter how quietly you try to move in my room, the way the floor squeaks, but Julian seemed to wait minutes, hours, between each step, until he was by the bed. I heard this froggy little whisper, "Jenny? Are you really, *really* sleeping?"

I didn't answer. A moment later, Julian put something down beside me, right on my pillow, brushing my face. It smelled pretty funky—not bad, just old, and somehow familiar, too. I heard Julian squeaking back to the door, and the door squeaking shut again. I didn't turn the light on, but after a while I reached out for whatever he'd left on the pillow. The moment I touched it, I knew. That damn one-eyed, beat-up stuffed gorilla he's had practically all his life—slept with, chewed on, probably peed on, too, more than likely. Trust Julian—every other kid has a bedtime bear, but Julian's got a gorilla named Elvis. I grabbed that thing, and I shoved my face hard into its stinky, sticky fur, and I cried my eyes out until I fell asleep.

So that's how Julian got to be my baby brother. The last thing in the world I needed right then, but that was it.

It's *noisy* in the country, in a strange way. You hear more sounds, just *because* of the stillness, especially at night. Instead of tuning out, the way you absolutely have to do in New York, you start tuning in, whether you want to or not. I don't mean just the geese going over, and the frogs and crickets and so on, and the cocks just as likely to start crowing at two in the morning. I got so I could hear a well pump cutting off and on and off, out beyond the dairy. Some frosty nights I'd even hear twigs snapping in the thickets, and that would be the deer foraging, eating the tree bark. And when you hear a cold, clear, sharp sort of yelp, with almost a metallic shrill to it, that's not a dog, that's a fox. It's always a little sudden and scary, that sound, even when you know what it is.

The Manor makes noises, too, the way all old houses do, settling in the ground—"working," that's what they say here. I've always thought it sounds like the little grunts and mumbles and sighs somebody makes getting comfortable in bed after a hard day. Even the West Eighty-third Street apartment made those, so that wasn't anything to be edgy about, most nights.

But every now and then. Just every now and then, from the first night, I'd hear something that didn't *fit*. Not so much the patter of little feet, or little snickery voices (you can always tell yourself it's mice running and squeaking), and not ghosts wailing or dragging chains around—no Halloween stuff like that. A sound like rushing water, in the air right above my bed. A sound that might have been somebody sweeping a floor, back and forth, over and over, in the middle of the night. A whisper so low I couldn't make out one word. But that was the one that always woke me up; that was the one I was scared of hearing when I went to bed. I'd have asked Julian if he ever heard anything, but I didn't want *him* to get scared, so I didn't.

There were smells, too—that cold vanilla the electrician smelled in the Arctic Circle, and a dark-toast one almost like Mister Cat. And just once in a real while I'd think I saw those same huge golden eyes from the dream outside my window. Only I couldn't ever be sure whether I was awake or dreaming when I saw those. They didn't frighten me, for some reason—I always wanted to go toward them—so maybe that was dreaming. I still don't know, even today.

There was one sound that everybody knew about, not just me— a sound that used to bring Julian flying into my room whenever we heard it. It usually had to be a really fierce night, with thunder and lightning, rain smashing into you like hailstones, wind shaking the house, stripping and snapping the trees—I mean, the *works*. Then you'd hear them, high over the storm, the hounds baying and the horses screaming—and people laughing, too, these terrible, hungry yells of laughter. That's what always got Julian, that laughter. He'd shut his eyes and cover his ears and burrow his head into me, hard, so it really hurt sometimes.

Evan would tell us it was just the wild geese calling to each other, the same as ever, only the wind was distorting their cries. He'd say, "Every country in Europe has that same legend—the Wild Hunt, the Wish-Hounds, the Chasse Gayere, the Sluagh— huntsmen and their dogs chasing after the souls of the dead. It's the geese, all of it—nothing but the wild geese, the wild weather, and a little wild imagination." And Julian would nod and be cool, but he'd spend the rest of the night in my room, and it was always nice to have the company. Because both of us knew what geese sounded like.

The Lovells gave Evan a totally free hand with the farm, as far as reconstruction went. They told him he could start from scratch—tear down everything except the Manor, if he wanted. He must have hired just about everybody in Sherborne and all the little nearby towns that he hadn't already hired to work on the house—men, women, some who didn't look much older than me or Tony. All the sheds and outhouses went first off, and all the tools and equipment got stored in one barn while they were demolishing the other. Then Evan started on the fences— he must have replaced every single post and every strand of wire on the whole seven hundred acres. And when he wasn't doing that, he was walking the fields, making notes and mumbling to himself and scooping up dirt. Sally did the best she could with his hands every night, but all that fall and winter they looked like ground meat.

Anyway, it was all just like the way it was when we were packing up on West Eighty-third, with everything half done, and nothing the same from day to day, and everybody knowing what was going on except me. And in the middle of all *that*, we started school in Sherborne.

I've been putting off talking about that first year of English school. It's not that it was so awful—I had way worse times at Gaynor when I started there. It's more that now absolutely everything in the *world* was out of balance at the same time, completely unfamiliar, from the food and the talk and the way people drove, to the house I was living in and the sounds I heard at night. The Sherborne Boys' school was new for Tony and Julian, too, but at least they knew the basics, they didn't have to think about how to *be* every step they took. If I'd met Meena right off, it might have been a lot different. If I'd had Mister Cat—but I didn't . . . worse than didn't. Okay, it was pretty awful, at the beginning. But so was I.

They do wear uniforms at the Sherborne School for Girls. It's not a bad uniform—navy-blue blazers, plaid kilt skirts, gray pullovers or white blouses—and there's more leeway about what you can wear as you go up through the forms, until you get to the Sixth Form, where you're practically God and you don't wear uniforms at all. But I was in the Third Form, down in the miserable middle of the pack and stuck with that blue blazer for centuries to come. Putting it on every morning, I felt years younger—a whole *life* younger—than I had in Gaynor Junior High. It was bad enough being the age I was, but I'd been getting almost used to it; now it felt like I was back being a sticky, whiny, scabby-kneed little girl all over again, and I hated it. I used to practically *undress* on the bus going home.

That was another thing, the bus. I've already said I don't make friends easily, and being a day girl didn't help either. There are about four hundred students at Sherborne Girls, and all of them were boarding at the school, living in one or another of the eight houses there, except maybe twenty who went home every day, like me. So I missed out on *that* bonding experience, too: The thing that happens when people spend months living and eating and studying, and being together all the time. You don't work up that kind of school spirit on a bus—anyway, I don't. We were all assigned to the different houses, just like real boarders, but it wasn't the same thing.

Meena Chari was a day girl, too, but I didn't notice her much on the bus. She wasn't one of the ones who came to sit next to me and ask me about life in the States, and did I ever see this or that band, this or that movie star. They tried me out one after another, for a while, but they all gave up pretty quickly. Which was too bad, because some of them were nice, and they never really spoke to me again, ever. My loss, I know that.

Sherborne Girls sits on forty acres of green hill at the western outskirts of town, and it looks like a *real* manor—just this side of a palace, even—with its two wings spreading out from a central tower. Evan calls places like those "stately piles," but all I can say is that it impressed the hell out of *me* that first day, and I was not planning to be impressed. It still does.

The work was so much tougher than Gaynor, I don't even want to go into it. I'd always gotten pretty good grades at Gaynor (which is different from being a good *student*, and I knew it then); but this was a different world, no comparison at all. Third form, and they had me taking stuff I wouldn't have had to deal with until high school—and half of it would have been elective then. English literature, maths, world history, British history, three different science classes, a language (I took Spanish, because of Marta)—and we're not even talking about Games or Information Technology. I was over my head, out of my league, and practically paralyzed that whole first term. And it didn't help a bit to know what my education was costing Evan and Sally. Tony and Julian both had partial scholarships at the boys' school—not me. Nobody ever said a word about it.

And everyone was so damn terminally sweet, you could scream. New girls each have an older girl—she's called your "shadow"—to go around with you for a while and help you get used to the way things are done at Sherborne. My shadow was named Barbara, and even now, writing this, I wish I could think of one single nice thing I ever did for her or said to her. The best I can come up with is that I hardly talked at all while she was showing me where my form room would be—like a homeroom at Gaynor—and introducing me to my teachers, and to everyone in the house I was assigned to. She and all of them kept telling me that my being a day girl didn't matter, that I was still going to be a real part of the house, fully involved in all the social activities, always invited to stay for dinner after classes—only I'd miss the bus, and Sally would have to come and get me—never a moment of feeling like an outsider. They meant it, too. I always knew they meant it.

And if I was a sulky, silent mess in school, I was worse at home. I dragged my feet, helped out exactly as much as I absolutely had to, and bitched every waking moment, when I wasn't brooding and moping. I really try not to remember things I said to people in those days—to Evan especially—because they make me cringe in my skin. I was sort of halfway decent to Julian, because somehow he wouldn't let me be any other way, but to everyone else . . . no, that's enough about that. I said I wouldn't lie in my own book, and I'm *not* lying, but that's enough.

No, there's one thing that I do like to remember, something that happened just before Christmas. That was an even edgier time than usual, with Sally and me being Jewish, the boys being used to trees and stockings and carols, and Evan being really nervous. Of course I let them all know that I didn't want anything to do with killing a tree for Jesus, and I made a thing out of stomping off to find the menorah Grandma Paula'd given to Sally before we left. Julian tagged along with me. I'd given up telling him not to by then.

Actually, he was the one who dug out the menorah, down at the bottom of a box in the second-floor room where Sally stashed all the stuff she was planning to deal with on the very first weekend after hell froze over. It's at least a hundred years old, and it's silver, though you couldn't have told that at first sight, tarnished and scratched as it was. But I showed Julian the silversmith's mark on the base, and told him how my great-grandparents used to hide the menorah in the barn when the soldiers came through town. "In the cow's stall," I said, "under half a ton of cowshit. Even the Cossacks weren't about to rummage through *that*." Julian loved it. Two of the candleholders were bent to the side, and I said that was because the cow had stepped on them. I don't know if that's true or not.

Julian wanted to know how the menorah worked, so I sent him downstairs to get some candles while I tried to polish it up a bit. We had all kinds of candles all over the place back then, because of the power failing every ten minutes. The ones Julian got back with didn't quite fit, but I made them fit, and I told him about Chanukah—about the Syrians and the Maccabees, and the one last little cup of consecrated oil for the new temple altar in Jerusalem burning miraculously for eight days, until somebody finally showed up with fresh oil. It's a good story, and while I was telling it, I almost forgot that I was pissed at everyone in the world.

When Julian asked me if Jews had Chanukah carols, I went completely blank for a moment—Sally and I weren't exactly the most observant family on the West Side—and then I remembered the blessing that you chant when you're lighting the candles. That one I know, because Grandma Paula taught me, and I sang it for Julian.

"Boruch ata Adonai,
eloheynu melech haolam,
asher kidshanu b'mitzvosav,
v'tsivonu l'hadleek nehr,
shel Chanukah . . ."

Julian's always been quick with songs. He had this one in no time, his Hebrew pronunciation no worse than mine, and we sang it together while I lighted the lead candle, the *shammes,* and then lighted the first-night candle from it, just to show him how it was done. So there we were, Julian and me, kneeling on the floor in that cold, cobwebby room, the walls lined halfway around with Sally's boxes, and with tattered old trunks and valises from some other Sally, who always meant to get around to going through them, one day soon. There we were, the two of us, chanting our heads off, praising a God neither one of us believed in for commanding us to light the Chanukah candles. You have to see us, it's important.

Because that was when I smelled vanilla.

Eight

Meena, if you're the least bit cool you'll skip this part. I'm going to have to pretend you'll mind me, because otherwise I'm never going to be able to write it. Okay?

Okay. In the spring, the girl who'd sat next to me in Lower Third form room dropped out because her father got a job in Namibia or somewhere, and Meena Chari moved down a row. We hadn't spoken two words to each other that whole first term, even on the bus. Not because she was Indian or anything, but because she was so pretty. I don't mean knock-down, drop-dead, movie-star gorgeous, like Stacy Altieri back home—Meena doesn't look like that at all. But she's got this incredibly smooth brown skin, which wouldn't know a zit from a jelly bean, and big dark eyes like pansies, even behind her glasses. And even in that school uniform, Meena's always really wearing some elegant sari—you can tell by the way she moves. You had just *better* not be reading this, Meena!

I don't go around with girls who look like Meena, that's one decision I made early on. A lot of girls do—at Gaynor, people like Tracy and Vanessa had their own little packs of groupies, all hoping it would rub off on them somehow, or that boys would try to get to the pretty ones through them. Which happened, I'm not saying it didn't work, but I couldn't. I just hung with Jake and Marta and was glad I had them.

But Meena. What are you going to do with someone like Meena, who doesn't know the rules about things, who doesn't *act* pretty? I know, right—when you look the way Meena looks, you can afford not to care, but she really *doesn't*. Girls mostly think she's conceited, and boys are mostly afraid of her, because she gets perfect marks and she's going to be a doctor, like her grandfather. She's as cool and neat as I'm hot-tempered and sloppy, and it was a long time before I could start to believe that she actually wanted to be friends with me. Nothing to do with modesty—I just understand the rules.

We've talked about it a couple of times. The first time, she took forever to get what I was asking. She kept saying, "Why *shouldn't* we be friends, tell me that? We like the same books, the same kind of music, we laugh the same—we have so much in common, you might as well have been born in Madras, or I in New York." Meena talks like that. Her mother and father have Indian accents, but with Meena it's not the way her English sounds, but the way she uses it. Same thing as the uniform—you see one thing, or you hear one thing, but you *feel* something else. And Meena doesn't even think about it.

When she finally caught onto what I meant, she didn't answer right away. She put her hands together and rested her chin on her fingertips, and she looked at the ground for a long time. Then she looked up at me, and she said, "Because I'm a very good girl. I'm an only child, and I'm everything my mother and father ever dreamed about. Very good student, perfect English, perfect manners—presentable enough, yes—right on track for a double First at Cambridge, where we always go. Nice if I were fair-skinned—you get a better choice of husbands that way—but there, you can't have it all. Jenny, do you see now?"

"No," I said. "No, I don't think I do." What I *thought* was that I probably ought to be angry, and I was trying to work up to it. "You mean I'm your absolute opposite—I'm so different from you I'm like a novelty? Like that?"

Meena looked as though I'd hit her. "Not that! Not that, no!" She jumped up and grabbed both my hands. "You have such *spirit,* you make your own plans—you wouldn't go along with what everyone else wanted, just so they'd go on thinking you were a good girl. You don't care what *anybody* thinks—that's what I admire so much about you. I wish I were like you, Jenny, truly."

Nobody else in my whole life had even come near saying something like that to me. Nobody. I told Meena so, but as smart as she is, there's no way she could ever really know what it meant when she said that. Meena understands a lot, but if she understood something like this, she couldn't be Meena. That's just the way things get set up.

Anyway. We first got to be friends when we both hid out in the girls' john, ducking Games, and then later when Meena started helping me with Spanish and I helped her with a music project she was doing, comparing the way Indian singers improvise with how Western jazz singers do it. Once I told her it didn't count like helping, because of my parents being musicians, and she got really angry with me. She said friendship wasn't a bloody cricket match, you didn't keep score, there wasn't a point system. I almost like watching Meena being mad, because she does it so well, considering it lasts maybe five minutes, no more. Meena can't ever work up a good sulk.

She lives just outside Yeovil—her mother's at the hospital there, and her father commutes to Dorchester to teach physics at the university. The first time I ever went to stay overnight at Meena's house, I was edgy because I didn't know if I should be different with Meena *there* than I was when it was just us, and she was edgy about how her parents would be with me. And *they* were edgy because Meena hadn't brought anyone home from school before, and they didn't know if I could eat Indian food, or how Jews were about graven images and shrines in the front hall. So between us we had the makings of a real disaster, but it worked out all right. Mr. and Mrs. Chari were as nice as they could be to their daughter's weird American friend, and I didn't knock anything over or say anything really stupid. And I know about Indian food—I'm from New York, for God's sake.

So it was a lot easier when Meena came to spend a weekend at Stourhead Farm. Tony and Julian fell in love with her the moment she walked in the door—okay, I was a little jealous, especially watching Julian following her around, offering to carry things for her—and I couldn't help thinking, *I bet Sally wishes I looked like that and acted like that.* But I was proud of her, too,—*she's my friend, what's that make me?*—and at the same time I felt guilty that I wasn't ever like that with Jake and Marta. Some days there's no damn way I can let myself alone.

Evan was out with a well-driller, and Sally was with the vet about some of the sheep, so Tony and Julian took Meena around the Manor, with me wandering along behind. Tony showed her the ground-floor room in the east wing that he'd been turning into a dance studio—he even had a bar on one wall, and he was putting up every piece of mirror glass he could find, fitting them together like a jigsaw puzzle. He was sanding the floor, too, on weekends, over and over, till it was practically transparent. So then, of course,

Julian had to show Meena his rock collection, *and* his pressed-leaf collection, *and* his sugar-packet collection. *And* the stuffed gorilla in my room, but he never once mentioned that it was really his. Julian. I still can't get him to take it back.

At dinner the boys were both talking to Meena at the same time, and Evan and Sally were asking her the same school questions Mr. and Mrs. Chari had been asking me. I didn't get a chance to talk to her in peace until we went to bed in my room. And *then* it took me half an hour to talk Meena into taking my bed and letting me get into Evan's old sleeping bag on the floor. Indians keep wanting to treat you like their guest, even when they're yours. They can wear you *out*.

But then, *finally*, we got down to business. We lay there and talked about our families, and people at school, and I told Meena about Jake and Marta, and she told me about Lalitha, who was her best friend in Madras, and we compared books and movies and songs, and who had worse periods, and who hated Mr. Winship more—he taught Organic Chemistry—and why the monsoons are so important, and why I was going to take her to meet an old man they call Poet O in Central Park. Today it's just a few years later, and already I can't remember why, when you're thirteen, all that stuff absolutely has to be talked about in the dark, when you're supposed to be asleep. But it does.

Meena told me about Karthik, her white mouse, and I talked about Mister Cat—or I did until my throat started to tighten up again. So Meena changed the subject without seeming to change the subject, which is something she's very good at. She said, "But what a palace he'll be coming home to, your Mister Cat. So much space, so many shadowy corners to investigate, so many interesting new sounds . . . I'd love to be a cat in this house."

"You don't know the half of it," I said. "Other people have cockroaches—*we've* got gnomes, or boggarts, or something." I told her about the voices in my bathroom, which I hadn't told anyone, and about the rooms Julian wouldn't go into, and the things the carpenters and electricians had said. The longer I went on, the crazier it sounded, but Meena listened without laughing or interrupting once.

When I got through, she said, "Well, Julian was right—you definitely *do* have a haunted house. Dollars to doughnuts." (Meena's crazy about American slang, and sticks it in every chance she gets.)

"In India we've got haunted houses all over the place—we've got haunted apartments, haunted gardens, even haunted garages. Our old house in Madras had a poltergeist, one of those spirits that breaks things, throws everything around. I saw her a few times as I was growing up."

I'm glad it was dark, so maybe she didn't see my mouth hanging open. "You *saw* it? Her? The poltergeist?"

"Oh, yes," Meena said. "Not very often, though. A little girl, about Julian's age, with a scar down one side of her poor face. Like a burn scar. Maybe that's why she was a poltergeist, who knows? We felt so sorry for her."

"What did you do? Do Indians have, like—I don't know—like with a priest? An exorcism?"

"Yes. In a way." Meena half laughed, but there was a little catch in it, too. "But Jenny, she *lived* there, she'd lived in our house longer than we'd done. What *could* we do?" Then she giggled outright and said, "Besides, she scared away a lot of relatives I couldn't stand. And she left my room alone, except once or twice. I think sometimes she almost liked me."

I thought about that for a while, and finally I said, "Well, whatever's in our house, it doesn't like *us* all that much. Not the way those nasty little voices sounded. I'd rather have a real flat-out ghost, if we're going to have anything. I'd rather even have a pooka."

Meena wanted to know what a pooka was, so I told her what Evan had told us, and about boggarts and the Wild Hunt. She said, "I don't see why you couldn't have both—boggarts *and* ghosts. I bet you do. It's just the sort of house that would."

I said thanks, I really needed to hear that, and Meena laughed a real laugh this time. "When you grow up with old houses, the way I did, you grow up with ghosts, too. They're people, they're always drawn to places where people have been living for a long time. You don't get ghosts in shopping malls."

"Great," I said. "I hope the ghosts at least run off the boggarts, that'd be something."

We didn't say anything for a while, and I was starting to think Meena was asleep. Then I felt her hand reaching down from the bed, bumping around to find mine and taking hold of it. She said, "When you go to get him. Your Mister Cat. I could come with you, if you like."

I didn't know what to say. I just squeezed her hand and mumbled, "Sure, I guess, okay." I think we fell asleep holding hands like that, but I don't remember.

It was a beautiful day when we drove to Goshawk Farm Cattery for the last time. You have to be careful with English springs—you can't ever turn your back on them, because they'll drop thirty degrees and start thundering and lightning while you're taking your shirt off. I know for a fact that the poet who wrote "Oh, to be in England, now that April's there" was living in Italy at the time.

But this one early April day stayed warm and clear all the way to Dorchester. There were pink and white blossoms on the trees, and daffodils everywhere, and new lambs in the fields with big red numbers painted on their sides. People were out on tractors, plowing and harrowing, and the car's front windows were partway open, so in the backseat I kept smelling raw turned earth from every direction. Not that I was paying any attention to it, or the lambs, or to Sally asking Meena more school questions in the front. I just hunched up around the pain in my stomach and tried not to think about how I used to imagine the way it would be, bringing Mister Cat home at last.

When we got to Dorchester, I was wishing Meena wasn't with us, because then I could have just waited while Sally went in and picked up Mister Cat. But they were all happy and excited, so there wasn't any choice. I still remember how heavy my legs felt, and how long it seemed to take to climb out of the car.

We went in, and Sally told us, "I'll handle the paperwork, you two go get the big guy." I was going to argue about it—he's my cat, I've handled every damn miserable bit of this all the way, I'll be the one who finishes it—but Meena grabbed my hand and pulled me toward the cat runs. So I couldn't stall even a minute longer.

Okay. This is hard, this is what I mean about trying to write how another person felt at one particular moment, six years ago. I may not be that same person anymore, but I'll never forget how it was for her, having to run with her new friend to find her best friend and bring him home, even though she already *knew* he wasn't going to speak to her or even look at her again. And she had to go through with it, there wasn't any way out, and the cat runs kept getting closer. And there was Martin, the nice guy from the airport, unlocking Mister Cat's run, and smiling at her, saying, "This is my favorite part of the job." And throwing the gate wide.

He didn't come out at first. He stood in the doorway and he stretched his front and then his back, the way cats do, and he yawned like a hippopotamus while he was doing it. I heard Meena say, "Oh, he's so *lovely!*" but she sounded somewhere far away. I knelt down by the gate, and he did look at me with those orange eyes of his. I said, "Please. I'm sorry." I don't think anybody heard me.

Mister Cat lowered his head and bumped it against my chin. Then he put his front paws around my neck and made a little sound he makes sometimes, which is always like a question I don't know the answer to. I picked him up.

"Oh, he *missed* you," Meena said. "*Look* at him." She stroked his back, but he didn't turn to look at her. He kept pushing his head against me and purring. I tried to say, "Come on, kid, we're blowing this joint," but the words wouldn't come out.

He didn't like the farm at first, I'm sure of that. He won't ever admit that anything's too much for him, but after a whole life in a New York apartment, and then six months in a cat run, he just couldn't handle it all, and he didn't want to. The first couple of days, he stayed in my room—under my bookcase, mostly—and he hissed at everybody except me, even Sally. Julian was really hurt about that, because he'd practically planned a whole welcoming party, with decorations and cat treats. I had to say something, so I told him that in another day or two he'd be able to pick Mister Cat up and wear him around his neck like a mink stole, so he felt better after that. Julian.

The third day was a Saturday, so I was home. Mister Cat woke me walking on my face, patting gently at my eyes. He's done that since he was a kitten, once he figured out I'm awake if my eyes are open. As soon as they were, he ran to the door, which usually means litter-box time. The box is in my bathroom, but that wasn't what he was after. Today, exactly like Julian, he was waking me up to go exploring.

"After I wash," I said. "After I eat something. Give me a break here, all right?" Same thing I was always telling Julian. So Mister Cat went off and used his box, and then he had something to eat, and a quick bath himself, and he was ready when I was.

Today it was just the Manor he had in mind—he wasn't quite ready for the great English outdoors just yet. We started with the Arctic Circle, me showing off the new range and the cupboards Evan had put in—not to mention *another* new refrigerator—and Mister Cat sauntering along beside me, tail up like a snorkel, digging on everything, just as though he might be thinking about buying the place. My throat got achy again for a bit, watching him.

West wing, east wing, corridors, closets, rooms . . . we walked the whole first floor, taking our time, letting Mister Cat go where he wanted. You can't ever figure what interests him—he hardly glanced into a couple of rooms that I'd have been curious about if I were a cat, but he took forever sniffing around one empty little alcove, looking up at me impatiently, as though I ought to know exactly what he was smelling and be doing something about it. I always disappoint Mister Cat, but he's used to it. Like Sherlock Holmes and Dr. Watson.

To get to the second floor, you climb a stair that curls around the west chimney—there's no stair in the east wing, I don't know why, but once we got to the second floor, Mister Cat's whole attitude changed. He sort of slunk along, not quite with his belly to the ground, but more as though he were stalking something—a bird, a big rat. His ears were down flat, his tail stuck straight out behind him, and he was growling a thin, mean growl that I'd never heard before. I said, "What? *What?* Those things in my bathroom?" but he didn't even look at me. Mister Cat was on the case, and there really are times when I wish I'd had a dog. Something fluffy.

Actually, he hadn't even looked at the bathroom, once he'd used his box. But up here you'd have thought he was snaking through a minefield: Everything was suspicious, everything was dangerous, or it could be. When we came to the two rooms Julian wouldn't go into that first day, Mister Cat stopped dead in his tracks. He didn't make a sound, he didn't lash his tail, nothing like that. He just sat down on his haunches and looked at me.

"*What?*" I said again. "What, boggarts? What is going *on?*" I bent to pick him up, but he backed off and sprinted away from me down the corridor, and there wasn't anything to do but follow him. I walked along after him, passing one closed oak door after another—all we'd done with the whole east wing in six months was to clear it out a bit, except for Tony setting up his studio there—

and even today no one really uses the rooms on the second floor for anything. You could, there's nothing wrong with them now. We just mostly don't.

Mister Cat had turned a corner ahead of me, and I caught up with him at what I first thought was another door and then realized was a stairway, boarded up like the one in the west wing. We still hadn't been up to the third floor, none of us, though you could get through pretty easily—here, all it would have taken was a squat and a shove. Not that I was about to, not unless I had to chase after Mister Cat, but he wasn't going anywhere either. He was crouching at the foot of the stair, his whole body tight as a barbed-wire fence, his eyes wide and wild as I'd never seen them. I didn't try to pick him up—I just kept saying, "*What?* What in the world is it with you?"

I couldn't see anything past the boards on the stair. I couldn't sense whatever he was smelling or hearing, or taking in through his whiskers or his tail. There wasn't a thing to do but shut up and wait, like Dr. Watson.

And then he was Mister Cat again, Ultimate Cool, sitting up to give himself a fast facial and a good scratch. Then he turned and I got The Look, the one that says—unmistakable, no question—"Well, you're deaf, dumb, blind, and funny looking, but we'll make do." When I knelt down, he jumped straight to my shoulder, which is how I used to carry him when he was a kitten. He's been way too big for that for years, but he won't give it up, even though he always skids and slides around up there and has to grab on so hard that I can't pull him off. But this time he balanced perfectly, hardly digging in at all, and purring right into my ear so loud that I could feel it in my teeth as we walked back. Some days I really do know exactly what's on his black furry mind. This wasn't one of them.

Sally came into my room that night, which was nice, because we hadn't had much time by ourselves for weeks, what with school and the farm, and me being with Meena a lot. She smiled when she saw Mister Cat asleep on my bed. She said, "So. All is forgiven?"

"I guess," I said. I wasn't handing her any blank check like that, even if it *was* like what Meena said about keeping score. Sally sat down near my feet and petted Mister Cat, who couldn't take the trouble to open his eyes. She asked if he'd been outside yet, and I said, no, he'd had quite enough excitement checking out the Manor. I didn't mean to, but I wound up telling her the whole thing about the way he'd been in certain parts of the house, and what had happened at the third-floor stair in the east wing. I didn't care how loony it all sounded. Sally listened without interrupting or saying anything. She looked tired—not bad, just tired.

"Well," she said when I finished. "This is a very old house, Jenny, and I haven't a clue about whatever's gone on in it over three hundred years. And cats do seem to sense things we don't, and nothing your big guy does would surprise me, anyway. So who knows?"

"Meena thinks the house really is haunted," I said. "She says they have them all over the place in India. No biggie."

Sally shook her head. "I don't do ghosts. Although I had a *very* strange harpsichord once, before you were born. . . ." But she stopped herself and shook her head again. "No. No ghosts. Brownies, gnomes, fairies at the bottom of my garden. . . . Did you *see* the kitchen this morning?"

I'd seen it. Like woodchucks had been slamdancing in the pantry. I told her about Meena's poltergeist, but she sighed and shrugged, and said it was probably altogether different in India. Then she asked, all of a sudden, "Baby, are you liking Evan any better? As a stepfather, I mean."

I shrugged. "I've never *not* liked him," I said, which was perfectly true. The only thing I really disliked about Evan was that I didn't dislike him; because if somebody wrecks and devastates your entire life, he ought to at least have the decency to be a full-out, David Copperfield-style, vicious rat bastard, not a skinny Limey farmer who liked to play the guitar. "He's all right. As a stepfather."

"Well, that's *something*," Sally said. She put her hand on my cheek. "He likes you a lot, you know. Admires you, in fact, though I can't think why." I didn't say anything. Sally sighed. "This is turning into a tough gig, Jenny. It's going to be a much harder, longer job than Evan estimated, reclaiming this relic of a farm. But he'll get it done. Of course, you may be pushing our wheelchairs by then, but it'll be done. And somewhere along in there, we *may* even have found the time to sneak off for a honeymoon. Right now, as far as I can see, from here to senility we're just going to be digging holes and tearing things down."

"Uh-huh," I said. "And the piano?" Sally looked at me. I said,

"You haven't touched the piano since we got here. I know you haven't, because it's way out of tune, you'll have to get somebody from Dorchester or wherever. Unless you're just going to let the boggarts have it—hey, it's your piano." I hadn't realized I was really upset about her not playing the piano until I got started. Mister Cat finally opened his eyes, yawned, and walked up the bed to see if I was being uncool again. He always knows.

Sally didn't get mad, though. She leaned forward and put her arms around me. Sometimes it used to make me prickly when she did that, and I'd turn into a bag of knees and elbows, but right then it felt good. I curled against her, with Mister Cat burrowed down against my stomach, so the three of us were comfortable and quiet together. I about fell asleep.

I think I *was* asleep when Sally said, "Jenny? Meena really said she saw a poltergeist?"

"Lil girl," I mumbled. "Felsorry."

"Because there's some evidence that there actually might be such things. Something to do with—what?—*emanations* from somebody else who might have lived here once. Lord, one minute it's *The Twilight Zone,* and the next minute you can get doctorates in it. Who knows anything for sure anymore?" She stroked my hair, but I felt it as far away as her voice sounded.

I think I said, "Nemnations, boogers," but I didn't hear myself. Just Mister Cat purring in his sleep, all night.

Nine

It's a good thing Mister Cat liked Julian. I don't think Julian could have stood it otherwise.

Mister Cat doesn't *like* a lot of people. He tolerates just about everyone, but it's not the same thing, and Julian would have known. But Mister Cat pushed his head into Julian's face, and did his paws-around-the-neck thing, and actually let Julian drape him around his shoulders, as I'd said he would. I've never seen him let *anyone* do that—I was just saying it to make Julian shut up, and hoping he'd forget. Mister Cat shows off sometimes.

He wasn't anything like that with Tony—polite but formal, that was about it. But what he really liked to do was sit in the doorway of Tony's practice room and watch him dance. It didn't matter if Tony was only doing stretches, or walking around thinking—Mister Cat was perfectly happy to sit there and watch him at it. Tony would close the door when he noticed him, but then the room would get stuffy and he'd have to open it again, and Mister Cat would be back like a shot. Absolutely, totally, utterly fascinated.

Tony wasn't. It went almost the same way every time—he'd come marching up to me and say something like, "Jenny, is it too much to ask for you to keep that animal away from my studio?"

"He's not doing anything," I'd say. "He just loves the way you dance. I'd think you'd be flattered."

"Well, I'm not. I don't like being watched. It makes me nervous."

I'd say, "Interesting career you're likely to have," and Tony would get furious and stamp away, yelling, "I mean by cats! I don't dance for cats!" And I really would try harder to make sure Mister Cat stayed outside or in my room during the day. But I already knew it wouldn't work. New York or Dorset, Mister Cat goes where he wants to go, and all I've ever been able to do is trail along after him. Which is why everything that happened happened, any way you look at it. If Mister Cat hadn't been so captivated by Tony's dancing, I don't know if I'd ever have met Tamsin. Meena thinks it was fated, but I don't know. You'll see. Any minute now.

Mister Cat took his own time about exploring his new outdoors. Cars and construction, manholes and dogs and crazies he knew about, but he'd never seen a cow or a chicken or a hay-baler in his life, and he found out fast why foxes are different from city dogs. (Albert was no problem—Albert didn't notice anything that wasn't a sheep.) But unlike me, he didn't waste one minute bitching and moaning and carrying on. I watched him prowling a little farther from the Manor every day, getting used to the whole idea of grass and dirt, sniffing everything and then sitting back and thinking about it. No hurry. He hung out in the dairy a lot, and he climbed trees after squirrels as though he'd been doing it all his life—I only had to help him get down once. The second day out, he was already peeing on things and rubbing against them, to mark them with his own smell. I should have done that.

By the time he'd been in residence a couple of months—say late April or early May—he knew everything there was to know about Stourhead Farm. He didn't like all of it, either. He might wander all day, but he mostly stayed in at night, though I left my window open for him when the nights started getting warmer. And when he did go out, he'd always wake me up coming back, which he practically never did in New York. Not just by digging down under my blankets and getting as close in as he could, but he kept *talking*—that sound he makes that isn't a meow and certainly isn't a purr, or even that questioning *prrrp?* that cats do. It's a rough, really urgent kind of sound—not loud, but *specific*, that's the only word I can think of. He only makes it when he's telling me something important that he already knows I won't understand. I will later on, but never in time.

So. Early May, and Sally had actually gotten the piano tuned, and even turned up a couple of pupils—sisters, I remember—in Dorchester. She told me that the money wasn't anything much, "But I need to be teaching again, just a little, just so the farm won't swallow me up. That's the one thing I'm afraid of." She asked me if I felt like coming along for company. "Lydia's not much more than a beginner, but Sarah's going to be good. You could listen, or you could go wander and meet me at the car."

I wandered. Dorchester's the county seat of Dorset, but it's still a town, not a real city. But it's not a Merrye Englande theme park either, even with the bungalows and developments and trailer camps surrounding it. I wandered down High East Street—the main drag, where Sally dropped me off—to where it becomes High West Street and there's a statue of Thomas Hardy, and I passed red and whitewashed brick houses and pubs, and a church that he could have walked out of yesterday. Narrow side streets, long thin windows with heavy old shutters, doors no higher than the top of my head, flowers absolutely *blazing* in back gardens, on windowsills. There were a bunch of people taking pictures of the Hardy statue and the County Museum—Tony calls them the Eustacia Vye groupies. They show up with the warm weather, crowding the Hardy Room in the Museum, where they've got everything the poor man ever owned, from his chair and his writing desk to his violin. I bought a couple of postcards for Marta and Jake there.

Then I went into a shop and bought a pasty—a little meat pie—and a ginger beer, and ate walking down to look at the River Frome. I got lost, of course, which is really hard to do in Dorchester, and by the time I found my way back to the car Sally was already there, waiting for me. In New York she'd have been scared out of her mind by now—here in Dorchester she was reading an opera score. Dorset really suited her. England suited her. It made her feel lonely suddenly, which I hadn't felt at all, walking alone.

She drove us out of Dorchester a different way than we'd come in, to show me the chestnut trees flowering along the Walks, and on the way home she took a detour around a hill and a couple of farms to look at pear trees and apple blossoms. That got me, too—she *knew* detours, she knew shortcuts, she'd been learning all kinds of things I didn't know anything about. She'd been becoming less my mother and more Sally every minute since we'd been here, and I hadn't even realized it. I'm not sure if that made me feel more lonely or not. Just more confused, probably.

I do remember that she asked me, not working up to it the way she usually does, but right out, "Jenny, is it better for you? Being here, I mean?"

This is another one of the hard spots to write. It *was* getting some better, and I knew it—not just because of Mister Cat, but because of Meena and Julian, and Mrs. Abbott, our Form Tutor, and because my room was starting to look the way I wanted it, and maybe the English climate really was doing something for my skin. And because I could *think* better, lying on my back on the downland, watching the butterflies. Everything was always clearer on the downs.

But I couldn't tell Sally. I *couldn't*, and it's no good blaming *her*, whoever I was then. It was me, all right, and damned if I was going to give up the least little advantage of having my mother feel guilty about me being miserable. Because things might be all right just then, but who knew when I might need that edge again? The way I saw it, Sally was the only one ever likely to care what I thought of her, and I wasn't letting her all the way off the hook until I had to. Meena's going to be so ashamed of me, but *there*, I've got it down. That's how it was.

I said, "I'm managing all right." Flat, no expression, one way or the other—God, I can hear myself right now! But Sally knows me, I always forget how well. She said, "And exactly what does that mean?"

"It means I'm managing. It means I'm okay, don't *worry* about me, I'm doing just fine. Okay?"

"Not okay," Sally said, which she'd never have done back home. "Jenny, I don't know what you've got in mind, but I almost like it better when you're throwing fits, bouncing off the walls. Now you're biding your time about *something*, and I want you to understand that whatever it is, it's not going to happen. However things turn out with the farm, we are not going back to New York. Get it out of your head, baby. This is it, this is our home and our family, and if you're not happy about it, I'm very sorry. Me, I'm happier than I've ever been in my life. I think you could be, too." She grinned at me suddenly, a real sidelong flasher that I'd seen on Marta, but never on my own mother. "I'll tell you, I think you even *are* at times—happy—when I'm not looking. Am I right?"

I didn't answer, and I didn't say a word the rest of the way back to Stourhead Farm. When we got home, I boiled out of the car and went to find Mister Cat, because I wanted to sit outside with him somewhere and do some major brooding. But he wasn't in the dairy or asleep in my room, so I headed for the east wing and Tony's studio. I was afraid that had to be it, and it was, and I got there just in time to scoop him up as Tony slung him out the door. I yelled, and Tony yelled back, "Well, I *told* you what I'd do, I *told* you, Jenny!" And he banged the door shut, and Mister Cat wriggled out of my arms—I thought the door slam had scared him, because he scratched me *hard* with a back foot, which he never does. He was down and gone before I even opened my mouth to call.

I caught up with him at the foot of the old stairway. He was just sliding between a couple of loose boards—and ahead of him, through the gap, I saw *something* flashing up the stairs. It looked gray in the dim light, or maybe gray-blue, and it ran on four feet, not making a sound, and it wasn't a rat or a mouse or any animal like that, I could tell that much. Whatever it was, I didn't want Mister Cat going after it, not for a minute. I grabbed, but you might as well grab rain as Mister Cat. He was gone, he was right behind the gray-blue thing, and it halfway turned to meet him, and then I couldn't see them anymore. I thought I heard Mister Cat make that *prrrp?* sound once—after that, nothing.

For one wild moment I was tugging and yanking at those boards, to widen the space so I could get through. Then I stopped, because I wasn't Mister Cat, and I was not going up those dark stairs by myself. With Meena or Tony, okay—even with Julian, I might have done it. Not alone.

For a while I sat there waiting for him, but that got old, so I gave up and started walking away, looking back every ten seconds or so to see if he was following me. He usually does, once he realizes I'm really going, pouncing and darting ahead of me to make it look like his own idea. Not this time. I waited in my room until Evan called me to help Tony set the table for dinner, but Mister Cat didn't show; and he wasn't around for the rest of the evening, either. I wasn't going to worry about him—in New York he'd have been out all night with the Siamese Hussy—so I cleaned up in the kitchen by myself, and I helped Julian with his geography homework, and he helped me with my maths—he *is* a whiz, just like he told me when we met—and I talked to Meena on the phone for a little, and went to bed early.

I woke up right before Mister Cat came into my room. I'd left the door a little way open, besides the window, so maybe there was a draft moving something. I sat up fast, groping around for my bedside lamp, thinking boggarts and pookas and Hedley Kows. But when I felt Mister Cat in my room, I didn't bother with the light, not then. I said, "You rotten, miserable cat, you scared the hell out of me! You get your butt on up here right now!"

I slapped the bed hard, and a moment later I felt him landing, heavy and light at the same time, down by my ankles. But instead of walking up to me, the way he always does, he went *prrrp?*, and in another moment something else landed on the bed. And I can't describe this properly, because there wasn't any *weight* to it—not a thump, not a rustle, not the smallest stir of the blankets. But there *was* something beside Mister Cat on my bed, and I almost knocked the lamp over turning it on. And the only reason I didn't scream the whole damn Manor down was that I couldn't get my breath. I didn't think I'd ever be able to get my breath again.

It was another cat. A long-haired, short-legged, blue-gray cat with deep-green eyes and a wide, pushed-in sort of face—a Persian, for God's sake. I don't like Persian cats much, but that wasn't the problem. The problem was that I could see through it.

Okay, not quite *through*—it wasn't really transparent, but almost. Its outlines were a little fuzzy, but Persians look like that anyway. It looked darker beside Mister Cat, lighter when it moved and had my blanket behind it; and when it sat down for a moment to scratch, I lost it altogether in the moonlight shining on the white wall. When Mister Cat nudged it with his shoulder, it opened its mouth and this tiny, tiny, faraway meow came out. Not a real meow. More like an old yellowing memory of a meow.

I was cold. I was so cold that I could feel it in my fingernails. Mister Cat kept prodding that *thing* toward me, and I kept scooting away, till I was as flat up against those fancy brass spindles as I could get. But it came on, making that little distant cry that didn't get any louder close to. It had really pretty eyes, but I couldn't see the lamplight in them, or me, or anything but deep, deep green.

It was a female—anybody could tell *that* watching Mister Cat fussing and nudging and carrying on around her. I didn't stop being scared, not with the way her shape wouldn't stay quite in focus, and the way her . . . her *texture* kept shifting, so you couldn't ever get a real fix on just what color she really was. But I was starting to get curious at the same time I was scared. I didn't try to touch her, even though she was solid enough for Mister Cat to rub up against. I didn't want to know what she felt like.

When I finally got my voice, I said to her, "So it was you, huh? You're the one he chased all over the east wing and up the stairway. Well, you sure must have shown him a good time, that's all *I* can say." She looked straight back at me, and if the rest of her was a little undecided, those eyes weren't. I didn't doubt for a minute that she understood what I was saying—better than Mister Cat, even. You tend to think like that when you've just been waked up in the middle of the night by two cats, and one of them's a ghost.

Because that's what she was, that green-eyed Persian—I never doubted that, either, though I hadn't ever seen a ghost, or believed in them, or even *thought* about believing in them. Or thought about cats having ghosts. But it was the only thing she *could* be—it's like Sherlock Holmes saying that once you eliminate the impossible, whatever's left has to be the answer, no matter how weird it is. I almost forgot to be scared, I was so anxious for it to be morning, so I could tell Meena.

Ghost or no ghost, Mister Cat obviously thought his new girlfriend was the greatest thing since the can-opener. He was showing her off to me, purring and crooning like an idiot, waltzing around her on the bed, practically turning somersaults. She seemed to be enjoying it, but I didn't like seeing him that way—it reminded me too much of the changes in Sally. I said, "Okay, okay, I get the picture, settle down already. I just hope the Siamese Hussy never hears about this, that's all."

The Persian came up close to me then, without any prompting from Mister Cat, and she looked right into my eyes. Mister Cat does that all the time, but this was different. Those green eyes were like those stairs to the third floor, but without the boards blocking the way. You could feel yourself leaning, tilting toward them, beginning to climb . . . only I didn't want to. No temptation, no hesitation. I shook my head, and I said, "Forget it. I'm tired and I'm going back to sleep. You can stay if you want, I don't care. Just be quiet, don't mess around. We'll talk in the morning, whenever."

And I did pull the covers up and wrap the pillow around my head and fall asleep again, with a ghost-cat on my bed, and my own cat fussing over her to make a complete fool of himself. I think I was more disgusted with him than I was scared of her. Mister Cat in love is not a pretty sight.

She was gone when I woke, and Mister Cat was snuggled under my arm, just as though he hadn't spent the night doing God knows what with God knows what. When he saw I was awake, he started running through his usual cool-cat-in-the-morning routine: the long stretch, the tongue-curling yawn, the serious scratch, the careful touch-up wash, and *then*, finally, it's the big bright eyes and what's for breakfast? I just looked at him, the way he looks at me sometimes. I said, "It's no good, give it up. I know everything."

But I didn't, and he knew I didn't. He came over and bumped his head against my hand, once only, and I said, "All right, but don't think I'm forgetting," and we went to see about breakfast.

Ten

I haven't worked on this for a few days now. Tony's dance company made it as far west as Salisbury for once, so we all spent the weekend there and caught every performance, even though he only danced in a couple of numbers. And then he came home with us and stayed until Sally and Evan took him back to London, leaving Julian and me in charge of each other. Julian wants to see what I've written in the worst way, and I keep moving it around, hiding it from him, stashing it at Meena's sometimes. Even Meena's just seen a few pages, because it's not ready. I'm stuck between who I think I was and who I think I am, between what happened to me and what I think really happened. All I wanted was to get it all down and done with, and now I don't know. Maybe I'm the one who's not ready.

Trying to write about seeing the ghost of a Persian cat doesn't exactly clear the mind, either. As I've already said, if ghosts were possible, maybe it was *all* possible, everything—boggarts, Hedley Kows, UFOs, alligators in the sewers. Mrs. Chari, Meena's mother, was in an earthquake once, and she said it felt as though the ground under her feet had all turned into water. That was how I felt after Mister Cat brought his new girlfriend around. I didn't tell Meena after all, or Sally, or anybody. Not because I thought about whether they'd believe me or not. I just did not want to deal with it. I didn't want to tell myself, even.

But I did come within *that* much of telling Tony. A few days after all this happened, he found me in a back pasture getting a cricket lesson from Julian. I can hit—I don't see how you could *not* hit, with a flat bat—but I can't pitch worth a damn. Bowl, I mean. Julian was showing me how to turn my wrist so the ball bounces away from the batter, when I looked around and saw Tony watching us. That made me nervous, but he wasn't interested in making fun of me. He waited until Julian asked him if he wanted to play, and then he said, "Not right now, but I'd like to borrow Jenny for a bit. I'm trying to work something out, and I need a partner. Just for a few minutes, I promise."

"I can't dance," I said. My heart started pounding, and I was running with sweat, that fast—not because of Tony, but because of the whole idea of dancing. "Take Julian, take Wilf—take *Albert.* You don't want me, believe me."

Both of them ignored me. Julian said, "You can have her, but only if I get to watch. I want to see Jenny dance."

"Not a chance," I said, just as Tony said, "Done, it's a deal. But you have to be *quiet.*"

They were still arguing about whether it would be all right for Julian to giggle if he didn't actually say anything, while I was being hustled off to Tony's studio. I didn't put up much of a fight, mainly because I was curious about what Tony actually did when he was pacing around in front of all his mirrors, mumbling to himself and slamming doors. And there was one stupid little part of me that kept wondering if maybe I *could* dance—if maybe panicking twice on the gym floor at Gaynor and running to the girls' john both times to have dry heaves and cry in Marta's lap didn't mean I couldn't learn a few moves. Maybe I wasn't born to boogie, but to float; maybe the moment Tony took my hand I'd *know.* I wondered if he'd try to lift me, and that was scarier than ghosts or the third floor.

It didn't work that way, of course. He just needed a body, something to take up space in his imagination while he paced and mumbled. All I did was stand in one place, and Tony moved me or moved around me, depending. Julian would have done just as well, only Julian got bored early on and went to practice his googlies. Tony didn't notice. Every once in a while he'd spin away from me, or he'd suddenly leap straight up and turn in the air, and come shivering down like a butterfly, and you could *see* the whole shiny floor turning into some kind of flower for him to land on. Then he'd be Tony again, shaking his head, really mad at himself for some reason I couldn't imagine. It took a lot longer than a few minutes, and he hardly said one word to me, but I didn't mind. I liked him like this.

Once, when he was either taking a break or trying to work something out—anyway, he was just sitting and staring—I asked him,

more or less the way Sally had asked me, "Is it better for you here?"
He blinked at me. "Better than London, I mean. Would you still
rather be living in London?"

Tony can look at you sometimes as though he hadn't quite realized just how stupid you were until right now. "For God's sake, I
could be *studying* in London. Studying with *real* dancers, watching
real groups every night. Meeting people—learning all the things
I'm never going to learn here." He stalked away from me across
the room, and then he turned around and came back to stand really close. "Of course, I'd never have a room like this in London,
so whatever I learned wouldn't do me a bloody bit of good, because I couldn't take it home and practice. So it's six of one, half
a dozen of another, I suppose. Why do you want to know?"

"No special reason." I took a deep breath. "About the Manor—I
was wondering, just out of curiosity—" God, I'd make a terrible spy.
"Do you ever hear any noises at night? I mean, you know—*noises?*"

Tony practically smiled, which he was not doing a lot of in those
days. "The Manor's a very old house. They make noises."

"I don't mean those," I said. "I mean . . . I mean *feet*, damn it!
Giggles."

I was expecting him to laugh at me, but all he did was sit down
on the floor and start doing stretching exercises. He said, "When
I knew we were positively coming here, no way out of it, I went to
the library and got out a lot of books on Dorset. History, agriculture, folklore, the lot. Do you know that there are two whole books
on Dorset ghosts alone? The county's up to its neck in hauntings,
revenants—everybody who's anybody has a Phantom Monk, or a
screaming skull, or a White Lady. Noises? I think if this house
doesn't have a ghost, Dad ought to sue the Lovells for breach of
contract. Or something like that."

It was the most he'd ever said to me since we'd been at Stourhead, except for when he was throwing Mister Cat out of the studio. He realized it at the same time I did, and went back to
stretching. I was getting up to leave quietly when he added, "A lot
of them date from 1685, the Dorset ghosts. Because of the Bloody
Assizes, you know."

"No, I don't know," I said. "What's an Assizes, and why were
these so bloody?"

Tony sighed. "They really don't teach you anything in those
American schools, do they? I thought it was just British chauvin-

ism. You wouldn't know about Monmouth's Rebellion, then?" I just shook my head. "Okay. Charles Stuart—that's King Charles II—had an illegitimate son named James. No big deal, as you'd say—quite common with kings, especially Charles. He acknowledges him, brings him to court, makes him the Duke of Monmouth, all very civil. Not that he's got a chance of succeeding to the throne—that's for Charles's brother, the Duke of York, also named James. You *are* following this so far?"

"James II," I said. "The Glorious Revolution, 1688. They teach us a few things."

"Oh, very *good*," Tony said. I couldn't tell whether he meant it, or was being sarcastic. I can now, usually. "Right. James II becomes king in 1685, over any number of objections—mainly because of his being a Roman Catholic, but also because he was always a nasty, treacherous piece of work. Charming, though, when he wanted, like all the Stuarts—they lived on charm. Anyway, Monmouth— that's James's half-brother, the *other* James—has been hiding out in Holland, because of maybe being involved in the Rye House Plot, but we can skip that part. Well, James II hasn't been James II for ten minutes before Monmouth's landed in Lyme Regis and starts raising an army to overthrow him."

I said, "Wait a minute. Lyme Regis? The tourist place, where we went for Easter?" We spent a weekend, and it rained, and Sally caught cold showing me where they'd filmed *The French Lieutenant's Woman*.

"They hadn't invented tourists then," Tony said impatiently. "It was a port, they built ships, and Monmouth was big in the West Country, don't ask me why. He went up to Taunton, in Somerset, and declared himself king, but his real following was right here, the Dorset people who met him on the beach. Farmers, miners, fishermen, a bunch of Dorchester artisans and shopkeepers—they were all mad about Monmouth. That old Stuart charm."

Most people get flushed and red when they're telling you something they're really excited about. Tony always gets very pale, even sort of shaky sometimes. He said, "They really did start a rebellion, Jenny, right here. They were sure the upper classes hated James as much as they did, and they thought the gentry would join them, you see, with their horses and guns and their money and their private armies, and they'd all sweep on to London together. But it didn't happen."

He got up again and began moving—turning, stooping, swinging around, not quite dancing, but almost. "It didn't happen. Most of the noble types just never showed up, and Monmouth scarpered, did a bunk, headed for the border, the way the Stuarts always did. Left his little low-class believers out there, high and dry, and the king's soldiers came down and crushed them, ate them alive. But James II wasn't finished with Dorset. He was going to show Dorset, once and for all, why you do not ever, *ever* mess with a king. He sent them Judge Jeffreys. Lord Chief Justice Jeffreys." A fast spin, not a pirouette, but close to the floor, like a top, pointing at me as he came up out of it. "And that's your Bloody Assizes."

When you grow up in New York, and your mother's absolutely crazy about old movies . . . Something clicked, and I said, "*Captain Blood*. Errol Flynn's a doctor, and he helps someone who's been hurt—"

"In Monmouth's Rebellion—"

"And there's a Judge Jeffreys in a wig, who sends him off to be a slave on a plantation. *That* Judge Jeffreys?"

"The very same. He set up shop in Dorchester, at the Antelope Hotel, and he had hundreds of people hanged, drawn and quartered—" He stopped, and he looked even paler than before. "You know what that was?"

"Don't tell me," I said. I didn't know, not then, but from his face I knew I didn't want to.

"No. All right. But he had their bodies boiled and tarred, and their heads stuck up on poles, and there were hundreds more whipped and transported to the West Indies. Oh, he had a grand time in Dorset, Judge Jeffreys did." Tony leaned against the wall and started putting his shoes on.

"What happened? Afterwards, I mean." I remember I felt dazed, giddy—maybe from what he'd been telling me, maybe more from the way he told it, the way he looked and sounded. He grinned at me, and this time he definitely *was* being sarcastic.

"Right, I forgot, you're an American—there has to be a happy ending around here somewhere. Well, in another three years, here came the old Glorious Revolution, and James II left town hastily, and went into business as a public nuisance, which was the family trade, you might say. Judge Jeffreys suffered agonies from kidney stones, and died in the Tower."

"Good," I said. "That's a happy ending, anyway."

Tony shrugged. "Didn't stick any heads back on any necks." He picked up a towel, mopped his face with it, and turned the light out. As we walked to the door, he said, "But I'd think it left a deal of angry ghosts around this part of Dorset. Noises would be the least of it."

Locking the studio—he did that to keep Julian out, and me, too, probably—he said, "Thank you for working with me," which was nice, as if we actually *had* been dancing together. I thought he might ask me again, but he never did.

Mister Cat didn't bring his Persian lady around to my room again. We sort of didn't talk to each other for a while—just came and went on our own business, me as much as him. We've had secrets together since I was little, but this wasn't like that. It's lonely when you know something nobody else knows, but it's exciting, too. That's the other side of the ground turning to water under you. Stourhead Farm felt like a completely new place, where every sound might mean something different than I'd thought—where suddenly every *thing*, not just cats or people, might be some kind of ghost from three hundred years ago. I really did want to tell people about it, and I really didn't. If that makes any sense at all.

One thing was certain—whatever it was that was playing games with us, wasn't likely to get bored any time soon. During the winter it had been an on-and-off kind of thing—stuff in the kitchen spilled and slopped or just *vanished*, a few mornings running, then nothing for a whole week or two. But come the warmer weather—about the time Mister Cat got sprung from quarantine—the boggart started expanding its horizons. Fuel lines breaking in the tractors and balers all the time, irrigation pipes coming apart, just where they were the hardest to get to, whole sections of Evan's fences collapsing for no good reason, Sally having apples drop on her head when she wasn't anywhere near the apple trees, *something* terrorizing Albert, the sheepdog, so on some days he wouldn't come out of his kennel, let alone go back to the pasture. As for the marshy upper meadow that Evan kept trying to drain . . . well, never mind, you get the idea. Julian said to me once, "I'm glad we know it's just a boggart. Otherwise I'd start worrying."

What's funny is that we really *did* know. Evan and Sally made a pass at sounding like rational, realistic parents, talking about coincidences and logical possibilities, but nobody paid any attention, including them. This wasn't West Eighty-third Street, this was old, old Dorset, and what we had had to be a boggart; and the only chance you have with boggarts is catch them in the act. All the tales say they're night creatures, so Sally set up a kitchen-watch rotation, making sure that she and Evan had the graveyard shift, and not even scheduling Julian at first. But he threw such a fit about being left out she finally penciled him in with me, from eight to eleven. I told him to bring his Snakes and Ladders game, because he's such a bad loser and a worse winner that I figured we'd stay awake, one way and another.

The first nights, nothing, not on anybody's watch. Evan said that figured. "He knows we're on guard, so he's going to sit tight for a while, considering. But he'll make his move soon, because he has to. Boggarts can't resist a challenge from humans, that's how they are."

I remember Sally asked, "What's with this *he* all the time? What if it's a lady boggart?" Evan said they were always male in the stories, and Meena—her parents let her sit up with Julian and me one night—said that in the little town where her father was born there was a lady boggart, or brownie, whatever, that swept out the temple at night. "Nobody ever saw her, but the priests would leave a bowl of milk out for her, and in the morning the milk would be gone and the temple would be clean. All the years my father lived there, every night, the same."

Tony wanted to know how the priests could tell the Indian boggart was a female, if they never saw her, and Sally said because she cleaned up after herself, which you couldn't get a man to do at gunpoint, never mind a male boggart. Evan said, "Right, then, we'll just call him *it*, let it go at that." Julian said he wanted to play Snakes and Ladders, so he and I and Meena played until Sally relieved us, and we didn't see a thing. That whole first week, it must have been.

But maybe ten nights into the boggart patrol, the weather suddenly turned bad. We'd had a week or so of pure summer, which is about the way you get summer in England—a week at a time, scattered around through the other seasons. That night we got rain like horses galloping on the roof, and we got thunder that felt as though someone were pounding the Manor with a huge baseball bat. Evan and Sally were actually out in the storm, trying to protect the new sapling fruit trees, and Julian was scared for them, and I kept telling him they'd be okay, just *play* already—and in the middle of all that racket, we heard someone laughing. Not a nasty, tittering kind of laugh, like the ones I'd heard in my bathroom— this one was deep and loud enough that Julian and I both heard it through the thunder. We turned around so fast that we knocked over Julian's Snakes and Ladders board, and we saw him.

It was a *him*, all right—I'd have known that much even if he hadn't had a beard, just from the way he stood there with his thumbs in his belt and his head back, looking around our kitchen as though everything in it was his. I've seen three-year-old boys stand like that on playgrounds—you can't miss it. He wasn't any bigger than a three-year-old, either: He came about up to Julian's chest, not counting his silly Seven Dwarfs hat with the green feather. He was dressed like a cross between the Seven Dwarfs and Robin Hood, in a kind of loose red smock, but with the belt, and brown leggings underneath, and heavy little boots, ankle-high— I'd have taken them for Doc Martens, except I don't think they make them in boggart sizes. And there wasn't a thing else in the world he could have been.

Julian had grabbed my hand, and I could feel him trembling right down my arm and into my stomach. He whispered, "Jenny, he came out from under the stove! How could he do that?"

I didn't answer. I just held his hand with both of mine, trying to stop his shaking. Julian said, in this small, sad voice, "I don't *like* this, Jenny."

The boggart looked at us for the first time. You could tell he was really, really old, but I can't say exactly how I knew, because he didn't have any gray hair, and no wrinkles at all, just a few lines on his skin, which was red-brown, the same color as the new lettuce fields closest to the Manor. He had a face like a goat's face—long and high-boned, with the little curly beard, and with big dark-red eyes, *wicked* eyes. I don't mean *evil*, I mean wicked. I know the difference now.

"Dun't ye goo a-ztaring," he said. "There's rude. Yer ma'd noo like it."

That's the way he sounded to me the first time I heard him speak. He had a deep voice for someone so small, but it didn't seem out of place coming out of that face, that big chest like my father's. He said again, "Dun't goo a-ztaring at me. Else I'll turn the pair of ye into crabapples and toss ye to the piggies. I will zo."

Julian gave a tiny whimper and burrowed against me with his eyes shut tight, like Mister Cat. It took me a couple of tries to make my voice work, but I said, "We don't *have* any pigs, and you're nothing but a dorky boggart, and you can't turn us into anything," all in one croaky rush. I don't know how I got it all out—I was just mad because he was scaring Julian, and enjoying it. Boggart or no boggart, I know *that* look when I see it.

The boggart's eyes twinkled. I've heard people say that all my life, but until then I'd never seen anyone actually do it. Like a birthday-cake candle flickering far down a tunnel. He said, "Maight be I can, maight be I can't. Dun't be in such a fluster to chance en." He pointed at me with a thick, stubby forefinger. "Mind yerse'n, or what boggart's doone's naught to what boggart will do." And he grinned at me like a horse with a mouthful of gray and black teeth.

"Oh, please," I said. "Trashing the kitchen every night, breaking down fences, throwing apples at people—that's about your speed. You'd be hot stuff at Gaynor Junior High." Julian was starting to get interested: He sat up, still huddling close against me, and gaped at the boggart. The boggart made a face at him—Julian yelped and dived into my lap again—and the boggart laughed.

"Noo, noo, tha's naught but what boggarts is zet to do on this earth"—only it came out *thik yearth*—"no harm in it, ner zpite." He was waving that finger at me, dead serious as Mrs. Wolfe at Gaynor used to get when she thought we weren't paying enough attention to the Congress of Vienna. "But *ye*—tak shame to yerself, ye ought, grieving yer ma zo wi' yer zulks and yer pelts and yer mopen to be off back wheer ye do coom vrom. And her a-worken and a-werreten hersen to plain boone vor to mak thikky farm be home vor ye, be home vor ye all. Tak shame, ye Jenny Glookstein!"

That's the best I can get it down, and that's all of *that* I'm about to do. I'd never heard old-time Dorset talk before, except in little scraps, like when Ellie John says a shriveled-up apple's all quaddled, or says she doesn't ho about something, meaning she doesn't give a damn. Or when William says the weather's turning lippy, which means it's going to rain. But nobody talks like Thomas Hardy people, they haven't for ages. Evan says it's because of radio and TV and movies. He'll go on forever about how regional dialects ought to be treated like endangered species before everybody winds up sounding just like everybody else. But that's what people *want*, most of them. I knew that in grade school.

Anyway, I was so startled by his coming on like Jiminy Cricket, the voice of my conscience, that I forgot to be scared. I yelled at him, "I don't believe this. You're the one who makes my mother's life hell, and it's all my fault? Okay, *that* is *chutzpah*." Let him chew on *my* native dialect, see how he likes it.

The boggart wasn't fazed a bit. "Noo, I do like yer ma, I do like her fine—she's a rare goodhussy, for an outlander, and pretty wi' it. There's bottom to en." It took me the longest time to figure out that hussy just means a housewife in Dorset talk, and bottom's like honor, integrity. "But she's noo raised her darter right, there's her zorrow. Proper darter, she'd a-zet hersen first thing to riddle out what in t'world might please a boggart. For us can be pleased, aye, us can be sweetened, na great trickses to it—any ninnyhammer'd a-figgured en out by naow. Any ninnyhammer as cared, that's to say." And he gave me that horse grin again.

I was catching on slowly, more to the rhythm than the words. I said, "There's a way to make you leave us alone? What is it, what do you want? Tell me, I'll be on it—five minutes, tops. What?"

But the boggart just shook his head. "Ben't *that* simple, can't be. *Think*, gel, use yer nogger—think like boggart, think like me." He folded his arms across his chest and stood there, reaching up now and then to play with his little beard, looking more self-satisfied than I've ever seen anyone look. Including Mister Cat.

Beside me Julian whispered, "Milk." The storm was still banging away at the house, rattling the windows until I thought the old frames would come apart, and Julian had to raise his voice. "Milk. Ellie John says her mother always leaves milk out for the—the Good Folk." He ducked his head back down so fast that I hardly heard the last words.

That got a snort out of the boggart—it sounded like somebody sneezing with a mouthful of hot soup. "*Milk?* Noo, that's all trot, that is—what's boggart want wi' milk? Is boggart a suckling piggy, then? Is boggart calf or lamb, chetten or poppy? Noo, and not Good Folk neither. Try us again, Joolian McHugh."

Julian couldn't manage it, but he'd got me thinking about the handful of fairy tales I still remembered in bits and pieces. I said, "Wait, wait a minute—hold it. . . . *Shoes!* That's it—we make you a terrific pair of shoes, and you're so happy with them that you dance all over the kitchen, and you never come back. That's it, right? *Has* to be." But the boggart was spluttering and stamping his feet before I was half through.

"Shoes, is it naow? Shoes, like them great clumsy hommicks you folk wear, and me wi' a grand pair of kittyboots of me own?" And he held them up, first one, then the other, to show Julian and me the perfect little sort of cleats on the soles, and the way the soles nestled into the uppers, as though there weren't any stitches at all. They were old, like him, but the best cobbler in Dorchester couldn't have matched them. Let alone us.

"Again! Try us again!" He was having a fine time, spinning on his heels, jumping up and down. I hoped he'd stamp his way through the floor, like Rumplestiltskin. Julian was whimpering again, and right then I wanted Sally more than I had in a long time—and Evan, too—because this was all way more than I could handle. But I didn't want Julian any more scared than he already was, so I put my arm around him and told the boggart, "Enough already, we give up, we don't want to play anymore. Just for God's sake tell us what would please you, so we can take care of it, and you can stop messing with us, and we'll *all* be pleased. How about it, okay?"

I had a feeling that wouldn't cut a lot of ice, and I was right. The boggart got really mad then. He stopped jumping around, and he grabbed off his dumb little feathered hat and slammed it down on the floor. "Noo, Jenny Glookstein," he said, and that weird deep voice had gotten very quiet, and scarier for it, "noo, ye'll play awhile wi' boggart yet, acause I say ye will. Ye'll goo on a-thinking what might soften boggart's heart, what might charm boggart to leave ye be. Acause I say so." And he took a couple of steps toward us, and Julian—I'll always remember this—Julian wiggled out from under my arm and wiggled himself in front of me. Scared as he was. I'll remember.

I never saw Mister Cat. You don't, until he's there. He hit the boggart like a bolt of black lightning out of that storm, landing on his shoulders with all four sets of claws out and busy. The boggart squealed and lurched forward—and here came Miss Fluffbucket, Miss Dustbunny, that Persian ghost-cat, flashing up from underneath to rake at his face . . . with real claws? I couldn't say, even now, but the boggart screamed like a trapped rabbit, falling flat, arms wrapped wildly around his head. Mister Cat pounced on his chest, holding him down, and the Persian stood off, ready for a fast slash anytime he raised his head. You'd have thought they'd been doing this sort of thing forever.

Julian was chanting, "Mister *Cat*! Mister *Cat*! Mister *Cat*!" like a mob cheering at a football game, but I made him stop. Mister Cat was making that creaky-door, mess-with-me-and-die sound, the way he'd done to me in Heathrow, and the boggart was absolutely cowering and crying, "Gi'm off me! Gi'm off me, missus! Boggart niver meant noo harm, boggart was on'y spoortin-like—gi'm off and ye'll nivver see boggart more, I zwear!"

I couldn't help feeling sorry for him. To somebody two feet high, Mister Cat has to look like Bagheera the Black Panther on a bad-hair day. Although the one who seemed to scare him more was the Persian—he wouldn't even look at her, but kept making funny signs with his fingers, more or less in her direction. Whatever they were supposed to do, they didn't. The Persian just watched him, licking her left front paw now and then. I wondered if a ghost's tongue could taste ghost-fur.

Julian was tugging my arm, whispering, "Jenny, don't believe him, don't believe him! He didn't say he wouldn't bother us, he just said we wouldn't *see* him do it." Julian's going to be a lawyer—I don't think I've mentioned that.

"Got it," I said; and then, to the boggart, "Okay, you, shut up and listen. Shut *up*, or I'll have my attack cat eat your face." Mister Cat might lose interest any time now, and I had to move before he strolled off somewhere with his hot date. In my toughest, meanest New York voice I said, "Now. No more bullshit. You tell us right now what we have to do so we don't have any more aggravation from you. Right now, buddy, or that sweet kisser is lunch meat." Jake and Marta wouldn't have stopped laughing for a week.

It did wonders for the boggart, though. He scrunched behind his arms even more, and started babbling so fast I couldn't understand him at first. "Zpectacles! Zpectacles, it is, so boggart can see past's nose again. Boggart's old, he is, boggart's eyen ben't what they was—zpectacles, they needs! Laive a pair on t'mat and boggart'll trouble ye no more." Mister Cat growled in his throat right at that moment, and the boggart *yeeped*—can't find another word for it. "Nivver no more! May kitties coom get me if I lie!"

I looked at Julian. He nodded. "They *have* to keep their promises. Ellie John told me."

"Okay, then," I said, still doing the New York gangster. "One pair of eyeglasses, onna mat tonight. Just remember, duh cats know where youse live."

I bent down and picked Mister Cat off the boggart. Mister Cat didn't like it, but he didn't argue about it. The Persian never moved, and I wasn't about to touch her, not in my entire life. Again it struck me that the boggart seemed more frightened of her than he was of Mister Cat. He watched her all the time he was getting up and finding his hat, practically groveling if she so much as flicked an ear. I said, "She won't hurt you," but the boggart plainly wasn't buying, and I got the feeling that he had reasons older than I was. He backed slowly away, still hunched and ready to run—then all at once he straightened up, set his hat on his head, and gave us the horse grin one more time.

"For yer ma's sake, a single word of advice, like. A warning." He pointed at the Persian, shaking his finger the same way he'd done at me. "Ware t'servant, ware t'mistress—and ware T'Other Oone most of all." And you could hear the capital letters on T'Other Oone. Believe it.

"The mistress," I said. "Who's that? The Other One—I don't know what you're talking about. Who's the Other One?"

But the boggart laughed like a bathtub drain, and did a sort of weird skip-jig on the kitchen floor. "A single word, a single word, I said, and that ye've had. To'morn's to be zpectacles waiting for boggart on mat—and so farewell, Jenny Glookstein, farewell, Joolian McHugh. Farewell, farewell."

And he was gone, the way I'd thought only Mister Cat could vanish. Julian insisted he went back under the stove, flattening himself out—"Like a piece of paper, Jenny, didn't you *see?*"—and slipping in through the little space there was. Sally and Evan came sloshing in just then, and Tony came down, and we all got busy running around bringing them towels, making tea, putting their Wellingtons and their rain slickers in the bathtub. They were all over mud, even with the slickers, and Evan had a huge bruise on one cheekbone where he'd fallen over something in the dark. But they'd saved the new fruit trees. There wasn't a thing on the planet more important, right then.

They sat there in the kitchen, laughing and holding hands, looking flushed and scratched up, and really tired, looking like kids—looking the way Julian and I should have been looking, instead of sneaking glances at each other and agreeing without a word that we wouldn't talk about *our* night for a bit. The Persian was as gone as the boggart, but Mister Cat was sitting between us, tail curled around his feet, looking utterly bored and sleepy. Julian picked him up and held him tight, practically strangling him, the way he used to hug that gorilla he gave me. Mister Cat usually hates that kind of thing, but he just purred and purred, while Evan and Sally drank their tea and picked little twigs out of each other's hair.

Eleven

The boggart kept his word. After everybody'd finally gone to bed, I sneaked back down and left an old pair of drugstore reading glasses Julian kept trying to start fires with out on the doormat. They were gone in the morning, and the kitchen was tidier than we'd left it.

The nighttime patrols dwindled away pretty fast, once it was obvious that the boggart had gone out of business. Julian and I never said anything—not even to each other, really. Julian more or less decided that he'd dreamed the whole thing, which was just as well. He did spend a lot of time hunting around the Manor for that Persian lady, though, and seriously asking Mister Cat where she was. I still feel guilty about that. I should have told Julian *something*.

I did tell Meena, one weekend when I was staying at her house and she was teaching me to put on a sari by myself. They're all six yards long, and there's a sort of blouse that goes underneath, and people from different parts of India wrap them around themselves differently, and throw the loose end over their shoulders in special ways. I was getting the hang of it pretty quickly, except for the damn pleats, which I still can't get right, and which Meena can do on herself in two minutes flat. I look like a big pink horse in a sari, but I don't care, I love them. And Meena always says I look nice.

When I told her what happened with the boggart and the cats, she got very quiet for a while. I said, "Don't you believe me?" and she said, "Oh, yes, yes, I do, that's the trouble. That's what frightens me."

"Come on," I said. "What *frightens*? You're the one who grew up with ghosts, poltergeists, all those stories you told me. Weretigers, for God's sake. What's so specially scary about a boggart?"

"Nothing much," Meena said. "In India. India's so old, Jenny. So many thousands of years, so many things happening to so many people, so much blood and birth—so much death that some things learned not to die, ever. The scary thing would be if India *weren't* full of ghosts and spirits and old, old curses. But England's not like that. I don't want England to be like India."

She was upset enough that she actually messed up her own pleats and had to do them over. I said, "Well, for a little baby country, England's up to here in weirdness. Eight months here, and I've heard more ghost stories, more legends, folktales, whatever, than I heard in New York my whole life. I think England's probably already like India, blood and all. You know about Monmouth's Rebellion?"

Meena laughed. "Oh, yes. In India we know English history better than our own. It's so much smaller and neater." She took me by the arms then, and looked straight into my face. She said, "Jenny, I don't know what that boggart meant about bewaring the servant, the mistress and the—that Other One. But you have to promise me that you'll take it seriously, what he said. You have to promise, Jenny."

With her deep-blue sari on and the blue dot on her forehead she could have been looking at me from any time at all. I'd never seen her like that. I said, "Yes, okay, I do, I promise, do the pleats look all right *now?*" But Meena kept at it, not just all that weekend, but in school, asking me almost every day if I was minding the boggart's warning. If I was staying away from the third floor.

That's what it came down to, after all. The third floor—still closed up, blocked off, and likely to stay that way for some while yet—was where Mister Cat's Persian ghost hung out. Haunted, I might as well get used to saying it. She haunted the third floor, where he'd met her, and probably just came down on special occasions. And if she was the servant, the way the boggart had said, then those other two were probably up there, too. And so was my cat these days, most of the time—he showed up for meals, and he usually came rolling in past midnight to sleep it off on my bed, but for the rest of it he might as well have been back at Goshawk Farm Cattery. I'd known him to be gone for a whole day, two days, on West Eighty-third, when the Siamese Hussy was exploiting his body, but then I just had cars and trucks and manholes and crazies to worry about. Now he was spending every waking moment on that third floor with ghosts, monsters, something called the Other One. And sooner or later, I was going to have to deal with it. Like making him quit eating lizards, the summer Norris rented the house in Southampton. You can't let your cat eat lizards, they're really bad for cats, and they're addictive, and you have to get the cat absolutely off them, cold turkey. Same way with ghosts. I can testify.

Because, of course, I couldn't stop thinking about the third floor, and not just because of Mister Cat, either. And the more I walked around thinking about it, the heavier it weighed on me, literally. Norris took me scuba diving once, that Southampton summer—once, and never again, because I couldn't handle it. The breathing-underwater part was fine; it was the weight, the mass, the whole *bulge* of the entire ocean, all of it, on my head—that was what I could not deal with. And the bulgy fact of the third floor was just like that, another ocean, except that this time I *was* going to have to cope. Sooner or later. I didn't live in Long Island Sound. I lived at Stourhead Farm.

But there were all kinds of perfectly good reasons to put off dealing with anything. The boggart was minding his manners, and school was getting interesting (though I wasn't about to admit it), and the weather was turning good for more than two days at a time, and Meena and Julian and I—and Tony, a couple of times—could have picnics on the downs. Once we picnicked in Julian's Hundred-Acre Wood, but that wasn't such a good idea, though nobody could ever say exactly why. It felt darker than it should have, even for an oak forest; maybe because it was so warm and bright just beyond the trees. Whatever, we packed up our picnic halfway through and moved out into the sunlight, and we never came back.

When I wasn't in school, I helped out around the Manor, like everyone else, but I dodged fieldwork whenever I got the chance—and so did Tony, I noticed pretty quickly. The Lovells were putting up enough money that first year that Evan could hire as much help as he wanted, and not need to press Tony or Julian or me into service. The problem was Julian: He kept volunteering the two of us, every time, for everything, no matter how much I threatened his life. He'd give me the big gray eyes and say, "But it's our *home*, Jenny!" That kid still has no idea how close he came, once or twice.

Mostly we weeded, whacking away with our hoes between the ridges of wheat and beans and peas and barley, sometimes even crawling to dig out stuff growing too close to the plants. We helped scatter fertilizer, too, either by hand or climbing on the back of the tractor to make sure the stuff was spreading evenly. Just as he'd told the Lovells, Evan was absolutely obsessed with getting nitrogen back into the soil—even Sally said there was only so much talking she could do about the nitrogen-fixing cycle. But he was finding out he was a *farmer*, which I don't think he'd really known before. Maybe it happened like that with old Roger Willoughby.

I don't remember the exact day that I finally went up to the third floor. You'd think I would, but I'm no good with dates—I can't remember my own birthday, let alone anybody else's. I know it was early in May, and I know it was a Tuesday afternoon, because Sally was in Dorchester with her two piano students—no, she'd picked up a third one by then. Julian had stayed in Sherborne after school for some cricket match. Evan was over at a neighbor's farm, helping out with some drainage problem, and I think Tony was with him. Either that, or he'd stayed for the cricket match, too, I'm not sure now.

I was sitting under the chestnut tree out behind the dairy, writing a letter to Marta, when Mister Cat's ghostly girlfriend trotted by. She looked different in broad daylight—fainter, for one thing, and definitely transparent, but more real, too, maybe because it *was* daylight. She got a few steps past me, and then she suddenly turned and looked at me.

I have never watched *Lassie* on TV. Not when I was little, not when I was thirteen—I'd watch game shows, which I hate, rather than watch *Lassie*. I'm making a big point about that, so it'll be clear that I didn't imagine for one minute that she was trying to get me to follow her. I got up and followed her just because I wanted to. Because I wanted to know what the hell ghost-cats do on a warm Tuesday afternoon in Dorset. That's all. I may wonder about it now, sometimes, but it was *my* idea then.

The Persian never looked back. She cut straight past the dairy, past Evan's workshop, that used to be the cider house, and right under the nose of Wilf's pet billygoat (he had the temperament of a werewolf and a thing about Mister Cat, but he never saw her) into the Manor. I thought she'd just fade through the door, like a special effect, but she used the cat-flap Evan had put in, the same as Mister Cat. It twanged back and forth a couple of times after she'd passed in, just as though a real cat had been there.

I was right behind her, practically stepping on her tail, but she didn't pay me any more heed than if I'd been a ghost myself. Straight up the stairs to the second floor, straight toward the east wing, swishing that feather-duster tail behind her like one of those fans slaves wave over emperors in movies. The house was so still that I could actually hear her feet padding on the hard old floors—or maybe I wasn't hearing real footsteps but the ghost of footsteps, the shadow of footsteps. Hard to be sure, when you don't know the rules.

I was following her so closely that I can't say exactly when Mister Cat materialized beside me. He was just there, for once not scampering after his deceased Persian patootie, but stalking along at my heel, all dignity now, sort of convoying me like a tugboat, escorting me—*where?*

At the foot of the east-wing stair, she turned again, and her eyes were glowing green as pine needles in sunlight. Mister Cat did go to her then, and they stood nose to nose, not saying anything I could hear—just looking over at me together from time to time. It got on my nerves, so I finally said, "Enough already. Let's do it." And I started for the stairway.

They went up ahead of me. Once I'd pushed the boards and rubbish aside, those two shot past me and vanished into the darkest darkness I'd ever seen—a darkness that didn't have a thing to do with the sun rising and setting. An old darkness that *knew* itself. When I started up, I felt it tasting *me*, licking at my neck and my face—daintily, carefully—the way Mister Cat will lick at something he isn't sure he wants to eat. But I kept climbing, out of pure plain stubbornness. I'm not proud of the cranky way I still get sometimes, but I can tell you it has its uses. There's a line in the Bible about perfect love casting out fear. That I don't know about, but orneriness will definitely do it every time.

It was lighter on the third floor, because of the high window at the far end. I could see clouds and sky, and the top branches of that same tree I'd been sitting under. The cats were halfway down the hall, and I walked toward them, already feeling a sneeze coming on, because the dust was so thick everywhere. But a sneeze was fine, a sneeze was *ordinary*—nothing ghostly or spooky about a sneeze. The third floor was turning out to be a floor, that was all—closed doors and cold dust, a couple of tottery old cabinets, a few faded portraits hanging above curved sconces, candleholders. Dimness, not darkness.

Mister Cat and the Persian were waiting for me, not at a door, but at a narrow panel on the left side of the corridor. It wasn't any different from any other section of the wall: same grungy oak trimmed with the same ivy-leaf molding, top and bottom, with the same chipped, bruised satyr faces peeking through at the corners. There was a bigger face about a third of the way down, looking like a lion, or maybe a sunflower with teeth. The other panels had that one, too, but this lion had little hollows for eyes, as though they were supposed to hold bits of bright glass, or jewels.

Just as I got there, the Persian gave that distant meow of hers and melted through the panel, the way I'd imagined she would when we came in from outside. She didn't actually walk into it, though—she sort of gathered herself into a shapeless gray-green *mist* for just a moment, and then she flowed right through, all at once. Five seconds—tops—and gone.

Mister Cat and I stared at each other. It's still the one and only time I've ever seen him looking as bewildered, dumbfounded and flat-out flabbergasted as I felt. He said, *"Prrrp?"* and I said, "How the hell do *I* know?" No doorknob, no hinges that I could see— maybe to everyone else who reads this, that's a dead giveaway to a secret room, but it wasn't for me. I felt over the panel, pressing hard on every single ivy leaf, or anything else raised. I even tried pressing the lion-head's empty eyes, because why not? Nothing. Mister Cat meowed impatiently. I said, "I'm *trying.*"

Then I thought, if there *had* once been stones of some kind in the lion's eyes, maybe they'd rested on something under the sockets. I dug in my pockets until I came up with a paper clip, bent it straight, and started poking around the hollows. Right eye, nothing—left eye . . . left eye, a little hole at the bottom of the socket . . . a soft *click,* and a louder *click* after that . . . and suddenly daylight around the molding, and the panel swinging back, very slowly. I remember, I saw one corner of a painting, and the legs of a chair.

Mister Cat was through the crack so fast you'd have thought his kibble dish was on the other side. But I stood right where I was, be- cause there was a third *click*—this one in my head—and I realized that what *was* beyond that panel had to be the room that we never could find in the house plan, or in any of the paintings of the house; the room whose pointy window never reflected the sun. And when I realized that, I wanted to run, but I didn't. I stood there, not moving, for maybe a month, maybe two, and then I pushed that secret door the rest of the way open.

And there was Tamsin.

Twelve

She was sitting in a chair with her back to me, looking out that window. The Persian was on her lap. I remember wondering crazily if a ghost could feel the ghost-weight of a ghost-cat, since I hadn't felt a thing when the Persian jumped up on my bed. Because there wasn't any more question about the woman than the cat—I could see the window through her, and the chestnut tree through the window; and when she put the cat down and stood up to face me, I saw that her hair and skin and gown were all the same color, a kind of pearl-gray, but with a light in it, the way rain clouds can look when the sky's almost purple behind them. She said, "Jennifer. Aye, I thought it would be you to find me."

I'd expected her voice would be as tiny as the Persian's meow, but actually it was clear as could be. Low and soft, but absolutely clear, with just a bit of what sounded almost like a Southern drawl. I couldn't answer her. I just stood there.

She smiled at me, and I guess that has to be when I fell in love with her. There was so much loneliness in that smile, but there was amusement, too, and understanding. She wasn't anything more than understanding; she was held together by memories of understanding, memories of laughter. No, of course I didn't know all that then. I didn't know anything, except that my life was never going to be the same again. And that was fine with me.

"I am Tamsin Willoughby," she said. With the chair behind her, I could see her better as she moved toward me. She wasn't tall—my height, maybe an inch more—and I couldn't have said much about her hair or her eyes (except that they were as delicately slanted as the Persian's), because everything was that glimmering gray color. And I can't say—even now—whether she was beautiful or not. Her face was a little round, and her mouth was probably too wide, with maybe a bit too much chin below it. But I couldn't stop looking at her, and I couldn't speak, not for the longest while. Tamsin just waited, never looking impatient, never looking as though she was patiently being patient. Time didn't mean anything to Tamsin—that was the first thing I ever really learned about her.

And the first thing I ever said to her, when I *could* talk, was, "How do you know my name?"

She laughed then, in a funny, breathless sort of way, like a child who's been running for no reason, just to run. "La, indeed"—she really did say that, *la*—"and how should I not know it, with you and your family abounding this way and that, filling the air with all your sweet riot—your jests, your labors, your songs, and your quarrels?" She pretended to count on her fingers. "Your father is Evan, your mother Sal, your brothers Anthony and Julian. As to Graymalkin here, I confess myself witling."

"His name's Mister Cat," I said. Graymalkin's out of *Macbeth*, which we had at Gaynor, in Introduction to Drama, so I knew. "And Evan and Tony and Julian aren't my family." I'd never said it just like that, not even to Sally when I was really pissed. I said, "They're my step-family, sort of."

Close to, I could see that the grayness had a slow pulse to it— clearer . . . dimmer . . . clearer . . . dimmer—like a heartbeat. Tamsin was looking at me altogether too shrewdly, considering she was dead and we'd just met. But all she said was, "You're not of Dorset—no, nor of England neither, I think. You'll be from the Colonies."

"The Colonies," I said. "Oh. Right. The Colonies. America, yes. There was a revolution. We're an independent country now. I guess you wouldn't know."

Her hair was a mass of corkscrew curls, drawn up on top and spilling down over her right shoulder. It didn't move when she shook her head. She said, "This house has not always stood empty, Mistress Jennifer—there have been a mort of other voices than yours passing my door, crying the news below my window. Well I know that Romish James is departed, and the Hanovers come long since, and those weighty men who visited my father by night as surely dust as I. Colonies gained and lost, powers arisen and fallen away, alliances sworn, alliances broken, poor Dorset long losel as a Jacobus . . . What may be the year now, child?"

I told her. It looked to me as though she swayed for a moment, but maybe that was just that come-and-go pulsation of the gray-ness. "So late? So late, and here am I still, when I should be as gone as James and . . . and Edric Davies, and *him*." I hardly heard the last few words, they came out in such a whisper. "Art certain, Mistress Jennifer?"

"I'm certain," I said. "And please, I wish you wouldn't call me Jennifer. I'm Jenny—no *mistress* about it. Everyone calls me Jenny."

Tamsin Willoughby smiled a second time, and everything in me just dissolved into marshmallows and Silly Putty. I have *never* been one of those girls who's always getting huge crushes on older girls, but Tamsin . . . It wasn't that she was so pretty—Meena's way pret-tier, if you want to measure these things. Maybe it was just the plain fact of her being a ghost, and smiling at me across three hun-dred years—I can't say it wasn't. But what I thought, and what I still think, and always will, is that she saw me. Nobody else has ever seen me—me, Jenny Gluckstein—like that. Not my parents, not Julian, not even Meena. Love is one thing—recognition is some-thing else.

Tamsin said, "Jenny, then. You must remind me when I forget—and I will forget, because that is what I do, that is all I am. You would think—would you not?—that after so many, many years, surely there would be naught left me to forget, who'd seen but twenty summers when I . . . when I *stopped*." She always used that word. "Yet the voices under the window do tell me names, speak of changes and wonders—teach me songs, even—and I learn these things for a little, then swiftly forget them, too. As I forget why I must be here at all."

Writing the words down the way she spoke them, it looks pitiable somehow, as though she were asking for sympathy. But that wasn't the way they sounded, not for a minute, and it wasn't in the way she carried herself, nor the way she looked at me. The Persian cat was rubbing against her foot, and that was weird: one see-through impossibility comforting itself by making contact with another. I asked, "Who's *she*? My cat's practically left home because of her."

Tamsin really laughed then, and it sounded like rainwater plink-ing off leaves and flowers after the storm's gone by. "Her name is Miss Sophia Brown. I could never forget *that*, as long as we have been together. She's all grand hogen-mogen one minute and a flirting flibbergib the next, but we fadge along pretty smartly—at least until your fine black gentleman presented himself. I've never known her gloat so upon a lover."

"Me neither," I said. "Mister Cat's got a girlfriend back home, but I think she was just using him. The thing is, he's alive, and your Sophia Brown . . . I don't know. I wouldn't exactly say they had much of a future."

"La, what odds makes that to a cat?" Miss Sophia Brown and Mister Cat were standing nose to nose, both of them purring in complete satisfaction with their own taste in pussycats. As we watched, Mister Cat began washing Miss Sophia Brown's face, and if there wasn't anything actually there to be washed, or held still with a paw behind her right ear, he didn't seem to notice. I wondered if ghost-cats got hairballs. I decided I wouldn't wonder about that.

Tamsin said, very quietly, "Cats have no cares for who's quick, who's . . . stopped. Shall we be like them?"

We looked at each other. I said, "You smell like vanilla."

Tamsin's eyebrows went up, but one corner of her mouth twitched just a bit. It seemed to me that she was looking maybe a bit less transparent—I could even see something like color in her face, and in the long, close-waisted gown she was wearing, or dreaming she was wearing. "I smelled you," I said. "When I was with Julian."

She'd forgotten. She stared at me for a long moment: *flickering,* halfway fading, then pulsing stronger as it came back to her. "Candles and singing—a strange tongue, but a sweet air. Aye, I do recall me."

"That electrician kept saying he smelled vanilla in the Arctic Circle—in the kitchen, I mean. Was that you? Were you bugging the workmen, too, like the boggart and the rest of them?"

"Bugging." Tamsin said the word a couple of times, as if she were nibbling it, turning it over with her tongue. "Bugging—ah, as t'were a harassment, a plaguing, a botheration. Nay, child, that was never me—I but spied betimes upon your hirelings as they hammered and tore at my house, vaporing endlessly the while. By and by I'd no heart to watch further, so I came away and left them to it. Are you contented with their work, Mistress Jennifer . . . Jenny?"

I couldn't tell if she was angry or not about what we'd all been doing to the Manor. I said, "Evan—he's my mother's husband—

Evan got hired to get this place going again as a real farm. To bring it back to life. It needed a lot of upgrading."

Tamsin didn't bother exploring *upgrading*. She said, "To bring it back to life. As though my home, my land, had stopped along with me. It is not so—you and yours know nothing of Stourhead Farm. I warrant you, there's more true *life* within these walls, between the fences that your stepfather spends his days butting together—aye, and walking your bean rows and apple orchards a' nights—than you've encountered in all the days of your own little life. Gorge me *that*, Mistress Jenny!"

Right then she looked practically solid, which is what happens to Tamsin when she gets excited or worked up about something. Her eyes were wide and bright—they were blue-green, I could even see that now—and her voice made the cats look up, just as they were settling into some serious necking. All I could think to mumble was, "Well, the plumbing really did need some work, it was pretty old. And the soil's old, too. Evan says the crops weren't growing because the soil was so tired. We had to do *something*."

Tamsin stared at me. After a moment, her eyes quieted down, and she smiled just a bit. "Truth enough, Jenny Gluckstein. I ask your pardon. The land is wearied indeed, and my fine house is a ruin, a daggy relic of antique times—as am I." She was starting to go filmy gray again, still pulsing slowly between this room and somewhere else. She said, "Truth for truth, I am greatly glad of you and all your family—of your stepbrothers' tumult and your mother's music. I am the better for commotion, the better for aught that rouses me, fetches me away out of this cloister of mine. Othergates, I sit as you found me, Miss Sophia Brown dozy on my lap—moonrise on moonrise, year on year, age on age—until the forgetting shall have me altogether. But that must not happen, must not. . . ."

Her voice was floating away, dissolving, and I was afraid that she would, too. I asked, "What *is* this room, anyway? It doesn't have a real door, and you can't see in the window, just out." There was hardly any furniture: just the chair, and a contraption in the corner like a trunk, but with a bedframe for the lid. The painting I'd seen from the doorway was a portrait of a big, ruddy man in a wig and a long sort of waistcoat, standing next to a shy-looking woman wearing a black gown and a frilly white linen cap on the back of her head. I asked Tamsin again, "What kind of a room is this?"

Tamsin looked a little surprised. "This? This is Roger Willoughby's priest-closet. Nay, we were no Papists, but my father—though he was always good Charles's man—saw Rome bound to come in with James, and persecutions with it, and nothing would do but we must build our own hidey-hole for our own chaplain, should we ever have one. My father was a prodigious romantic, you must know, Jenny, with a headpiece full of notions my poor mother never fathomed. But we loved him dearly, she and I, and it grieves me still to think how he suffered when . . ."

She didn't finish, and I didn't know if I ought to prompt her to go on. I didn't have any idea what the rules were with a ghost. Did they only have so much juice at a time, like a car battery? Would they just fade and go out if you pushed them too much? When she sat alone with her Persian cat in this room, years at a time, the way she said—was she visible then? I said, "When you died—stopped, I mean. That must have been really awful, watching him mourning for you." Tamsin didn't say anything. I thought I should probably change the subject, so I asked, "Who's the Other One?"

Tamsin looked at me as though *I* were the ghost and she'd just seen *me* for the first time. I said, "We had some boggart trouble a while back. The cats took care of him"—Mister Cat and Miss Sophia Brown were chasing each other around the room, playing tag like kittens—"but he told me to beware of the servant and the mistress—I guess that's you and your cat—and the Other One. Who's that, when he's at home and properly labelled?" I picked up that last bit from Julian.

A ghost can't really turn pale, but Tamsin came close. She put her hands out toward me, and I think she'd have grabbed me by the shoulders and shaken me if she could. She said, "Child, Jenny, never ask me that again. Never ask again, not of me nor of any—not of *yourself*, do you understand me? Promise me that, as we stand here. Jenny, you *must* promise, if we are to be friends."

Her fear—and she was terrified, ghost or no ghost—had brought her back to being untransparent enough so that I could smell that odd whisk of vanilla, and even see a bit of a dimple under her left cheekbone. Her hair was a kind of darkish blond, and her eyes had gone deep turquoise, but the exact shade kept changing as I looked into them, as though she couldn't ever quite remember the color they'd been. Something about that twisted my insides, and I'd have promised her anything to comfort her. I said, "Okay, I won't. Cross my heart, spit twice, hope to die—I won't ask about the Other One anymore."

I knew I'd break that promise when I gave it. Sometimes I think Tamsin knew, too. But she cheered up right away, and after that we just talked, watching Miss Sophia Brown and Mister Cat taking turns ambushing each other, until I really did feel that we were like that, totally unconcerned with who was alive and who wasn't. I told her about New York and my friends there, and Norris, and how I'd felt about Sally marrying Evan and dragging me off to Dorset—I was *pretty* honest, anyway—and about the boys, and Meena, and the Sherborne School, and even about grubby old Wilf and his goat. And Tamsin listened, and laughed, and grew more and more visible—more *present*—until her hair and the flows of her gown swayed with her laughter, and I couldn't see through her at all, although maybe that was because the room was getting darker. And I actually forgot what she was, just for that little time. I did.

For her part, Tamsin talked mostly about Stourhead Farm, and about Roger Willoughby. "City man, merchant, son and grandson of merchants, why he should have so fancied the life of the soil, who can say? Yet my father believed with all his heart that anyone, man or woman, may learn anything he truly wishes to learn, if only his enterprise be a match for his desire. And if that were never so for any other, yet it was true for my father. For he was no farmer, but he made himself over into one, and never was poet or painter gladder in his trade. Indeed, I never knew a happier man."

I thought she might turn sad again, the way she had the first time she spoke of her father, but instead she giggled suddenly, sounding just like Meena when she tries to tell a joke and *always* cracks up before she gets to the punchline. "Jenny, he labored like any hero to cozen his neighbors into draining their grasslands— into daring, even for a season, to fertilize their fields some other road than letting their cattle do it for 'em. Nay, but surely you know farmers by now"—and she dropped into an old-Dorset voice, like the boggart's— "*Nah, nah, zir, mook's your man, there's nothing beats your good ripe mook for not overztimulating the zoil, d'ye zee?*" We were both laughing into each other's eyes, and the cats turned around to hear us.

"They heeded not one word of his advice," Tamsin said. "They went on farming as they were used, and my father farmed as he would, and time proved him the wiser, though I was not there to see." She looked away then, out the window. I could hear Tony and Julian calling to each other somewhere.

I asked, "How did it happen? I mean, you dying—stopping—when you were only twenty?" I didn't know if that was something else I shouldn't ask her, but you can't be *always* changing the subject, even with a ghost. Tamsin's face did change when she turned back to me—I saw her mouth thin out and her eyes lost some of their color—but she answered clearly, "A flux of the lungs, it was, a catarrh that grew to a pleurisy, then to a pulmonary phthisis. And no one to blame for it but my own bufflehead self, for lacking the wit to come inside on a wild night. Not a soul else to blame, and well-deserved."

That was all she said about it. Julian was yelling for me now, and when I looked at my watch I was surprised to see that it was coming up on dinnertime. I picked up Mister Cat, who wasn't pleased about it, and looked at Tamsin over his black head. She said, "We will meet again, Mistress Jenny."

"Yes," I said. "That's good. Can I just come and see you here, like Mister Cat?"

Tamsin smiled. "Indeed you may. Or I might become Miss Sophia Brown and seek you in your own chamber. You'll not be afeard?"

I shook my head. Tamsin reached to stroke Mister Cat's throat, and he closed his eyes and purred as though he felt it. I said, "Could I ask you one thing? When you talked about all the life in this house, and running around at night all over Stourhead Farm, I was wondering . . . what kind of life did you exactly mean?"

Tamsin looked at me long enough without answering for Julian to bellow twice more. Finally she said, "I will show you. When I come to you, I will show you."

Thirteen

Nobody. Not even Meena. All the way down the stairs—all the time I was putting the barriers back in place—all during dinner—as soon as I had a minute to myself I was going to call Meena and tell her everything about Tamsin Willoughby, my own ghost on the third floor. I almost did it the next time I saw her at school, and I *almost* did it when I spent a whole weekend in London with Meena and her parents. But it was like Julian and me with the boggart, only more so. Keeping secrets, knowing something that no one else in the world knows, no matter how powerful or smart or beautiful they are—it's deadly addictive. At least it is for me, and it's something I'm going to have to watch out for all my life. Not that a secret like Tamsin is likely to come along ever again. I know that, too.

I wanted to go right back up there the next day, after I got home from school, but I didn't. It wasn't so much that I thought she'd mind; it was more me needing time to *believe*, to take in what I'd seen, who I'd been talking to—where I'd been, in a way. Because, up in that little hidden room her father had built to hide Church of England ministers . . . up in that room, there were moments when Stourhead Farm was practically just built, and the first crops just in the ground, and Roger Willoughby was out front roaring at his neighbors about overgrazing, and Tamsin and I were giggling together about whom *we'd* like to be hiding up here, never mind any chaplains. That's the way it felt, anyway; and for days—three or four weeks, anyway—even after I came down, I was sort of seasick in time, not completely sure of when I was. Julian noticed it, but he didn't know what he was seeing. Like me.

Meanwhile there were finals coming up, and Julian forever after me about helping out on the farm, and Meena having a kind of long-distance love affair with Christopher Herridge, who sang in the mixed choir Sherborne Girls shares with the boys' school.

What I mean by long distance is that they mostly just gazed at each other across a lot of heads and pews and violins, singing their hearts out. It was very romantic and doomed, because however large a fit Chris's family might have had about him dating an Indian girl, it would have been a sneeze, a hiccup, a burp, compared to what Mr. and Mrs. Chari would have done if their daughter brought an English boy home to dinner. So Meena cried a lot— Chris was as cute as they come, no question—and we hung on the phone for hours, me doing my best to console her. Really trying, too, because I was wildly jealous of Chris, and I knew it, and wanted to make up to Meena for *that*, some way. I'd have days at a time, back then, when it was just impossible to be human, whichever way I turned. I still have them, once in a while.

I kept Tamsin to myself—even from myself, in a way, because I'd make a point of not thinking about her at all until I was in bed at night. Then I'd lie there and wonder what *she* was thinking about right at that moment, sitting in her chair watching the moon coming up, not knowing or caring whether it was tonight's moon or tomorrow's, or a moon from a hundred years ago. Most nights Mister Cat would be on my bed, but sometimes he wasn't, and I'd be sure he was out with Miss Sophia Brown, being shown around all the old secret places of Stourhead Farm. And I'd decide one more time that Tamsin never meant to come find me and show *me* things—she'd just been being polite, the way ladies were raised to be in sixteen-whatever. She was probably off with the cats herself, none of them wasting a single minute on me. Around then I'd indulge in one quick sorrowful sniffle and go to sleep.

I'd been braced for disaster when the exam results were posted, so they didn't look too bad the way they came out. Thanks to Julian, I sneaked through maths, just barely; thanks to Meena, I did better than that in my science classes. I was dead in Spanish, never mind that I had the best accent of anybody—I don't understand pluperfects and past imperfects in *English*. But I ate up Literature and World History, and British History, too—I did almost as well as Meena, who'd been raised on that stuff. I was terrible in Games. Could have been worse.

As for Stourhead, I still wasn't paying a lot of attention, for all the grunt work Julian had me putting in, but crops were coming up thick and fast everywhere you looked, so I figured the farm had to be back in business by now. But Evan wasn't a bit happy. I'd hear him talking to Sally at night, always saying the same thing. "I *knew* it was wrong, from the beginning. I was trying to impress the Lovells—showing off, just bloody showing off, after all that talk about not expecting miracles. I should have gone ahead and done what I was meaning to do in the first place. But the Lovells would have backed off, and I was afraid of losing the situation before I even got started. But I *knew*, Sally."

I'd usually have tuned out by then—I really don't like eavesdropping. Besides, I wanted to go on knowing as little as I could get away with about Stourhead Farm, even if I had to live there. So I had no idea what was bothering Evan, and I managed to keep Sally from telling me, which she'd have done in a second. I'd lived through an English winter and an entire year of English school. I had my cat, I'd picked up a best friend and—face it—a kid brother; I'd met a boggart, and I knew a ghost. Dorset or no Dorset, I had a summer coming to me.

And we actually had a genuinely hot summer night, somewhere around the middle of June. Dorset does not have a whole lot of hot nights, no matter what the day was like. Come sundown the temperature drops off fast, and the air always feels moist, even when it hasn't been raining. That's because of the Bristol Channel—you can't ever get away from the Channel in Dorset, even inland. It's not unpleasant, it just never feels to me like real summer.

But that evening was pure funky, sticky, breathless asphalt New York. My clothes felt as though they'd been ironed right onto me. Everybody wilted, even Sally, who can look like crisp lettuce in the worst weather. Julian got some kind of prickly rash all over him, and fussed until he had to go to bed. Evan and Tony kept making more lemonade, drinking so much of it that you could almost see it evaporating out of their pores, like a mist. Mister Cat flopped down on his side with his legs out behind him, the way a dog does, looking small and damp. When I sat by him and petted him, he rolled over, away from me, so I stopped. Too damn hot even for that.

Finally I got up and walked a little away from the Manor by myself. I felt like Mister Cat: too hot to be around people. The moon hadn't risen yet. I stood still under a tree whose leaves weren't stirring an inch, and listened to utterly nothing, which was the strangest thing of all. I've already said that it's *noisy* in the country, once you know how to listen, and a completely silent country night is scary in a special way. No insects, no frogs, no owls, not so much as a creak or a clunk, or a faraway scurry—none of those nameless nightsounds you get used to, living on a farm. And the silence builds and builds, until it becomes a sound by itself, until it's just like one of those West Eighty-third Street jackhammers, and all you want is for it to *stop*. As though something were going to fly apart, burst, split wide open, any minute now, but you can't tell what it's going to be. Like that.

Tamsin came toward me through the trees. I hadn't noticed it up in the hidden room, but outdoors in the darkness there was the faintest sort of glow about her, greeny-violet, the way seawater gets at night sometimes. You can see it a surprising way off, and at first you think it's fireflies. Miss Sophia Brown didn't have it—I can't say if even all human ghosts have it. The three I ever knew did.

"Good evening to you, Mistress Jenny," she said. "You see, your name remains." She was wearing a different gown to come out in, this one puffy at the sides, with something almost like a bustle in back. I didn't like it as much as the first one, but she'd remembered bunches of ribbons over her ears, and those looked lovely. She dipped me a curtsy, and I actually made her one back, which is tricky in shorts.

"I didn't know you ever left the house," I said. "Your room." It was different talking to her outside: She seemed more alive, if that makes any sense—dangerous, even, in a way.

When she smiled at me, I felt her remembering me, just like those ribbons in her hair. "Oh, I may go where I choose, so I remain within the bounds of Stourhead." Close to, glimmering under those old trees, she looked like a beautiful moth. "But what odds the freedom of a prison?"

There was a soft bitterness in her voice that I couldn't have imagined. I said, "I didn't know you felt that way about . . . I mean, it's your home." I sounded like Julian.

"Aye, so it is. And will be while it stands—and after." Tamsin put her hand on my arm, the first time she'd ever touched me. I didn't feel anything, but I stared at her fingers against my skin the way people stare at newborn babies. *"Oh, look at the perfect little nails, the darling little toes!"* Tamsin said, "But Jenny, do we not every one leave home when it comes time to find another? A father's home for a husband's—is that not so? And that in turn for a third, for the long home where all will meet again at last. All, all . . . except

such as are bound, ensnared, barred away forever from such joy."
The moon was just beginning to rise, and I could see her hand
tightening on my forearm, but there was absolutely no sensation.

"I don't know what you mean," I said. "I'm sorry." And I *was*
sorry, because she'd been speaking to me as though we were the
same age, even out of the same century, with the same experience,
the same understanding. And all I could do was remind her that I
was thirteen, from New York, and didn't know what the hell she
was talking about, and I hated myself for it. I really expected her
to vanish right there—just forget me completely, like one of the
pretty girls back at Gaynor—and I wouldn't have blamed her for a
minute.

But Tamsin . . . Tamsin only looked at me with such pity in her
imaginary eyes as I never saw in my life, before or since. She said,
"Child, no, sure I am the blind buzzard here—it's you must forgive
my foolishness. Indeed, how *should* you know? How *should* you
comprehend what I myself cannot?" She clapped her hands
soundlessly. "It's all mystery anyroad, live or die, leave or stay. Let
be—did I not promise to show you the true Stourhead night?
Come, so." And she put her arm through mine.

No, I didn't feel that either—I couldn't have, I know I didn't—
but I *thought* I did, and I can't explain it any better than that. She
looked so solid, not transparent at all, and her eyes were as bright
as Julian's when he's got a surprise for you. At the time I'd have
sworn up and down that I felt the pull and bump of another
human body in the bend of my arm, and when I think back on it
now, I *remember*. Like Tamsin remembering the world.

I yelled back to the house that I was going for a walk. Sally called
that she might want to come with me, but I pretended I hadn't
heard. Tamsin led me down the rutted tractor path that runs to
the south fields, but she turned away from it before we got there,
toward a row of huge beech trees that the Lovells kept after Evan
to cut down because most of them were half-dead. Evan wouldn't
do it. He said they were as old as the Manor, and belonged there
as much as we did. By day they looked a mess—all bald and twisted
and shedding bark, putting out leaves on one branch in ten—but
now they stood up over us like fierce, proud, horrible old men.
No, I don't mean *horrible*; more like people who've suffered so
much that it's made them mean. But Tamsin was so happy to see
them she let go of me and ran ahead, floating through the moon-

light, not quite touching the ground. When she reached the first tree she swung around it to face me, and if the trees looked like men, she looked as young as Julian.

"Still here—oh, still here!" she called—halfway singing, really. "Oh, still holding to Stourhead earth, they and I." She hooked her arm around the tree and swung again, as though she was dancing with it. I knew she couldn't have touched it, felt the bark or the dry leaves, any more than I could have felt her arm against mine— but nobody looks as beautiful, as joyous, as Tamsin looked right then when they're feeling nothing. *Nobody*, ghost or not, I don't believe it.

"I saw my father plant these trees," she said as I came up with her. "Jenny, they were such minikins, hardly saplings—truly, I must bend down to pet them good morning, as I do Miss Sophia Brown. And see them now, grown so great and grim—stripped and battered by the years, yet still here, unyielding." She wheeled toward the beech trees again, asking them, "Were you waiting for me then, little ones, all this time? Would you ask my sanction before you fall? Well, I do not grant it, do you hear me?" Her voice didn't change at all; she might just as well have been talking to me. "Nay, if I'm to stay on, so shall you—and I am even older, so you'll mind what I say. Whiles I remain at Stourhead, you're to keep me company, as Roger my father bade you. Hear!"

There was the tiniest flick of a breeze just now beginning to stir, and that's probably why the trees seemed to be bowing their raggedy heads to her. Tamsin turned back to me. She said, "Beeches are kind, beeches will help if they can. Elders, too, and even ash, if you speak them courtesy. But ware the oak, Jenny, for they love men no whit more than they love the swine who eat their acorns. Ware the oak, *always*."

It sounded as much like a command as when she'd told the beech trees they couldn't die as long as she was at the Manor. I said I would, and Tamsin took my arm again. "Now, Mistress Jenny," she said. "Now I will take you to meet another old companion of mine."

I tried to find it the next day, that path Tamsin took me by in the hot darkness, but I never could. It had to be on Stourhead Farm, because she couldn't pass its boundaries, and it had to be somewhere near the barley fields, because they take a lot of water and I could hear the auxiliary pump working. There's a regular path, of course, that runs right to the fields, but that's not the one we were on, I *know* that. Six years, and I've never been able to find it again, no more than I've ever found that feeling of utter, absolute, total safety that I had walking with Tamsin that night. I'm as scared of the dark as anyone else—with more reason—but not then, not with Tamsin beside me, glimmering and laughing, teasing me that my family had let the path go to hell. "La, what a shaggy tumble it's become, where once one saw clear to the high road. What horses then! aye, and how we heard their hoofbeats for miles, as it seemed, before the brave carriages whirled into view. Well, well, never fret, dear Jenny, it must have been long ago, I'll warrant." But she wasn't *sure* it was long ago—she was still listening for those horses. You could tell.

I don't know when it hit me that we weren't alone. First I looked around for Miss Sophia Brown and Mister Cat, but then I realized someone or something was pacing us, just off to my left. I can't say how I knew, because I couldn't see it, whatever it was, and it didn't make any sound. No crackling brush, no growl—no breathing, even—but the thing was *close*, and I would have been scared out of my mind if I hadn't been with Tamsin. She put her arm around my shoulders, which I couldn't feel any more than I'd felt her hand on my arm, but I was glad of it just the same. She said quietly, "Do not fear. There is no danger."

We stood together, waiting. I didn't know for what, but I wasn't afraid, because Tamsin had said not to be. We stood there, and after a while the thing that had been walking with us came out into the moonlight.

It was a dog, the biggest dog I've ever seen, the size of a cow. It looked like the Hound of the Baskervilles, except that it was totally black—so black that the moonlight made it look even blacker, as though it was soaking up the light and turning it to darkness inside itself. Its eyes were glowing red, but it didn't look savage: more like really dignified, almost sad. I whispered to Tamsin, "What is it? What kind of dog is that?"

"That is the Black Dog," Tamsin said. I just blinked at her, which seemed to surprise her. "The Black Dog. He appears always as a warning."

"Warning about what?" Tamsin didn't answer me. She moved toward that huge creature, and I *thought* he wagged his tail the least bit, but maybe not. Her voice was different than when she talked to me. She said, "Why have you come, tell me? What need for such as I am to beware?"

She beckoned to me without taking her eyes off him, but I couldn't move. *I* knew I wasn't scared, but my legs didn't. Tamsin turned and saw how I was standing, and called softly, "Jenny, to me! No harm, no harm," as though she were coaxing a skittery animal. I went to stand beside her, and I made myself look straight into the Black Dog's red eyes.

To this day I don't have any idea what the Black Dog is. Maybe he's nothing more than a presentiment, a way of telling yourself to watch out for something you already know to watch out for. I could believe that if he hadn't looked so real—he even *smelled* like a real dog. I've never yet had a presentiment that smelled.

Tamsin asked him again, "Why have you come?" He didn't bark or whine, the way dogs do when it's killing them not to be able to talk. But she listened to his silence, and once she nodded. She glanced sideways at me, and I said, "What? I don't understand a thing!" and when I looked back again the Black Dog was gone.

"Well," Tamsin said. "Passing strange." Her voice was so soft I could barely hear her. "This is passing strange, Jenny. The Black Dog is come to warn us both, though of what I'm not aware. He came just so to Edric and me, but my understanding failed us then. It must not fail again."

"Who's Edric?" I asked her, but she didn't answer. The moon was so bright that I could even make out a small frown line between her eyes, and that melted me more than I can write down now. The idea that she could make herself remember something as human as a frown, with everything else she was trying to hold on to. . . . I wondered suddenly if Miss Sophia Brown ever used to paw her eyes open in the morning, three hundred years ago, the way Mister Cat does with me.

"It's late," I said, "Sally's going to start worrying. I guess we can meet your friend another time." Tamsin looked at me without answering. There was a moment when I felt like the ultimate idiot, talking about lateness and worry to a ghost. But then she said, "Indeed, my own mother was greatly given to apprehension," and we started back.

She didn't talk much on the way, but she stayed visible and distinct in the darkness, which I took to mean that she was thinking hard about the Black Dog. Which was why I did something I shouldn't have done, something she'd made me promise I'd never do. I asked her, "Do you suppose the dog was warning us about the Other One? You know, like the boggart?"

The moment the words were out of my mouth I was desperately hoping she wouldn't recall what I'd promised. But I just had to look at her, and I knew. I was sure she'd be furious at me—and for a bit she was, which was frightening, because with a ghost you can really *see* a feeling, all the way down. Somebody who has to remember all the time what feelings are isn't going to be any good at hiding them. Tamsin looked at me for a long time without saying anything, while I was apologizing and apologizing for mentioning the Other One at all. Finally she smiled, and it was all right, like *that*, the same way it had been absolutely, horribly wrong a minute before. That's how it always was with Tamsin.

"He is gone," she said. "Long gone, Jenny, long away past returning, even that one. And if he did, be sure that I would know of it. The Black Dog is wrong."

"Well, who was he?" I asked, but that was pushing it. Tamsin turned and started on, and although she seemed to be barely drifting through that sludgy air, I had to skip to catch up with her. She said, "Jenny, all that matters is that he is *not*. Words are dear to me, and he will consume no more of mine. The Black Dog is wrong, and your boggart is wrong—be greatly thankful, and be still." And I was, the rest of the way, until the lights of the Manor came into view through the branches of Tamsin's beech trees. They seemed very far away, although they weren't really. I think that was the first time I was even a little homesick for someplace that wasn't West Eighty-third and Columbus Avenue—even for the people who had snatched West Eighty-third away from me. It was an uneasy feeling, and I didn't like it.

Tamsin stopped before we reached the trees, putting her arm out in front of me. For a moment I thought the Black Dog was with us again; but *he* never made a sound, and there are too many dead leaves under the beeches for a big animal to move quietly. Tamsin whispered, "Stay" to me; and then, louder, "Will you have forgotten me so soon, old friend? Not you, surely?"

There was a sudden raspy grunt up ahead, and one loud crash in the undergrowth, and something darker than the night loped away beyond the line of trees. It looked as big as the Black Dog—bigger—but I couldn't make out whether it was running on two legs or four. It turned once to look back at us, and its eyes were yellow as gold. Tamsin said softly, "A pity."

"What's a pity?" I asked her. "What was *that?*" Tamsin pretended not to hear me. She did that a lot when she didn't want to answer a question, just as I did with Sally. She said, "And yet, one turn around Stourhead Farm in your fair company, and here are folk I've not seen since my father died, waiting to welcome me. Not only those two, but others, others . . . I think you must be my good fortune come to find me, and calling yourself Mistress Jenny." She made to ruffle my hair, and I will swear to this day that I felt the one little breeze of the night cooling my sweaty neck. I know it had to be a coincidence. I'm not saying it wasn't.

"What others?" No chance. Tamsin said, "Child, we will part here, an it please you. Your mother will be waiting, and I . . . I have affairs left too long untended. Stay on the path, and it will have you home before you can say my name entire, which is Tamsin Elspeth Catherine Maria Dubois Willoughby. I will come for you again."

Even this close to the Manor, I wasn't crazy about being left alone in a night that was turning out to be practically as inhabited as West Eighty-third Street. But I didn't have a vote—Tamsin blinked out with her last word, and I made my way home, looking over my shoulder a lot. Sally tried to be angry with me for being gone so long, but it was too hot. Julian was still up, fussy and miserable, so I read him one of his William books until he fell asleep. I took the book to bed with me, because I was afraid I wouldn't be able to sleep either, but I was, and I dreamed all night of the Black Dog.

Fourteen

Night's never been the same for me again.

I'll never know exactly how wandering over Stourhead Farm with me at night became a habit of Tamsin's—if ghosts even *have* habits. She'd be there, waiting by the South Barn or under the chestnut tree behind the dairy, every two or three evenings; and sometimes it felt as though we were two old ladies out for their regular constitutional stroll, the same way they'd been doing for years. But for me, each time had to be the first—I couldn't ever afford to take our meetings for granted, even if she could. Tamsin might forget me any time at all, just forget forever to come and find me, and that would be that. So whenever I smelled vanilla and caught sight of her, glowing so gently in the twilight, smiling to see me (she was always careful never to pop out of nowhere, like a ghost in a movie), all my insides would jump right up from a standing start, the way crickets leap up out of the grass. I suppose I'll be that way about a man someday, but it hasn't happened yet.

The thing is, we were the only people who knew what moved around the Manor and the farm after nightfall, Tamsin and me. I mean, Julian did see the boggart, and Sally's always had her suspicions, but nobody *knows*, not even after everything that happened. Right now it's about ten o'clock, and I'm writing this in Sally's music room, which she's very sneakily turned into the most comfortable place in the whole house. Tony's dancing in Edinburgh, Julian's off somewhere with his newest girlfriend, and Sally and Evan are in the North Barn with Lady Caroline Lamb, who's due to drop a calf tonight, and always needs company. Your typical rural Dorset evening. Nothing much going on that Thomas Hardy wouldn't recognize.

And if I just stand up and walk to the front door, and open it, and look outside, past the courtyard, past both barns and the dairy and the cowpen and the workshop . . . out there in the dark there are creatures moving around who have been out there since before the Manor was ever built—since before there were people in Dorset, for all I can say. And I've seen them. I've spoken to them, I've run from them, and two of them maybe saved my life, and maybe more than my life. You can pave Dorset over from Cranborne to Charmouth, Gillingham to Portland Isle—they'll still be there, come nightfall. I really know this.

The funny part is that before we got here Stourhead Farm came *that* close to being declared an SSSI (Site of Special Scientific Interest), because of one particular species of vole that doesn't seem to exist anywhere but in this part of West Dorset. Which would have meant the end of Stourhead—you can't farm an SSSI—but there isn't a country in the world that has a Strangeness Preserve, so we were all right. Nothing that lives on our land counts as an endangered species.

Since I couldn't ever know for certain when Tamsin would show up, I always had to go by feeling, and whether I had it right or wrong, it made for some bad moments. Once we were all in the car, bound for a movie in Yeovil, and I backed out at the last minute—literally jumped out on the driveway—because I suddenly just *knew* that Tamsin was waiting for me. She was, too, that time, but it took a ton of explaining when everybody got home. And when I went out at night—"to stretch my legs," "to clear my head," whatever excuse I used—I'd have to deal with Julian at one end, wanting to come with me, and Sally at the other, because she never fell asleep until she knew I was in the house. One time I was on the phone to Meena, and I saw a pale shiver at the window that I was *sure* had to be Tamsin, and I just cut Meena off—just hung up and ran outside to be with her. But it was some sort of bird, a nightjar, whatever, and I had to call Meena back and apologize. I never did that again, hang up on Meena, even when it *was* Tamsin.

We covered Stourhead Farm on those walks, Tamsin and I, and sometimes the cats, chasing each other practically under our feet and vanishing again. Tamsin just wafted along beside me like dandelion fluff, like a toy balloon that got away. The truly amazing thing was that she absolutely remembered every field, every crop: She'd say things like, "Ah, you've let this meadow go back to ryegrass; my father was forever making trial of the French grasses—lucerne, sainfoin and those." Or, again, "I vow, Jenny, how wonderful well they do drain in these times of yours. We'd no such pipes and culverts, no such siphon engines—only spades, only ditches filled with stones and bramble. Oh, could my father have seen those *pipes!*" And she'd actually sigh, and we'd move on. She was a country girl, all right, Tamsin Willoughby, dead or alive.

The sheep weren't ever aware of her when we'd cross their downland pasture (sheep are barely aware they're sheep), but she used to scare the hell out of the collie, Albert. Nothing short of foxes threatening a new lamb ever roused that dog; but whenever I passed by with Tamsin, he'd race to head us off, plant his feet and go into an unbelievable frenzy of barking until he actually lost his voice. And that did scare the sheep, so we stopped walking there.

She wanted to know *everything* about me, about Sally and Evan and the boys—even Norris, even the Lovells. Especially the Lovells, come to think of it—she knew the farm wasn't in her family anymore, but she didn't have a clue about the hands and changes it had passed through in the last fifty years. I explained what I could, which wasn't a lot. Tamsin seemed to understand most of it; but when I started in on the twentieth century, she wasn't much interested. It took me a while to realize that for all her father's money, she'd never once been out of Dorset, except for a couple of holidays in Bath; for all her education, Dorset was the world, and all she really cared about was how much Dorset had changed. She said it herself: "Jenny, Jenny, what should I do in this place where I am—stopped—but dream my long dreams of what was? Yet I need to know what *is*, I must know, if I am ever to—" She broke off right there, and didn't say anything more for a long time.

I told her the hills were still there, and the butterflies and wildflowers, and the evening fog off the Channel. I talked about dark, soft little coombes like the one where Julian caught his foot in the stream, about barns and cottages that she'd have recognized, and farms where I'd seen horses pulling binding and threshing machines so old that Thomas Hardy probably helped uncrate them. I went into a whole lot of detail about the time Meena and I met a man in the woods making sheep hurdles by hand, weaving split hazel stems together and singing to himself. And I never said a word about plowed-up heathland and air pollution and housing developments on the hills. What for?

"If I could but leap these bounds of mine," she kept saying. "If I could walk my Dorset but once, one time only, before I pass to . . . to wherever I should be. Dear and close as it clips me yet, Stourhead is no more my home, nor has been since Edric—"

And she'd quit there, every time, like a record with the needle caught in a scratch. And I'd ask her again who Edric was, and Tamsin either wouldn't answer or she'd change the subject entirely and tell me how her mother used to make conserves out of rose leaves and sugar, or how her father kept bees. "He would say to me, 'Catty'—for that was his pet name for me—'Catty, girl, if a man would be solaced, if he would find respite from daily harassments and grievances, let him observe these creatures at their labor. *There's* amnesty for you, *there's* plenary absolution for all sins, all sorrows.' Oh, I do think of him still, Jenny, and I am so sad that the bees are gone."

Which may all have been her way of keeping me from asking any more questions about Edric—or even the Other One—and if it was, it worked. Ghosts can't cry, but I about did, every time she remembered something that small from three hundred years ago. The more time we spent together, the more things like that came back to her—just as she herself was growing clearer, easier to see. Her father called her mother "Magpie," short for Margaret, and the two of them privately called *him*—roaring Roger Willoughby, the Prodigious Romantic—"Sir Fopling Flutter," after someone in a play. Her favorite horse was a mare named Elegance; her favorite smell came from the lavender hedges that her mother planted all along the front of the Manor. They're long gone with the Willoughbys, of course, like her father's beehives.

She'd had an older sister who died of the Black Plague—the same Black Plague we'd had to study in British History—"and how I failed of catching it, I am sure I do not know, Jenny, for we slept together always. Her name was Maria, so I put it straight into my own name, thinking to make my mother less forlorn. But she grew terrible wroth with me and beat me, which she never did, and bid me not ever use my sister's name so again. But I kept it anyway." That one time I thought she remembered tears.

She was looking for someone, I knew that; someone she really especially wanted me to meet. I thought it must be that old friend of hers who'd loped away through the beech trees, on two legs or four, that first night—the one with the golden eyes. I asked her about it, but she wouldn't ever say.

Whenever we passed an oak grove—especially Julian's Hundred-Acre Wood—she'd warn me again about oak trees. "It is a thrice-cut coppice, Jenny, for all these seem virgin. Twice was it cut before my time, and once since, and each time saplings sprang from the stumps with speed uncanny. The old of these parts, they've a saying, *'Fairy folk are in old oak,'* and a thrice-cut wood harbors Oakmen, always. Never, Jenny, *never* step foot under oak after sundown." She made me promise that one over and over.

Which is why when I first saw the billy-blind I went probably six feet straight up. He wasn't in any oak grove, but standing on a barrel in the North Barn. He was about the same size as the boggart, but slighter, not as burly. He wore a sort of old-style suit, with an eggplant-colored cravat fluffed around his neck, and a waistcoat to match. No hat, thank God. I don't think I could have handled a hat. Ankles crossed, one hand in his pocket, bracing the other against the wall—a mini-Jimmy Cagney, Sally's all-time favorite. Only in the moonlight slanting through the window behind him, he looked more like that English actor who played Long John Silver in the old Disney movie. Robert Newton, that's it.

Tamsin introduced us, very formally, like people meeting at a party or a fancy dinner. "Jenny, this is the billy-blind. The billy-blind, I have the honor to present to you Mistress Jennifer Gluckstein." I almost didn't mind the Jennifer when she said it.

I'd had a lot of practice with curtsies by now, so I made him a really deep one and he put his right hand flat on his belly and bowed. Then he straightened up fast and said, "Oughtn't wear your hair all strained back like that, child—doesn't suit, doesn't suit. Take my advice, you'll comb it forward."

He had a Dorset accent, but not old Dorset, not like the boggart. You could hear the *Z's* buzzing around in there, and the *I's* wanting to come out like *oi*, but I didn't have any trouble understanding him. What I *did* have trouble with was the whole notion that a two-foot-high Robert Newton was telling me what I ought to do with my hair. I said, "Look, Mr. billy-blind, I really appreciate your interest—"

Well, he turned absolutely pink at that. Fuchsia. He pulled himself up as tall as he could, and he actually stamped his foot as he shouted at me, "I'm noo *Measter* billy-blind! You call me *the* billy-blind, same's her does, that's what you call me! I am *the* billy-blind!"

I took a step back, he was so angry, but Tamsin moved in in a hurry. "The billy-blind, she's but young and meant no harm. I was just so myself when first we met, you'll remember."

That calmed him down a bit, and he tidied his cravat and smoothed out his vest. "I do that, I remember. No bigger than the billy-blind, you were, and no more manners than a hedge-pig." Now he was all mush, that fast, with real tears in his eyes. He bowed to me again and said, "Your pardon, Mistress Jennifer—"

"Jenny—"

"Mistress Jenny, then. You've all my apologies, but you'd do better to take my advice about your hair. And now I'm at it, yellow's noo your color. Green's what you want, mind me, greens and blues. The billy-blind knows."

And he just went on like that, nonstop. He told me my sinuses would clear up if I ate red clover, and that I wouldn't keep waking up with headaches if I moved my bed to the other side of the room. "And there's noo use in your friend, the dark girl, greeting her eyes out for that boy in choir. W'ole family be gone away come fall, moved off to Afriky somewhere. You tell her *the* billy-blind said so."

I said I would. The billy-blind gave me a really long stare, studying me all up and down. His eyes weren't Disney eyes at all, but they weren't wicked either, like the boggart's. They were more like jewelled passages leading a long way backward or a long way forward, I couldn't tell which. He nodded suddenly.

"Aye, you'd be needing the billy-blind's counsel, the pair on ye." He was looking at Tamsin now. "*You* want to sit still, that's what you want. Sit *still*, don't be running about so." Giving a ghost lessons in deportment sounded like the dumbest thing I'd ever heard of, but Tamsin nodded. The billy-blind turned back to me. "You," he said. "You'll do best to stay away from that place. And stop eating them grapes."

I couldn't take it in. I gaped at him like a baby bird. I said, "*What* place? And what's wrong with me eating grapes?"

"You'll be eating them all," the billy-blind said calmly. He went back to talking with Tamsin, and I was too busy blushing to hear what they were saying. Because it's perfectly true about me and grapes. I always *mean* to leave some, but I'm just not reliable.

I was going to ask him again about whatever place I was supposed to stay away from, but right at that moment I heard Evan's voice saying, "Jenny? Is that you?"

Tamsin went out the way a match goes out, and the billy-blind was through the window and *gone* in a blur of eggplant. I turned and saw Evan standing in the doorway, absently rumpling his hair the way he was always doing. He said, "We were getting a bit anxious."

"I lost track of time," I said. "Sorry." I'd gotten a lot better with Evan by then. I didn't blame him anymore for wrecking my life—I even had long stretches when I thought maybe he hadn't wrecked it at all. But I didn't like him *knowing* that, and I had an uneasy feeling he did. I'd invested a lot of time and thought and energy in hating Evan. I wasn't ready to call it a waste and let it go. That's how I was then.

"I was looking for something," I said as I came out. Evan gave me a funny look. Back then the North Barn was more of a glorified storage shed, all farm machinery and things under tarpaulins, and mysterious old barrels like the one the billy-blind had been standing on. But Evan didn't push it, and we started back toward the Manor together.

Even in the darkness I could see he was looking tired. He said, "Your mother worries about these night walks of yours. I do myself. It's easy to step into something, a furrow, and break an ankle, if you don't know where you're going."

"I'm careful," I said. "I really do know this place pretty well by now." Of course the *moment* I said that, I tripped—not in a hole, but over Mister Cat, flopped right down in my path, the way he does sometimes. He yowled at me, and I yowled back at him to *watch* it, stupid *cat,* and he scatted away into the brush with his feelings hurt. I figured we'd make it up at bedtime.

Evan started to say, "I think it'd be a good idea if you had someone—Julian or Tony—" but I headed him off by asking if he knew what a billy-blind was. You can almost always sidetrack Evan with a question like that, about legends or folklore. The boys do it all the time.

"Billy-blinds?" He shook his head and smiled a little. "Lord, I haven't heard that word in years. Who told you about billy-blinds?"

"Just a friend," I said. "Someone at school. She said they're supposed to give advice?"

Evan laughed. "That they do. Your billy-blind absolutely lives to give advice. Doesn't matter what subject, never mind the time or the place or the person—the billy-blind will tell you what to do, whether you ask or not. It's their nature, and there's only the tiniest problem with it. They aren't always right."

I asked if there was only one billy-blind at any one time, like the phoenix. Evan said he'd never heard that, nor that you had to call each one *the* billy-blind. "But maybe it's different in Dorset. There's a lot of regional variation among British bogles. Like the way our boggart just vanished—I've never heard of that before. You maybe make a deal with boggarts, but you don't get rid of them."

He was glad we were talking, and it was easy to keep him from asking any more questions about me wandering the farm at night. I felt a bit guilty about that, and guilty all over again for not telling everyone what had really happened with the boggart. But Evan was telling me a story about a Yorkshire family who moved from their farm to get away from a boggart, only to find that they'd brought it along with them. And I was thinking of Tamsin, and wondering again who Edric was, and what the Black Dog and the billy-blind knew that we didn't. And where Tamsin was supposed to be, instead of here, where I wanted her to be.

All the same, I was feeling guilty enough that I actually asked Evan a question about himself before we reached the Manor. "What is it that's not going right with the farm? I hear you and Sally talking, but I don't understand. It's looking great, as far as I can see."

Evan stopped in his tracks and blinked at me. I don't think he could have been more amazed if Tamsin had walked up to him and tried to bum a cigarette. He messed his hair again, sighed, stared around vaguely, and finally said, "Jenny, people have been plowing up this land for over three hundred years, and the soil's exhausted, played out. It's losing topsoil, it's starved for nutrients, and what it's been given is bloody rivers of chemical fertilizers. I went along with that style of farming this whole last year, because the Lovells expected it—because the land's literally addicted to it. Maybe it looks good to you now, but the yield's half what it should be, and it'll be less next year, less than that the next. It's my fault, and I know what I have to do. And I'm scared to do it."

We were at the house by then, and Evan walked in without saying another word to me. I waited around outside for a bit, hoping for a quick moment with Tamsin. But she didn't show, so I went up to bed, waiting for Mister Cat instead. No luck there, either. I lay awake forever, holding Julian's funky old gorilla, with my head too full of too many things to think straight about any one of them. I'd have settled for snickery little voices in my bathroom right then, just for the distraction.

But I must have fallen asleep sometime, because I was awakened by Mister Cat going round and round with something outside. I know that sound he makes when he's in a fight: low and evil, like a saw cutting bone. I stuck my head out of the window and yelled for him to get up here, and he came scrambling in a moment later, while something I couldn't see clearly scuttled out of sight under Evan's Jeep. Mister Cat was panting hard, and his eyes were as red as the Black Dog's. There was blood high on his chest. I wanted to look at it, but he backed away from me and settled down to licking the wound, still growling to himself. He was still doing it when I dozed off again.

He was fine in the morning, cool and sleek as ever, though he still wouldn't let me inspect the slash on his chest. I went into my bathroom and started doing things with my hair, trying to see what bangs would look like. I got Julian to help me move the bed.

Fifteen

A couple of weeks later, Christopher Herridge told Meena his family would be moving to Africa in September. Meena cried more than ever, and I felt terrible, because I'd *known,* and maybe I could have found *some* way to warn Meena even a little, to soften the blow. But I hadn't said anything, because Evan had warned me billy-blinds don't always get things right. More secrets.

I didn't see Tamsin for some while after that night. Every evening I'd find some reason to wander off to the places where we usually met, but she wasn't ever there. Once I even went up to the third floor and spent maybe half an hour walking back and forth outside the secret door. I could have opened it and walked in, but I didn't. It's hard to explain why now. Most of me missed Tamsin in a way I'd never missed anybody—not Marta and Jake when I started school here, not even Mister Cat when he was in quarantine—but one small part of me was scared utterly out of its mind, because this was getting too big for me, and I knew it. One night I had a dream about that big golden-eyed creature Tamsin called "old friend," and another night I dreamed about the Other One. She'd told me he was gone, vanished, but the dream didn't think so. I was back at her door, and this time I pushed it open, and *he* was waiting, sitting in her chair. I didn't see his face, but it was him.

To keep from thinking about her so much, I started being help-ful around the Manor. I cleaned up my room without anyone's having to ask me, and then I went ahead and cleaned the boys' rooms, which got them both mad at me—Julian especially, be-cause his spiders got loose. After that I hung around Sally, volun-teering for every damn thing she needed done—washing, cooking, weeding her little kitchen garden and stirring up the compost pile—even refinishing musty old furniture or running errands to Evan out in the fields, when she couldn't stand it and

had to get rid of me. I made everybody really nervous during that
stretch, including Mister Cat. He'd either disappear for the whole
day—probably with Miss Sophia Brown, whom I didn't see either—or else he'd follow me around, saying sarcastic things in
Siamese, which he only ever speaks when he's really mad, or when
I've surprised him. Mister Cat hates surprises.

Tony was the one who called me on it. He just came straight up
to me one afternoon when I was out hanging laundry and asked,
"All right, what have you done?"

I had a mouthful of clothespins, so I had to mumble, "Drying
your damn legwarmers, you really want to know. *And* your sweaty
old Fabrizios." Tony goes through tights like Julian through crawly
things.

"You're being good," Tony said. "You're being unbelievably, un-
naturally, abnormally good. Julian's the same way when he's done
something really awful nobody knows about yet. Let's have it,
Jenny."

I got furious, of course. Tony can still do that to me once in a
while, sniffing out something absolutely true and getting it totally
wrong. I said I wasn't *up* to anything, and hadn't *been* up to anything, and what the hell did he know about anything, and about
Monmouth's Rebellion—did he think old Roger Willoughby
might have been involved in it? Tony's harder to sidetrack than
Evan, but you can do it.

"Roger Willoughby? Possible, but I doubt it, rather. He wasn't
gentry-born, but he wasn't a little Dorset yeoman, either. He'd
have known what the Stuarts were like, and he'd probably have
waited to see how things fell out." He rumpled his hair, exactly like
Evan, and added after a moment, "But I'd bet at least some of his
farmhands took off with Monmouth, poor sods. Why do you want
to know?"

"Just curious," I said. "Just wondering about stuff." Tony gave
me the kind of look Mister Cat gives me when there's only dry kibble in his dish, but he left it alone. I went on hanging laundry and
thinking about Tamsin. As much as she'd told me about herself—
family, childhood, the farm, the Black Plague, even the name of
her horse—there were pieces missing. I could feel their shapes
sometimes, when we were together, actually feel the empty outlines of things she wasn't telling me. I didn't know if she'd been
around for the Rebellion, or what she'd thought about it when it

was happening. Or why the billy-blind had warned her twice to sit still—or why she hadn't come inside on a wild night, and died of it, for that matter. I didn't know what questions I ought to ask her, and I didn't know what questions I didn't want to hear the answers to. Only that I wanted to be with her.

Late one July afternoon, I went off for a walk by myself, feeling glumpy, which is one of Julian's words for being stupidly miserable. Meena's mother had been supposed to drop her off with us to stay the weekend, but something family came up and she had to cancel at the last minute. Between that and not being sure if I'd ever see Tamsin again—*and* not even knowing where the hell my cat was—I was glumpy enough to realize that I hadn't been this glumpy in a pretty long while. Which only made me glumpier, dumb as that is.

There's a place I still go to when I'm feeling like that. It's on the downs, above the sheep pasture, what's left of a shepherd's hut. No roof, one wall, a few foundation stones, a few rainy splinters of a floor. Evan thinks it's a hundred years old, no more, but it could just as easily be from Tamsin's time, you can't tell. I hike out there, and I sit on the ground with my back against that last wall and the sun on my face—or the fog, either—and I watch the butterflies and feel sorry for myself. Love it.

I was amazed to see the black pony grazing peacefully right by the old hut. There's never anything bigger than a rabbit on that long slope, except for the sheep, away off—but there he was, stocky and small as the New Forest ponies, and black as Mister Cat himself, almost purple in the shadow of the wall. No saddle, no bridle, no shoes, mane and tail stiff with burrs, he never looked up as I came near, being so careful not to spook him. "Look at *you*," I said, keeping my voice really low. "You're *wild*—you're a genuine wild horse. Hello."

The black pony didn't even flick his ears. I said, "You're also a *mess.* I've got a friend named Meena—she'd spend a whole day currying you, combing you out. Me, I couldn't care less, I'm not much into horses. Just shove over a bit, I want to sit down."

He raised his head then, and I saw his eyes. They were golden as the rising moon, before it turns pale and small; they had long horizontal pupils, like Wilf's billygoat, and they were too big for that shaggy, slanty face. And they held me. They made me come closer, one step after another, until I had one hand in that brambly mane and was just about to scramble up. I knew what he was, I remembered what Evan had told me—*a fine black horse, absolutely black, inviting you to get on his back and take a ride*—but I couldn't look away. He blew softly through his nostrils and nibbled my sleeve, just like a real horse.

I heard Tamsin before I saw her. *"Ah, no!"* and it sounded like a trumpet, ghost or not. "That I'll not have! Get from him, Jenny!"

The big yellow eyes let go of me, and I stumbled back so hard I almost fell down. Tamsin blew by me as though a hurricane were driving her and blazed up between me and the black pony, clearer and more solid than I'd ever seen her, even in daylight, she was so angry. "Rogue, scoundrel, swinger, is it thus you'll dare treat my friend? When you've seen us together, when I've called you time and time to acquaint with her—"

And the black pony spoke.

"I do not come when I am called. You knew that once." His voice was deep and even—no whinny in it, nothing like that—and his mouth didn't move at all. But there wasn't any question that it was him speaking. The voice went exactly with those eyes—the same eyes I'd dreamed those first nights at Stourhead Farm—it went with the way he held his head, with just a slight quirk in the neck, as he looked at us, and with what I felt looking back, which was a weird kind of calm fear. Nobody's going to understand that. I knew what he was, and I knew he was dangerous—miles more dangerous than boggarts or billy-blinds or voices behind the bathtub. But I wasn't afraid of him. I should have been, but I wasn't.

Tamsin was still steaming, absolutely furious. "When I knew you, I'd her age, and you never would have done with me as you planned for her. You were kind to children then, Pooka."

"I have never been *kind* to any," the black pony answered her. "I am I, and I do what suits me. You understood that, too, Tamsin Willoughby." But he lowered his head briefly before her, and she reached out to touch him—just for a second—before she remembered that she couldn't. He said, "I did not grieve you gone. I cannot. But it suits me to see you again."

She wasn't letting him off that easily. "Aye, well, it does *not* suit *me* to find you cozening my Mistress Jenny to mount your back and be hurled into some mire, miles from her home. She is my friend, as much as you were—more—and you'll treat her as you did me, or answer for it. Jenny Gluckstein, she's called." She whipped around to face me, one arm thrown wide, burning bright as a lacy cinder flying up the chimney. "Jenny, this creature is the Pooka. Pay no mind to the shape he wears, for he's none of his own, and no soul neither. Ware him ever, trust him never, but when the wind's right he has his uses." She turned back to the black pony. "Say, have I proclaimed you fairly, then?"

"Indeed." The black pony was cropping grass, not looking at either of us, not even raising his head when he said, "I see you, Jenny Gluckstein." Nothing more than that.

"Come," Tamsin said to me. I wanted to stay and talk to the Pooka, or anyway hang around and watch him a while longer, but there wasn't any arguing with Tamsin in that mood. She swept ahead of me without looking back, and I followed her over the downs. I turned once, but the shadows around the ruined hut had lengthened a lot, and I couldn't see the black pony.

"Evan told me about pookas," I said when I caught up with Tamsin. "I thought it was just a story." Tamsin didn't say anything. I said, "He wouldn't really have hurt me, would he?"

"God's death, who knows what a pooka will do?" Tamsin's answer came so short and hard and impatient that I actually stopped in my tracks, as surprised as I'd been to hear a pony speak to me. She knew right away, even though I was walking behind her, and she stopped herself and actually put her arms around me, which she'd never done before. I felt a tiny vanilla breeze on my skin, moving in my hair.

"Dearest Jenny, forgive me, forgive. I was most affrighted, as I've not been since . . . since I was just so affrighted for another—long ago, when I was as you are. My anger was never at you, but with myself, who even then knew far better than to call a pooka *friend*." She stepped back from me, and she sighed a little. "He is no one's friend—no one's—yet he proved truest friend to me once, when none were by. You may trust him well enough now, Jenny, for he knows you as mine—but never forget that you will never know *him*. The Pooka's mystery even to the Pooka, I think."

"He really can change his shape?" I asked. Tamsin nodded. I said, "Could he look like you, or like my mother? Or Mister Cat? I need to know."

"Always you may tell the Pooka by his eyes. All else changes, not those." The setting sun at her back struck right through her just then, and made her face glow and tremble like a candle's flame. I can still see her. She said, "He will not bait you again with such sport, have no fear. One day you may yet ride him to a safe ending, and no thorn bush. Come, Jenny, your dinner will be cold, surely."

I think about that, too, her bothering to consider my needing to eat, when she couldn't keep centuries straight in her ghost of a mind. She wouldn't say anything more about the Pooka the rest of the way, because she was set on teaching me a song her sister Maria had taught her—the one who died of the Plague. It was a ripply, simple tune, repeating and repeating like a birdcall, but I've forgotten most of the words. It starts out like this:

"*Oranges and cherries,*
sweetest candleberries—
who will come and buy?
who will come and buy?
Daughters I have plenty,
ten and twelve and twenty,
fit to please the gentry—
who will come and buy?"

I wish I remembered all of it. I still go around singing the bits I remember to myself, because sometimes the rest of a song will come back if you do that. Maybe if I could call back the whole song, Tamsin would come with it, the way she was then, shivering so brightly in the sunset. It's not right to wish that, but I do.

When we were almost at the Manor, I said, keeping my voice as light as I could, "So many weird things running around on just this one farm. Pookas, Black Dogs, boggarts, billy-blinds—"

"Oakmen," Tamsin interrupted. "*Remember*, Jenny. And the Old Lady of the Elder Tree—though you'll not see *her*, surely, and more's the pity of it. Even the Pooka steps aside for her when she moves."

"Oakmen, right," I said. "Oak groves and Oakmen. And the little whatevers I heard in the bathroom, and probably whatever Mister Cat was fighting with the other night. I don't want to know anything about mean old ladies—I just want to know, are there a whole lot more? I mean, is this normal for England, or is it just Dorset?"

Tamsin laughed that spring-rain laugh of hers. "Alas, my poor

Jenny—awash in hobgoblins, besieged by bogles. Truly, there are no such creatures in your New York?"

"Only in junior high school," I said. "Never mind. Just introduce me as they come along."

Julian ran out of the house, yelling, "Jenny! Jenny, *dinner!*" I expected Tamsin to vanish like a shot, the way she always did when there was the least chance of anyone else seeing her. But this time she stepped back until the shadows hid everything except her eyes and the swing of her hair. Her voice was really quiet. She said, "My Jenny, I will never see your own land, yet well I know night's as dark there as in Dorset. And night is not ours, and never will be, not till all is night. I tell you it will not, Jenny—never any more ours than the sea, for all we plough and harrow up *that* darkness. What yet swims in the deepest deep, I'm sure none can say—and not even the Pooka knows all that may move beyond the light. But you have friends there now—do but remember that, and you'll come to no harm. You have friends in the night, dear Jenny."

About then Julian caught sight of me, and started waving his arms and bellowing, "Jenny, Jenny, come on, it's cock-a-leekie!" He knows that's my favorite soup, ever since Evan's sister Charlie taught Sally how to make it. He came running and threw his arms around me, and started dragging me toward the house, telling me about some experiment he'd been doing with sliced cucumbers, sugar, and three snails. I'd gotten so I could usually feel it when Tamsin left me, but I never felt it this time. I think she stood there in the shadows and watched us go.

After dinner, Tony and I washed up, and then I went outside and sat in the double swing that Evan had rigged to a branch of the old walnut tree near the tractor garage. The evening was still warm, practically balmy; we hadn't had one of those since the sweltering night when I first walked with Tamsin. I was looking around for her without really expecting to see her, and I was keeping an eye out for other things, too—maybe the Pooka, maybe the billy-blind. I still wasn't sure he was right about bangs.

Evan made that swing with a nice high back, so it's really easy to fall asleep in it. I dozed and woke a couple of times, and the second time I had a bad dream. I was still in the swing, in my dream, and it was still night, only now the Manor was really far away, practically on the horizon. There was someone walking toward me, slowly, his face half in shadow, half in moonlight. I tried to jump off and run, but the swing turned into the Pooka, and I was on his back and couldn't get down. The Other One came right up to the Pooka amd mounted right behind me, wrapping his long arms around me. I screamed, and Sally said, "Shush, baby, it's me, it's just me. You were looking so adorable."

She was in the swing next to me, with my head bumping on her shoulder. My skin was really cold, my mouth was dry, and my neck hurt. Sally said, "You looked so much the way you did when you were little, I just couldn't help giving you a hug."

I mumbled something and sat up, trying to straighten my hair. The moon was high, which always makes the night darker here, I don't know why. Sally told me Meena had called, and I said I'd call her back tomorrow. We stayed in the swing for a time, not saying much, but Sally kept trying to cuddle me and *look* at me at the same time, and you can't do that, not the way Sally looks at you. Finally I said, "What? Say it already, and let's get some sleep. What'd I do?"

Sally got all indignant. "Nothing—you haven't done anything— why are you so *suspicious*?" She went on like that a bit longer, and then, without missing a beat: "It's just that you've become so—so *solitary* lately. Going off by yourself so much, not asking Julian or anyone to come with you. Julian's feelings are really hurt, did you know that? And Meena—Meena's been noticing it, too. She asked me about it when she was over the last time."

I felt horrible. I said, "I'll talk to her. I'll do something with Julian, we'll play croquet or something. It's just that I've been sort of needing to be alone these days. To work a few things out."

She didn't immediately ask, "What things?"—Sally's much cooler than that, and much trickier, too. She nodded, and didn't say anything right away; but when I started to get up out of the swing she said, "Could I help? Is it something I could maybe—I don't know . . . just tell me, Jenny. If it is."

These days I have a pretty good idea why Evan fell in love with my mother. Norris, too, for that matter. Back then . . . back then, what the hell did I know about love and grown people? But I did have my moments, once in a great while, and that was one of them. I looked at *her* for a change, staring hard through the darkness, seeing the dead leaf in her hair and the motheaten collar of that gray cardigan she'll never give up on, seeing that her eyes were as wide as Tamsin's, and brighter in the moonlight. I flicked the leaf away, gave her a kiss on the cheek, took her hand, and we walked back to the house.

"I just love that swing tree," she said. "I always feel it's holding me in its arms, and I'm safe as long as I stay there."

"It's the last one of those old walnuts," I told her. "There used to be a dozen. Roger Willoughby planted them when his first daughter was born."

Sally opened her mouth, closed it again, and went inside. I stayed on the doorstep a moment longer, wondering if Tamsin might still be near. Even with the moon, and with lights in the Manor windows, I couldn't see much past the barns, except for the bulk of an old sprayer Evan had told Wilf to get rid of a month ago. Just beyond it, two golden glints could have been a lot of things besides the Pooka's eyes. Tamsin had told me I had friends in the night now, and I went up to bed telling myself that, over and over.

Sixteen

A couple of nights later, half an hour after his bedtime, Julian came padding into my room to say he couldn't sleep and would I tell him a story? Sally and Evan were in Dorchester for dinner and a movie (no infants wanted, thank you very much), and in those days you'd get a bedtime story out of Mister Cat faster than you would out of Tony. But Julian's always had my number—and anyway, it wasn't much payback for a passing grade in maths and a stinky stuffed gorilla when I needed one. I made him get back into bed first, though, and promise he'd go to sleep after *one* story. He's as crafty as a boggart about the small print, but he keeps promises when he makes them.

Between Sally and Norris, I know a lot of stories—I even know some Indian fairy tales that Meena's told me. But that night I couldn't get started, and I knew why right away. My mind was so full of Tamsin's shadow world that I'd been dreaming about her and the Pooka almost every night—and about the Other One, too—and I couldn't get into witches and princesses and dragons, even for Julian. So just on an impulse, I did something really dumb. Even for me.

"Okay," I said when he got settled in. "Once upon a time there was a girl who lived at Stourhead Farm, right in this house where we live now. Her name was Tamsin Willoughby."

Because suddenly I wanted to talk about her. Not to tell anyone, exactly, not to try to explain that she was still here with us in the Manor, but more like Tony telling me about James II and Judge Jeffreys—real people, a long time ago, but still real to him. I guess I thought if I made Tamsin someone in a story for a child like Julian, it might be all right.

"Is this a true story?" Julian demanded. "How do *you* know?" He was big on how-do-*you*-know? that summer.

"Somebody told me about her," I said. "You want to hear this or not?" Julian pulled the blankets up over his face, leaving just his eyes peeking out. I said, "Her father was Roger Willoughby, the guy who started this farm. Her mother was called Margaret, and she had an older sister named Maria. Two brothers, too, but I don't remember their names. But it's all true, and if you even *think* 'How do *you* know?' I'll shove those blankets down your throat and leave you for the vultures. You got that?"

"Mmmph," Julian said, but he nodded.

"She was the youngest child," I said. "The farm was too small for her family to be really rich, but they were a lot better off than most people in Dorset three hundred years ago. They had servants, and there were a lot of farm workers, and Tamsin had a tutor and a horse named Elegance. The worst thing that happened was when her sister Maria died of the Black Plague—that was terrible for her, for all of them." Julian was staring at me, and I realized I'd better slow down, rein in, or there'd be too many questions waiting the moment I stopped for breath. I said, "This was her room, matter of fact."

Actually, Tamsin couldn't ever remember which bedroom had been hers, but she thought Evan and Sally's room might be the one. But it gave Julian something else to think about while I went on. I told him how different the Manor looked in those days, and how the Willoughbys raised lots more sheep than the Lovells do now, and what it was like plowing and irrigating and harvesting with nothing but hand tools. It was all stuff Tamsin had told *me*, but I could always say I'd gotten it from Evan. That part went fine.

But then Julian had to ask, because he's Julian, "Did she ever get married? Did she have children?"

"No," I said. "No, she never did."

"Why not?" The blanket was all the way down off his face now.

"Because she died very young."

"Oh, *no.*" Julian's eyes actually started to fill up. He took stories absolutely seriously, even at ten, and I kept forgetting that. "Did she get the Black Plague? Like her sister?"

"The Plague was mostly gone by then," I said. "It was some kind of lung trouble." I remembered Tamsin talking about *"a flux . . . a catarrh that grew to a pleurisy . . . pulmonary phthisis . . ."* I said, "She was twenty years old. I think she got caught out in a storm, something like that."

Julian was quiet for a while. I thought he might be falling asleep, and I was just getting ready to sneak out when he asked, "Jenny? Did she at least have a boyfriend?"

He wanted her to have been happy, even a little bit. That damn kid. Before I knew it, I heard myself saying, "Yes, she did, I know that for a fact. His name was Edric Davies."

I didn't know a thing about Edric Davies. I made it all up, just because of Julian. Davies is a Welsh name, so I told Julian he was a Welsh fisherman who wandered all the way down to Dorset and fell in love with a wealthy farmer's daughter. I said that Roger Willoughby wasn't about to have his only girl marrying a penniless fish-jockey. He wouldn't let Edric even come to the house. But Tamsin used to slip off and meet him anyway, in a ruined shepherd's hut on the downs. Use what you've got, right?

"You said they didn't get married." Julian had turned on his side, head propped on his hand, alert as a damn chipmunk. Not a chance of him dropping off until I finished the story somehow.

"Well, they wanted to," I said. "They ran away together one night, and Roger Willoughby had dogs out hunting for them." I hated badmouthing Tamsin's father, knowing how much she loved him, but I'd gotten myself into this story, and I had to get out of it some way. "It was storming and raining, the way it gets here in the winter, so the dogs lost the trail, but they got lost too, Tamsin and Edric. He wanted to take her home, but she wouldn't let him. She said she'd rather die than go back."

Julian was wide-eyed, hardly breathing. I was pretty caught up myself, considering. "Is that how she died? Tamsin?"

I thought about the Other One, about the face in my dreams that I couldn't ever quite see. I said, "No, not then. There was a man, an older man. He took them into his house, out of the storm, and they thought they could trust him. But he fell in love with Tamsin, too—or anyway he wanted her—and he killed Edric. They fought a duel, but what does a fisherman know about dueling? The man killed him."

I practically had tears in my own eyes, it had gotten so real, and it explained so much that Tamsin wouldn't tell me. Julian whispered, "What about *her*? What happened to her?"

"She ran out into the storm," I said. "Back into the rain and the wind and everything. They found her body the next day, and old Roger Willoughby died of a broken heart." I threw that in like an afterthought, something extra. Lost to all shame, as Meena would say.

Julian slid back down in the bed. He asked, "How do *you* know?" but the question was a shadow of its usual snotty self. I told him I'd heard the story from Ellie John, who'd just come to work part-time for Evan. Ellie John's very nice, but she's a *big* woman with a sort of gruff voice, and Julian was a bit scared of her in those days. I figured he wasn't likely to check on me.

"That's a *terrible* story," he said, the same way he used to say, "That was a *scary* movie," and with just the same satisfaction. "Did they ever get that man—the one who killed poor Edric?"

"No," I said. "Dueling was legal then, I think. Anyway, who cared about one Welsh fisherman? I guess he got clean away with it, whoever he was. Go to sleep."

I tucked him in, gave him a quick little nuzzle—he wasn't eleven yet, you could still get away with it—and headed for the door. Behind me I heard a mumble, "Guess he's dead by now, that man."

I turned at the door. "Well, it's been three hundred years. *I'd* guess."

"Too bad. Wish he was still alive, so we could kill him." And with that childish dream on his childish lips, my adopted baby brother went bye-bye. I tiptoed out and went back to my room.

But now *I* couldn't sleep. I'd made that whole story up, like I said, just to occupy Julian, and told him it was true without turning a hair. But thinking about it I started wondering if it could be at all near the truth of what really happened with Tamsin and Edric Davies. What *was* she doing out on a night wild enough to cause her death? And who was Edric if he wasn't her lover? And if the Other One wasn't his rival for Tamsin . . . but I didn't want to think about the Other One any more than I had to. He was all right in a story, but not out of it.

Sally and Evan weren't back yet, and Tony was in his studio. I gave sleep half an hour, and then I got up and dressed again and went outside to hunt up the billy-blind.

We'd met him in the North Barn, but I didn't imagine him living there like the boggart in our house. I figured he'd have a place of his own—a burrow or a den, or even a treehouse—somewhere near the Manor. I didn't know how to find him—I hoped maybe I'd get lucky and have him come looking for me. Dogs like Albert don't feel right if there isn't at least one sheep around to herd somewhere. Maybe it was the same with billy-blinds and people.

It was a mild night, with an apple-smelling breeze making the new metal sheds squeak and grumble; but there was autumn way down under it, like a little cold current nibbling your ankles when you're swimming. I didn't go beyond the main buildings. I just wandered more or less aimlessly, trying to look like someone in huge need of advice, which wasn't difficult. Dairy, nothing—North and South Barns, farmworkers' parking lot, tractor shed, nothing—workshop, nothing—nameless shed where you stash the stuff that doesn't belong in any other shed, nothing. Mister Cat kept me company for a while, pouncing at shadows like a kitten, but then he got bored and just never came back out of one shadow or another. I was watching out for the Pooka, and for whatever it was Mister Cat had gone a few rounds with the same night I met the billy-blind; but there didn't seem to be anybody but me prowling around Stourhead Farm that night. Today that would tell me something.

He was the one who found me. I was trudging back to the South Barn, thinking that I hadn't checked the loft, when he actually tugged on my pants leg. "You'll be looking for me, no doubt," he said, when I got back from wherever I'd jumped to. "Come, I've been expecting you."

Waistcoat, fluffed-up cravat, and this time a long coat, like the kind gunfighters wear in Westerns. I have *never* found out where he lives, by the way, or who does his laundry. He led me, very importantly—your average billy-blind can strut sitting down—over to a stack of scrap lumber, hopped up onto it so he could look down at me, put his hands on his hips, and announced, "Well, I'll tell you one thing, child, and that's not two—nowt but porter and an egg will help that hair. Porter and a brown egg, there's your ticket. I use it meself, and look at me, would you?"

He did have a great head of curly hair, about the color of stone-washed jeans. I said, really carefully, "I'll try it, the billy-blind, I promise I will. But that's not what I was wanting to ask you about."

"Aye, well, it should have been," the billy-blind growled, just like Robert Newton. "It's as well you sought me out, mind, for I've meant and meant to speak sharply to you about your friend. The Willoughby."

"Yes!" I said. "Yes, that's it, that's what I wanted to ask!" The billy-blind grinned like a magician who's just shown you the card that he couldn't possibly have guessed you chose. I said, "There's so much I want to know about her, and she won't . . . I mean, like how she died, or why she keeps saying she's supposed to be somewhere else—or where the Other One fits into all this. And Edric Davies." I was talking so fast I ran out of breath, while the billy-blind stood on that pile of wood, not moving, not saying a word. "And why did you tell her twice to sit still, and what place is it I should stay away from? You're *the* billy-blind around here—you tell me."

The billy-blind wasn't smiling anymore. If you just looked at his face like anybody else's, he could have been twenty-five, fifty, sixty. I'm terrible at guessing ages, anyway. But when you stared into those jewelled eyes—I couldn't have told you what color they were, then or now—you had to realize that he was older than Tamsin, way older. He said, "I give advice, lass. I don't explain. There's different."

"Oh," I said. "Well, couldn't you just once make an exception? I mean, she's your friend, and it's *very* important."

Snort. "My friend, oh aye—yet she'll not heed the billy-blind's counsel, never, not she! Sit still? Don't I see her traipsing the night with you, showing herself to any who'd wish her ill? Don't I, then?"

Snort. Stamp. Billy-blinds don't just hand out advice, it matters like mad to them if you take it or not. I said, "*Who* is it who wishes her ill? If I knew *that*, maybe I could do something, get her to stay out of sight the way you want. What would it hurt you to tell?"

I was starting to snort a little myself, and the billy-blind was looking almost amused. "Always so, always so. The ones I fancy, they never know how to behave with the billy-blind. Not her, not you, always so." When he scratched his head with both hands, I still think I maybe saw a pair of bumpy horns, the same color as his hair, but maybe not. "Well, I'll say this much to you, for that's a good girl, Tamsin Willoughby, manners or no. But you've roused her, that's your doing, and that shifts things, that makes things to move, d'ye see? And I can't signify what's to come of it, indeed I can't, but there's *looking* now, there's waking and hunting besides hers, *beyond* hers. Do you see, girl?"

His eyes had hold of me the way the Pooka's yellow eyes had done, except that these eyes were almost pleading, almost human for that moment. I said, "That's the Other One." The billy-blind didn't answer me. "But he's gone," I said. "She told me—Tamsin told me. He's gone, and he can't come back."

The billy-blind said, "You'll remember to drink eight full glasses of water a day. Grand for the system, that is."

"I could have gotten that off a damn cereal box!" I yelled at him. "What about the Other One?" But the billy-blind was looking past me, he was listening to something I hadn't heard yet. When I did hear it, I first thought it was Evan and Sally driving in, and I went on telling myself it was them as long as I could, because I didn't want it to be what I already knew it was. I'm going to come back and fix that sentence later.

Most times, like I've said, it had to be a really fierce night for you to hear the Wild Hunt in the sky. But this night was as calm as calm, even with that bit of a breeze, and that's what made it so terrible. Because suddenly they were up there, right overhead, the horses and the dogs, the howling and the horns and the rattling hoofbeats, the screechy laughter that didn't sound like wild geese for a damn minute—all of it, all of it. And I wasn't safe in the house, behind walls and a window with Julian holding my hand too tight, but out on the open ground, where they could see me—and they saw me, I *felt* it—*that* was the storm, their awareness bursting over me. I stood where I was, not because I was brave, but because there wasn't any room under the woodpile, with the billy-blind already there. I just stood alone in the storm, like Tamsin, looking up.

Anyway, I *was* alone until Mister Cat landed on my shoulder. I hardly felt him, I was so paralyzed, until he dug in his claws and shoved in close to my neck and yowled like a banshee at the Wild Hunt. His fangs were bare to the gums, and his fur and tail were fluffed up so he looked twice his normal size; and if those Huntsmen had understood Siamese, they'd have turned and come for us in a flash. But Mister Cat didn't care if they did—he was ready to take them all on, and the horses, too. Maybe he was just showing off for Miss Sophia Brown, but I've never been so proud of him.

They didn't turn. They passed over. Probably it didn't take more than ten or fifteen seconds, which I read somewhere is all the time dreams are supposed to take, at most. They passed over, and the rage of their passage faded off toward Sherborne, and I stood still, straining after them, listening for a sound I'd never heard before when the Hunt went by. It was a voice, a man's voice, but shrieking in such awful terror that I almost couldn't tell it was human. We don't have pigs at Stourhead, but the Colfaxes do—they're the next farm over—and you can hear pigs screaming all that way when they know they're about to be slaughtered. It's horrible, it's the most horrible thing I know, but it sounds more human than that voice, that night, flying just ahead of the Wild Hunt.

They were gone. Mister Cat quieted down to the kind of growl he'd use for some idiot dog, and the billy-blind crawled out of hiding, looking scared, but not the least embarrassed at having grabbed the one bit of shelter for himself. He cleared his throat. "Aye, so, advice you want, advice you'll have. Stay clear of *them*, stay away from that place I've told you about—"

"You never did, you never said *what* place—"

"—and you'll stop *rousing* the Willoughby, stop walking out with her! There's no good can come of it, nowt but danger for you and worse for her. Let be, girl, there's the billy-blind's advice for you—she was well enough till you came worreting at her—"

"No, she *wasn't*, and I *didn't*—"

"—and what's moving, what's waiting, it can't come into that little secret place of hers. It didn't know then, it can't know now—"

"*It?* What, the Wild Hunt? No, you mean the Other One, that's it, right?" Mister Cat hissed in my ear, because I was losing my cool again, but I was miles past listening even to him. "What *then?* What *then* are we talking about? What can't it know? What's waiting for Tamsin?" I was reaching for him, I was actually going to grab him and shake him. I wonder what would have happened if I had.

Headlights bouncing off the sky; the sound of a truck engine climbing the hill. Evan and Sally. The billy-blind and I stared at each other in absolute silence for a moment. I couldn't read his eyes at all, but he didn't seem angry at me. He said, "You go back to school, don't be asking that big Whidbey girl for help—she don't like you above half. And sit near the window in that Spanish class." He had to yell that last bit after me, because I was already heading for the house, with Mister Cat bounding along beside me. We were in bed—me still in my jeans, but with my eyes tight shut—by the time Evan and Sally came in.

Neither of us slept that night, not me and not Mister Cat. He knew a lot better than I what he'd been challenging, and now he crept under the blankets with me and snuggled into my armpit, and stayed there. But every time I looked at him, his eyes were open, and all night he kept moaning really softly to himself, no matter how much I petted him and told him what a hero he was.

He only stopped doing it after Miss Sophia Brown showed up toward morning—she just *appeared*, popping into sight like a silent movie projected on a bedsheet. I almost jumped out of bed when she got under the covers, too, and curled herself right next to Mister Cat. But I didn't, and that's the way the three of us stayed until the first cocks went at it before dawn. I remembered a snatch of an old, old ballad Evan sings with Sally sometimes:

> "*The cock doth craw, the day doth daw,*
> *The channering worm doth chide . . .*"

I don't know what a channering worm is, or what it's chiding about, but the song's about ghosts. Miss Sophia Brown stood up and stretched herself, just like a real cat, and she gave Mister Cat's nose one quick lick and disappeared. And I fell straight off to sleep, and got a good five or ten minutes before Julian barged in to tell me it was stupid canteloupes for breakfast (Julian hates fruit), and he wanted to go visit Albert and the sheep afterward. There are days, even now, when I'm quite proud of myself for letting Julian live. Because there *were* options.

Seventeen

We started school again sharp at the beginning of September, and we landed running. The English don't believe in easing you back into the classroom—I had all I could do just to keep halfway even with people who must have been studying all summer. The boys were pretty much in the same mess: Tony hadn't done a thing but dance, and Julian had mostly been doing very weird experiments and reading Asterix comic books in French. As for me, there's not much to say. I was ready for *something* that fall, but it wasn't Sherborne Girls.

As the billy-blind had advised me, I kept away from Penelope Whidbey, and grabbed a seat by the window in Spanish class. (Yes, my grades *did* go up—not a lot, but some.) When anyone asked me how I'd spent the summer, I'd roll my eyes and sigh, and do my best to look too expensively debauched for words. It didn't work worth a damn—everyone knew I didn't have a boyfriend—but I liked doing it anyway, just because I'd never have dared to try it at Gaynor. Meena said it embarrassed her, but it made her laugh, too. Which was good, because Chris Herridge was gone, and they hadn't even been able to get together for a decent farewell scene. She hardly spoke in class, and hardly ate at all, and she stopped making any sound when she cried, which bothered me more than anything else, I don't know why. So then I started clowning around, especially at school, doing and saying every silly thing I could think of to get her at least to smile. I got called for it a lot, until Meena made me stop. But it did help—after that, sometimes, I could just look at her across a classroom and she'd giggle a little. So that was something.

The Dorset rains were even worse that fall than they'd been the year before. They actually started before harvest was quite over, which meant we were all helping out in the fields—Sally cancelling her piano lessons, the boys and me right after school, and Evan and the hands going nonstop, dawn to dark, getting in as much of the crop as we could. It was muddy and cold and endless, and miserable, and I broke all my nails, but I still did as much work as Tony and Julian. Then we went and helped with the Colfoxes' harvest. They had a bigger farm, but not as many workers, and they lost more than we did.

I've never been that tired. It got so just lifting my feet to get from one field to another—one *row* to another—felt like way more trouble than just standing still in the rain forever. I didn't catch cold, like Tony, or pull a muscle in my back, like Evan. What I did was, I stopped thinking. I stopped thinking about everything except slogging along this row, cutting things off stalks, scooping sodden blue-black things up from the mud, wiping rain out of my eyes, moving on to *that* row. I learned more about Thomas Hardy that harvest than I ever learned in any literature class. A lot of his people stop thinking, too.

One of the things I didn't think about was Tamsin—Tamsin and the night world she'd introduced me to. No, that's not true. Sometimes, when I was most worn out, it was really easy to see myself being one of the people who'd have worked for Roger Willoughby, and all the Willoughbys after him: trudging their hills, plowing their fields, talking old Dorset, having children, losing half of them at birth, living on bread and cheese and beer, and whatever they could glean after the harvest; getting through one winter like this after another the best way they could—and still somehow feeling like part of the Willoughby family. It confused me—I didn't know if Tamsin was to blame for the way they lived, just for *being* a Willoughby, or whether she'd never had any more choice than any of them.

I worked until we'd saved what we could from the rains, and then I had to catch up with my schoolwork, which took until practically Christmas. Either way, it was weeks before I went back to that secret room that Roger Willoughby had built to hide his chaplains in.

I saw the Pooka twice. He was different each time: Once he was a little red fox in the shadow of a tree, watching as Tony and I were trying to salvage a few scrawny ears of corn from the muck; and the second time he was a deer stepping as elegantly as Mister Cat along a row of soggy cabbages, nibbling here, noshing there. Tamsin was right—you couldn't mistake the eyes, even at a distance. And when he looked straight at me he knew me, just as Tamsin had said he would. He didn't speak, or come toward me, or do anything that a fox or a deer wouldn't have done, but it was him. I wasn't scared, and I wasn't thrilled either. I was too damn tired.

Mister Cat and Miss Sophia Brown went on being an item, though nobody knew that except me. Nobody else ever saw them together. Some nights I'd have no cat in my room, because he was out somewhere in the wind and rain, carrying on with her; some nights I'd have them both piled together on the quilt, and I'd just lie there watching them sleep, the live cat and the ghost, and Julian's gorilla. At least Miss Sophia Brown *looked* asleep, but of course I'll never know. Tamsin never exactly slept, I know that, but she did doze now and then, in a sort of way. She tried to explain it to me once.

"Jenny, have you known it ever, that zone between aware and asleep when dreams float through you—or you through them—as though you and they were of the same substance? Beyond control, beyond words to name them, yet there's an exchange, a penetration, for all one knows them to be baseless phantoms. So with me, often, as I wait by my window. And is what I see truly what *is*? or are these visions of what has been? what might be? I can never tell."

She was sitting on the edge of my bed when she said that. I'd *felt* her there, as deeply as I was sleeping—the way I always felt Miss Sophia Brown—and I opened my eyes to see her petting the cats. They purred and stretched under her hands the way cats do when anybody, an ordinary person, strokes them. Everything's different with cats.

Tamsin gave a sort of half-embarrassed laugh, nothing like the way she usually laughed. She said, "In fair truth, Jenny, you and your Mister Cat are my touchstone, my Pole Star, my ground bass of existence. But for you two, I'd have no notion at all of which way lay reality, lapped round as I am in my dreams and my near-dreams. This is why I came seeking you tonight."

I didn't know how to tell her that I'd been afraid of opening her door and finding the Other One waiting in her chair. I muttered, "We've been helping to get the harvest in."

Tamsin nodded. "Aye, we did just so, even when I was small. It rained the same then, if that's any comfort."

"And I'm trying not to rouse you," I said. Tamsin looked at me

as blankly as any living, breathing human could have done. I said,
"That's what the billy-blind warned me about. He told me I was
waking you up, the way we talk and visit and go for walks, and that
rousing you meant rousing something else, other things, I don't
know what he meant. Maybe you do. I don't know anything—I just
want to keep you safe. From whatever."

Tamsin went on petting Mister Cat and Miss Sophia Brown, and
she didn't answer me. It was too hard to keep my eyes open, so I
let them float shut. Tamsin began to sing her sister's nursery song:

> *"Apricocks I'm selling,*
> *peaches, plums and melons,*
> *who will come and buy?*
> *who will come and buy?*
> *Daughters I've so many,*
> *Jean and Joan and Jenny,*
> *selling two a penny—*
> *who will come and buy?"*

I opened my eyes again when she sang my name. She was smiling, and there was never one damn thing I could do when Tamsin
smiled. It's hard to say why, especially when you figure that we're
talking about a guess of a memory of a smile—how does a ghost
recall teeth, or what happens to the eyes when the mouth corners
turn up? But maybe that was exactly it; maybe Tamsin's smile got
me the way it always did because three hundred years of Tamsin
went into that smile. Anyway, all I could manage was to say, "I've
missed you. I miss you more than I miss *anybody*—people back in
New York, anybody. But you're supposed to sit still, the billy-blind
kept saying it. I just don't want to get you into trouble."

Tamsin patted my leg through the blankets. I didn't feel it—I
wanted to, but I didn't—but *she* did, some way, I could tell. I could.
She said, "Jenny, I have never missed but four folk, if by that you
mean being more aware of their absence than of my own presence. Now of those four, three are as long stopped as I—my father
and my mother and . . ." and she actually mumbled the next
name—*Edric*—on purpose, like me when I don't want to be understood. For just that moment, just that moment, Tamsin Elspeth
Catherine Maria Dubois Willoughby was exactly my age.

She went on, really quietly, "But that fourth—that fourth is a child from the colonies, a living girl whose world can only be one of my dreams, but whose soul somehow takes my soul by the hand. Dear Jenny, it is too late for the billy-blind. I *am* wakened, and I *am* already in trouble, and there's naught for it but to see it through, come wind, come weather. Yet I am glad—is that not strange?"

I was wide awake myself now. I sat up in bed, joggling Mister Cat, who didn't like it. "Well, it's my fault, so I have to see it through with you. And even if it weren't and I didn't, I would, you know that." Tamsin smiled at me again. I said, "But you have to tell me some things. You know that, too."

"Yes, Jenny," Tamsin said, but she didn't say anything else for what seemed like a long time. Outside, one of the cocks crowed, but not because the day was dawing, like in the old song—cocks go off like car alarms, at all hours. It was raining again, so maybe that did it. I couldn't hear any other night sounds through the rain, but for a moment I *thought* I heard what *might* have been the click of unshod hoofs across the new driveway, and I wondered if the Pooka was watching the house. I hoped he was, though I couldn't have said why.

Tamsin said, "Edric Davies is a musician?" That happened a lot—her meaning to state a fact and having it come out a sad little question. I actually said, "No!" before I could stop myself—that's how totally I'd fixed my face for Edric being a Welsh fisherman. I said, "You mean, like my *mother?*"

"Indeed, just so." Tamsin was really delighted by the idea, you could see. "A music master, like your mother, teaching his art and playing for grand balls and brawls alike, all through the county. My father *would* have my portrait done when I turned nineteen, and Edric was thus engaged for my entertainment while I must sit for the painter. So it was."

Another musician. Up to here in musicians my entire life, and here comes another one—keyboards, yet. A fisherman, a sailor, a gypsy tinker would have been more romantic than one more damn piano player. "Shall I say what he sang, Jenny? I tell his songs over to myself, like a nun with her beads, and could name you every one, when I cannot always recall the hue of my own hair. 'Lawn as white as driven snow,' 'Ombre de mon amant,' 'Vous ne sauriez, mes yeux,' 'Still I'm wishing,' 'What can we poor females do?'—you see, you see how I remember?"

I'd never seen her looking the way she looked now. It wasn't just that she was absolutely clear, perfectly distinct, as solid and real and *alive* for that moment as Mister Cat snoring between us. What it was was a light, that faint, faint ghost-light all around her, growing bright enough to throw my shadow on the bed. I don't believe in angels and halos, and I've never seen anyone's aura, but Tamsin looked like all that stuff when she talked about Edric Davies.

"My parents quite approved of him," she said. "As singer, as musico—as a gentleman, even, for he was better educated than they, while never making show of it, and they'd have been shamed to have him eat with the servants. But had they known what was passing between our eyes, while the hired dauber toiled away and my mother knitted in a corner . . . Jenny, we said no word of it to each other—what need? It was our good fortune that the painter was slow and clumsy, and cross with it, and must be forever scratching out and starting over. My father grew impatient, but as for Edric and me, we'd have stopped time and the world in that music room, could we have done so. Perhaps we did. I think sometimes we did."

I didn't know how to take it. I never used to get squirmy about other people's big romances—as many crushes as I saw Jake Walkowitz through, let alone Meena's broken heart over Chris Herridge. But this was something altogether else, this wasn't anything I knew anything about, and I didn't even know how to look back into Tamsin's eyes. I said, "So you ran off together."

Tamsin sighed so softly that I almost didn't hear her, because of the rain. I still don't understand how ghosts can make sounds at all. "We had such plans, Jenny. It was to be Bristol first, then to Cardiff, where Edric had family, and where we might be married—and then London, oh, London! There was work for a musician, and friends who might yet arrange an introduction at Court—for James does prize music, I'll grant him that."

She'd do that sometimes, slipping between past and present, like a radio at sundown, when the little faraway stations start coming in. Now she said, "I love him so, and dare tell none. I fear to sleep—what if I should cry out his name, and my mother or a servant hear? My parents will be destroyed to lose me, and I will surely be destroyed to think of them finding me gone—but there's naught for it, Jenny, there's naught for it. Bristol first, then, tomorrow night, and chance the elements." The rain started falling harder right on those last words. Dorset weather is *very* dramatic.

"And you got caught in the storm," I said. It was working out practically the way I'd made it up, except maybe for the duel. But Tamsin shook her head, coming back to the present tense so hard that her outline shivered like a candle flame.

"A storm, yes—a storm it was indeed, but not the one we knew to beware." She put her hands on mine, so that I could see our fingers laced together even if I couldn't feel it. "There came a man to Lyme Regis. Lyme Regis, the eleventh of June. I could never forget that if I had been stopped twice as long as I have. I'd forget Edric's voice ere I forgot the eleventh of June."

And I knew. Tony hadn't told me the date, and we hadn't gotten up to it in British History, but I knew. I said, "Monmouth's Rebellion."

"Was that his name? Monmouth?" Tamsin thought about it for a moment, then shrugged. "Very like. There were folk who followed his banner, crying that he should be king. My father was not of their number." She laughed a little. "He said to me, 'Catty, never you go trailing after a Stuart, not one step. The best of them love their dreams, the worst love none but themselves, but no Stuart born cares for you, or for me, or for any of the poor fools who love them. Follow a moontouched zany, follow an *ignis fatuus*, but never a Stuart. Mind what I say, little one.' "

It was making sense, it was even better than my story. I said, "But Edric followed him. Edric went with Monmouth."

"No, not Edric," Tamsin said. "Not he, but his pupil, Francis Gollop. For Edric did take students, as does your mother, and Francis was all his pride. A yeoman's son, nothing more, but he *would* learn the harpsichord, and Edric told me often that Francis had the same gift of love as his own for the music he played. He said . . . he said that was better than having clean hands, better than quick, slender fingers. Oh, Jenny, I do remember everything!"

There was joy in her voice, but more pain—even I could tell the difference, even back then. It woke Miss Sophia Brown up, or whatever; anyway, she came and put her paws around Tamsin's neck, the way Mister Cat does with me. "Right. So this Francis joined Monmouth's Rebellion. But Edric *didn't* go with him."

"Nay, Edric went after him. Francis's mother came pleading to him, on her knees, that he would bring her son home—but be sure that Edric would have gone to find him had she never done so. For he was greatly fond of the boy, and had no mind to lose him to such madness. 'What cares music who's king?' he would ask me, expecting no answer, and getting none. 'Thieves, murderers, the lot of them, crowned and uncrowned alike. Francis's left hand, Francis's improvisations—these are worth all the thrones of all the world, all the kings and queens, all the bloody wretched seaports, frontiers, principalities. And the worse for that idiot boy if he doesn't know it. I'll fetch him straightway back, for his mother's sake and my own. The kings shall not have this one.' "

For that moment I could actually see Edric Davies. That can happen with ghosts, when they're thinking of a person who meant as much in their living days as they did to themselves. Tamsin's face *changed*—not a lot, but just enough for me to glimpse a pointed, off-center nose, a chin like a football, and cheekbones you could borrow money on. Long dark hair, not quite shoulder length—eyes much darker than Tamsin's . . . a quirky face, sort of lopsided. Not at all handsome, but nice. Then Edric was gone and she was herself again, looking a little lonelier for the memory. She said quietly, "But they did. They did, Jenny."

I didn't know my throat was hurting until I tried to talk. "He was killed? Francis?"

"At Sedgemoor, fighting on foot against mounted men with swords. Edric found his body in a ditch, still clutching a broken shepherd's crook. It was over by then, Monmouth already taken, and rebels ordered left where they fell, for the dogs and the ravens. But Edric would not have it so, and he brought Francis by night to his parents on a handbarrow." She was smiling now, holding Miss Sophia Brown close. "I was never so proud of him as I was when we buried Francis in a wheatfield, with his music and that broken stick at his side. Even my father said it was well done."

It was too much. It was all too much, and it was all coming too fast, and it was too *real*, at three or whatever in the morning, with a ghost sitting on my bed, petting her ghost-cat and remembering. People running and shouting and falling, horses screaming, armored men battering peasants down into the mud of meadows and pastures I actually knew—and Tamsin's Edric Davies, Edric the musician, who wanted nothing to do with any of it, struggling in the same rainy Dorset darkness as this, pushing his barrow along lanes lined with bodies just like the one he was lugging home . . . it was still *happening* in her voice, everything that had really happened here three hundred years ago. It wasn't me making up a silly story about Tamsin and Edric for Julian—it was real and right now, and I couldn't handle it. I started to cry.

Tamsin took my face between her hands. It *seemed* to me that my hot skin cooled just a bit when she did that, but what do I know? I was busy gulping and coughing and hiccuping, trying to hold it all back, because I was afraid of waking people, and because I can't stand to cry in front of anybody, even her. She said, "Little one, Jenny, hush, hush, there, never mind," but I couldn't stop, and she didn't know what to do—poor Tamsin, how could she? So finally she went back one more time to that song her sister taught her:

"Watercress and quinces,
fit for kings and princes,
who will come and buy?
who will come and buy?
Daughters all are married,
far away they're carried—
would that one had tarried—
who will come and buy?"

Which gave me time to sniff and burp (I *always* start burping like mad when I've been crying), and wipe my eyes on the sheet, and mutter, "They still wouldn't let you marry Edric." Tamsin didn't answer. I said, "What happened to Edric?"

I think she would have told me right then—no, I *know* she would have—if Julian hadn't wandered in, rubbing his eyes and holding a couple of his French comic books. He said, "Jenny? Why are you doing that?"

I didn't know whether he meant crying or burping, or just being awake—you can't ever tell with that kid. Tamsin was gone before he was halfway through the door, and my room suddenly felt really dark again, and I almost started bawling again, but I didn't. I told him, "I can't get back to sleep, and I'm so tired," which was true enough. And Julian said, "Me, too. I know what—I'll make chocolate milk and I'll *read* to you!" Julian would sell out the entire British Commonwealth for chocolate milk. I'm just mentioning it now, in case he ever gets into power.

So he went to the kitchen and stirred up chocolate milk for us

both, and then he curled up on my bed and read me both of his
Asterix books—doing all the different voices, naturally. Mister Cat
was pissed at him, because Miss Sophia Brown had vanished with
Tamsin the moment Julian showed. But he got into Asterix after a
while, and I dozed and woke and dozed until dawn. Julian fell
asleep at my feet somewhere along in there.

Eighteen

The rains don't exactly *stop* in a Dorset winter—there's a reason so many places are called Puddletown, Tolpuddle, Piddlehinton, Piddletrenthide, and like that—but they do ease up from time to time. Once he could get out to the fields, Evan started mounding up strips of earth straight across the muddy stubble and rotten leftover bits, everywhere there was going to be any planting. "To keep the soil warm," he told Ellie John and Seth—right, Seth was there by then—and they stared at him, and then told everybody else about it, and *they* stared, but they went ahead and did what he told them. The fields looked weird when it was done—welted up like an attack of hives—and the Lovells damn near got hives themselves when Evan invited them to come down from Oxford and take a look. But Evan didn't care. He was as cool as Mister Cat with the Lovells that time.

"It's called no-till farming," he told them. "I studied it fairly extensively when I was in the States. Very much the new thing. Very popular in the Midwest."

The Lovells weren't buying. They particularly weren't buying Evan's explanation that with this method you don't do any plowing at all—just lay the seeds down on the ground and walk away. Not really walk away; you need to be using special improved seeds, and just the right amounts of the right kinds of fertilizer. Sometimes you don't get as big a crop the first year or two, because the ground's so used to disks and blades harrowing it up. And if it sounds for a minute as though I know what I'm talking about, forget it. I just live here.

Tony and I were on floor-mopping duty when Evan laid it on the line for the Lovells. "I know it's hard to imagine, after so many millennia of people all over the world doing exactly the same thing with their land. Good soil or bad—you turn it over, you break it up, you hack furrows into it, you sow—you weed, you spray, you harvest, you market, you start over, world without end." He shook his head solemnly. "All those centuries, basically unaltered. Amazing, when you think of it."

Masses of Lovells glowered back at him. (Actually, they never came more than three or four at a time, but they always managed to look like an entire Board of Directors.) One Lovell said, "Nothing wrong with that. Civilization's always built on people farming their land."

"Civilizations change," Evan said. "People change. And land changes—that's what I've been trying to make you see. This soil, this earth we're standing on has had the equivalent of a hurricane blowing through it every year for a thousand years. There's nothing left. I want you to understand this. *There is nothing left.* The only reason Stourhead Farm and all the farms in West Dorset produce so much as a dandelion, a bloody burdock leaf, is that they're absolutely saturated in chemical fertilizers. Zombie farms, the walking dead!" The Lovells' mouths were hanging open like steamshovel jaws. Evan said, "If you're serious about wanting to restore Stourhead to what it was when the land was young, then you're going to have to change with the land. This is what's needed, and this is how I'm going to be managing here from now on."

A big bald Lovell was the first to stop spluttering. He said, "And I suppose there's not a thing we can do about it."

Evan smiled. "You're my employers. You've always got a choice."

The Lovells didn't exactly call for a time out and a huddle, but close enough. There was a lot of silent shrugging, grunting, head shaking, mouth twitching, hand spreading, and general eyebrow athletics going on, while Evan leaned back in his chair and stretched his legs, just as though none of their antics meant a thing in the world to him. When he looked over and saw Tony and me leaning on our mops and watching, he gave us a long, slow wink. Cool as Mister Cat.

And he got away with it. The bald Lovell finally grumbled, "Might have *said* something . . . well, in for a penny, in for a pound, hey?" and the rest of them went along. Evan could have two years to try out his no-till method, with an option for a third year if the second crop at least equaled this last harvest. It didn't seem like much of a shot to me, but it was plainly all he was going to get out of the Lovells. He told them what kind of new equipment he'd need, and how much it would cost, and the Lovells pissed and moaned some more, but it came out consent. Evan got them to put everything in writing before they left, just in case.

"They could have fired you," Tony said afterward. "They could have bloody bounced you, right on the spot. We'd have been back bunking in with Charlie."

Evan shook his head. "They'd lose at least a year and a harvest finding another manager this late—they know it, and I know it, and they know I know. *Now*, on their way home, they'll start looking around in a hurry, but it'll keep them busy for a while. All I've done is buy us a bit of time, which was all I wanted. Who's for chess? Julian, I'll give you a rook, how about it?" Evan would have made a great chess hustler, like the ones in Central Park, if he weren't a crazy farmer.

Later, with the rain coming down hard again, with the lights going on and off and the TV completely dead, and everyone piled together in the music room listening to Sally playing Rolling Stones songs the way Bach or Schubert or Mahler would have done them, I asked on an impulse, "Evan, does anybody know anything about Roger Willoughby's family?"

Evan was leaning against the piano bench with his head resting lightly on Sally's leg. By now I was almost used to seeing them like that, as though they'd been married forever; it only got to me once in a while, when I was offguard or in some kind of mood. He said, "It depends on what you want to know, Jenny. I could show you a copy of Roger's will, which is quite detailed about who gets what, and I could describe the changes his oldest son, Giles, made when he took over the farm in 1699. But that's not what you're after, is it?"

"No," I said. Tony was propped on an elbow, thumb-wrestling with Julian, but he was watching me really curiously, which is why he was losing. I said, "What about the other children? There were the two boys and two girls, only one of them died of the Black Plague." *That* was a mistake—now *everybody* was looking at me. Well, in for a penny, like the Lovells. "I mean, that's what I heard, anyway. I was just wondering about the other daughter, and about—I don't know . . . if any of them could have gotten mixed up in Monmouth's Rebellion or anything like that? Tony doesn't think so, but I was wondering."

If human life on this planet ever depends on whether or not I can tell a lie without blushing, humanity had better start packing. I wasn't even lying—I was just trying for casual, and I can't even do that without my whole face spontaneously combusting. Everybody was polite about it, though, and nobody asked any of the questions I'd left myself wide open for. Evan did give me a *long* look, way too thoughtful—Tony gets it from him, it just occurs to me now—but all he said was, "You should talk to old Guy Guthrie."

Sally stopped playing for a moment. "The man at the market? What would he know about the Willoughbys?"

"Guy Guthrie knows everything," Evan said. "Everything about Dorset, anyway. The Celts, the Romans, the people who cut the Cerne Abbas Giant in the turf, the ones who lived in Maiden Castle, the ones who went with Monmouth—the Tolpuddle Martyrs, Thomas Hardy, Barnes, the lot. *And* their ghosts." I must have dropped my teeth, because Evan smiled his long, slow smile at me. "He collects ghosts, old Guy does. Hobs and bogles too—get him to tell you about the Screaming Skull of Bettiscombe Manor—but mostly it's Dorset history, the bits and loose ends that don't fit into books. He'll know about the Willoughbys."

He did, too. *Does*, I mean: Guy Guthrie's still alive, still doesn't look any more than seventy-five—though he's got to be ninety—still wears Sherlock Holmes tweeds and ulsters, and still works part-time at the Dorchester Museum, though you don't see him running the cattle auctions at the farmers' market the way he used to do. He lives alone in Puddletown, a few miles east of Dorchester, in a stone cottage that smells of old books and a nice old dog named Clem. Sally dropped me off there one Saturday afternoon when she had pupils to see.

Mr. Guthrie served me milky Indian tea, the way they have it at Meena's house, and little cakes, the kind that taste like sweet sand, and which you can actually feel rotting your teeth while you're eating them. He's a tall man, with a big broad face, Crayola-blue eyes, and a hayrick of white hair that used to be red. He poured tea for himself, leaned forward, and asked me, "Now why on earth would a child like yourself be wanting to know about Tamsin Willoughby?"

Sally hadn't told him about Tamsin—she couldn't have. She'd simply gotten his phone number and called to say that her daughter was very interested in the history of Stourhead Farm and the Willoughby family. And there he sat, smiling a little over the rim of his teacup, and getting straight to the heart of things first crack. I said, "Well, I didn't mean Tamsin—I mean, not *just* Tamsin—"

"Of course you do," Mr. Guthrie interrupted me. "Tell me, does she still smell of vanilla?" I sloshed tea into my saucer, and Mr. Guthrie's smile got wider. He said, "I'm sorry, my dear—that was a silly parlor trick, and I do apologize. But you see, Tamsin Willoughby has appeared a number of times over the last three centuries. Always to young women—girls, really, none very much older than yourself—and always accompanied by the scent of vanilla." Mr. Guthrie was born in the north of England, not the west, so his accent isn't really Dorset, and people tease him about it, but I liked it right away. He said, "Please do tell me about her."

I didn't tell him everything I knew, but just to be able to talk about Tamsin at all was like early spring in Mr. Guthrie's little parlor. When I said that I'd spoken with her, and that we'd gone walking together, he didn't answer me for a while. Then he said, very carefully, "As a rule, Miss Gluckstein—ah, Jenny, then—as a rule the sightings of Tamsin Willoughby have usually been very brief, and *always* occurred within the walls of the Manor itself. And no one has ever reported—ah—any sort of actual conversation with her. Are you absolutely sure . . . ?" He let his voice trail away then, the way people do when they're too polite to call you a liar, so they offer you a way out. Like in all those English movies Sally took me to, when they leave the villain alone with a drink and a pistol. I said that I was telling the truth, and he gave a sigh, leaned back in his chair, and didn't speak for another while. But it was a different kind of not speaking.

"The story of Tamsin Willoughby," Mr. Guthrie said, "is to my mind the most romantic legend between Winchester and Exeter. I call it a legend because the people involved were most real, but every other aspect of the tale is guesswork, there's no other word for it. It begins with a chap who was apparently engaged to play to her while she was having her portrait painted—"

"Edric Davies," I said. I didn't *mean* to say it—it just came out of me, that fast. Mr. Guthrie looked at me. I said, "He was Welsh—I *think*." Because it was his story to tell, after all.

"Edric Davies," Mr. Guthrie said. "Yes. Yes, he was indeed a Welshman. Of course they fell in love, quite properly—what sort of a legend would this be if they didn't?—and made plans to elope together, since her family would never have consented to such a marriage." He stopped, narrowing his eyes, which made them look even brighter. "You know all this, I can see."

I nodded. "She told me," I said. "I'm really not making it up, Mr. Guthrie."

Mr. Guthrie sighed again. "Eigh, dear, I rather wish you *were*. Because I know what to do with fabrications, Jenny, with all the ridiculous nonsense that always collects around stories like this one of Tamsin Willoughby. I sieve them out, like one of your American goldminers—I shake them up and turn them on their heads, and I shake them some more, and in time all the silliness and all the superstition sift through and sink. And most of the time there's nowt more than that to the business, but once in a while, once in a while . . . some bit of gold is left behind, and that's what I collect, do you see? Those tiny flecks of inexplicable truth that won't dissolve, won't wash away." He smiled again, a little sadly now. "It's not a very big collection, for as long as I've been at it, but you're welcome to what's there."

As far as he knew, Edric Davies had been lost in Monmouth's Rebellion. When I told him about Edric's student, Francis Gollop, being the one who went, and how Edric had gone after him and brought the body home by night, he gave a funny, nice little yelp, the way Julian still does when the crossword puzzle suddenly falls into place. "*That* accounts for it!" He set his cup down too hard, spilling tea himself, and clapped his hands. "*That* accounts for it!"

"What? Accounts for what?"

"Why, for the way he disappears from the story," Mr. Guthrie practically shouted. He hopped to his feet—then saw I didn't have a clue what he was carrying on about, and he laughed and sat down again. "Jenny, in all the years I've been asking Dorset people about the ghost stories their parents and grandparents told them, I've come across four versions of the tale of Tamsin and Edric. And in every one of them, Edric vanishes into the Rebellion and Tamsin never learns what becomes of him—nobody does. Maybe he was killed, maybe Judge Jeffreys had him hanged or transported; maybe he simply fled to safety in Wales. I must tell you, it's never felt right to me. Wrong *shape* to the story, Edric never coming back. Wrong shape."

"Well, he did," I said. "He came back, all right, and he buried Francis Gollop in a wheatfield. But I don't know what became of him after that. Tamsin won't ever say."

"She died," Mr. Guthrie said. "Maybe that's all that happened." There was one little sugary cake left, and he waved it to me, but I wrapped it in a paper napkin to take home to Julian. A kid gives you his damn gorilla, you have obligations.

I said, "I don't believe that. And you don't either." Mr. Guthrie didn't answer right away. Clem wandered over and slobbered on my shoes. I scratched his ears, keeping Julian's cake well out of range. Once Mr. Guthrie started to say something, but then he didn't. The old stone cottage got really quiet, but not scary. You could hear a clock ticking somewhere, and smell something on the stove, and a bird scratching for shelter under the eaves. I studied a framed photograph on an end table: three little girls, each one holding a doll. They must have wanted them in the picture, too, the same way I still don't like to be in a photo without Mister Cat. I need all the diversions and evasive maneuvers I can get.

"Do you know anything about Judge Jeffreys?" Mr. Guthrie finally asked me. I told him what Tony had told me about the Bloody Assizes, and he nodded his head, but he was sort of shaking it at the same time. He said, "You can't imagine him. You can't imagine what he did here. The Irish still damn each other with the Curse of Cromwell, because of the terrible way he drove them off their land, and the thousands and thousands who were killed when they resisted. We in Dorset could call down the Curse of Jeffreys on our enemies, but we never would—no one could deserve that, and it's no name to be conjuring with. Oh, I talk about him to the tourists all the time, but I don't *think* about him, do you see? I don't like to think about him."

He was looking flushed and agitated, and *old* for the first time. He saw me seeing it and snapped his fingers to call Clem, calming himself some by smoothing the dog's messy coat. I almost didn't hear him when he said, "Jeffreys knew the Willoughbys. I'm sure he knew Tamsin."

My entire inside turned to ice-cold mashed potatoes, that fast. When I could talk, I said, "No. No, he couldn't have. Roger Willoughby stayed out of the Rebellion, they didn't have anything to do with it. I *know* that."

Mr. Guthrie's northern accent was getting stronger, and his rough, easy voice had turned pinched and harsh. "Jeffreys convicted an eight-year-old girl of treason. He raved at her in his courtroom until she collapsed and died. He didn't *care* who was involved with Monmouth and who wasn't. King James had sent him down to make an example of Dorset—he was after the whole county, not just a handful of miserable peasants. He was a bloody terrorist, Jenny. Guilt or innocence didn't matter tuppence to Judge Jeffreys."

Clem yelped, and Mr. Guthrie looked down at his hand, clenched hard in the dog's fur as though it were somebody else's hand. He let go and petted Clem, crooning and apologizing to him. I said, "You can't be sure. That he actually knew them. Her."

"He kept a diary," Mr. Guthrie said. "Not a real diary—more of a schedule, you'd call it. A few scribbled notes on the trials—you wouldn't want to read those—but most are social things. Visitors, dinner invitations. He was a very popular dinner guest during the Assizes, the judge was."

I stared at him. I said, "That's crazy. With everything he was doing every day?"

"Well, that's precisely why." Mr. Guthrie made himself smile. "Just you think about it. Here's a man can send *anyone*, anyone he chooses to the gallows or worse. Commoners can't offer him an evening's entertainment, but the gentry can. Wouldn't you want to keep in his good books—make certain he doesn't decide you might have *thought* about supporting Monmouth, even for five minutes together? Oh, take my word, they fought to have him to their homes, people like the Willoughbys, people far greater than they. That's how it was then, during the Bloody Assizes."

I didn't want to hear what he was going to tell me. I looked at my watch to see when Sally would be back to pick me up. Mr. Guthrie said, "His journal is in the County Museum. There are several entries for the Willoughbys."

"She wouldn't have had anything to do with him," I said. "I don't care how many times he came to dinner, I don't care *what* he could have done to her family, she wouldn't have talked to him, *looked* at him. You don't know her." I was getting red-faced myself, I could feel it—not gracefully around the cheekbones like Mr. Guthrie, but pop-eyed and smeary and awful. I said, "I'm sure that sounds incredibly dumb, saying I know someone who's been dead for three hundred years, but I *do*."

"And I know George Jeffreys—Baron Jeffreys, Lord Chief Justice Jeffreys of Wem," Mr. Guthrie answered. "Haven't I looked in his face, forty years, time and time, and seen what that poor little girl saw? Haven't I looked in his face?"

He was on his feet now, though I don't think he knew it, and he had to grip the back of the chair to steady himself, he was trembling so. For a moment I was sure he meant he'd actually *seen* Judge Jeffreys, just as I saw Tamsin. But then he went on—quickly, as though he knew what I was thinking—"There's a portrait in the Lodgings. Ask them to show you."

It got awkwardly, embarrassingly quiet again after that, and I couldn't think of a thing to say, except to ask if I could have some more tea. Mr. Guthrie seemed relieved to go and make it. I sat there, so caught up in imagining Judge Jeffreys at Stourhead Farm, dining with the Willoughbys in the Manor, that I kept forgetting to stroke Clem. Then he'd shove his head into my hand for attention, and I'd get back to my job. But all I could think about was Tamsin, Tamsin looking across the dining table, seeing that man staring at her. Because he would have stared. And she'd have looked straight back into his face, like Mr. Guthrie, and seen what she saw. I didn't taste that second pot of tea at all.

Sally was tired from teaching when she came to get me, and I felt guilty about it, but I talked her into taking me by the Judge Jeffreys Restaurant, back in Dorchester. The Restaurant is on High West Street, around the corner from the Antelope Hotel, where they held the Bloody Assizes. It's a three-story, half-timbered building, all stone and oak, over four hundred years old, and it's so real that it looks absolutely fake, if you can figure that. Judge Jeffreys's picture is on the sign hanging out front, but you really can't make much out of it, except that he's wearing a wig. I've passed it any number of times without giving it any thought, even after Tony told me about the Assizes.

But upstairs, in the Lodgings, where he slept and wrote in his journal and where people probably came to beg him for their lives, or their children's lives—upstairs they have the portrait Mr. Guthrie was talking about. It was late, and the Lodgings part was closed, but the restaurant people knew Sally—she eats there a lot, in between pupils—so they showed us up and left us alone. And we stood there and looked at Judge Jeffreys together.

The thing I wasn't the least bit prepared for was that he was *pretty*. I can't say it any other way—he was out and out pretty, that mad, evil man. And he was *young*—the painting wasn't done at the time of the Assizes, but maybe seven or eight years before, so he'd have been around thirty at the most. It's almost a woman's face: delicate, calm, even thoughtful, with big heavy-lidded eyes and a woman's soft mouth. You can't possibly imagine that face screaming and raging and foaming—which is what everybody says he did—sentencing people by the hundreds to be hacked into pieces, and ordering their heads and quarters boiled and tarred and stuck up on poles all over Dorset. There's no way you can see that face doing those things.

I told Sally that, and she said, "Well, you know, in those days portraits didn't necessarily look much like the people who were paying for them. Oliver Cromwell's *supposed* to have told a painter that he wanted to be shown warts and all, but I don't think that was ever much of a trend. I'll bet nobody was about to chance painting Judge Jeffreys the way he *really* looked." She put her arm around me—I guess because of the way I was staring at the portrait. "Too bad they didn't have Polaroids back then, huh?"

But he did look like that. He looked exactly like that.

Nineteen

The Wild Hunt was out almost every night that second winter in Dorset—or that's the way it seemed, anyway. Most of the time I'd be awakened, not by the horsemen, but by Julian scrambling frantically into bed with me, or by Mister Cat slamming through the window I always left partway open for him. Once or twice Meena was staying over, so it would be all of us huddled together: Mister Cat hissing and growling, Julian trying not to whimper, and Meena doing her best to stay cool and logical. Which is tricky when you're dealing with that crazy howling and baying and laughing, all riding on an icy wind that never seemed to come from any one place. Nothing with feathers sounds like the Wild Hunt, and everybody knows it. I *know* everybody knows it.

And Meena heard the other thing one night—that awful, hopeless almost-human wail crossing the sky just ahead of the Hunt. Julian didn't hear it, but Meena's face went almost transparent, as though you could see right through her brown skin to the trembling underneath. She said, very softly, "We have demons in India, demons with a hundred terrible heads—even demons that can be gods at the same time, it depends. We don't have *that*. We *don't*." She wasn't over it in the morning, like Julian; she didn't get over it for days. It's still the one time I've ever seen Meena afraid.

Other people were hearing the Hunt too—there was even a squib in the Dorchester paper about it. The Colfaxes, next farm over, said their chickens couldn't sleep and were off their feed; and at school everyone told me their parents were really spooked and pretending not to be. It didn't matter whether they believed in the Wild Hunt or not—it was *there*. People are different about stuff like that in England.

I'd been frantic to go find Tamsin the same night after I'd talked with Mr. Guthrie and been to the Lodgings with Sally. But I

couldn't, not then, and not for more than a week. There was
school, and there was fixup stuff around the Manor—as there is to
this day, it's *never* done with—and there was always the farm. The
Lovells had clamped down hard on Evan's hiring budget, so Tony
and Julian and I got pressed into more fieldwork than anybody'd
bargained for. In some ways the no-till business was easier for us
than deep plowing would have been; in other ways it was a lot
more delicate, because you have to use *exactly* the right amount of
fertilizer—you can't slather it on anymore—and we had to be spar-
ing with the seeds because the new kind Evan needed were really
hard to come by that first year. And the weather never quit being
mean and messy. That's another thing that accounts for a lot of
Thomas Hardy.

Finally I had the Manor more or less to myself one afternoon—
Evan and Sally were working, Tony was locked in his studio, and
Julian was at a school friend's house, the two of them totally involved in some experiment I didn't even want to think about. I
couldn't find Mister Cat anywhere, so I figured he must be off with
Miss Sophia Brown. The Wild Hunt never bothered *her*, by the way.
If it got too noisy overhead, she might open one eye and yawn, but
that was it. You could plop Miss Sophia Brown down on an ice-
berg, and she'd probably burst into flame.

I grabbed a paper clip and went up the east-wing stairs to the
third floor. It was as comfortably desolate as ever, dim as it was,
even in midafternoon, I could actually see Mister Cat's footprints
in the dust on the floor. I found Tamsin's door, straightened the
clip, poked around in the lion's left eye, heard the double *click*,
and I was in the secret room. I could do it almost as fast now as
Miss Sophia Brown could pour herself through the panel.

Tamsin wasn't there. I called for her a few times, which was silly,
and then I wandered around the little room, investigating the
bedframe-chest combination, staring at the painting of Roger and
Margaret Willoughby for a long while, looking for Tamsin—and finally I sat down in her chair. I felt like her, a little bit, sitting there,
looking out into a world that couldn't see me. I saw the chestnut
tree, and the clouds heaped up like fresh laundry, and I saw the
back of a woman going into the dairy, and William slogging past
in the mud with a feed sack on each shoulder. I thought about
New York, I thought about having been in Dorset for a whole year
and a half, and about being practically fifteen and a Fourth For-

mer, and what Marta and Jake would say if they could see me doing no-till farming. Tamsin's chair was more comfortable than I'd expected, and the room was warmer than it should have been, considering the weather outside. I fell asleep.

When I opened my eyes, I was looking straight into Judge Jeffreys's face.

It was the portrait at the Lodgings come perfectly to life: robes, brown wig, white lace at the throat, gentle expression and all. Even the hands were right, long and graceful and . . . *reposeful* as Tamsin's hands. It's a good thing I saw the eyes before I screamed, because I'd have brought the whole east wing down. But the eyes were angled, golden, mocking, and I didn't scream. I said, "Evan warned me you had a really crude sense of humor."

Judge Jeffreys shrugged lightly, and the Pooka said, "My humor suits me well. What else should concern me?"

"Nothing, I guess," I said. "But could you please look like something different? Anything, I don't care what—just not *him*, okay?" The Pooka shrugged again, and became Mister Cat, crouched at my feet, tail whipping back and forth. I yelled that time—not screamed, there's a difference, just yelled *"No!"*—and the Pooka chuckled. I can't describe that sound, as well as I came to know it: The best I can get into words is that there's never any smile in the Pooka's laughter. But he did change himself into Albert the sheepdog, and I was grateful for that.

I said, "You ever turn into things that hide under bathtubs?"

The Pooka sat back on his haunches and lolled his tongue out, which is the other thing Albert can do. "No fear, Jenny Gluckstein, I do not often come peeping at you or yours. I am here with word for Tamsin Willoughby."

"Sorry, she's in a meeting," I said. "You want to leave a pager number or something?"

The main trouble with shapeshifters is that it's too easy to forget what they really are and get careless. The Pooka didn't turn into some other form, but slobby old Albert suddenly reared up over me like a grizzly bear, drooling blood, those giveaway eyes gone streaky-red and his chipped yellow teeth bulging his mouth. That time, all right—*that* time I screamed, and I knocked Tamsin's chair over, trying to get to the door . . . and then it was just old Albert again, the only dog who smells like a wet dog when he's dry. The Pooka said, quite calmly, "I am no billy-blind, Jenny Gluckstein."

"No," I agreed. I was pretty shaky. I said, "I'm sorry. I honestly don't know where Tamsin is."

"With the dancer," the Pooka said. "She watches the dancer."

I couldn't take that in. "Tony? You mean she's in Tony's studio right now?"

Albert always seems to be grinning like an idiot, but the Pooka was definitely overdoing it. "Indeed, she had always a great fancy for galliard or brawl, or even a running-battle, such as men dance with swords. It often comforts her to watch the dancer."

And like *that* I was jealous. My God, I was roaring jealous, howling jealous, Gaynor Junior High School jealous—horribly, disgustingly jealous. *Tamsin belonged to me—I was her comfort, nobody else.* I didn't have a minute to brace myself; it rushed me like one of those waves that slams you down and tumbles you in so many different directions you can't remember which way the air is—there was a moment where I was really fighting just to get my breath. It was absolutely horrible, and I was so ashamed.

And the Pooka knew. He didn't say anything, but I took one look at that stupid old dog's face and I couldn't look at him again. I said, "Would you mind? Somebody I don't actually know, please."

The Pooka nodded politely, and turned into something that would have had me wetting my pants at some other time. It was more or less a naked human from the waist down—and so hairy I couldn't tell if it was male or female—but the upper part was like a huge stoat or weasel, with a weasel's short clawed forelegs, a weasel's humped back, masked face and pointed muzzle, and a mouth way too full of white teeth when it put its head back to laugh at me. It said, "Will this do, Jenny Gluckstein?"

The weird thing is, I couldn't be bothered with it. The way I was feeling right then was so much worse than any monster the Pooka could have come up with that I just nodded and said, "Fine, sure," as though he'd been a waiter asking me if my dinner was all right. I said, "How come Tony can't see her?" Because I'd have known if Tony had seen Tamsin. I can't say why I'd have known, but I would have. Jealousy has its own awful magic.

The Pooka said, "Not everyone is given to see such as Tamsin Willoughby. Indeed, not every ghost can perceive another. As for your brother—"

"*Step*brother—"

"Your brother sees his own ghosts," the Pooka said. "Dances yet undanced, paces invisible to others that he must set down on the air for them. There is no room in his vision for Tamsin Willoughby, just as you cannot espy the spirits who come to partner him when he calls." He gave me a weasel's chattery grin, and added, "And so be easy, Jenny Gluckstein."

I had myself pretty much under control by then. The shame and anger at myself hadn't gone anywhere, but I figured I could face them later. "Well, if you know where she is, why didn't you go there to give her your message? Why come to me?"

"The message is as well for you." The Pooka came closer. He smelled like an entire weasel, not just half of one, and he towered over me in this shape, but I wasn't afraid. He said, "You are the first she has ever spoken to."

"I know that," I said. "Mr. Guthrie told me."

"It was not wise, that." Far beyond the cold, thoughtless flare there's always something a little like sadness in the Pooka's eyes, only it's not safe to look for it. He said, "Wisdom is no concern of mine—but for the dead to linger so long that they come to have speech with the living . . . this is not *right*. The least of boggarts would know that."

I remembered the way Mr. Guthrie had looked at me when I said that Tamsin talked to me. I said, "Then you tell me where she's supposed to be. Because she doesn't *know*."

The Pooka shook his fierce weasel head. "Not here. It is dangerous, it makes wrongness, and in time other wrongness follows. Somewhere a single stream runs backward—one tree flowers in deep winter—in one nest a hatchling devours its parent. A door meant to close behind Tamsin Willoughby bides open." He didn't say anything more for a moment: We just stood looking at each other, me and this completely impossible creature in a room only cats could find. The Pooka said, "This concerns me."

"Well, me, too," I said. "Whatever it means. Look, she knows she shouldn't still be here—it's not like she *wants* to stay. Something's holding her, there's some kind of *reason*. Maybe you ought to be concerned about that, instead of trees and doors and baby birds."

The Pooka looked at me for a long time. Weasels have eyes like round maroon pinheads, but the Pooka's eyes were as yellow as ever, and just as deep with danger. The weird thing was, though, that he also seemed the least bit uncomfortable—embarrassed, even—which was ridiculous. We hadn't spent a lot of quality time together, but if there was one thing I already understood, it was that the Pooka doesn't get *embarrassed*. He's the Pooka.

What he finally said was, "That is not in my power."

I said, "What? Oh, *please*."

The Pooka actually almost smiled, I think—it's hard to tell with weasels, even big weasels with human legs. He said, "I do not lie about such things, Jenny Gluckstein. If I could have been of help to Tamsin Willoughby, I might well have done so long ago, but I cannot. It is forbidden, which is only to say impossible. She is not of my world."

"*Please*," I said again. "She's a lot more of your world than she is of mine or anyone else's. She's like a damn tour guide to your world, for heaven's sake."

"Tours . . . I have seen such things," the Pooka said, which surprised the hell out of me. Though I guess it shouldn't have, when you think about it. "But this guide belongs no more to the world she reveals than do those who trudge behind her. Quick or dead, Tamsin Willoughby remains human, and even I"—and when the Pooka said *even I*, you *heard* it—"even I cannot guide her in her turn. I might as well be the Black Dog, silently foreboding, or I might be the billy-blind, forever offering the right advice at the wrong time." The weasel-head leaned over me; the Pooka's golden eyes drew me up and in. The Pooka said, "Quick or dead, there's no helping a human, but if anyone is to succor Tamsin Willoughby, it must be you."

And if anything could have snapped me out of the blank enchantment the Pooka's eyes always laid on me, that was it. I jumped back, right away from him. I yelled, *"What?"*

"Only you. And no chance of that unless you come rightly to understand her plight—which you do not, no more than she." The Pooka got bored with the weasel and became a little gray rabbit with yellow eyes. He said, "Listen to the Wild Hunt. The Wild Hunt will tell you what you must know."

"The Wild Hunt," I said. I'm not even sure the words actually came out. The rabbit sat up on its haunches and began washing its face and fluffing its whiskers, just the way cats do.

"Listen to the Wild Hunt, Jenny Gluckstein," it said again. Then it turned and leaped straight through that pointy dark window, in a flurry of wings that looked too big to fit. And left me standing alone in Tamsin's room, which didn't smell at all of vanilla when she wasn't there.

* * *

So that was also the winter when I learned a lot more about Tony's dancing than I ever expected to. If Tamsin was spending time in his studio, maybe I wouldn't be so jealous if I were there with her, at least trying to understand what she got out of it. Tony was *not* crazy about the idea, even though I'd already been in his damn studio, and let him try out his moves on me, and generally behaved a lot better than his brother. I could have told him that there was a ghost watching him get into his tights and put on the legwarmers that Sally had knitted for him, but I didn't. It took us a while, but we cut a deal. I promised to sweep the floor when it needed doing, and absolutely never to comment unless asked. And not ever to bring Mister Cat.

Personally, I think he'd been ready for a long time to have someone see him practicing. He just would have liked it to be someone who understood what the hell he was trying to do. Sally and Evan both love music, but even Sally doesn't know much more about dance than I do. Poor Tony. Working by himself in a real vacuum—no one to study with, no one to talk to him or trade ideas with, hardly ever getting even a glimpse of real dancers—he finally had to settle on me as an audience, the best of a bad lot. *Maybe.*

And he couldn't know that he had another one, a better one than all his family put together. I didn't see Tamsin the first time I dropped in when he was working. (I'm saying "dropped in" because I tried hard to make it casual—just sort of sidling through the door, don't mind me, and sidling over to sit in a corner.) I could smell her, but it took a while before I made her out, almost invisible on a chair that Tony was using for some of his stretching exercises. She wasn't more than a few inches away from him—when he braced his foot on the chair to bend over it, he actually stepped through Tamsin's own foot, and the hem of her white dress. It was a nightgowny sort of thing, and she looked like a little girl in it, staring up at Tony as he touched his forehead to his knee, then straightened, then did it again, and again. Usually he wears a headband when he works, but he didn't have it on that day, and his sweaty brown hair kept flopping into his eyes. Once or twice Tamsin lifted her hand, as though she wanted to brush it away.

It took me a while to get her attention, because she was so totally caught up in watching Tony at work. He didn't do anything terribly glamorous or dramatic: It was all fits and starts—a slow half-turn here, a sudden little run there, or a burst of jumps, and then most likely a shake of the head and a mumble, and he'd be trying it over a different way. It wasn't dancing, it was *making* a dance, which is about as boring as making anything, unless you're the one doing it. Believe me, I know.

But Tamsin couldn't stop looking at him, couldn't stop *breathing* with him, if you can imagine that, considering that she didn't breathe. The more she watched, the clearer she grew, until she was practically as distinct as Tony, and still he was too absorbed to notice her. He was using the chair as a center to work around, now spinning away from it, now sort of bouncing off it, now actually picking it up and dancing with it—holding Tamsin in his arms, though he didn't know. He didn't see her, and she didn't see me, and there was a moment when I really couldn't have said just whom I was jealous of.

Then it was past, and Tamsin did notice me, and came to be with me in my corner while Tony went on dancing with the chair. She didn't look like such a little girl now, but someone closer to my age, or Meena's—that's it, she looked like Meena watching Chris Herridge playing football. She said without looking at me, "Oh, Jenny, but he's a springald, your brother—a gerfalcon, if ever I saw one—"

"*Step*brother. You *know* he's my stepbrother." I was whispering as low as I could but Tony said, with his head practically touching the small of his back, "No comments from the cheap seats. That's part of the deal."

"La, stepbrother then, what of it?" I'd never seen Tamsin this wound up. "Jenny, I'd no notion—we never had such a mode when I . . ." Tony was scribbling something on a yellow pad—he has his own kind of dance notation—and Tamsin watched him at it, fascinated, not taking the least note of me. "How Edric would love this," she whispered, so low I could hardly make it out. "Edric would play such music for such dancing."

"He's just practicing, for God's sake," I said. "Listen, I have to talk to you." Tony turned and pointed at me. He didn't say anything, but I shut up and waited it out, until he'd worked himself down to a dripping rag—Tony never knows when to quit, even now that dancing's what he does all the time. Then he said, "That's it, show's over," and limped off with a towel around his neck to take a shower. I really thought Tamsin was going to follow him, but she came outside with me instead.

February still, but this was one of those gentle afternoons that Dorset slips in now and again, even in the middle of a miserable Dorset winter. Two of those in a row, and tiny green and white things start peeking out of the mud, and I always want to run around pushing them down again and yelling at them, "Don't fall for it, stay low, it's a trick!" It is, too, always; but right then it was what people here call a soft day, with a breeze pushing against me like a dog's wet nose. Tamsin's white dress seemed to flutter a little, even though it couldn't have.

"He's there every day," I said. "But you know that." Tamsin didn't answer. I said, "I've never seen anybody that obsessed about anything. I mean, school's just something that gets between him and that studio."

We were walking down toward the dairy, and Wilf passed me, humping a couple of fence posts along on his shoulders, actually doing something. He gave me a weird look, hearing me talking to myself, and turned around slowly to stare after me, so the fence posts *clonged* against a metal stanchion. Somebody yelled at him to bleeding-Christ *watch* it.

Tamsin said again, "Edric would have played and played." She was quiet now, and maybe not as distinct, as different from the air, as when she'd been watching Tony. She said, "Jenny, it is not any dancing I know, what your brother does. I see no form or course to it, no rule that I might follow, no design that I understand. And yet . . . and yet I *dance,* Jenny. Past any fathoming of mine, I see your brother dancing, and I, too, I, too . . ." She put her hand to her breast, as though she could touch herself. "I feel, Jenny. It cannot be, but I feel."

I was good then. I like remembering that I was all right. It didn't matter if it was Tony's dancing and not me being with her that made her remember she was somewhere still human, the way the Pooka said. I looked straight at her, shimmering in the pale sunlight like dew along a spiderweb, and I said, "Yes, Mistress Tamsin. I know you do."

I headed us back toward the chestnut tree where I'd been writing to Marta the day I met Tamsin, a hundred years ago. I sat on the damp ground, and Tamsin floated down beside me, careful and precise as any well-brought-up, young seventeenth-century lady settling herself. I said, "He's Judge Jeffreys, isn't he? The Other One. I have to know, Tamsin."

She vanished. Instantly. One second of the purest terror and plain shock I've ever yet seen on a human face, whether you could see bare chestnut branches through it or not—the next second, so *gone* you could practically hear the air snapping to behind her. I jumped to my feet and yelled after her, top of my voice, not even thinking what I was doing, "You come back here! Tamsin Willoughby, you come back!" To this day, I can't believe I did that. Three people and a goat whipped around and gaped, and Mister Cat and Miss Sophia Brown strolled out of the dairy together and gave me a Look. Mister Cat almost seemed to be apologizing for me. "She gets like that, it's embarrassing, I'm sorry. Just ignore her."

But I wasn't letting Tamsin get away with it. After dinner that night I went to the secret room—Tony wasn't in his studio—but she wasn't there. I plunked down in her chair, bound and determined to wait her out, until it got . . . I guess *scary*'s the only word. I'd *never* been frightened in Tamsin's room before: But this time, as the last light went, all the shadows seemed to be drawing in around that chair, and each of them looked more like Judge Jeffreys than the one before. I *knew* how stupid it was, but knowing didn't help. The night mist was gathering, and it made a soft, raspy sound when it stirred against the window. I knew that couldn't be happening either. My mouth was getting drier and drier, and I kept feeling like I had to pee. You can't think straight when you're like that. The mist was coming into the room, through the leaks around that ancient window frame. It felt cold and sticky, and it smelled of sour bedsheets.

Between one rustle and the next, one more tongue-tip of cold air against the back of my neck, I just suddenly lost it. I ran out of the room, down the hall, with the old dust not quite muffling the echo of my footsteps, and down the stairs, and I didn't stop running until I almost fell over Julian. He was trying to get a rubber-band-powered model plane to take off and fly straight down the corridor, but it kept spinning in circles on one wheel. Julian never has any luck with things like that.

"Trample me and I'll put a curse on you," he warned me in that rasping little rumble of his. He was into putting curses on people then—I think he got it from Ellie John. "All your hair will fall out, and you'll always want to sneeze, only you won't be able to." Evan used to go on at him about it, but it never did any good.

"Don't talk about curses," I said. "Not here. Just shut up about curses, Julian." I think I was actually shaking. I know I was yelling.

Julian looked really hurt for a moment—I'd never once raised my voice to him before—and then he *saw*, the way he still does sometimes, even now that he's a foul teenager, and he just came and leaned against me without saying anything. He got something sticky and permanent on my sweater, but what the hell.

Twenty

Tamsin came to me late that night. Not in my bedroom, like the other time, but in my damn bathroom, when I was standing naked at the mirror, mumbling to myself, just checking the damage. These days I can look pretty straight into a mirror, not flinching away or making idiot faces; but back then it took me weeks to work up to something like that, staring head-on at what I'm going to be staring at for the rest of my life. Skin actually not too hideous for once—maybe Sally's right about the climate. Hair . . . well, the billy-blind's brown egg just made a mess, but the porter actually helped some. Shape absolutely hopeless—live with it, that's all. Too much mouth, too little nose—makes my eyes look too close together, but I don't *think* they are. No, eyes probably okay—eyelashes too damn stubby. Meena's got such pretty eyelashes. Live with it.

I didn't see Tamsin in the mirror—ghosts don't reflect—but I knew she was there even before I smelled her. She was balancing on the edge of the bathtub, poised on one foot—doing Tony, for God's sake!—and I caught my breath to warn her not to lean against the curtain rod, because it comes down if you look cross-eyed at it. I *was* going to be embarrassed or annoyed or something at being caught and inspected like that, but Tamsin smiled, and all I said was, "Where'd you *go?*"

Tamsin didn't answer that right away. She looked me up and down very thoughtfully, not smiling now. At last she nodded firmly and she said, "I remember."

"You remember *what?*" I got back into my bathrobe, not because of being shy or anything, but because of drafts. Tamsin went on studying me in a way she hadn't ever done—so clear for the moment that I almost couldn't see the shower curtain behind her. So clear that what I *could* see was something I'd never noticed before:

a crooked right eyetooth, crowding just a bit over the tooth to its left, whatever it's called. Not grotesque, not a deformity—just something I didn't expect, and it startled me. And Tamsin knew. "We call it a wolf tooth," she said. "I cannot say what your time's name for it might be. But the hours I spent staring at it in my glass—oh, Jenny, the foolish years! My parents were kind, but what could they do for me, save pretend it made no matter and increase my dowry? And well they might indeed, for a daughter who never smiled at them, let alone at a suitor? When my father told me he'd engaged a painter for my portrait, I wept all night to think of it, and I vowed that I'd no more smile for him than for the hangman." Her voice softened then, and she remembered a face even younger than mine, the way she did sometimes. "And I kept my word, too, Jenny, for it was never the painter I smiled at."

"You've got a beautiful smile, for God's sake," I said. "I never saw a smile like yours. I'll do anything—I mean, *people* would do anything when you smile."

And Tamsin pounced—she even sort of swooped her head down close to mine, like a butterfly landing on something sweet. "Aye, well then—and your eyelashes are in no way too short, and your eyes are perfectly set in your head, and your mouth is a womanly mouth, a sister's vow on't." I didn't take it in at first, that word, *sister.* Tamsin said, "Mistress Jenny—I call you so a'purpose, mind—you've all the makings of a proper beauty, and a sympathetic heart beside. Trust me, there will be more than one man comes to grief over you in a little time."

My womanly mouth was hanging open, and all I could think of was Mr. Hammell and Introduction to Drama. But Tamsin went on looking at me as proudly as though I really were her sister, dressed for a ball in her borrowed clothes, instead of my mildewy old bathrobe. Mister Cat looked like that when he was first showing Miss Sophia Brown off to me.

I asked her again, when I could talk, "Where did you go? When I asked you about Judge Jeffreys? Why did you disappear like that?"

She didn't do it again this time, though you could see how much she wanted to. She went all filmy and indistinct, fragile as a dragonfly wing, but without any color, and without that pulse of light that she always had. But she stayed visible, and she *seemed* to take a long breath and let it out again, though she couldn't have. She whispered, "I was afeared."

"He's gone," I said. "He's gone, and he can't come back, you told me that. He died in 1688, three years after you." Tamsin had grown so faint in the air that I remembered being a kid watching *Peter Pan* and clapping my hands wildly to save Tinker Bell from dying. I said, "But he was here, I know that. You remember him."

"He came often to dine with us." Tamsin's voice wasn't even as loud as those squeaks and chitterings I'd heard under the tub. "My parents despised him to their souls, but what could they . . . ?" She broke off for a moment, and then she burst out, "My father feared no man born, you must know this, but in the presence of that— that . . . Jenny, I'd not have known him, he was grown so small, as though all the marrow were out of him. And my mother the same, tiny and white, not able to swallow so much as a bit of bread, and her hand so cold . . . and *him* smiling at me across the table, peeling oranges to make me share with him, and talking, talking, all evening long, about the *things* he'd done that day. The *things*, Jenny."

Robe or no robe, I was freezing, and my throat was closing up on me. I got her out of the bathroom and into my room, and we just sat together on the bed, with Tamsin's voice going on in the dark, soft and toneless, and I couldn't even put my arm around her. "Courting me, from the very first—there, at my parents' table, before their eyes—and taking such grand pleasure in his knowledge that there was naught they could do against my Lord Justice George Jeffreys. And leaning forward, whispering, offering slips of orange between his fingers, like to a man feeding a pet bird. I see him still, Jenny. I see him now."

"He was sort of handsome, wasn't he?" I said. "Pretty eyes." Tamsin was staring at me. "I mean, in his pictures, anyway."

If nobody ever again, for the whole damn rest of my life, looks at me the way Tamsin did then, I'll be just as happy. I honestly thought she might never be going to *speak* to me again, but after about a year she said, "Pretty eyes. So they were—nor did he ever take them from me in all that time, not for two minutes together. Edric would be playing, and the portraitist daubing and scratching, my father snoring—and those *pretty* eyes so softly on me. . . ."

"He came to see you being painted?" I should have figured that—Meena would have. "So he saw Edric, and . . . he saw Edric and you?"

"He saw everything." She began to sound a little more like the

Tamsin I knew then, speaking faster and with a bit of expression back in her voice. "Aye, he knew the truth of us, I think before *we* did! He never spoke word to Edric, but whiles that gentle gaze would rise to take the two of us in—never more than a moment, a single breath—and Jenny, the *pit*, the fiery, filthy cavern just below that gentleness! Afterward—him having taken his leave at last—I'd weep and shiver all night, and bite my fingers with fear, and no way Edric could ever come to comfort me. And one still night—once only, somewhere in the house—I heard my mother weeping as well."

I felt like Edric, unable to cross three hundred years to hold her and say, *It's all right, it's all right. I won't let anything bad happen,* as though that would have helped. All I could do was ask helplessly dumb things like, "Did he ever get you—I mean, were you ever alone with him?"

"Always," Tamsin said. She was turning her hands over and over in her lap, and she looked like a child being scolded for something she hadn't done. She said, "Jenny, when he was in this house, it made no matter who else was here. Not servants, not my parents—not Edric, even. Dissolved, *vanished,* every one, leaving me alone . . . there was nothing but *him,* no one to stand between us, do you take me? And no hope, for all knew he would surely ask for me when his horrible Assizes was done, and who in Dorset would say Judge Jeffreys nay? Who would dare?"

She tried to grip my hand, and I felt that little cool breath that sometimes happened between us. "Do you wonder I fear him still, Jenny, even to speak of? Do you wonder I forget?"

"No," I said, "no, of course not, of course I don't." Her smell had changed—not vanilla now, but sharper, drier, almost making me sneeze. I took a gamble. I said, "But Edric said nay, didn't he? *No,* I mean. Edric dared."

A big, fuzzy moth was thumping and flopping against the window, just crazy to get to the faint ghost-light, which was the only brightness in the room. I pushed again, like the moth. "You did run away. You made your plans, just like the first time, and you ran away together. *Tell* me, Tamsin."

I didn't call her often by her name; maybe that's what got her attention. She looked straight in my eyes, and her voice grew stronger, with a calm pride in it now. She said, "Yes. We chose our night once again."

I didn't exactly jump in the air and yell my head off for Guy

Guthrie and Julian—"I was *right*! *Yes*! They *did* run away! I was *right*!"—but I came pretty close. Tamsin said, "No ladder to my casement, no whistles or birdcalls for signal. We were to meet in twilight, at a crumbling old cow byre to which my parents knew me accustomed to walk in the evenings. Little margin it left us before our flight were noticed—but the portrait was near done, and Edric had two days' hire left at best. No choice, you see."

Outside, in the hallway, Sally: "Jenny? You still up, babe?" Nights when she can't sleep, she prowls like old Albert, making certain that all her sheep are tucked in safely. I mumbled something about working on an oral presentation for school. She didn't especially believe me—I can always feel that with Sally—but she just called, "Well, get some sleep sometime," and left it alone. I really, *really* like my mother.

"I was clever, Jenny," Tamsin said. "I walked out to the byre the day before, and there concealed a portmanteau containing a change of clothes and sturdy shoes as well. No food—Edric was to bring that—and no keepsake but a miniature of my sister, Maria. Which was not theft, for my father gave it me." Tamsin was always picky and precise about things like that. After a moment she added, "I saw the Black Dog that day."

Better and better. I hadn't even thought to put the Black Dog in the story. "He came to warn you not to go," I said. "But you went anyway."

Tamsin was far away, not looking at me now, but ages beyond me. "I cannot tell you his errand, nor how I responded, for I hardly saw him at all, so full I was of plans and dreams and terrors. Next day's weather was cool and blowy, with a smell of rain. My father and brothers were in Dorchester, not to return till late afternoon—my mother was advising a friend's daughter on her wedding. I came down the stairs for the last time as bold and trembling as though I were already a bride myself, saying farewell to all I loved, all I understood, walking away with my husband. I wept, dear Jenny, and I blessed my family a dozen times over and begged their forgiveness, and I walked away."

I saw her, you know. I did. Probably partly because of the way ghosts *change* when they remember something that intensely—but I'll swear forever that it was more than that. Her eyes were brighter than I'd ever seen them, bright as flowers in moonlight, and she was *there* in them, three hundred years before—she was on the stairs in this same house, so frightened she could hardly stand up, and so wildly happy, and so brave. It was there still, that moment, in her own eyes.

"But you didn't go to meet him? What *happened?*" My voice sounded like a dry little cricket chirp, far away. The room had grown darker; or maybe that was Tamsin's brightness gathering—I don't know. I thought she'd take a long time answering me, but she didn't.

"I did set forth to meet Edric," she said. "But he was not the one I met." Miss Sophia Brown appeared on her lap half a second before Mister Cat eased through the window and poured himself into mine. They were both looking very pleased about one cat thing or another, and promptly settled down to washing each other's faces. Tamsin said, "I had taken but a dozen steps beyond my doorstep when *he* was there. Smiling, bowing over my hand, murmuring that he should be properly disappointed to find my family gone from home, but could not, so enchanted was he at this chance to speak with me in sweet solitude." Her voice had dropped into a nasty dry whisper, like insect wings rubbing together, and she kept going back and forth between that voice and her own as she talked.

"I told him that my parents would return quite soon, and that he might await them within and welcome. He answers me, nay, but he'll pass our farm quite by and rate such hospitality poor stuff indeed if I'd not bide him company a while. And truly he means more by that than the mere words. There's naught in England to hinder him from declaring my father Monmouth's fellow and agent—naught but his fancy for me, and well he knew *I* knew it. We looked each other in the eyes, Jenny, and both of us knew *all.*"

She laughed suddenly, which spooked me about as much as if she'd cursed or screamed. "Aye, there was a droll moment, if you will, set snug in horror like a currant into a Yorkshire pudding. I told him I was in the habit of my evening stroll, and he replied on the instant, he was bound to convoy me, to see me safe from just such vile rebels as he'd that day been sending by the score to meet their black Master in hell. And ere I could speak, there's my arm tight through his, and him guiding me down the path to the byre where Edric waits for me." She looked at me as though she'd just now remembered I was there, and she smiled, almost mockingly. "As good as a play, is't not, Jenny?"

And it was that, all right. I couldn't speak for *seeing* her: alone, arm in arm with that soft-eyed monster, him bending down to her, breathing on her, moving her along . . . and her unsuspecting lover in the cowshed: a rebel himself, or the next thing to it. I just about managed to croak out, like Julian, "What did you *do?*"

"Do? I did nothing—a blessed wet rock did it all. The rain had begun—my ankle turned—I fell, drawing him down with me." The laugh was closer to a gasp this time, as though she was falling again, right there. "He bore me back to the house, arranging me on a couch, and propping up my ankle, tender as a nurse—indeed, I believe he would have salved and bandaged me, had I let him. And all the while crooning to me, vowing he's never been so ensorcelled, and I must truly be a witch, and he knows what to do with witches. And then he laughs, to show 'twas all meant as love-talk. I think it was, Jenny. God's mercy, but I think so."

She stood up, pushing Miss Sophia Brown off her lap (the Persian reacted just as indignantly as though she'd been a real cat), and walked to my window. I'll always wonder what she saw, standing with her back to me, looking out into one night or another. I could see the moon through her left shoulder.

"He spoke to me of marriage," she said quietly. "Marriage and hanging—the same voice, the same passion, 'twas all one to that man. Oh, aye, he was already wed, but what of that? his wife was rotten with consumption, unlikely to last the year. I would be a baroness, the lady wife of the Lord Chief Justice, living a life as far above this jumped-up croft as it would be above a shepherd's hut. Land, society, horses, servants—and him merely the first among those, ever at my side, as now, asking only my love and approval." She turned, and when she smiled this time I saw the crooked wolf tooth. "Oh, it does come back in your presence, my Jenny," she said, "it comes back. There was a reason the cats brought you to me."

"And all that time you were worrying about Edric," I said. "He was carrying on, proposing to you and everything, and you must have been just frantic, thinking about Edric—"

Tamsin laughed a third time, and this one came out dry and small and rueful. "Oh, aye—nor was I the only one. For of a sudden, between this fond word and that, Judge Jeffreys's hands were gripping my arms like fetters, and his face was kissing-close to mine so I could only see his eyes—his great, gentle, terrible eyes. His lips did hardly move when he spoke to me again, saying, 'And as for that twangling fool in the cowshed, you need have no dismay on his score. He never purposed to wait your coming, but was gone from there ere you had set out. And I know this, Mistress Willoughby, because I passed that way coming here.' His hands on me, Jenny. I cannot feel, and yet I feel them now."

I felt them myself. I said, "He knew? About Edric and Francis Gollop and everything?"

"He knew," Tamsin said. "He held me there, and he told me what he knew, and told me further what fate Edric and my father merited, who had knowingly harbored a damned rebel against His Majesty James II—aye, and even dared remove the body for the Christian burial it had forfeited, in direct violation of the King's own command. Oh, Jenny, Jenny, it comes back."

How can I write what she looked like—my Tamsin—made so bright by her own memory, and cringing away from it at the same time? She said, "He went on, on, half raving, half singing—now swearing eternal adoration, now threatening horror to my entire family if I were denied him. After a time I but half heard him, Jenny, so hard was I listening for my father's returning—and for Edric as well, come at last to carry me safe away. But there was no one, and the rain fell harder."

I couldn't just sit still. I dumped Mister Cat, stood up and went to her, standing as close—*kissing-close*, she'd called it—as maybe the Judge had been that day; so close that the ghost-glimmer seemed to fall right on me, like moonlight. Tamsin touched my hair, but I couldn't feel it.

"I ran," she said. "The moment those hands loosened on me in the slightest, I was up and out, splashing and sliding toward the cow byre once again, for I would never credit that Edric had abandoned me. Behind me I hear *him* calling furiously, but I dare not look back, hard as it was to keep my balance on the wet stones. I fall, I fell—the ankle turns grievously under me a second time—and I was near crawling when at last I reached the byre." She turned away, back toward the window. There hadn't been any rain that day, but the buildings and fences and bits of machinery I could see were all glinting in the moon like new grass.

Tamsin said, "Edric was not there. My portmanteau was there still—and his traveling bag beside it—but not he. I stand in the rain, holding to the byre door, staring and staring within—and then I truly run, Jenny, lame ankle and all. I cannot say *where* I ran, for my wits were as gone from me as Edric, whose name I shrieked into the storm until I fell. This time—or perhaps the next, or the next—I lay where I'd fallen."

I couldn't say anything, and she didn't speak again for a long while. " 'Twas the Pooka found me, else I'd have stopped there. He'd taken the guise of my brother Hugh, but I remember yet those yellow eyes looking down at me as he carried me home. My mother put me to bed."

Saying that, she suddenly realized that I was standing barefoot beside her, and she got really upset, almost angry with me. "Get into bed yourself, child, at once! Am I to have you catching a chill and dying of it"—and that was the *one* time she used the word—"as I did? *That* I'll not have." Just the way she'd said it to the Pooka when she came flying to rescue me. In the middle of everything, I was absolutely thrilled.

"That's how it happened," I said. "It really *is* like my story, sort of."

Tamsin blinked in puzzlement at that, but she went on talking. "I lingered some days—just how long, I cannot say, for they swam all around me, the days, in and out, like fish. My parents and brothers were always at my bedside, whenever I should open my eyes; and *he* came every day, his labors at the Assizes done, to clasp my hand and gaze tenderly upon me by the hour. But my mother made sure never to leave me alone with him, dread him as she might, for she guessed something of what had passed between us. Indeed, it was he who was nearest when I drew my last breath in this world."

I'd gotten into bed by then, and she meant to sit on the edge, but she couldn't do it. It was as though she'd suddenly forgotten sitting, forgotten what bodies have to do so they can sit down on a bed, or in her own chair in her little secret room. She looked frightened—anyway, I think she did, because she was beginning to fade, and it was hard to be sure. I said, "Tell me. Tell me what you remember." Because I *knew* it was important, though I couldn't have said why, not then.

She tried to tell me. "He spoke," she said. "He leaned close—for a moment he was Edric, but the eyes . . . the eyes betrayed him. . . ." Like the Pooka again, I thought weirdly. Tamsin said, "He whispered to me. He took both my hands in one of his, and he leaned over me, and he *whispered* . . ."

And she was gone.

I couldn't even call after her, for fear of waking someone. But I couldn't just fluff my pillow and crash, even if I'd wanted to, which I didn't, because I knew what I'd dream. So I sat up and hugged my knees—and Julian's gorilla—and I thought about things until morning came.

Twenty-one

Spring came the way it does in Dorset, like a really small child hiding behind a curtain to pounce out at the grown-up world for a moment, and then dash right back into cover. Tony's mustache actually took hold, and Julian quit sleeping with the stuffed turtle that was Elvis' successor. The first no-till crops looked promising—although Evan kept warning us and the Lovells that there'd probably be a yield hit this year, until the soil got used to the new regime. But when he spaded up a chunk of black dirt, it crumbled pretty easily in his hand, and there were a lot of earthworms, which even I know is a good sign. Evan said it was too stiff by half, wouldn't be proper for a couple of years yet, but he looked happy.

The April nights were way too cold to go walking with Tamsin, so I mostly went to her room (which was cold enough—we didn't have any heating in the east wing then), or in Tony's studio, where she used to watch him practicing and sigh now and then: a long, liquid, three-hundred-year-old adolescent sigh that used to embarrass me even more than it made me jealous. Tony never heard it, never noticed it at all, and tried really hard not to notice me. I envied him his gift and his devotion, and I envied him Tamsin's worship; but for once that seemed to be happening far away, in some other region of myself. I had bigger, scarier fish to fry.

She didn't remember a single word that Judge Jeffreys had said to her on her deathbed. She didn't even remember a lot of the things she'd already told me; that's how hard she shrank away from thinking about that man, three centuries later. I made things worse because I kept asking her if it could have had anything to do with Edric Davies. Because I couldn't get rid of the idea that Judge Jeffreys might have met him at the cow byre on his way to the Manor to make his awful proposal to Tamsin. And Edric might have been younger, and maybe even stronger, but he wouldn't have stood a chance. I knew that much.

It took me a while to understand that what she *did* remember was her desperate anger at Edric for not being there when she scrambled up that rainsoaked path, not coming to protect her when those hands were pinning her arms. She felt it still, that anger, but by now it was all mixed up with three hundred years' worth of regret and confusion and fear—three hundred years of never *knowing*. Guy Guthrie says that there are ghosts who go mad after their deaths. I don't know why Tamsin didn't.

That cow byre isn't there, of course—nothing left but a kind of impression of the floor. I'd never have found it if Tamsin hadn't guided me out there one afternoon when I should have been helping Sally in her garden. There wasn't anything to look at, but I stood still for a long time, trying to see into the past the way Tamsin did. But I couldn't find a foothold, a place to begin imagining . . . except maybe one thing. The wild grasses had long since taken the place back completely; all but a single small area, about the size of a bath mat, bare and bald as a brick. I pointed it out to Tamsin, and she said it was right where the door had been—maybe a few inches inside and to the right. Some things she remembered like a photograph after all the years. I just couldn't ever be sure which they'd be.

"Seems weird, the grass not growing in that one place," I said. "I wonder what would cause that."

"My mother says—" Tamsin began. She stopped herself, and then she said it again, very deliberately. "My mother says that nothing will grow where a murderer lies. Or where a virgin has been martyred—for she inclines just a bit to papistry on some points, does my mother. Or where the Wild Hunt has set foot."

I froze on the spot—it actually felt as though hands had reached out of the tall grass and grabbed my ankles. The whole notion of those mad, laughing horsemen wheeling down from the night sky, leaping to earth, stalking this ground where I stood, where Tamsin Willoughby had come running desperately to find her man . . . to find *what?* You'd think seeing the Wild Hunt close to would be something that stayed with you, but Tamsin went completely blank on that—all she remembered was Edric's absence and the Pooka carrying her home. But I kept standing in that empty place, staring at the patch where nothing grew.

*   *   *

On the first halfway warm weekend Meena and I went on a picnic. Julian wanted to come, but he also wanted to go to a big football match in Dorchester, and football won. Meena brought an
Indian box lunch for the two of us, and I chipped in Sally's stuffed
mushrooms, which Meena adores, and a thermos of iced coffee.
We got started late, because Dr. Chari had an emergency to handle at the Yeovil hospital before she could bring Meena, so Sally
told us not to worry about getting back, as long as we were home
for dinner. She did want to know where we'd be picnicking, and I
told her probably around the Hundred-Acre Wood. Not *in*—not
after that first time—but somewhere around.

It's a good hike to the Hundred-Acre Wood: uphill, pretty much,
but not *too* uphill, and the path mostly runs through land that
probably hasn't been cultivated since Roger Willoughby's time. All
kinds of berries growing wild, and some elm and ash trees that look
even older than Tamsin's beeches, and a lot of snug little dells just
perfect for spreading out the tablecloth and unrolling the mats.
Meena sang songs from Indian movies as we walked. She says
they're incredibly silly, but I'm getting so I like them. After that we
sang practically the entire score of *My Fair Lady*.

It was a nice picnic, maybe the best we ever had. We took our
time about everything—didn't even start eating right away, but
dozed in the sun a bit, "like bears coming out of hibernation,"
Meena said. She'd brought a book of poems with her, and we took
turns reading a few aloud. I can't remember which ones now, but
it was fun.

We'd skirted wide around the Hundred-Acre Wood when we
came up to find a picnic spot; but by the time we were ready to
start home, the late sun was shining on it at an angle that made
the young new oak leaves glow like emeralds, and the forest itself
look golden and sleepy and magical. Meena kept glancing over at
it while we were packing up the picnic stuff, and all of a sudden
she said, "It would be so much shorter to go back straight through
the Wood. Let's do that, Jenny."

"Let's not, how about that?" I said. "You *hated* the place—we all
did. Very bad idea."

Meena scowled. She doesn't do it well, but it's cute. "I was
scared," she said. "I don't like being scared. It'll bother me until I
do something about it."

When Meena gets locked in on something, that's the end of it. She'll always listen, she's always polite, but you might as well not bother. Even Chris Herridge would have found that out, sooner or later.

We were halfway to the Hundred-Acre Wood, making good time on the downhill walk, when I saw the Black Dog.

He was flanking us on the right, keeping between us and the Wood. Daytime or not, he looked just as black as he'd looked in moonlight, and maybe even bigger. Not a sound out of him—no bark, no breath, no footsteps in the grass—nothing but those red, red eyes fixed on me. I stopped where I was. I said, "What do you want?"

Meena was walking a little way ahead of me. She turned around, blinking. "What? Did you say something, Jenny?"

The Black Dog had stopped walking when I did. I asked again, louder this time. "What the hell do you *want?*"

"Jenny," Meena said. She came up to me, partly blocking my view of the Black Dog. "Jenny, who are you talking to?"

"The Black Dog, for God's sake. Don't you see him?" Because Tamsin's one thing—I can imagine how some people might not notice a wispy, transparent ghost, even if she's practically sitting in their laps, the way she always was with Tony. But the Black Dog looks like a solid chunk of midnight that somebody hacked into the shape of a dog. Other people *have* seen him, I know that, there are books. I still don't understand how it all works.

"The Black Dog," Meena said. She turned to look where I was pointing, and then back at me. "Jenny, I don't see anything." She was keeping her voice as even as she could, the way people do when they're really worried about you. "I don't see a dog."

"It's all right," I said. "I'll explain." I moved her out of the way, very gently, and I asked the Black Dog again, "*What?* What *is* it?"

Nothing. I don't know what I expected—he'd never made a sound, even to Tamsin, or told her anything useful, except to watch out for some aggravation or other. But when I started walking again (with Meena sticking close and looking anxious), so did he, always edging us away from the Hundred-Acre Wood, like Albert steering those idiot sheep. I'm not quite *that* dumb, so I told Meena, "The Black Dog always comes as an omen. He's telling us to stay out of the Wood."

Meena stopped studying me as though I were crazy and just started to laugh, standing there with her hands on her hips. "And that's it? That's what all this is about? You don't want to cut through the Wood, so—*voilà!*—here comes the Black Dog to warn us off. *Really,* Jenny." She was trying to look stern and severe, but she was giggling too much to pull it off. She said, "Well. You *and* the Black Dog will just stay out of the Wood, and *I* will be waiting for you at the Lightning Tree," which was a storm-splintered alder where we'd veered away from the oak forest on the way up. "Just don't take too long. I want my tea." And she started straight off into the Wood, walking right past the Black Dog. He didn't move to follow her, or block her path again—didn't even look after her, any more than she looked back to see if I was coming. Just at me.

Well, there wasn't any damn choice, obviously. I met the Black Dog's red eyes, spread my hands, lifted my shoulders, mumbled, "Yeah, I know, I know," and followed Meena. I looked back once, and of course he was gone. He'd done *his* job.

I walked a little way into the wood, along the path Meena had taken. Tamsin had only made me promise never to walk in an oak forest after sundown, and we still had plenty of daylight left. But oak forests are different from pine woods. Under the pines it's dark and cool almost from the moment you step into their shadow; but with oaks, at first you still feel that you're walking in sunlight. For a while. Scuba diving's like that, I remember: warm and sparkly near the surface, with the light drifting down through the water; but the deeper you go, the scarier it gets, until it's ice-cold night and going to be night forever. That's the way the Hundred-Acre Wood is, once you're inside.

Meena was already half out of sight, bending to duck under an overhanging branch, when I saw the red cap. Just the one, with no face under it, no body. It looked like a toadstool—no, more like a fat red thumb bobbing up from behind a scrubby berry bush and disappearing so fast I wasn't even sure I'd seen it. I stopped in my tracks—still just on the edge of the wood, and I called to Meena, but she didn't hear me.

I couldn't tell if the second red cap was the same as the first or different: It popped out of a rotten log—bloodred, sticky blood just starting to dry—and gone again. I yelled then, as loud as I possibly could, "Meena! Get back here! *Meena!*"

To me it seemed as though the oak trees were swallowing up my voice, but a moment later Meena reappeared around a bend in the narrow path. "What? Did you call me, Jenny?"

She hadn't seen the red caps at all. I didn't want to scare her, so I lowered my voice a little. I said, "Come back here. Please. Now."

Meena stared at me. "Oh, don't tell me the Black Dog has made another appearance? Jenny, you can do what you like, but I am walking straight through this wood and out the other side. That's all there is to that, I mean it."

My throat was dry and tight, and I was shaking, going burning hot and then absolutely icy by turns. I told her, "Meena, if you take another step, I will drag you back out of this place by the hair. And I mean *that*, and you know I do."

She did know. I spotted another red cap over her shoulder, flirting through branches, quick as a squirrel's tail, no chance to get a fix on it. I was frantic for Meena to *move*, but she only stood looking at me for what felt like hours. Then she started back along the path toward me, walking slowly, not saying a word.

"Move!" I said, but she wouldn't come any faster. I was afraid she'd stop altogether if I pushed her any more, so I just stood waiting until she reached me and stalked on past. When her hair brushed my face, she jerked her head away.

Just before we came out of the Hundred-Acre Wood, I turned and saw a face. It looked like melted candlewax, the color of bacon fat, except for the blobby red nose. The eyes were round as a doll's eyes, and they watched us from a hole in a hollow tree with a no-color hatred that made me stumble against Meena. There was a smell, too, I remember, all around us, like a refrigerator that really needs cleaning out.

Meena saw the face, too. We didn't say anything to each other. We just got out of there. When we looked back at the forest, we didn't see a single red cap anywhere, but the branches of the oaks were lashing as wildly as though a storm were on the way. Beyond the fence, where we stood, the air wasn't moving at all.

Meena and I did start running then, and we didn't slow down until we were completely out of sight of the Hundred-Acre Wood, and we didn't talk for a while after that. The sun was setting fast, but I could have gotten us home in the dark. Finally I said, "I'm sorry I talked to you that way."

"Well, you had to, didn't you?" Meena said. She stopped walking and turned to face me. "You *knew* we shouldn't go into the wood," she said. "A *thing* came to warn you—a Black Dog, or whatever it was. You tried to tell me, but I wouldn't listen."

"It's hard to believe stuff like that, first off." I couldn't tell if she was still mad at me or not—and with Meena you know—but I had an uneasy feeling, looking at her.

"But what you *aren't* telling me is how you knew. And you haven't been telling me for a long time now." She was mad, all right, but mad in a different way than I'd ever seen her, level and cold. She said, "Talk to me, Jenny."

I can't remember what I answered, and it doesn't matter—I'd probably be ashamed to recall whatever I tried to get away with. Meena just stood there looking like that, saying, "It's been going on for months—even Julian's noticed the way you've been behaving. How stupid do you think I am, Jenny?"

So, at last, I told her about Tamsin.

I *would* have told her—I was *planning* to, whenever the right moment came up—but the fact is I hadn't, and she was my best friend, and she had every right to do what she did, once I was through, which was to chew me up one side and down the other in that same flat, un-Meena voice. I took it without a word, not looking at her, until she ran out of gas, and then I just said in the silence, hoping I wasn't going to cry, "Meena, I'm sorry."

Meena said, "You could have trusted me. I don't mean just to keep your secret—I mean to believe you. Of all people, do you think I don't know about ghosts? About night creatures? About spirits, fairies, things that can change their shape?" Her eyes were getting brighter and brighter, and I was afraid *she* was going to start crying, which would have been even worse than me. "You *know* I would have believed you, Jenny."

I couldn't say anything. We stood still, the two of us, both *twanging* like fiddle strings about to go, and me wishing I were dead. Only time in my life so far I've ever wished such a thing, but I'll know it if it happens again. Then Meena began to smile, just a little bit, brushing the back of her hand very quickly across her eyes. "But you went after me," she said. "You followed me into the wood, even though you were warned not to. You brought me back."

"Well, I'm not *all* dork," I mumbled. "Not all the way through." So then we *both* cried, and we hugged each other, and we went on home together, not saying much. With the lights of Stourhead Farm in sight, Meena suddenly turned to me and asked me, "Jenny, what do you think they wanted with us, those things—what did you say *she* called them?"

"Oakmen," I said. "I *think* those were Oakmen, but I don't know what the hell they are, or what they'd have done. I don't know anything about this place, Meena. I thought I did, but I don't. You remember that if I ever start saying I know."

The first time I brought Meena to Tamsin's secret room, Tamsin wasn't there. I was starting to get as jumpy as the billy-blind about all her roaming around—because it was my fault, I'd started her doing that—but Meena was fascinated by the hidden lock, and by that little closet with the one dark window, and I was too busy explaining everything to her to worry much then. But later we sneaked a glance into Tony's studio and didn't see Tamsin there either, and that's when it started to get to me. I kept thinking about Judge Jeffreys—the Other One, whatever that really meant—and all the bewildering things the Pooka had said about me being the only one who could help. I told Meena all that stuff, too.

But Tamsin did show up, just before Meena had to go home. We were sitting in that double swing Evan had made, waiting for Mr. Chari to arrive—and like that, there she was, perched between us on the back of the swing, smiling at me in that way that always turned my insides to chocolate syrup. I said, "Meena, she's here."

Meena whirled around, her face actually flushing with excitement. "*Where,* Jenny? Show me!"

I pointed grandly and made my introduction. "Mistress Tamsin Willoughby, this is my dear friend Meena Chari. Miss Meena, I have the honor to introduce Tamsin Elspeth Catherine Maria Dubois Willoughby, of Stourhead Farm." And I bowed and waited for them to discover each other.

But it didn't work out like that. Tamsin was shaking her head sadly, and Meena was looking wide-eyed in all directions, still asking, "Where, Jenny? Where is she?" I'll never forget the sound of her voice right then. Like a little girl growing more and more afraid that the parade or the show or the party has already started without her.

She hadn't seen the Black Dog. She didn't see Tamsin. I didn't know what to do. I asked, "Can you smell her?"

Meena nodded. In the same small voice, she said, "I know she's here. I just . . ." She let it trail off. Tamsin leaned forward and put her hand on Meena's cheek. Meena stiffened where she sat, and her eyes got very wide. She looked at me, and I nodded, and Meena said, "Oh," but not so I could hear it. I had to turn my head away for a moment. I didn't think I ought to see her like that.

"It's not fair," I said. "It should be you."

That snapped Meena out of it fast. "What? Why? Because I *look* right?—because you think I *look* like someone who should be able to see ghosts? You have to stop that, Jenny, right now. It's degrading to you, and it makes me feel really bad. She chose you to talk to, when she's never spoken to anyone else, and if that doesn't tell you something about yourself, then I don't know what will. I think that's my father coming."

It was. Meena stood up and turned toward where she thought Tamsin was sitting—I had to move her just a little. She said clearly, "Good-bye. I'm happy that you speak to my friend Jenny. She's the best person you could have on your side, you can take my word for that." She stopped for a moment, touching her cheek, and then she said, "If you can hear me—I'm on your side, too." Then she ran to meet Mr. Chari, and I stood with Tamsin, watching her go.

Twenty-two

Tamsin scolded me about the Oakmen. I'd thought Meena had really worked me over, but after Tamsin got through, there wasn't enough left to recycle. "Witling, gommeril, logger-head, are you mad then? After all my cautions, to walk in that accursed wood of your own choice, *knowing*? Mistress Jenny Gluckstein, what can have possessed you? What cloud came over your brain-pan, tell me?" There was a lot more. She was so furious that she lost all her usual transparency—she looked as solid as Sally while she was laying into me. I was so fascinated to see her like that, I know I missed some great seventeenth-century words.

It didn't help at all when I pointed out that I'd only gone in a little way, and only after Meena—that I couldn't let her go alone just because she wouldn't pay any attention to my warning. Tamsin ran right over that one. "Never gainsay me, child—it was for you to keep her out of danger in the first place. *There's* where you should have laid hold of her hair, the very moment she spoke of entering the wood." Oh, she was sizzling, she was wonderful!

In time she cooled down (though she remembered how angry she'd been—and why—well after I expected she'd have forgotten). She stood in front of me and touched my cheek, the way she'd done with Meena.

"Jenny," she whispered. "My dear Mistress Jenny, do you not yet know that I fear losing you even as I fear . . ." She didn't finish, but started over. "Dear Jenny, you well know the perils of your own world, but now you walk somewhat in mine as well, and you must heed what little I can tell you of it. There are worse than Oakmen abroad in what you call night."

"I love it," I said. "I don't care what's running loose in your world, I love it a lot more than mine. I love walking around at night, even when I'm not with you, just *knowing*. Even in the day-time, everything's different, because I *know*."

"No," Tamsin said sharply, "no, you do *not* know," and we were right back at why I shouldn't have let Meena set one foot into the Hundred-Acre Wood. But her heart wasn't nearly as much in it: She kept fading, reappearing, fading out again, as though she were being pulled back and forth between her own time and this one, memories grabbing at her this way, things she wanted to tell me yanking her back the other way. Finally she just gave up and vanished, but even that wasn't quite right—she didn't blink out instantly, but lingered for a moment, a soap-bubble Tamsin, with dust motes falling through her sad eyes. I didn't see her for days after that.

I saw the Pooka a lot that spring, though: never again face-to-face in a room, but always from a distance, in the shape of a bird, a hare, a badger rolling along on its toes, a young red deer with the velvet still on its antlers. He might not be able to be any help to Tamsin, but he was definitely keeping watch on the farm—or on her and me. Meena said from what I told her about him, the Pooka reminded her a little of Hanuman, the Monkey King: wise and strong, and very mischievous, but always on the side of good. I wouldn't have gone that far—I still wouldn't, even after what he did for us—but I was glad to see him. More glad than not, anyway.

Because something *was* moving around Stourhead Farm that spring, just as the billy-blind had warned me, and finally even I could feel it. It wasn't only my on-and-off dreams about Judge Jeffreys, and it wasn't Mister Cat's occasional nighttime go-rounds with things that always seemed to have too many legs and weren't ever there when I went down in the morning to check out his body count. It wasn't even the Wild Hunt baying across the sky time and time—once I even halfway slept through it, I was getting so used to them. It was Tamsin.

She was increasingly restless, in a way I'd never seen before. By now I knew her as well, I guess, as you can know someone who died three hundred years before you were born. I usually knew where she was likely to be if I couldn't find her in her room or Tony's studio—out talking to those beech trees of hers, or curled in Evan's swing with Miss Sophia Brown, and probably Mister Cat as well. Once in a while she liked to be in the kitchen when Sally or Evan was cooking. She couldn't explain exactly why to me; one time she said, "I have no sense of smell, but an *imagination* of smell—can you comprehend such a thing, Jenny?" I couldn't. Tamsin said, "Besides, there's comfort in a kitchen, always, for me as much as any other." That one I did understand.

But lately I couldn't tell, not only where to find her, but just how she'd be when I did. I'd see her sometimes in places where I'd never come across her before: walking the fields among Evan's workers, or sitting at Sally's piano with her poor transparent hands stretched out over the keys, as though she could make them move up and down by plain will. Most often, when I spoke to her, she'd wheel around, looking absolutely terrified, and vanish. It would take me forever to get her to come back, and *then* generally she wouldn't know me, sometimes for a couple of days. Once she didn't even know Miss Sophia Brown.

The worst thing was, I had a terrible feeling that I knew why it was happening to her. *She* certainly didn't, and there wasn't any point asking the Pooka or the billy-blind—neither one of them was worth a damn at saying anything useful straight out, anyway. So I talked to Meena.

I'd kept my promise about that, even though I was so much in the habit of not saying a word about Tamsin to anyone that it was really work. But it was worth it, too: Not just for the plain relief of dropping all my fears and confusions in someone else's lap, but because of who that someone was. I said, "It's the Other One, Judge Jeffreys. The billy-blind kept warning me. Meena, he's not gone, the way she told me—he's somewhere close by, and the more restless she gets, the more active, so does he. And she knows it, or she halfway knows it, and she's so frightened she can barely hold herself together. That's what I think, anyway."

We were in the Charis' kitchen, and Meena was showing me how to make a *pillau*. Over her shoulder she said, "You think he might still be here, still waiting on earth, because of his obsession with her? Is that how it is with ghosts?"

"Is it? You're the one who grew up with them—you tell me. I'm just starting to wonder if maybe *she's* held here because of some obsession of her own. Something to do with Edric, with what happened to him. I don't *know*, Meena."

"In the south they put coconut milk in with the stock," Meena said. "My mother doesn't do that, but I like it. Do you know what

I wish?" I didn't say anything. Meena said, "I'd like to see that painting of her."

"I asked her about it once," I said. "She didn't have any idea where it might be, after so long. I've looked for it a few times, but if it's in the house I'm not seeing it. Anyway, I don't know what help it'd be. She says the guy was a rotten painter."

"This isn't an art class. Watch now—when you put the rice in for frying, you have to do it with your fingers, so the grains fall separately. *Watch,* Jenny! I still think it might tell us *something,* the painting."

So we went looking. Whenever Meena was over for an afternoon or a weekend, we slipped off and went through the Manor—east wing, west wing, all three floors, and every damn room we could get into, including my lady's chamber, just in case Roger Willoughby'd been into hiding more than chaplains. Nothing. Meena was all for scraping off some of the older portraits, on the chance that the one of Tamsin might have been painted over, but I was afraid to try that. We did pry a lot of them out of their frames, though; and we spent a whole miserable day in the cellar, digging blindly around under incredibly dirty drapes and sheets, and layers of rotting cloth that crumbled away to black powder the moment you touched it. Nothing. Wherever that portrait of Tamsin was, if it was still in the house, we'd never find it.

It wasn't in the house. It was hanging on the wall in the Judge Jeffreys Restaurant.

I'd never gone in, out of pure snobbery, so I wouldn't have known. Meena had, and she'd actually noticed the picture, but of course she didn't recognize it. The only reason I ever saw the thing was that Sally dragged me into the Restaurant one afternoon when we'd been shopping for a long time, and I was suddenly hungry enough that I didn't care where we ate. Even under the sign with that man's dreadful gentle face on it was all right with me.

The portrait hangs in a dark corner at the rear of the Restaurant, so I didn't see it until I was on my way to the john. Then I about wet myself right there, but the ironic thing is that I forgot I had to go. I just stood staring at the painting—not *seeing* it, you understand, just gaping, slowly realizing what it was. Because there couldn't be two like that: Tamsin Willoughby, nineteen years old, but looking not much older than me—maybe because the loose white gown she wore was a bit too big for her—with her hair done up high in tumbly curls, the way she remembered it, and her eyes full of someone who wasn't on the canvas. I don't know how the painter got it, as awful as he was supposed to be, but somehow you could see Edric in the turn of her neck and the lift of her chin. Just across the room, playing for her, trying like mad not to turn his own head, and turning anyway. . . .

It took forever for Meena and me to get into Dorchester together, until we managed to arrange to meet her father at the university for dinner. That gave us time to have tea by ourselves at the Judge Jeffreys Restaurant, and we stood in front of the portrait of Tamsin for a long time, neither of us saying a word.

"Is that really how she looks?" Meena's voice was very quiet and young.

"Yes," I said, "exactly. Except sometimes, when she forgets."

We didn't say anything more for some while after that, and then Meena said, "There's somebody else."

I said, "*What?* No, there isn't. *Where?*"

Meena pointed. The painter had posed Tamsin in a chair with a tall, narrow back and no armrests. There was a small table to her right, with a book open on it, and to her left a bigger table with some kind of beaker made of copper, or even gold; the painting was too old and dirty to be sure. Meena said, "Look at that. Closely, Jenny."

In the surface of the beaker—and you had to squint to be sure it wasn't one more smudge on the canvas—I could just dimly make out a face. Only part of a face, really, but I didn't need more than a part. I felt my hand at my mouth, though I couldn't remember how it got there.

"He's in the portrait," Meena said. "The painter put him in."

I didn't waste time saying no, no, impossible, it couldn't be. It was him, all right. Maybe the painter thought it helped the composition somehow; more likely he did it out of flattery; most likely Judge Jeffreys ordered him to do it, and who was going to refuse? But why did the Judge—the Other One—why did he *want* to be in Tamsin's portrait? The man might have been completely loose in the flue, but when it came to Tamsin he didn't do anything without a reason. So we just stood there, Meena and I, looking and wondering, while our tea got cold.

On our way out of the cafe to meet Mr. Chari, we ran into Mrs.

Fallowfield. I was *always* running into Mrs. Fallowfield back then. She lived alone on a tiny farm not far from ours, mostly growing apples, pears, cherries, and I think walnuts. How she managed everything by herself, nobody could quite figure, but she never hired anyone to help with the harvest, or with the grafting and fertilizing either. A tall, skinny woman who could have been sixty or ninety-five, all knobby bones and bundles of gristly muscle, with no lips—just a down-curving slash, like a shark—and bright, hard blue eyes. She wore jeans, thick woolen shirts, and army boots, winter and summer, and she always had a kind of Russian fur cap crammed on her head, rain or shine, summer or winter. With earflaps.

I didn't like her much, but Mrs. Fallowfield liked *me*, in her extremely weird way. The reason for that was that one time the yippy little dog she always carried in a pocket of her duffel coat—it looked like a kind of pink possum with mange—got lost and wound up at Stourhead Farm, with Albert the collie about to turn him into dog jerky. Albert's *very* territorial. I scooped the nasty thing up—it bit the hell out of my finger—and took it home to Sally, who called Mrs. Fallowfield, and she came right over and got it. I still remember shivering to see it scuttle up her sleeve like a mouse and dive into her pocket. I'd never seen a dog do that before.

"Thank 'ee," she said to me. "I wun't forget." And God knows she didn't. She kept turning up, from then on, in the fields, or stumping along a back road or a Dorchester street—where she didn't belong any more than a boggart would have—or crossing our land to check out Evan's no-till technique. And somehow she'd always come by at just the right time to stop me and ask how I was doing in school, or how a city girl was getting along on a Dorset farm these days. Her voice went with the rest of her: It sounded like chunks of coal rattling down a chute. But I'd stand and answer her questions as politely as I could. I was always polite to Mrs. Fallowfield.

This time she just grunted, "Nut seen you in here before, I han't. Who's this one?"

I introduced Meena. Mrs. Fallowfield gave her one swift up-and-down sweep with those small blue eyes, but didn't say anything. I said, "We go to school together. We were just in for tea. Very nice tea. Great scones."

Mrs. Fallowfield's dog—or whatever—stuck its head out of her coat pocket and yipped at me. I'd saved his miserable life, and he hated my guts from that day. She scratched his head with a hairy forefinger, tilting her head and squinting sideways at me. She said, "Been looking at 'er." It wasn't a question.

"Her," I said. "Yes. Never saw that picture before. We were supposed to study it for class." I'm a really stupid liar when I'm nervous, but that's the only time I lie.

Mrs. Fallowfield said harshly, "Right bad 'un, she was. Family suffered untold grief, along of that girl."

I wasn't having that. I didn't know I wasn't having that until I heard myself saying, "That is not true." Meena says I turned absolutely white, which would be a change anyway. I said, "Tamsin Willoughby loved her family! She never did *anything* to harm them! *She* was the one who suffered, and she's *still* suffering, and you don't know what the hell you're talking about!" I didn't even realize what I'd done until I saw Meena's face, I was that angry.

Mrs. Fallowfield didn't answer me. Instead she smiled, which I'd never seen her do before—I'm not sure anybody ever had, from the work her face muscles had to do to squeeze out a kind of pained twitch around her mouth. But it wasn't a mean smile, and the blue eyes seemed somehow larger for a moment. Just as hard, but maybe a little larger. Then she turned her head and said something to Meena—not in English—and Meena's mouth fell open, and Mrs. Fallowfield clumped on into the Judge Jeffreys Restaurant.

"What was she speaking?" I demanded. "What language was that?"

"Tamil," Meena said faintly. "With a Madras accent."

"What did she *say?*" Meena shook her head, and then she smiled a little bit herself, almost like Mrs. Fallowfield.

"She said, 'Keep an eye on her.' " I waited. Meena blushed—she can't even lie by omission. "Actually, she didn't say *her.* She said, 'Keep an eye on that child—she's not fit to be let out alone.' But she wasn't making fun of you, I'm sure she wasn't. There was something else, something about her."

"Oh, right," I said. "Let's go meet your dad."

I kept going back to the Judge Jeffreys Restaurant whenever I was in Dorchester. Mostly I was with Sally, but she came for tea, and I was there to stare at that portrait of Tamsin. I got to the point where I literally knew every brush stroke that made up that painting, from the hundreds of fussy little ones that created the highlights in her hair and every detail of her gown, to the half dozen or so that put Judge Jeffreys on that gold beaker, watching Tamsin forever with his mild, tender eyes. I wasn't looking for anything exactly—I was waiting for the picture to *tell* me something, which is different. And it did tell me something terribly important, but I didn't understand. I couldn't possibly have understood then, but I still think I should have.

Tamsin couldn't tell me a thing, of course. All she remembered of the painting sessions was Edric, and Edric's music—she didn't even know that Judge Jeffreys was in the portrait, too, and I could see her forgetting it almost as soon as I'd told her. I actually thought of bringing Tony to look at it, because of him knowing so much about Dorset history, but I decided against risking his curiosity. As for asking the Pooka or the billy-blind . . . no, there wouldn't be any point to that. The Pooka was right—it was my problem, my business. And I hadn't a clue.

The weather got warmer, even in Dorset. Wheat and barley, corn and peas and hay were popping up in Evan's unplowed fields, fruit trees were blossoming overnight, and Meena and I had to start dodging football and field hockey again. Mister Cat was shedding his first real winter coat all over my room (he'd never needed to grow one in New York), and swaggered Stourhead Farm like Roger Willoughby. Sally finally got her first vocal student, in Frampton; Tony actually found a ballet class in Dorchester started up by a retired, slightly alcoholic Sadler's Wells dancer; and Julian the Mad Scientist discovered what happens when you run experiments involving the electrical conductivity of water in the Male Faculty toilets at Sherborne Boys. Evan yelled at him about it, but it made him a celebrity for the rest of the term, and I was proud to be his sister.

Me, I went to see Guy Guthrie again, to ask if it seemed the least bit odd to *him*, Judge Jeffreys's face being reflected in Tamsin Willoughby's portrait. But the most even he could tell me was that the thing had always had a strange sort of reputation, almost from the time it was painted. "Maybe it's owing to her dying so soon after, or perhaps it does have to do with Jeffreys—hard to say these days, when he's become such a cash crop for Dorchester. In any case, the last Willoughby left it for the Lovells, and the Lovells gave it to the Restaurant." He chuckled suddenly. "Very nearly the day it opened, as I recall."

I said they certainly didn't take much care of it, and Mr. Guthrie nodded agreement. He said slowly, "They're afraid of it, too, I think, but they don't know why. They won't put it upstairs, in the Lodgings—they keep it in shadow, they never clean it, and I think they'd leave it for the dustman tomorrow, if they could. But it's Dorset history, it's part of the atmosphere they sell—they can't quite make themselves get rid of it. I don't know whether that's any use to you, Jenny, but it's the best I can do."

Well, it was and it wasn't. It convinced me that I was right to feel the weird way I did about the portrait, but it didn't get me any closer to understanding *why*. So I finally gave up on it, and on the Judge Jeffreys Restaurant, and on anybody being much help to me but me. And I went looking for Tamsin.

It was still chilly to be walking out at night, but there wasn't much choice if I wanted to be with her, restive and fretful as she'd become. No more sitting in her chair, both asleep and awake, decades at a time—now she was truly haunting the Manor, wandering endlessly, upstairs and down, leaving a hint of vanilla in the laundry, or the Arctic Circle, or Sally's music room; giving Julian scary, bewildering dreams and giving Evan a sense of being constantly followed in the fields by something he didn't want to turn around and see. Tony complained to me that lately he couldn't concentrate in his studio well enough to choreograph jumping jacks for a Phys Ed class. He blamed me for it, which figured.

As for Sally . . . Sally just watched me and didn't say much. It's taken a long time for me to realize that I'd probably never have learned how smart that woman is if we hadn't moved to England. She knew *something* was going on, and she knew me, and she *almost* felt the connection somewhere. She'd have understood Tamsin better than I ever did, my mother.

One flukey warm evening in May, I spotted Tamsin from a distance, whisking across a cornfield like a scrap of laundry blown off a clothesline. When I ran to catch up with her and she turned to face me, for a moment I was more frightened than the Oakmen could have made me. She was *tattered,* as though dogs had been tearing at her, ripping away her memories of herself. There

were *holes* between shoulder and breast, I remember, and another one gaping below her waist . . . and you couldn't see
through them—there was *nothing* on the other side. I read about
black holes now, where comets and planets and all the light in
the universe get sucked in forever, and I think of those holes in
Tamsin.

"*Who are you?*" Her voice was like a wind over my own grave.

"It's me," I said. Squeaked. "Tamsin, it's me, it's Jenny. Don't
you remember?"

She didn't, not at all, not at first. Her eyes were still Tamsin's blue-
green eyes, practically the one undamaged thing about her, but I
wasn't there. And I was twice as scared then, feeling myself being
drawn into those black holes, and all I could think of was to squeak
out those first lines of the song her sister Maria had taught her:

> "*Oranges and cherries,*
> *sweetest candleberries—*
> *who will come and buy?*
> *who will come and buy . . . ?*"

Nothing . . . and then—very, very slowly—she came back. It's
hard to describe now. It isn't that she became clear and whole and
solid, recognizing me, because she didn't; what happened was that
the old transparency returned, little by little, until you could see
irrigation pipes and skinny young cornstalks through her, and I
was as overjoyed as if she'd come back to me in the flesh. The
holes—or whatever they really were—faded as her memories knitted themselves back together; when she looked at me again, her
eyes took me in, and she smiled.

"Mistress Jenny," she said. "I'faith, but how much older you've
grown since last we met." It hadn't been that long at all, though I
surely felt a deal older than I had when I'd run after her. "Jenny,
did I know you at first? You must tell me truly."

"No," I said. "Not right away." Tamsin was already nodding. I
said, "What *is* this? What's *happening* to you?"

She wouldn't quite look at me, and that was just about more
than I could bear. I held my hands out to her, which was something we'd gradually begun to use as sign language for a hug. I
didn't think she'd remember, but she put her own hands out,
slowly. She whispered, "I do not know. It comes on me often now."

"There's a reason," I said. "There has to be. Something's happening, and maybe it's a good thing. Maybe it means you're breaking loose, about to get out of here at last. To go wherever you're supposed to be." But I said it pretty lamely, because I was afraid it was true, and it's hard to sound encouraging about something you hope isn't going to happen. Even if you're ashamed of yourself.

Tamsin shook her head. "I would know if that were so. This is far other, this is a rending such as I have not known, and each time there's less of me comes back able to say where I have been." It was turning chilly: A little wind blew through her, and I smelled her vanilla and the musty scent of the green corn together. Tamsin said, "Jenny, I am afraid."

"I'll help you," I said. "I will. We'll stay together, I'll watch you every minute, some way, so any time it starts coming over you, I'll be there, I'll remind you." But it was crazy, and we both knew it. Tamsin didn't say anything. I said, "It's my turn to make dinner," and we started back toward the Manor, but she vanished before we were out of the cornfield. I called her name, and I thought she answered me in the wind, but if she did, I never caught a word.

The cornfield was pretty near the Manor—I could see the lights and both chimneys from where I stood—but with Tamsin gone the house seemed as far away as New York, and with a deeper, colder sea between me and it. I wasn't scared, but I was afraid that I was going to be, so I walked fast—*not* running—and I kept telling myself that I'd be home in a minute, in a warm kitchen with people all around me and Sally pissed because I was late. And I was practically on top of the Black Dog before I saw him.

I can feel him now, most of the time, the way Tamsin could. It's a little like smelling rain a whole day away, or like knowing the phone's going to ring. But then he was just there in front of me, where he hadn't been a second before: big as a Harley-Davidson, and so *black* there has to be another word for it; people just call him the Black Dog because they don't know the real word. Nothing—not a cave, a mine, not the bottom of the ocean, not even deep space—is the color of the Black Dog.

"Get *away*," I said. "No hard feelings, but the last thing I need right now is one more bad omen. Excuse me, okay?"

He moved aside to let me by, but when I started on, he walked along with me, pacing me exactly as he'd done at the Hundred-Acre Wood. I was really losing patience fast with mythical creatures, and I told him that as he padded beside me. "What the hell use are you, for God's sake? Go around predicting all kinds of trouble and danger without ever telling people what to look out for—what good's that? I'd rather not know, you know that? You wouldn't be any damn help if trouble showed up right now, anyway." The Black Dog watched me out of his red eyes as I bitched at him, and he seemed to be listening, but he never made a sound.

He stayed with me past the front gate, past Evan's swing and Sally's garden. That did shut me up in time, because whatever he was supposed to be warning me against, it had to be *near*. When he stopped, I mumbled, "Sorry about the Oakmen," and he gave me one last fiery stare before he stepped away into the shadow of a shed. Mister Cat shot out of it in a hurry, turned, and hissed at him, then stalked over to me to complain about the company I was keeping these days. I picked him up and started toward the house.

I was close enough to hear dishes clattering and Julian singing "I'm 'Ennery the Eighth, I am, I am"—which is my fault, because I taught it to him—when somebody said my name, and I turned.

He was standing almost exactly where the Black Dog had vanished. He wore the same robes and wig that he had on in his portrait, the one upstairs from the Restaurant. I could see his face clearly in the light from the kitchen—pale and handsome and young—and he was smiling at me. His voice was dry and whispery, just the way Tamsin had said—it sounded like tissue paper burning. I shouldn't have been able to hear it from that distance, but I could. He said, "I am here. Tell her." Then he bowed to me and snapped off—you could practically hear the switch click—and Sally called for me, and I went on into the house and did the best I could to help get dinner together.

I didn't sleep at all that night. Sometime between moonset and dawn, Mister Cat woke up on my bed, stretched, growled, went to the window, made his prepare-to-meet-your-Maker-however-you-conceive-him noise, and launched himself. I said a word I'd learned from Tamsin and threw on my bathrobe.

It was a good thing I was awake, because what Mister Cat had backed up against the right front tire of Evan's car was Mrs. Fallowfield's repulsive little pink dog-thing. It was whimpering and showing its fishy teeth, while Mister Cat lashed his tail, deciding whether he wanted steaks or filets. I grabbed him up, tossed him in the house, grabbed Mrs. Fallowfield's dog, slapped its nose when it tried to bite me, and sat down on the front step to wait for Mrs. Fallowfield. I figured she'd be along any time now.

Twenty-three

Actually, she showed up just around dawn, when I was about to throw her pink beast into one of the sheds for safekeeping and try to salvage a couple of hours' sleep. But I heard those army boots on the gravel before I even saw her, and I got up and went to meet her. The dog squirmed so much in my arms as she got nearer that I had to let go, and the thing hurled itself through the air—a *lot* farther than it should have been able to—to plop into the pocket of her duffel coat like a slam dunk. Mrs. Fallowfield bent her neck and said something sharp to him, but I didn't catch the words.

"I can't figure why he comes over here," I said. "I mean, he doesn't know anybody." The moment it was out I realized how dumb it sounded, but Mrs. Fallowfield made that funny, painful-looking almost-smile again.

"Happen he might," she grunted. "A chicken, mebbe, a sheep. Nivver know with that one—he's got some strange friends, he has." She was looking at me when she said that, and you could have cut yourself on those blue eyes. She said, "Second time you've delivered him."

It seemed a strange word to use. I hadn't told her about snatching her pet practically out of Mister Cat's claws, but I was too tired to wonder how she knew. Probably happened all the time with that creature. I mumbled, "No trouble," and started back toward the Manor. Mrs. Fallowfield walked along beside me.

"Evan's up, if you want to see him," I said. "I heard him moving around a while back." She hardly ever said a word to Sally, but she seemed to like talking to Evan about drainage and manure. Mrs. Fallowfield shook her head. She didn't say anything more until we reached the door and I said good-bye and started to go in.

Abruptly she said, "Coom over to my house sometime. Scones." She didn't wait for me to answer—just turned around and tramped off. I watched her all the way out of sight. She never looked back, but that dog stuck its head out of her coat pocket and snarled at me.

I didn't tell Tamsin that I'd seen Judge Jeffreys. I didn't have to. She *felt* him, the way Mister Cat had sensed the pink dog's presence on his premises. But where Mister Cat's natural feline response was to remove every trace of the intruder from the planet, Tamsin fled. She was less and less to be found in her secret room, less and less in the house at all. When we first met, she'd told me that she could go anywhere within the boundaries of Stourhead Farm; now she caromed around the place like a pinball, or like a hamster on a very big wheel. Some days I tracked her down, and most of the time she knew me when I did, but not always. The black holes didn't come back, or anyway I never saw them. Generally, she looked like the Tamsin she remembered, only a bit more . . . tentative. I can't think of another word.

But she was frightened almost literally out of her mind, and she couldn't tell me why. You have to try to understand what that might be like for a ghost, the way I had to. That's all she was, after all, as I've been saying—memory, recollection, *mind*—and here she was, so terrified of another ghost, or of the person he'd been, that she couldn't even remember the cause of her fear. I kept pushing and pushing her, whenever I had the chance. "It's nothing he did to you—it's Edric, something about Edric." Tamsin would shake her head vaguely, wearily. "Something he *said*, then. Whatever he said to you when you were sick, when you stopped. The last thing you heard him say—it'll come back, *think* about it."

But she *couldn't* think about it, that was exactly it. I learned even to avoid speaking that man's name, because each time it would blow straight through her, scattering her like clouds before a Dorset gale, and then I wouldn't see her for days at a time. I think it took her that long to gather Tamsin again, and each time was harder.

I told Meena what there was to tell about my seeing Judge Jeffreys, including what he'd said about having come for Tamsin. She didn't agree with me that Edric had to be at the center of the trouble. "Jenny, have you ever heard of Occam's Razor? My father always talks about Occam's Razor—he can drive you crazy with it. It's a philosophical idea that says, look first for the simplest solution—

don't make anything more complicated than it has to be. I think you are doing that with Tamsin. It's that horrible man she is frightened of, and well she should be. He is the one you saw, not Edric. This is nothing to do with Edric."

"Maybe," I said. "Maybe not. I keep wondering—how come he's back, anyway? The Pooka says ghosts don't return, once they're really gone—how did he manage it? It's important, Meena, some way. I know it is."

Meena put her hands on my arms. "Either way, you are to stay out of it. Understand me, Jenny."

She sounded so totally unlike herself—so much older, so tense and bleak—that I gaped at her for a moment. "I have to help her. Nobody else can help her but me."

Meena gripped my arms tighter. "*How* will you help her? What plans do you have? You don't have any plans."

"Yes, I do," I said. "I can't be with her every minute—it's all I can do to keep up with her, the way she's zigging and zagging around the place. But if I can keep a watch on *him,* if there's some way I can stay on *his* trail—"

"No!" Either Meena actually shook me a little or else she was trembling so hard that I felt it myself. "Jenny, this is like me and the Hundred-Acre Wood—I really will drag *you* away by the hair this time, if I have to. I don't care about your Tamsin, whatever happens to her—I'm sorry, but I don't. I care about you."

For one really crazy minute I almost imagined Meena actually being jealous of Tamsin and me, the way I'd been so wildly jealous about Tamsin's fascination with Tony. *That* notion passed in a hurry, and I was just me, flushed and clumsy as always, trying to say something that wouldn't sound too stupid. "I know you do," I said. "I mean, I really do know." Not much, but that's me, every time. "But he's dead, and I'm alive—what can he do to me? I've never understood people being scared of ghosts. Poor Tamsin can't even touch me."

"Tamsin doesn't wish you harm," Meena said stubbornly. "You will not go near him, Jenny. You have to promise me."

"I can't do that," I said. "*I'm* sorry."

We looked at each other. Meena finally sighed, and laughed a very little bit, and stood back from me. "Well," she said. "In *that* case."

*　　*　　*

If it hadn't been for Mister Cat, I don't know what might have happened. He'd plainly been having the same sort of problem with Miss Sophia Brown that I was having with Tamsin. I'd see them together once in a while, and sometimes get a glimpse of her by herself, trotting off on one of those important cat errands that even ghost-cats have. But she didn't sleep on my bed with Mister Cat anymore, or materialize to join us when we were hunting through the Manor for Tamsin. Mister Cat was distressed about it, too, and kept saying so, loudly and constantly. I told him I couldn't do a damn thing about it, and he said he already knew that, but still.

Meena and I had started with some notion that the two of us could somehow keep track of Judge Jeffreys's comings and goings, and stay close to Tamsin that way. Not a chance, not even with school out. Meena spent as much time at Stourhead Farm as she could get away with, but her family had Cotswold-vacation plans, no way out of it; and anyway, she wouldn't have been able to see Judge Jeffreys—she was just determined to be there when *I* did. When I look back at us, all I can do is laugh. Now that I can.

One thing that helped was the fact that Judge Jeffreys wasn't nearly as easy moving around the farm as I'd expected he would be. Tamsin had lived her whole short life there: three centuries dead or not, there wasn't anything she didn't remember about Stourhead—at least, when she wasn't panicky. But Judge Jeffreys stuck pretty close to the Manor when he appeared—maybe because he was afraid of getting lost, maybe just because he knew she'd have to return sooner or later. I still don't know how it really works with ghosts.

Mister Cat knew. He began to come looking for me, day or night—not even bothering to stay cool, but bursting in with a full-throated, full-tilt, red-alert Siamese yowl—and I learned to drop whatever I was doing, make whatever excuse I could get away with, and follow him down to the cellar, up to the Arctic Circle, out to one of the barns—the North Barn, usually—or even to Sally's garden. For his own personal reasons, Mister Cat had taken the case.

And *he* was always there, wherever Mister Cat led me: tall and still, looking much more like a living person than Tamsin did. Maybe that was because of the robes and the wig (wigs, really—he remembered three or four styles); or maybe it was that he knew what he wanted, dead or alive, so being dead didn't make any difference to him, the way it did to Tamsin. Meena thought he didn't know he was dead. She said there were a lot of ghosts like that in India. "They come marching in to dinner and expect to sit down with everyone. Or they get into bed with their wives or husbands, because that's where they always slept. It's very sad."

Nothing sad about Judge Jeffreys, not in his own time and not now. He hung around, pacing a bit now and then, murmuring to himself sometimes, but never the least bit impatient, never anything but waiting. I don't think he knew for a minute whether he was standing in Albert's water dish or Sally's tomato patch, and I know he didn't see the farm workers as they passed him by, or Evan, Sally, Tony, or Julian, even if he was in the kitchen when we sat down to dinner. Nobody else ever saw him, of course—although Julian kept looking right at him and shaking his head a little, as though there were some insect buzzing around him. But of everyone and everything on the whole damn farm, Judge Jeffreys only saw me.

Even after everything that happened, I still think those were the worst moments of all, those times when he'd stand behind my chair, or beside me while I was washing dishes and *talk* to me in that rustly voice of his. It wasn't that he said anything that creepy or terrifying; mostly he just repeated over and over, "I have come for her. Tell her." But what he *felt* like, there at my shoulder, whether he spoke or not . . . I don't know how to write about that. The best way I can put it is that the presence of him rustled like his voice, like an attic full of old dead bugs: the empty husks of flies in ragged spiderwebs, still bobbing against the window—the beetles and grasshoppers that froze to death winters ago—the dusty rinds of little nameless things stirring on the floor in a draft, crunching underfoot wherever you step. Judge Jeffreys didn't just *sound* like that. He *was* that.

I couldn't speak to him, not with people there—besides, most of the time I couldn't have gotten a word out if I'd wanted to. But once, when I was by myself, waiting outside the South Barn to meet Julian for a cricket lesson—I saw him coming toward me over the young grass, the way I'd dreamed it and wakened to find Sally holding me. Now it was real, and everything in me wanted to run, but it was funny, too, because Mister Cat was stalking right beside him, looking as professional as Albert when he's got his sheep all lined up. Judge Jeffreys ignored him.

I spoke first—I'm still proud of that. I said, "You won't find her.

And if you could, you couldn't touch her. You can't do anything to her." I squeaked a little on the last bit, but otherwise it came out all right.

Judge Jeffreys smiled at me. He had a tired, thoughtful, *attentive* kind of smile, as though he really was considering the merits of what I'd said. Tony told me that a lot of Dorset folk who were tried at the Bloody Assizes honestly believed that he'd understood their innocence and was going to let them go. He said, "She will come to me."

"Oh, no, she won't," I said. "Not ever." My voice was still pretty wobbly, but the words were clear. I picked up Mister Cat and held him against my chest, because I was shaking.

Judge Jeffreys said, "She belongs to me. Since first I spoke her name and bowed over her hand—since first our eyes kissed across her father's table." I hadn't imagined he could talk like that. He said, "From that moment, she was mine. She knew then—she knows now. She will come."

Mister Cat snarled in my arms. I thought it was because I was holding him too tight, but when I eased up he kept glaring at Judge Jeffreys and making that jammed-garbage-disposal sound of his. Judge Jeffreys pursed his lips, made his own mocking *puss-puss* sound at Mister Cat, and smiled again. "*Her* cat disliked me also. I grieved that greatly once."

"Grieved?" I said. "Grieved over anything? You? I don't believe it."

Judge Jeffreys's chuckle was like the gasping hiss of our old steam radiator on West Eighty-third Street. "Aye, of a certainty, for the wretched creature held more sway with Tamsin Willoughby than any notions of her imbecile Monmouth-loving father. I entertained certain hopes that she might endear me to her mistress by fawning upon me, but she showed her detestation so plain that I took a cordial pleasure in teaching pretty Puss to swim, the day following the burial. She proved a poor pupil, but no matter. Tamsin Willoughby already belonged to me, as surely that beast belonged to her."

I said, "She loved Edric Davies. She hated you with all her heart. You had to know that."

That got him—only for a second, but it was something to see. The handsome dead face absolutely convulsed, like something hit by a car, flopping in the road. Out of control. "That damned Welsh villain! That canting, cozening, rebel-loving rogue! Jesus

God, to see him—to sit watching, day on day, as he plied his vile sorcery against her susceptible innocence. A hundred times—a thousand!—oh, but I was hard put not to leap from my chair and strangle him where he sat, twangling at the jacks and looking sideways, looking, *looking* at her. . . ."

Tony says that he used to foam at the mouth when he got properly up to speed in court. I didn't think a ghost could do that, but I didn't want to find out. I said, "They loved each other. They were going to be married."

He stopped raving like *that*, on a dime, and he stared at me in a new way, really seeing me. His face smoothed itself out, getting back that gentle, patient, almost fragile look he'd had before. "Married, you say? Good God, the villain would have betrayed and abandoned her ere they'd gone ten miles. But she was the purest innocent ever drew breath, my Tamsin." My stomach turned right into a bowling ball when he called her that, in that voice. "What could a shining angel know of the snares and ruses of so licentious a knave? I will bless the name of the Almighty for three centuries more, and three yet after those that I was in time to offer her an honorable love and a marriage such as no jumped-up tradesman's family could have dared imagine. As to Master Davies, he fled before me as a demon flees the face of the risen Christ. I told her so, at the last. She died in my arms, at peace, knowing herself cleansed and free."

And here comes another one of those moments that I wish I hadn't promised myself to write down honestly when I got to it. Because it's very embarrassing to say that just then, just for a bit, I believed him, even knowing what he was. Or maybe I believed that he really had loved Tamsin—or at least that *he* really believed he had. I'd never met anyone like him. He was completely out of my league, that's all.

But then he blew it, even so. He'd been keeping a little distance between us—as though he didn't want to get too close to Mister Cat—but when I said, "No, she's not at peace, and she won't ever be at peace until she finds out what happened to Edric," he took two long, floating strides and he was *there*, towering and whispering, his face suddenly gone dim, almost featureless, and his eyes glaring white. I tried to back away, but I couldn't move.

"I tell you again, Edric Davies is gone," Judge Jeffreys said. "Rebel, seducer, false Welsh traitor to his anointed king, Tamsin

Willoughby need concern herself no longer with fears of the scoundrel's returning. I've seen to *that*, by God."

He was standing so close to me that I could feel things like little static sparks crackling between us. I couldn't see anything, but I've read since that that can happen with ghosts and people. It never did with Tamsin. Judge Jeffreys's voice had gotten very quiet. "A great power was granted me when we met last, Edric Davies and I. I was the unworthy instrument of the Almighty, humbly privileged to speed him to such a doom as all the saints together could never lift from him. There will be no return from where Edric Davies is gone."

People write and talk about their hair standing on end, their hearts standing still, their blood freezing in their veins. I never knew what that meant until then, when all of it happened to me at once. Between one word of his and the next I was too cold to breathe, too cold even to tremble—and my mouth dried up and tasted like pennies. Judge Jeffreys looked down at me from the gray afternoon moon. He said, "She knows."

"No," I said. "Oh, no. No way in the world does Tamsin Willoughby know anything about whatever happened to Edric Davies. No way in the *world*."

I saw Julian trotting past the North Barn, loaded down with cricket bats and balls and stumps—he wanted us both to wear white flannels, but I threatened to back out of our lessons, and Julian just loves to be teaching someone something. I said again, really loudly, "She *doesn't* know. You're a liar."

He didn't like that. He leaned over me, with his face doing that floppy, melting thing it did before, and the sound that came out of him wasn't words. My legs turned to string—I can't think of another way to describe it. I'd have sat down right there, flat on my butt, except that suddenly I was seeing Julian through him, which I hadn't been able to do a moment before. Then there was only Julian, staring at me out of those impossible gray eyes, saying, "Jenny, you look all funny. Are you all right?"

"Yes," I said. "Yes, I'm fine." But I sounded funny even to me.

"Because if you're *not* all right, we can practice later," Julian said. "Jenny, what is it? What's the matter?"

My baby brother. I didn't even send away for him. I said, "Julian, knock it off, I'm fine—a goose just walked over my grave or something. Show me what a shooter is again."

*　　　*　　　*

The weather got warmer, Evan's no-till crops got taller and better looking than he expected. The new corn was taking hold, the new wells were pumping more water than the old ones ever had, and the Lovells seemed happy as clams. Oh—and the "malaria swamp" in the upper meadows finally got drained, probably for the first time ever. Evan's got pear trees there now.

But there were other things happening, and only Mister Cat and I had the smallest clue about them. (Miss Sophia Brown, too—she must have known everything, for sure.) You can't have two three-century-old ghosts in the same place without *unsettling* things, without swinging that door between now and whenever wide open. And what was beginning to come through wasn't just Dorset night creatures, or more of Mister Cat's scuttling sparring partners. We were getting an altogether different class of scary now.

The first ones weren't ghosts—not unless whole scenes, whole *landscapes*, can be ghosts or have ghosts. I was washing dishes one morning with Sally, the two of us arguing lazily over who played who in some old movie, when Mister Cat was suddenly on my shoulder—digging in—and the kitchen was filling up with *hills*, for God's sake. Sally didn't notice a thing, which was just as well, since she was being crowded at the sink by shadowy oaks that made the Hundred-Acre Wood look like a Christmas-tree farm. Me, whichever way I turned—with Mister Cat permanently welded to the back of my neck—I came up against great chalky slopes and banks of downland, all tilted on their sides, running away into the ceiling. All transparent, of course, gauzy as Meena's silk scarves, rippling gently when Sally or I walked through them, as though we'd moved in front of a slide projector. No plowed land, no animals, no people. Just the hills.

That was how it started, but it didn't stay that harmless for very long. Some of the mirages were always ghostly, even flimsier than Tamsin, but others looked so real that I kept jumping aside to keep from tumbling down a slope that some Willoughby had leveled, or from bumping into huge old boulders looming up in the cornfield or the sheep pasture. As long as it happened in the house it was actually funny, especially with me being the only person aware of anything unusual. Once I forgot and warned Tony about the boggy, weedy pond right in the middle of his shiny studio floor; other times, I'd stand blinking in the doorway of the music room without coming in, until Sally got really annoyed at me. But I couldn't see her because of the stony meadows between us, or the wild woods.

Outside, under an ordinary Dorset sky (generally a sort of windy gray-lilac, spring or no spring) . . . outside was something else. Outside, half the time I couldn't be sure where or when I was. I'd come out of the house some mornings and every shed and outbuilding would be gone—everything but the Manor itself. Nothing left but hills this way, a deep green coombe off that way, and maybe a game trail between. Nothing for me to do but stay close to the house until the mirages cleared away, which they always did, sooner or later. It was almost like being Judge Jeffreys, from the other side, with both of us clinging to the Manor as the only truth in a world of fever dreams. Anyway, it's the closest I ever came to understanding anything about him.

I keep calling them *mirages, dreams, shadows*, but they were more than that, and I knew it then. Meena knew, too, even though she couldn't ever see them. "They are visitations," she told me, "and I think they are perfectly real. Not real here, now, but real in their own time and place, which is still going on somewhere." She asked me if I understood, and I said maybe you had to be a Hindu. Meena said no, you didn't, but it would help if I'd read a book by someone named Dunne. I said I hadn't, and Meena said in that case I'd have to take a Hindu's word for what was going on. I said *please.*

"I think what you are seeing is Stourhead Farm before it *was* Stourhead Farm," Meena said. "Long, long before Thomas Hardy and William Barnes—long before Roger Willoughby moved down from Bristol. Before the Saxons, before the Romans, before there were farms here, before there were any people at all. Somehow it is all unrolling for you, like running a movie in reverse—"

"Not for *me*," I interrupted her. "It's *him*, it's not me, that's the whole point. He's the one making it happen, just by being here." I told her what the Pooka had said about the wrongness of Tamsin's lingering on at the Manor and speaking to me, and Meena listened and nodded. "Yes," she said, "yes, like what most people think about reincarnation. They think, if you're a bad person you have to return as a snake, a worm, a cockroach, but it doesn't work like that, it can't. You don't go backwards, Hindu or not—the world could *unravel*. Yes, I see, Jenny."

"More than I do," I said. "All *I* know is that it can't go on. What happens when *people* start showing up?" Meena didn't know. I said, "And I'll tell you something else—those visitations, or whatever, they're getting more solid every time. I can still walk through them—but what about when I can't? Meena, is the seventeenth century coming back for real, for *good*? And everywhere, or just here?"

"No," Meena said. "Absolutely, positively *not*. Not possible." She took my hands and held them tightly between hers, and that felt comforting, but what I saw in her face didn't make me feel any better. She stayed over that night, but she didn't want to hear anything about the stretch of heathland, ashy-purple with moor-grass and ling, that floated into my room like Mary Poppins while we were lying awake talking about boys. I don't know whether she fell asleep, but after a while I couldn't hear her voice anymore. I just lay holding Mister Cat and feeling my bed under me, but looking up at a thousand-year-old sky that couldn't be there, and smelling rain that had fallen a thousand years ago.

There was a young Lovell, just about my age. I didn't know about him until it was too late.

His name was Colin. He came down with a bunch of Lovells one afternoon to bug Evan about exporting or something. Colin looked like a string bag of yams, his skin was worse than mine, he whined like a gnat, and he homed in on me like a heat-seeking missile. Julian hacked him with a croquet mallet accidentally on purpose; even Tony came out of his studio to glower silently at him. Tony's got a glower that blisters paint at fifty yards, but old Colin never noticed. His nose was wide open, as Marta would have said: He followed me wherever I went on the farm, and there wasn't a thing I could do except be nice to him. It was fun, in a way, feeling like a siren for once, but I could have done without it right then, with the world of Stourhead Farm shifting around me so constantly that just crossing a barley field was like trying to find your seat in a pitch-dark movie theater, where the only light comes from the screen, and faces and scenery go flickering over you until you have to stand still and wait for your eyes to understand and adjust. And with Colin Lovell buzzing after me I never had one instant that whole day to stand still. Which was why we ran slap into Kirke's Lambs.

No, to be fair, it wasn't really Colin's fault. I'd been getting glimpses of people—as opposed to landscapes—for a few days already, though I didn't tell Meena about them. Mostly I saw them from a distance, either driving sheep and cattle along roads that weren't there anymore, or plodding off somewhere through the rain in weary little groups of two and three. I hadn't seen any real faces yet, or heard voices. I didn't want to hear voices.

What happened was this: I was showing Colin through the new walnut orchard, and he was pretending to know a lot more about grafting than he did—he really was trying to impress me—and between one damn minute and the next, the entire orchard seemed to fly away, and we were standing on what felt like that path I'd walked with Tamsin and never found again, the one where she remembered waiting to see the visiting carriages come sweeping into view on the high road. It was foggy and cold, and there were huge, shapeless figures moving all around us, making me back up close against Colin. He liked that, because he thought I was being friendly, but I was too scared to tell him to piss off because I knew what those creatures were. They were big men riding big horses, and even through the mist I could tell that they were wearing scarlet coats and plumed silver helmets, and jackboots, like pirates. Like soldiers.

Colin was telling me how many different kinds of walnuts there are, and why English walnuts are the best, but I was hearing the soldiers talking to each other. They sounded very far away, but so did he; their voices were deep and thin at the same time, and distorted, as though the tape were dragging, but I could make out most of the words. They were talking about the rebels.

"... *Sedgemoor, the week after Sedgemoor . . . ah, you should have seen the colonel then. Hanged a hundred of them in the market at Bridgewater—practically with his own hands, he did. . . .*"

"... *Codso, do you tell me that? You weren't with him in Tangiers—*"

"... *Aye, Tangiers, and no bloody Bishop Mews there to prate of innocence and force him to spare the lives of such filth. . . .*"

"... *A gallows every three miles—every three miles, a gallows and a chopper and a cauldron of pitch, you'd see this country quiet fast enough. . . .*"

"Jenny? Jenny, did you know that your American pecans are from the same family as walnuts?"

I snapped. I forgot where I was. I hissed at him, "Colin, shut up! Don't you know who these guys are?"

It's amazing, when you think about it, but I've never yet had anyone look at me as though I were genuinely crazy. I mean, when you really think about it, there should have been dozens by now. But all I've got is the memory of Colin, gaping at me and starting to back away, honestly expecting me to start drooling and foaming and jump at his throat. I guess he'll have to do. He said, "Jenny, what are you talking about? They're just walnut trees."

They were, too, and I knew that. I *knew* that, that's what I'm trying to explain. But I knew those soldiers, too, just as surely as I knew what was ripening on those trees. Tony had told me all about Colonel Kirke's dragoons—"Kirke's Lambs," they called themselves—and it wasn't something you forget once the history test is over. Kirke's Lambs were the military equivalent of Judge Jeffreys, a lynch mob in uniform. Judge, jury, and executioners, the whole crew, and they didn't even need to wear wigs. When I imagined people like them being turned loose in the Colonies, a century later . . . I don't think I've ever been that proud again of being an American.

Colin kept backing off. "What are you *looking* at, Jenny? What *guys*—what do you mean? Jenny, there's nobody there."

"Oh, yes, there is," I said. "And they can hear us, too, so for Christ's sake put a sock in it." I was just saying that to keep him quiet—I didn't think Kirke's gang actually could hear us, away off in 1685—but three of the dragoons reined in their horses and looked straight at us, right on the money. One of them had one blue eye and one brown eye; a second man had a scar running from the left corner of his mouth to his left ear. A third was the handsomest man I've ever yet seen, except for his mouth, which was like another scar, thin and white, a bloodless welt. I'd know every one of those faces if I saw them again.

"Voices," the scarred dragoon said. "I heard them."

The handsome one said, "Cornet Simmons, you're drunk as a fiddler's bitch." His mouth hardly moved.

Colin called, "Jenny, I'm going back to the house. I think my father's leaving, anyway."

"There!" Cornet Simmons said. "*There*, by the stump. I heard a bloody voice, I tell you."

There wasn't any stump where I stood, but he was staring right into my eyes. His were a streaky blue—he *was* drunk, back there in the seventeenth century, hunting rebels on the Yeovil road—and he kept blinking and shaking his head . . . but he saw me. I know he saw me.

The dragoon with the mismatched eyes laughed suddenly: one short machine-gun burst. He sounded closer and clearer than the other two, I don't know why. He said, "Ghosts, it's ghosts you're hearing, Simmons—and why not? Country's full up, as many of them as the Colonel's made around here."

"Aye, that'll be it," the handsome one said. "Ghosts. Close ranks, Cornet Simmons. Business in Yeovil tonight, and Taunton after. Close ranks."

He didn't raise his voice, but the last two words cracked out across three centuries like bones breaking. The scarred dragoon hesitated for a little—then he wheeled his horse and followed the others, who were already trotting on into the fog. But at the last moment he spun the horse on its hind legs—practically popping a wheelie—and rode at me, grabbing for his sword hilt. I can still hear the soft whir the thing made coming out of its sheath. Behind him, the handsome one shouted something, sounding really pissed.

I couldn't move. I stood still and watched him coming for me. God, when I write this I remember so much I've never told even Meena—the crusted blood in his mustache, the slobber flying from his horse's mouth, the glint of *somebody's* sunlight along the sword blade, the funny deep, humming sound he was making in his throat right up to the moment when the sabre swept through *my* throat. No, I didn't feel a thing—though the berry bushes just behind me hissed and rustled—but maybe the people he killed like that in 1685 or whenever didn't feel anything either. Anyway, he swung his horse around, stared right at me one more time, made one last sort of half-pass with his sword before he put it away, and then he cantered off after the rest of the Lambs, whistling loudly through his teeth. I heard someone yelling back at him, but I couldn't see the others anymore.

I stood where I was, with the walnut orchard drifting slowly into place around me again while I just *shook*. Colin was long gone, probably already telling every Lovell within range that I was a serious double-barrelled loony, and I saw his point myself. Seeing Tamsin, talking to her, having feelings about her . . . well, you could call that a special case, and you could even say that about Judge Jeffreys—at least *I* could. But meeting Kirke's Dragoons on a road that only a ghost remembered, and believing that one of them was aware enough of me to try to kill me—no, I never told Meena about that. I never told anyone until now.

Mister Cat came flowing out of a bush, one of those same berry bushes that Cornet Simmons's sabre had set swaying. He did his stiff-legged Frankenstein walk over to where the dragoons' horses had been standing. *Would* have been standing, if they and the old road had really been there. He sniffed the ground very carefully, and then he scratched it hard with his back feet, as though he'd just taken a major dump. Then I knew that I'd seen what I'd seen, and I picked him up when he sauntered back to me and said, "Thanks. I was having a bad ten minutes or so there."

I put him on my shoulder, and we started back through the walnut orchard, me trying to think of something nice and sane to say to the Lovells in case they hadn't left yet. Suddenly Mister Cat stiffened, spat, got a grip (my right shoulder looked like a dart board for two days), and made an entirely new sound, like a bandsaw seizing up in wet wood. I had no idea he could make a sound like that.

I turned to see where he was swearing, and got a quick glimpse of Mrs. Fallowfield's little pink dog-thing scuttling away from us among the trees. Mister Cat wanted down in the worst way, to rend and devour, but I wouldn't let him. I said, "Forget it, leave him *alone*, we've got enough troubles." But Mister Cat bitched about it all the way home.

Twenty-four

That summer Sally landed a gig as musical director for a women's choir in Yeovil. I liked that, because I could usually go with her and visit with Meena while she was working; and *Meena* liked it because she knows more about the Byrd and Bach and Dowland stuff Sally had them singing than I do, and I was raised with it. Meena thinks my mother is the best piano player south of Horowitz, and Sally's flattered by that, as who wouldn't be? It doesn't make me jealous to watch them together; but sometimes it does make me wish that I understood my mother's music—*really* understood, down deep the way my best friend does. I talked to Tamsin about that once. I said, "Maybe it's not possible if it's your mother."

Tamsin smiled. I don't really expect anyone ever to smile at me the way Tamsin used to do. "Dear Mistress Jenny," she said, "*my* mother was such a gardener as Dorset has never seen. There was no flower, native or no, robust or tender, failed to thrive under her hands. Our folk swore that Squire Willoughby's gardens flourished as they did because even the most delicate, contrary bloom fair worshipped my mother, and would have budded in the deeps of winter to please her. Yet it was never so with me—I admired flowers well enough, but there was no intimacy between us, no liaison. And I sorrowed greatly over this—oh, not for myself, not for the poor blossoms that dropped their petals and began to die the first moment I looked at them—but because I so, *so* wanted to know the truth of my mother's joy in her garden. But I never could, Jenny. I could only look on and admire, and wonder."

"I guess," I said. "But I just wish—"

Tamsin's face changed then, closing against me as I'd never seen it do since the day we met. She said, "Child, never speak to me of wishes," and that was the end of that.

Anyway, Meena and I spent a lot more time at those choir rehearsals than I'd ever bargained for, scrunched in bare-metal folding chairs at the back of the auditorium while Sally took those women through four bars of some cantata over and over again. I told Meena everything I could—I honestly didn't hold much back, except the stuff I thought would only worry her—and she listened carefully to all of it and told me how much the whole business worried her. "It's you and *him* now," she said one evening. "It's not simply a matter of helping Tamsin anymore, is it? It's you and him, and I hate it, Jenny."

I said, "I read a story once about the way some cowboys used to trap wild horses by walking after them, slowly, day after day after day. After a while, the horses would get so frightened, so bewildered, finally they'd just stand still until the men caught up with them. That's exactly what he's doing with Tamsin. Waiting until she gives up and comes to him. He's told me."

"But she won't do it," Meena said. "All this time, and he hasn't seen her once. She can hide from him, she has the whole farm—"

"He can wait forever," I said. "She can't. I'm starting to understand a little bit, Meena, the way the Pooka said I had to. It's the painting—he got himself into that portrait of her, and I think somehow that *connects* them, that's why he's been able to hang on or come back, whichever. Or maybe it's because she didn't leave when she was meant to—maybe that left a door open for him, like the Pooka said. I wonder what would happen if we could steal the painting and just destroy it? That might be all it takes to set her free."

"And *him*, too?" I didn't have an answer. "Besides, Edric Davies is in that picture too—in her face, in her eyes. He's not painted in, but he's there. What would happen to him, wherever he is?"

"I don't know," I said. "I don't know how any of that stuff *works.*" We sat without talking for a while, listening to Sally trying to get her sopranos to sing on pitch. Finally I said, "The Pooka told me the Wild Hunt would tell me what I needed to know. How do you ask the Wild Hunt for advice?"

"E-mail," Meena said. "Faxes."

Actually, the Wild Hunt hadn't passed over Stourhead in weeks, almost as long as I hadn't seen Tamsin. You mostly hear the Hunt in the autumn and winter, not too much in spring. I asked Guy Guthrie why that was so, and he peered over his glasses at me and said, "A lot of people would tell you it's because that's when the geese are traveling south, and between their carry-on and perhaps the howling of a winter storm . . ."

"Yes," I said. "That's what Evan thinks."

Mr. Guthrie grinned. "But you don't. And what do *I* think?" He wouldn't say anything more until the tea was ready—he makes tea the way Evan rumples his hair and Mr. Chari plays with cigars he doesn't light half the time. At last he said, "Well, if I thought much about such things, I *suppose* I'd think that more folk everywhere die in the cold months, as the year dies, and perhaps the Wild Hunt have their best pick of poor souls to hound through the sky then. Perhaps they seek them on the other side of the world, come springtime. There's not a great deal known about the Wild Hunt, I'm afraid."

I asked him, "Do they . . . are they on their own, or does someone, somebody—"

"Direct them? Ah now, I can't tell you that for certain either, nor how they choose their quarry. Some say the Devil's their master—in Cornwall they're called the Devil's Dandy Dogs—and that you can find refuge from them in churches, in prayer. Others will have it that there's no sanctuary once they're on your track. Living or dead, saint or sinner—no sanctuary." He took off his glasses and leaned forward, one hand scratching behind Clem's ears, but his old blue eyes as intent on me as Cornet Simmons's had been. "Why do you need to know, Jenny?"

I think I told him I was working on a folklore project for school. I'm not only a bad liar, I'm an over-elaborate one. I don't think he bought it for a second; but just before I left, he said, "There's one other belief about the Hunt. I've only come across it a few times, and only here in Dorset. Supposedly they can be *summoned*—called down and actually set to run a victim to his death—by someone who knows the proper spell, and has the required force of personality to achieve it. But it's a risky thing to attempt, as you might imagine, and in any case the pursuit only lasts for one night. So there'd be a bit of a chance of escape that way. I don't know if you'll want to bother with that one for your project, though."

Between that and what the Pooka had said about the Wild Hunt, I started finding myself looking out for them, listening for them, almost in the way that I looked for Tamsin all the time, and with just the same result. The only thing assuring me that she and Miss

Sophia Brown hadn't vanished for good was that Judge Jeffreys hadn't. I saw him most often in the morning and early twilight, never far from the Manor: solid-looking enough that you might take him for an ordinary person on first sight, but casting no shadow, motionless, *waiting* for Tamsin the way nothing human ever waited. He didn't speak to me anymore, but sometimes our eyes met from a distance, and the patient, patient hatred in him would slam into me right below my ribs. *He* might be dead as road-kill, but that hatred was every bit as alive as I was.

One day in mid-August, when Dorset's as hot as it ever gets, and the poor sheep lie down in each other's shade, Julian and I were out on the downs, him trying to teach Albert to fetch (Albert does not do dog stuff), and me flat on my back, same as always, eyes almost closed, trying not to think about anything but a couple of blue butterflies about to settle on my forehead. Then they were gone, and I was staring straight up at Mrs. Fallowfield. Practically nobody looks good from that angle, especially a bony old woman in a big fur cap, with no lips. She said nothing but, "Scones. Five minutes. Bring the boy." And she tramped off, the way she always did, as though she were breaking a trail through the snow for people to follow.

Julian hadn't ever met Mrs. Fallowfield. He came running up to watch her leaving, and when I told him who she was, he wanted to know if there was a *Mr.* Fallowfield. I said I didn't think so, and Julian said, "I'll bet she ate him. I'll bet that's what happened." But he's crazy about scones, so he hauled me to my feet and hustled me after her. We didn't get there in five minutes—you can't possibly, from the downs—but it wasn't Julian's fault.

She made it in five minutes, though. I'd swear to that, because by the time we arrived, she had those scones and muffins hot from the oven—no microwave, no toaster—and set out on her kitchen table, along with half a dozen kinds of jam and tea with clotted cream. Her farmhouse was a funny little place, wedged into a grove of white-flowering elder trees. Mrs. Fallowfield said it was about a hundred years younger than the Manor, but it *felt* older, maybe because it hadn't ever been remodeled, or had anything added to it, so it was all one thing: dim and damp smelling, not much bigger than a three-car garage, with ceilings so low that even Julian could touch them if he stood on tiptoe. I remember a few dried flowers shoved into a medicine bottle on the window, and candleholders everywhere, although she *must* have had electricity. Everything was built around the oven, which was huge enough to heat the entire farmhouse, and probably half her orchards as well. It wasn't any witchy lair, nothing like that—only musty and close and worn out. The scones were the best I ever had, though.

Mrs. Fallowfield watched us eat, but didn't say much. I didn't see her pink dog-thing around anywhere. When Julian asked her if she'd always lived here, she answered him, "That I have, boy. Always." When he asked if anyone lived with her, to help her take care of the farm, she gave him a major Look and didn't answer—just stuck out an arm and indicated for him to try and bend it. Julian told me later that he could have swung on it, walked on it, done handstands; that arm wasn't going anywhere. "I'll bet she pumps iron," he said. "I'll bet she's got a weight room back there somewhere." I said he ought to ask her, but he never got the chance.

A storm hit while Julian and I were getting ready to leave, with me not a bit wiser about why she'd asked us there in the first place. It blew up with no warning, the way it happens in Dorset, and all we could do was wait it out. Mrs. Fallowfield gave Julian a crumbly picture book that looked as though King Arthur had teethed on it—Julian loves *anything* old—and she had me sit with her at that one kitchen window to watch the storm. The rain was coming in practically sideways, and the wind was shaking the house so hard that it groaned in the ground like trees do. Mrs. Fallowfield leaned forward, so I could hear her, and said, "Nothing to be feared of. She's got deep roots, this house."

Actually, what she said was "thikky hoose," like the boggart, but I had the feeling she'd done it on purpose—just as she'd spoken in Tamil to Meena—and not slipped back into Old Dorset talk. The more I saw of her, the less I could make her out; all I could tell was that she *knew* it, and she enjoyed it. "Put up wi' worse, house has," she said now. Then she added something I couldn't catch, because of the wind, except for the last words: ". . . and worse yet coming."

"What?" I said. "*What* worse?" Mrs. Fallowfield only grinned at me with her long gray teeth and turned away to look out the window. I repeated it—"*What* worse?"—but she didn't answer. Instead she suddenly reached back, grabbed my arm and pointed it where she was staring, into the roiling violet heart of the storm. She still didn't say anything. She didn't have to.

I heard them before I saw them; or maybe it was that I couldn't take in what I was seeing right away. They weren't in the clouds, but just below them, so that the lightning flared over the faces of the Huntsmen and made their spears and harness *twinkle,* for God's sake—green and red and blue, like decorations spinning on some horrible Christmas tree. There were dogs racing ahead of them, but they weren't any more like real dogs than the beasts they rode had anything to do with horses. Too many legs, some of them—like Mister Cat's midnight playmates—too many laughing red tongues, too many faces that were nothing but bone and teeth and fire-filled eyesockets. I pulled back from the window, but Mrs. Fallowfield wouldn't let go of my arm.

"Look," she ordered me, and I looked. Some of the Huntsmen were men, some women, some neither, some never. Some wore armor and helmets; some were stark naked, carrying no weapons at all, stretched along their mounts' necks like spiders. I couldn't make out any faces, not until Mrs. Fallowfield pointed with her free arm, and then I could see them all. I still see them, on bad nights.

Julian dropped his books and came running to be with me, but Mrs. Fallowfield said, *"Back* you, boy," and he stopped where he was. But I could feel him being scared and lonely, even though he couldn't see the riders, so I put my hand back for him to hold. He grabbed onto it, and the three of us stayed like that, while the storm pounded down on Mrs. Fallowfield's old, old house and the Wild Hunt bayed and screamed overhead.

It didn't last very long, considering how many of them there were, arching from one horizon halfway to the other, like the opposite of a rainbow. The storm dribbled and piddled off toward Dorchester, and the Wild Hunt faded with it, though the Huntsmen's howling still flickered around the sky after they were gone. Julian came up close beside me, and Mrs. Fallowfield patted his head clumsily. "There, boy," she said. "There, boy." But she looked at me for a long time before she spoke to me. Before she finally said, "You saw."

I didn't say anything. I just nodded.

Because I'd seen too much and not enough, both. I'd seen the tattered *human* figure flying before the Wild Hunt, and heard that desperate, hopeless scream once again, even through their clamor. I couldn't talk—I could barely breathe—and I couldn't look away. Once, in some science experiment back at Gaynor, when I touched a piece of dry ice, it stuck to my fingers, and the cold actually burned them. Mrs. Fallowfield's blue eyes were like that: They hurt my eyes, they hurt my chest and my mind to meet, but I had to, until she let go. At last she nodded herself, and said again, "You saw. Go home now."

I don't remember leaving her house. I don't remember a thing about walking home with Julian, except that suddenly we were in front of the Manor, and he was still holding my hand tightly and saying, "I don't think I like that old woman, Jenny. Do you like her?"

"Who cares if I like her or not?" I said. "It doesn't *matter* if we like her." And I pulled loose from him and took off, running past Sally—who'd been frantic about us being caught out in the storm—upstairs to my room. I didn't just lie down on my bed, I crawled into it, clothes and shoes and all, and I pulled the blankets up as high as I could, and I lay there *not thinking, not thinking,* until Evan came and got me for dinner. He asked me if I was all right, didn't believe a word of what I told him, but didn't say anything. Evan's good that way.

I was perfectly charming at dinner. I talked a lot, and I made jokes, and I took turns with Julian talking about Mrs. Fallowfield's scones and her weird house. Julian did mention that we'd thought we'd heard the Wild Hunt, but I didn't back him up on that one, and nobody else paid much attention. Sorry, Julian.

Sally had her Yeovil choir that evening, but I didn't go with her. I went up to the third floor, to Tamsin's room—with Mister Cat following me every step of the way—and I let myself in with my bent paper clip, like always. Tamsin wasn't there. I sat down in her chair and watched Mister Cat sniffing out every corner of the room for Miss Sophia Brown, as though she had her own smell for him, ghost or no, the way Tamsin smelled of vanilla to me. Finally, reluctantly, he came over and climbed into my lap, looking weary. I've never seen Mister Cat look just like that. Lazy, yes; pissed off, sure—but not tired and sad. I stroked his throat, and under his chin, but he didn't purr.

"Yeah, right," I said. "Same here." I raised my voice a little and spoke to Tamsin, wherever she was. I said, "I've seen him. I've seen Edric Davies. I know what happened to him." Then I sat still as Roger Willoughby's secret room darkened around me until I couldn't see the chestnut tree outside the window, or the window itself, or even Mister Cat silent on my lap, but not asleep.

I couldn't find her.

Stourhead Farm is about seven hundred acres, maybe a little less—I've already said that. That sounds like a lot, but I covered every damn one of them on foot, looking for Tamsin. Sometimes Meena was with me, but more often I was by myself, just trudging from one fence to another, from the creepy fringes of the Oak-men's Wood—which was the way I thought of it now—to Evan's walnut orchard where I'd seen Kirke's Lambs; zigzagging between fields, cutting across the downland, actually getting lost in sudden fogs a couple of times. Once I found a place that Evan himself hadn't ever seen: a kind of brambly mini-meadow, covered with a kind of grass whose name I forget, but which doesn't grow any-where else on the farm. There were wild apple trees, too, most of them dead, but a few still putting out papery blossoms, almost transparent. I wondered if Roger Willoughby had ever seen them, or if he'd missed them, too, like us. It would have been wonderful to find Tamsin there.

The worst of it was that I couldn't *feel* her. I'd gotten much bet-ter at that over time: sensing her presence even when she wasn't around—in the house, out in the fields, it didn't matter. Some-times I could feel her wanting me, needing my company, needing to be around *me*, which was a sensation I'm not about to try to put into words, but it made me more vain than I'll probably ever be again. Now, nothing—a kind of nothing I never knew existed, be-cause you have to have lost something incredibly precious for that, and you have to have not quite known how precious it was. I hadn't ever taken Tamsin for granted—not ever—but I hadn't known.

And watching *him* waiting for her didn't help. He had all the time in the world; he didn't have to move, or think, or pretend to be living a normal human life with a family and a best friend and a cat, with chores to remember, and conversations to keep up. All he had to do was wait for Tamsin to come to him, like those cow-boys. He knew she'd come.

I wouldn't have known if it hadn't been for Mister Cat. And even *he* wouldn't have known if not for Miss Sophia Brown. I'll never have a clue where or when she finally showed up—the important thing is that the two of them found me in my room one bright, windy afternoon, trying to get into the sari that Meena gave me to practice with. They didn't have to jump around me, or yowl meaningfully: The moment I saw that fluffy blue shadow whose feet never quite touched the floor, I was back in my jeans and out of the house, running like a maniac after the two cats, who were flashing across the courtyard, scurrying between barns and tool-sheds as though their tails were on fire. I almost knocked Ellie John over, almost stumbled into a half-dug drainage ditch, *did* crack both shins on a wheelbarrow heaped high with fresh cowshit, and swivel-hipped around Wilf's billygoat so fast he had no chance for a clear shot at me. This one time in my life, I moved the way Mister Cat's always been trying to teach me to move. I think he'd have been proud of me, if he could have been bothered to look back.

Tamsin was in Julian's potato field, of all places. Julian's got no interest in gardens, but he was experimenting to see if he could grow potatoes the size of pumpkins, which he was getting really close to before he got bored. His patch was right at the base of a hillside, with KEEP OUT notices everywhere, so the place looked like a construction site. Tamsin came drifting down that hill and through Julian's warning signs, and I never saw anything more beautiful in my life. When I dream about her today, most often that's the way I see her.

He was there, standing at the edge of the potato field, watching her come toward him. I have to say that he'd put on his Sunday best to receive her: not his judge's robes, but a long deep-red coat with absolutely dozens of little buttons, a kind of broad white cravat around his neck, and a curly brown wig that fell down past his shoulders. Gloves, too—fringed gloves, like a movie cowboy. He looked grand. He looked like a perfect match for Tamsin.

She didn't seem to be awake. I mean, her eyes were open, but it was as though she couldn't remember *sight*, or didn't want to. Something was moving her down that hillside and slowly across Julian's potato patch toward *him*—moving her like a chess piece, like a shadow puppet—and it wasn't her own will. She was lovely in a way I'd never seen her before—she might have been all those shivering, transparent Dorset twilights bent into a human shape—but she was dead twice over like this, somehow: doubly gone, both from the world and from herself. I'm saying all this now, ages later, but at the time I didn't think any of it. I just knew that she didn't look like Tamsin, and I ran.

It *is* true, that thing that happens in dreams, where you run and run harder than you ever could awake, but it's like running in water, and you can't get anywhere. I ran toward that damn potato patch, waving my arms and calling like that woman I used to see on Eighty-third Street, shouting at the cabs—and I'll swear to this day that it took me hours to get a few yards closer to Tamsin . . . Tamsin and Judge Jeffreys, him standing and smiling and waiting for her, and me yelling, "No! Don't go near him! Stay where you are, I'm coming! *Tamsin, no!*" until my voice shredded. I sounded like Julian by the time I reached his first KEEP OUT sign.

Neither of them paid the slightest bit of attention to me. Tamsin floated to a stop in the middle of the field, and they faced each other for the first time in three hundred years. Judge Jeffreys said her name— *"Tamsin Willoughby"*—just that and no more. In his mouth, in that voice like dead leaves, it sounded like a curse, like a witch's spell.

Which you could say it was, I guess, because it started her moving again. The ocean-colored eyes were completely without light, empty of any memories; and the closer she got to him, the less of her there was—she was so barely *there* that sometimes I couldn't make her out at all against the green hillside. A cobweb after rain, a breath on a freezing day—even those don't tell you how it was to see her like that. My heart hurts now, just writing this little about it, and it always will.

It hurt to see Miss Sophia Brown, too. There was a lady who could have given Mister Cat lessons in cool: nothing in this world or that one *ever* ruffled her fur, or disturbed her poise for half a second—whatever the act, she'd already caught it, she'd been to the show, thank you very much. But now she was frenzied, hysterical, looking back and forth from Judge Jeffreys to me, meowing so desperately that I almost heard her. Miss Sophia Brown was asking for help, and she was asking the wrong person.

Judge Jeffreys spoke Tamsin's name a second time. No mad laughter, no "Ha-*ha*, me proud beauty, I have you in me power at last!" Her name, nothing more, softly, but it cracked across her like a whiplash, and that ragged remnant of Tamsin Willoughby twitched toward him again. And right around there I went seriously crazy.

I threw myself between them—and that's definitely the word, because I tripped over something and fell flat in Julian's potato patch, practically at Judge Jeffreys's feet. (He wore high-heeled red boots, I remember, with big floppy red bows on them.) Judge Jeffreys didn't look at me, not even when I stumbled up and started shouting at him, "Get *away* from her! Get *away*!" I actually grabbed a rock—or maybe a potato, who remembers?—and threw it at him, catching him right below that elegant nose, bang on the mouth. Of course it went on through him and hit an old outhouse, but it's the thought that counts. I placed myself in front of Tamsin—as nearly as I could guess where she was—and I yelled, "You can't touch her! You'll have to walk over me first! Try it! Go ahead, just try it!"

Yes, I *know* people only say things like that in movies, but that's all that comes to mind when you're crazy. Me, anyway. So there I was, screaming my head off, snatching up fistfuls of stones and earth and God knows what and hurling them at the ghost of a seventeenth-century psycho with great taste in clothes. I did get his attention at last, though I can't say how: he took that savage focus off Tamsin long enough to give me another long, narrow smile. He said, "How now, girl? I cannot touch her, say you? But I *will* touch her—here, in your sight—as the wretch Edric Davies never had power to do, not with all her guiltless connivance. For I will make her a part of myself—I will make her a *sharer* in myself, intimate equal in deed and memory, until there shall remain no singular Tamsin Willoughby, but a greater Jeffreys withal, a Jeffreys enhanced, not merely possessing the object of his desire, but *including* her. See now, how 'tis accomplished. See now."

I'm slow about some things. I know I am. Meena would definitely have caught on faster than I—hell, Julian and Tony both probably would have—about the reason for Tamsin's looking so dreadfully changed, and why he hadn't needed to hunt her down. He *had* been hunting her, all these silent, motionless weeks—he'd been drawing her back to him, wherever she fled over Stourhead Farm's seven hundred acres, by the pure power of want, by the power of hating Edric Davies beyond death, beyond whatever waits for everyone as he'd waited for Tamsin Willoughby. I don't know if a ghost's ever done that—stopped the whole bureaucracy of passing on, whatever it is—right in its tracks, but it shows you what's possible if you really put your mind to it. Inspiring, actually, in a way.

And I can't believe—not now—that any ghost could do what he

was out to do: just assimilate, just *consume* another ghost, take another spirit into itself. But I don't know the rules now any better than I did then, and I don't want to know. All I'm saying is that back in that potato patch, with the sun going down and Tamsin dwindling to nothing while I looked on, I believed him. If I hadn't believed him, maybe I'd never have thought to do what I did. I've wondered a lot about that.

I caught the tiniest glimmer of a white dress out of the corner of my eye, and I turned away from *him* and called out—and there wasn't much more left of my voice than there was of Tamsin—"He gave Edric Davies to the Wild Hunt! That's what happened, that's why Edric couldn't meet you! The Wild Hunt's got him!"

Nothing happened. Nothing happened to me, anyway, though that wasn't Judge Jeffreys's fault. For one instant I saw him as he must have looked in his courtroom: not when he was foaming and raging, but right at the moment when he pronounced the death sentence. The story is that he'd get suddenly quiet—weary, almost regretful—and that's when you knew you'd had it. That's the way he was gazing at me now, as though he really would have spared me if he could. The Wild Hunt couldn't have been any more frightening than that look.

I wasn't even sure if Tamsin had heard me—if there was enough Tamsin left to hear me—so I shouted again, "It's true! I've seen him! Judge Jeffreys must have called down the Wild Hunt to take him, I don't know how. That's why you're still here—because Edric needs you! We have to save him!" I didn't mean to say *we*, it just came out.

And this time she heard. She began to back away, she began to pull against whatever was reeling her in; she began to remember her own real shape, the color of her hair and her skin and her clothes, her own texture in the world. I saw her growing Tamsin again around that last poor fragment of herself, until she was facing me, as solid looking as *him*, with her wide eyes full of what I'd just told her. She didn't speak, but she knew me. She knew us both.

Behind me Judge Jeffreys whispered, "No matter. It begins again."

"Oh, no, it doesn't," I said. I turned around to say it right into his delicate, sad, handsome face. "No, it doesn't, because she *knows* now. Finally, she knows what she's supposed to do, and she'll fight the Wild Hunt *and* you to do it. And I'm going to help her.

You'll never get near her again, not if you hang around another three hundred years. You've had your shot."

"My *shot?*" He laughed outright then, for the first time. I wonder if I'm the only person in history who ever heard Judge Jeffreys laugh. He said, "Fool, what need for me to wait another hour, when all that woman's immortal soul yearns to lose itself in mine a thousand times more than it yearns for heaven? This is the moment she was born for, and nor you nor Edric Davies, nor any multitude of devils like you will keep Tamsin Willoughby from her destiny. Behold it now."

He stretched his left arm out toward her and he beckoned. He didn't say a word, just crooked his forefinger once, smiling that sleeping-snake smile of his. Miss Sophia Brown opened her mouth for what must have been the longest, most despairing cat wail I never heard. Mister Cat pressed as close against her as he could, considering that she wasn't there, trying to comfort her. And Tamsin vanished.

For a moment my insides fell off the World Trade Center, because I thought that was it—*all over, all over*—I thought she'd merged with him, her tender ghost-light lost forever in his endless night. But then I saw the look on Judge Jeffreys's face, and I heard the wordless sound he made, and I wheezed, "Yes! Yes! *Yes!*" I scooped up Mister Cat, and I danced through that potato field with him—and I'd even have tried to pick up Miss Sophia Brown, too, but she'd disappeared the instant Tamsin did. She probably wouldn't have cared for being half-strangled and waltzed with, anyway. Mister Cat loved it.

And Judge Jeffreys came completely unglued, as though he were back in his court with a whole gang of Monmouth's rebels facing him, instead of just me and Mister Cat. It was a Rumplestiltskin fit, a Wicked Witch of the West tantrum; it was Captain Hook dithering between rage and panic, slashing the guts out of the nearest pirate at hand. "Devils, devils—devils, imps, demons and cacodemons! I am God's own, and by the holy names of Jesus and His Father, I charge you—back, back to your burning cesspools, back to your stinking pits of abomination, back to your eternal filth and vileness! Tamsin Willoughby is mine to me, and not all Hell itself shall keep us from being joined as we were destined to be joined! Not all the loathsome might of Hell shall keep me from her!"

You don't have to believe in Hell. All you need is to hear someone who really does, who believes in it this minute, today, the way people believed in 1685—all you have to do is see his face, hear his voice when he says the *word* . . . and then you know that anyone who can imagine Hell has the power to make it real for other people. I don't mean I understood any of that right then—just barely do now—but at that instant I understood Judge Jeffreys, and why I ought to be even more frightened of him, dead or alive, than I'd known to be. There's a lot to be said for never quite grasping the situation.

Then it was gone, that one flash of comprehension—and so was he, with his last words hanging in the air like the burned-out skeleton of fireworks—and I was running for the Manor, still hugging Mister Cat against my chest, knowing beyond any doubt where Tamsin had to be, and knowing that *he* knew, too.

Twenty-five

Except that we were both wrong.

She wasn't anywhere in the Manor—and by now I knew how to search that house. *He* must have been searching, too, though I never saw him. The billy-blind said he wouldn't be able to come into Roger Willoughby's secret room—anyway, that's what it had *sounded* like he was saying—but the billy-blind hadn't just seen Judge Jeffreys beckoning Tamsin to her doom, commanding her with no more magic than her name. I wasn't about to assume there was anything Judge Jeffreys couldn't do.

But there was a whole lot *I* couldn't do. I couldn't ask anyone for help—not even Meena, not with things gone this hairy—and I couldn't lurk and slide around home looking as though I were trying to rescue a ghost from a crazy ghost judge who'd somehow condemned her boyfriend to being chased across the sky forever by a howling pack of ghost huntsmen. There is no really good time or way to break something like this to sensible people like Sally and Evan and—all right—Tony. Julian was weird enough to believe me, but he was also entirely weird enough to wind up running the Wild Hunt. Master of the Hounds, or whatever. Uh-uh.

And I couldn't go to Mrs. Fallowfield, either. That was my first impulse—after all, she'd shown me what had happened to poor Edric Davies, which I'd never have found out if she hadn't let me see the Wild Hunt with her eyes. But I didn't dare assume that she was on my side, or on Tamsin's, or anyone else's but her own. The one thing I knew for sure about Mrs. Fallowfield was that I couldn't take one thing about her for granted.

I didn't tell Meena about Edric, but I did tell her about Tamsin's face-off with Judge Jeffreys. Meena was too smart to be optimistic: She knew way too much about Indian ghosts. She said, "Jenny, you must be so careful, more careful than ever. Now it's not just Tamsin—now it's personal. He will harm you if he can."

"Thanks," I said. "Exactly what I needed to hear." But Meena looked so worried that I told her, "I don't think either of us are going to see her again, him or me. I think she's broken free of him, and free of the Manor, too. I really do think that was it."

Which I didn't think for a minute, but Meena seemed to feel better, so *I* felt better. But what I knew was that this time I couldn't afford to wait for Judge Jeffreys to locate Tamsin, the way I'd been doing. This time I had to get to her before he did, and the only edge I had was that I knew Tamsin better than he did. Or I thought so, anyway, but maybe I was totally wrong about that, too—maybe I didn't, couldn't, mean any more to her than any other unreal figure in this half-dream world she'd lingered in. But I had to believe I did; and I had to believe that if dead, mad Judge Jeffreys could call Tamsin to him, so could I. I just had to find the right place and the perfect moment. And the words.

It took a while. The secret room wasn't it—I had a sense that Tamsin wouldn't ever come back to that room—and no other place in the house felt right. I was going to have to find the one spot in the seven hundred acres of Stourhead Farm where the daughter of Roger Willoughby might choose to make her stand. Because she wasn't running from Judge Jeffreys, not this time. She was going after Edric Davies—she was going to find Edric and rescue him from the Wild Hunt, whatever it took, however she could. Like I said, it took me a while to understand, but once I did, then I knew where she'd be.

A lot of stuff got in the way of my finding her, though. It's funny now, but at the time I was at least half-convinced that it was all Judge Jeffreys's doing, all the delays and distractions that landed on me together right then. School was starting again, for one thing, and there was farm work to help out with almost every day—hoeing and singling, mostly. (That was one thing about Evan's new no-till system—the weeds were crazy about it, especially thistles.) And Tony picked that time to use me again as a sort of dressmaker's dummy for some new dance; and Julian got left off his form's cricket team and tagged after me more than ever, being miserable and making mournful plans to blow up the school. I talked him down to a scheme involving piranhas in the water supply, but it was so complicated that I think he lost interest. I think.

So between one damn thing and another, it seemed a lot like forever until I was finally free to go search for Tamsin. By then I was out-and-out frantic—and unable to let *anyone* see it—because there was not only no reason why Judge Jeffreys wouldn't have thought of the same place, there was one major hell of a reason why he would have. I hadn't seen him since the shootout in the potato field, but ten angels could have sworn that he'd left town on the two-fifteen train, and I wouldn't have believed them. For all I knew, he was shadowing me this time; so there was something else driving me to that ruin of a seventeenth-century cow byre, with nothing remaining but a bald scorch mark near where the door had been. Because that was what it was, I knew it for sure now: the footprint of the Wild Hunt, called down by Judge Jeffreys to hound Edric Davies far from Tamsin Willoughby, if he survived at all. That was where they found him waiting for her, as he'd promised he would.

And that was where I went to find Tamsin, one evening after dinner, with everything anyone could possibly stick me with out of the way. Sally stopped me, all the same—I was actually opening the door when she called to me, "Take a brolly, it's going to rain."

"No, it's not," I called back. "Ellie John says it's not, and she always knows."

"Take it anyway—do me a favor." Sally came close and put her hand lightly on my arm. "Where are you off to?"

"No place special. Just walking around, to clear my head. I'll be back soon."

"You've been doing a lot of that," Sally said quietly. "Clearing your head. Is everything all right?"

I don't get great whopping visions and insights into the human condition—I don't think I'm made like that—but for one moment I did have an image of thousands, millions of mothers all over the world asking their daughters the same question at that same moment. I said, "Fine, I'm fine, really," and Sally said, "Don't be out too long, I don't care *what* Ellie John says," and I said, "Right," and I practically ran out of the house, in such a hurry that I forgot to take the umbrella. It wouldn't have helped.

Tamsin was exactly where I thought she'd be, though I couldn't make her out right away. She sat huddled like a sad little girl in what would have been a far corner of the cow byre: All there, all fully present—not like she'd been when Judge Jeffreys was dragging her into him—but so transparent that I felt I could see through her all the way to Mrs. Fallowfield's house among the elders, or all the way to the seventeenth century. . . . It was a warm night, and very still, but there was heat lightning sputtering on the horizon.

She knew me when she saw me. She said softly, "Mistress Jennifer. So you are come."

"*Jenny,*" I said. "No Mistress, no Jennifer. Just Jenny." I went and sat down next to her, I said, "Yes, I'm come. And we're going to talk about what happened on the night that Edric Davies *didn't* come for you."

Tamsin shivered—or maybe that was a breeze rising. She said, "Jenny. I know what you did. Until you called to me, I was lost, truly lost beyond your imagining. While I remember anything, I will remember—"

"Never mind that," I said. "Do you remember *what* I called? What I told you?"

She didn't reply for a few moments, and when she did, her voice was very low. "That the Wild Hunt . . . that *they* took him. Yes, I know—I know that must have happened, and who it was summoned the Huntsmen—"

I interrupted her again. "This isn't about Judge Jeffreys—I don't think so, anyway. Yes, he's a bad guy, he's a psychopath, he's the only real *monster* I've ever met, and somehow he learned how to sic the Wild Hunt on a rival like Edric Davies. But that would just have been for one night, and Edric's out there still, running the way he's been running from the Hunt, night after night for three hundred years. Do you understand me?" Because I couldn't be sure she was taking any of it in, sitting there so wide-eyed. "No way Judge Jeffreys could have done that to him—that took somebody else. Somebody with more power than Jeffreys, a kind of power Jeffreys never had in his whole rotten life. Do you understand?" Tamsin didn't move or answer me.

"I used to go nuts," I said, "drive myself absolutely crazy, trying to figure out what Judge Jeffreys could possibly have whispered to you when you were . . . you know, at the last. Then I got to wondering about *you*—if *you* maybe said something to *him.*" I waited, but she didn't say anything, so I just plunged ahead, point-blank. "Do you remember? It's really important, it might explain everything. Even a couple of words."

No answer, no sense that she was trying to remember a thing more than she wanted to. And suddenly I was really pissed at her, Tamsin or no Tamsin. I shouted at her. I said, "Damn it, you owe me a damn effort! I'm knocking myself out to help you learn the truth, even though I don't want to, because once you do learn, you'll go wherever you go, and I'll never see you again. But I'm doing it anyway, because it's the right thing for you, and I love you. Now you *think*, and you think *hard*, and you help *me* for a change!" I could have cut my tongue out, even while I was yelling, but I only stopped because of what was happening to her face.

When people write about living people facing up to something shocking, some awful memory that's just come back to them, they always have them turn pale, bloodless, or else they get weak-kneed and have to sit down, or press their hands against their mouths and start to cry. Tamsin didn't do any of that, and it wasn't that her face got twisted with horror or distorted with fear, like in books. Tamsin's face *stopped*, the way she always talked about herself stopping. I'd seen her go really still at times, but that softly pulsing ghost-light would be there, if you knew how to look. But this was different, this was something so *else* I don't think anybody's yet got the right words for it. They just call it the stillness of death.

"O, Jenny," she said. "O, Jenny."

I didn't say anything. I didn't breathe.

"O, Jenny," Tamsin said. "I cursed him. I cursed my love."

I was the one who began to tremble, the one who put her fingers to her dry, cold mouth. There was a half-moon rising behind clouds. The wind was definitely picking up, and I could smell rain. Tamsin said, "Jenny, I remember."

"Don't," I said. "Don't, you don't have to, I'm sorry."

But she didn't hear me. "I was in such despair. I so needed him to be there—to be here, where we are—and he was not, and he had sworn, sworn to me . . . And I was *frightened*, Jenny—frightened of being abandoned to Judge Jeffreys, frightened of such things as he might do to my family—and then I was sick and all a-fevered, and truly not in my proper senses. Jenny, my Jenny, I remember."

Her eyes were burning. I never knew what that meant before. She was growing more and more clear and solid—I couldn't see through her anymore. She said, "I spoke evil words against Edric. I cursed him for deserting me, and I vowed that he should wait as

I had waited, wait on forever and forever for someone who never came. Jenny, do *you* understand me now?"

"Oh, God," I said. "Oh, no wonder you forgot." My teeth were actually chattering, dumb as that sounds.

Tamsin said, "The last breath of a passing soul has such power— the power of a transient angel, of a momentary demon. . . . And I loosed it against him. It was I sent him to his eternal torment—I, not Judge Jeffreys. My doing, my doing—three hundred years." She was rocking herself slowly, like a grieving old woman.

The big, warm drops of rain were starting to fall, one at a time, but Tamsin couldn't feel them, and I didn't care about them. Of all the damn, damn things, I wanted to see Evan. Evan would think of something. I said, "I don't know what to *do*. I don't know what we can do to save him."

Tamsin smiled at me. I know I've written all over the place about the way I felt when she smiled, but this one didn't turn my heart and my insides gooey: This was a smile like Marta's, like Jake's, on my last night on West Eighty-third Street. An old friend saying good-bye.

"*Do*, Mistress Jenny?" she said. "Why, there is nothing for you to do, having aided me so far beyond my deserving. What I do now is for me."

And with that the storm broke, and the Wild Hunt came.

There wasn't a lot of rain, not like when Julian and I were caught at Mrs. Fallowfield's farmhouse. This was mostly wet wind, but it was the strongest wind I've ever been out in. It knocked me back down when I tried to stand, punching at me from every side; it slashed my hair across my face and into my eyes so it stung like mad, and it *shook* me the way I've seen Albert shake a poor little mole to bits before he tossed it up and swallowed it. I saw Tamsin's face, bright as the moon, if there had been a moon. She touched her right-hand fingers to her remembered lips, blowing me a kiss—and then she was gone, swept away by the wind like a rag snatched off a clothesline.

I screamed after her—couldn't hear myself, of course—and then did something a lot more useful, which was pushing myself to my feet. The Wild Hunt was right overhead, shrieking and banging and yammering like the D train barreling uptown, but for once I hardly paid any mind to them. I had one glimpse of Tamsin, not being driven by the wind but riding it to meet the Huntsmen, flashing like a meteor, up and out, on an angle that would intercept them somewhere over the downland. Then I lost sight of her for good, and I sank back down in total despair, because there wasn't any way for me to catch up, to be with her when she turned to deal with the Wild Hunt and fight them all for Edric Davies, if she had to. I'd always figured I *would* be there at the end, without thinking much about it, but I wasn't going to be, and I couldn't even cry about it, because of the damn wind. I *think* that's the lowest I've ever been—though I'm sure there's worse waiting, as Mrs. Fallowfield would say.

The black pony materialized slowly out of the storm, as though it were drifting up from the bottom of the sea. It looked at me out of its yellow eyes and remarked, "I had thought better of you. Slightly better."

That got me on my feet fast enough. I yelled, "Pooka!" and stumbled to him against the wind, but he backed away, shaking his shaggy head. I kept yelling, "You have to, you have to! I have to get to her!"

"Do you remember her words on the day we met?" The Pooka's voice was as calm and low as though the Wild Hunt weren't still raging over us, and his mane weren't trying to whip itself loose by the roots. "She warned you never to trust me, never to mount my back, for I would surely hurl you into a bog or a briarpatch and abandon you there. I am still what I am, Jenny Gluckstein."

I put my hands on him. I said, "I know, but I can't worry about it now. Just try to dump me someplace near where she's gone." And I grabbed his mane and scrambled aboard, not giving myself time to reconsider anything. I was braced for matted, soaking horsehair, but the Pooka's back was completely dry, even warm. I actually yelped in surprise, and the Pooka slanted one eye back at me in the usual wicked amusement. Then he took off.

I'm not a big horse person, and I never have been. I know young girls are all supposed to go through a stage of thinking about nothing but horses, but there wasn't a lot of that on West Eighty-third Street. The boys both like horses better than I do, and Meena's nuts about them—it's the only time she's ever boring, when she starts in on horses. Not me. I used to have a thing about snakes, though, when I was really young. I still like them.

But the Pooka isn't a horse. The Pooka is the Pooka, and he didn't run like a horse at all. He didn't gallop, he *bounded*, like

Mister Cat, like a lion or a cheetah, the way I've seen them on nature shows. He was in top gear around the second stride, driving off both hind legs together, with his back bowing under me, moving in great flowing leaps that melted together into a hunter's glide that felt as though it could outrun the Wild Hunt itself. I flattened myself along his neck, because the storm and his speed together would have had me on the ground in a minute if I'd tried to sit up like a real rider. It was hard to breathe: All I could do was grab onto his mane, and bury my face in it, while we tore through orchards whose branches almost raked me off his back, fields that I could only pray he wouldn't trample, pastures where sheep gaped sleepily up at us and the wind froze my fingers and pounded at my face. I knew where we were, more or less, but I was as groggy and stupid as those sheep. All I could do was hang on.

The Wild Hunt was downwind of us, their nerve-numbing howl making me want to throw myself off the Pooka's back and crawl away into the dark and wet, where they'd never find me. But each time I opened my eyes, we'd drawn closer to that terrible rainbow, because the Pooka was *traveling.* The half-moon was a crayon scrawl on the horizon, and the trees on both sides of us had blurred into a sort of grayish tunnel, but I could see the Hunt clearly—and I could see Edric Davies now, running and running in the black sky. The Huntsmen were so close behind him that it seemed to me as though they were playing with him, that they could have caught him any time they wanted to, but maybe not.

What did he look like, Tamsin's lost lover? What do you think *you'd* look like after three hundred years like his? Horrible, right. I'll tell you what's horrible. What's really horrible is that *I'd seen worse.* I see worse than Edric Davies damn near every day, and so do you—on TV, in newspaper pictures, in photographs we get so totally used to that they don't make us puke our guts out every time we look at them, the way we should. There's only so much you can do to a person, to a human body, even if you're the Wild Hunt or Judge Jeffreys. I grew up knowing that, and you probably did, too.

The Pooka said quietly, under the storm and the Huntsmen's baying, "It ends here." And I saw Tamsin directly up ahead of us, standing in a field of young corn. Her head was thrown back, her hair fallen loose—though she hadn't wasted any time remembering how it would have blown around—and she was stretching her arms up toward the Wild Hunt, and Edric Davies. She was calling, crying out words, but I couldn't hear them, because of the wind.

But the Wild Hunt heard. The riders out in front, so close on Edric Davies's heels, swung away from him, banking straight down toward Tamsin. The others followed as they caught sight of her, filling the sky with their spears and their skulls and their screaming laughter, lunging forward over their mounts' necks as if they couldn't wait to get at that small white figure in the cornfield. But she never took one step backward—she kept on beckoning, challenging them down, away from Edric to her. I was too dazed and too scared to be proud of her then, my Tamsin. But I dream that moment sometimes, these years later, and in the dream I always tell her.

Then the Pooka dumped me. Nothing dramatic about it—he just stopped dead and I shot over his head at about a hundred and fifty miles an hour, and landed on my butt in soft mud, practically at Tamsin's feet. I jumped right up, howling like the Wild Hunt myself, but the Pooka actually bowed his head to me and I shut up. He said, "Here is your friend, and here is the Wild Hunt. This is your affair, not mine. Tend to it, Jenny Gluckstein."

And he was gone, exactly that fast—I thought I spotted a frog hopping away through the cornstalks, but it was dark and crazy, and you can't ever tell with the Pooka, anyway. Tamsin hadn't turned her head for a moment, because the first of the Huntsmen had touched down, the wet earth hissing under their horses' feet. The rest were circling like stacked-up planes, coming in one by one, as they must have done when Judge Jeffreys called them to the cow byre where Edric Davies waited for Tamsin Willoughby. The corn was smoking where they trampled it, and I wondered, somewhere far off, what I'd say to Evan when nothing ever grew in this field again.

They didn't keep up their racket once they were on the ground. Even the hounds quieted down and dropped back alongside their masters, and the horses—or whatever they were—stopped foaming flames, though they kept on growling very low, meaner than the dogs. Tamsin just stood there, solid as a living woman, *smiling* as each rider dropped to earth and moved in on her. You'd have thought she was welcoming company at the front door.

I didn't know *what* the hell she had in mind, and the Wild Huntsmen were as hung up as I was. They kept advancing, but they did it slowly, fanning out a little bit, as though she were Sir Lancelot or someone, ready to leap at them and mow them down five and six at a time. I was just behind her, shaking so hard I could barely stand, watching them come on.

I'll never know who they were. Who they had been. I'll never know how you get to be a Wild Huntsman, nor if you have to be one forever. What I remember—this is weird—is their *smell*. If Tamsin smelled of vanilla, you'd have expected these guys and their beasts to smell all meaty and hairy and blood-sticky, like the lion house at the zoo. They didn't: Close to, even the worst of them, the ones with no real faces, but only a smeary collection of holes and skin and cindery snot—even those had the faintest smell of the sea, of fishing boats, and sails drying in the sun, the way you see them at Lyme Regis. Maybe they were all old pirates— who knows? The one thing I'm sure of is that I can't ever be afraid of anyone again. The Wild Hunt gave me that.

Tamsin spoke to them, proud and clear over their fearful still-ness. She said, "I take back what belongs to me. You have no claim on him, nor did you ever. The evil was mine alone, and long will I be in atoning for it. I take Edric Davies back from you now."

The Huntsmen didn't do anything. They sat their horses and stared at Tamsin, and not one head turned when Edric Davies walked between them to her side. I'd lost sight of him when the Pooka dumped me, so I'm not sure exactly where he'd been, but I can tell you that he walked as though he were afraid the planet would buck him off at any moment, back into the sky. Tamsin hadn't glanced at me once in all this time, but Edric did as he passed me; and although he looked like an entire train wreck all by himself, he winked at me! He *winked,* and I saw what it was that Tamsin had loved three centuries ago. She took her eyes off the Wild Hunt for the first time, and she and Edric stood there look-ing at each other, and they didn't say a thing. Not a hello, not a cry of pain or sympathy, no apologies—not one single word of love. They just *looked,* and if somebody ever looks at me the way the ghost of Edric Davies looked at the ghost of Tamsin Willoughby, that'll be all right. It won't happen, but at least I'll know it if I see it.

By and by, Tamsin turned her attention back to the Huntsmen. "We will go," she said, haughty as could be. "You will pursue Edric Davies no further, nor me neither. You have no power here. Go back to your home beyond the winds—go back to the bowels of the skies and trouble us no more. Hear me, you!" And she stamped forward, right at them, and swung her arms the way Sally does when she's shooing Mister Cat out of the kitchen.

For one crazy minute, I thought she was going to get away with it. The Wild Huntsmen seemed paralyzed, in a funny sort of way: They might almost have been human, ordinary Dorset people, sitting their shuffling horses in the rain, sneaking sideways peeks at each other to see if anyone had a clue about what they ought to be doing next. A couple of them even backed away, just a step, but that's how close she came. I really thought she'd make it.

Then Judge Jeffreys screamed.

Twenty-six

You wouldn't have thought that soft, scratchy voice—a dead man's voice—could make that sound. He was hanging in the air over the cornfield like some awful glowing kite, and he screamed like someone losing a leg or having a baby—there was as much pain as rage in the sound, maybe more. I couldn't even make out the words at first, simple as they were. "*Never!* They'll not walk free of me, neither of them, *never!* The Welsh bastard fell at my hand, there in the muck of the byre, which was nothing but his vile due—and I did enjoin you by certain cantrips to harry his spirit away, which was his due as well, as it ever shall be! Obey me! Living or dead, I command you yet!"

When I think about it now, I'm sure even the Wild Huntsmen must have felt anyway the least bit bewildered and pushed around, what with Tamsin running them off on one hand and now Judge Jeffreys badgering them to get after Edric Davies again. They weren't making any sound among themselves yet, but their beasts were growling and shifting, and I saw the riders who had edged away from Tamsin nudging their horses back toward her. Judge Jeffreys saw that, too.

"*No!*" he rasped, and the Huntsmen were still. That's when it struck me that he'd maybe had dealings with the Wild Hunt before Edric Davies. They *knew* each other, anyway—I'll always be sure of that much. Judge Jeffreys said, "The woman is mine, as God yet wills her to be. The Welshman is yours, as *I* mean for him. As for that one—"

He glanced over me, not at all as though I weren't there, but as though my being there was something he'd always meant to take care of and kept forgetting about. I got one last clear look at his eyes—dead as newsprint, they would have been, if not for the hatred that had been holding him together all these centuries, the way Tamsin's memories kept her who she was. All *his* memories were of pain and vengeance, and—I'm really ashamed of this—there was one moment, just one, when I felt sorry for Judge Jeffreys. I've never said that until now.

I never did find out exactly what he had in mind for me, because Tamsin cried out, "Jenny, fly, on your peril!"—and the next moment she and I and Edric Davies were abandoning ship and heading for the hills. Or for the wheatfield, as far as I could tell, because I can get lost in a phone booth. Even in daylight, even when I'm not being chased by the Wild Hunt.

And I just might actually be the only living person in England who's ever *been* chased by the Wild Hunt. They made one long sound together, like a fiery sigh of relief, and came after us, not yelling now, but silent as the Black Dog. Which was much worse, strangely, because of course I couldn't keep from looking back, and they always seemed nearer than they were. But they weren't racing through the clouds now; they were on the muddy Dorset earth, like me, and if it sucked at my skidding shoes amd made me fall twice, it slowed their horses, too. The Huntsmen may have been ghosts themselves, but those beasts were alive, wherever they came from. Maybe in the sky the wind and rain didn't touch them, but down here they were as soaked as everything else, and having to pick their way over the crops they crushed and the ditches and irrigation pipes under their feet, and they didn't like any of it. As long as the fields kept slanting uphill, I actually had a bit of an edge.

Tamsin never left my side. She could have flown on to be with Edric, even if it meant running from the Hunt with him forever, as she must have known it would. But she stayed close to me, leading me through the storm, that glimmer of hers almost bright enough to see by. Every time I stumbled, she reached out to catch me, and couldn't, but the terror in her eyes always got me back on my feet right away, yelling at her to go *on*, the way Edric was calling, "Tamsin, beloved, *hurry!*" He'd have abandoned me in a hot second, if he'd had the choice—I know that, and I can't blame him. He'd had the Wild Hunt after him for a lot longer time than I had—or Tamsin either—he knew what we were dealing with, and all he cared about was getting Tamsin the hell away from them. But she wouldn't leave me.

I don't honestly know what kind of danger I was in. They'd been ordered to get Edric back on the rails, and to bring Tamsin to Judge Jeffreys, but I'm not sure even the Huntsmen knew what he had in mind for me. But Tamsin did—I'm sure of that—and she kept driving me on when I could have lain down right there and gone straight to sleep in the rain and mud. Absolutely crazy, when you think about it: scrambling and stumbling through what people here call a real toadstrangler of a storm, with a ghost who couldn't even touch me trying to protect me from another ghost—who maybe could—and also save her ghost-boyfriend from the pack of immortal hellhounds hunting us all. But I *think* if not for her I could have wound up where Edric had been, and with no Tamsin to come and find me. I *think* so. I don't know.

I remember the maddest things about that flight; in fact, the mad stuff is about all I do remember. I'd swear I remember Tamsin singing to me, for one thing—just snatches of her sister Maria's nursery song—

"Oranges and cherries,
sweetest candleberries—
who will come and buy . . . ?"

I *know* Tamsin had us running through a deep place called Digby's Coombe—that's where I lost my shoes—and I remember Miss Sophia Brown running with us, bounding along like the Pooka, and keeping up, too. The rain was flashing through her as she ran, turning her blue-gray coat to silver.

And I couldn't tell you for certain how we reached the Alpine Meadow without crossing the wheatfield, because you can't, but we did. The name's just a joke of Evan's: It isn't alpine, and it isn't a real meadow at all—maybe it was long ago, but now it's useless to anyone short of Wilf's billygoat. It's just a huge stretch of brush and sinkholes and twisted, nameless shrubs, with a few dead cherry trees left from some Willoughby's vision of an orchard. It's a blasted heath, like in *Macbeth*, and nobody goes up there much. Evan says you could still do something with the land, but Evan always says that.

I've never gone back to the Alpine Meadow since that night. I do dream about it once in a while: me scrabbling along out there in the storm, with the rain bouncing off me like hail and the Wild Hunt on my track—sometimes they're right on top of me, sometimes not—and it's so dark that all I can see is those two lights fluttering just ahead. Tamsin and Edric, twinkling away like Tinker Bell, for God's sake. My legs are unbelievably painful, and I can't get my breath at all—it's like my lungs are full of broken glass— but Tamsin won't let me give up, so Edric won't either, even though there's no point, no hope, no damn *reason*. I'd rather breathe, I'd rather breathe than anything in the world, and those damn ghosts won't *let* me. In the dream I'm always angrier at them than I am at the Wild Hunt and Judge Jeffreys.

The Huntsmen's horses were still having trouble with the mud and gaining only slowly, if they were gaining at all. But Judge Jeffreys was on us all the way, swooping and howling, popping out of the dark so close to my face that I'd jump back and fall, and then slashing in at Tamsin or Edric when they came to me. And he was *hurting* them, though I couldn't see how. I don't know what ghosts can actually do to other ghosts, but when the light that pulsed around him even came near them, their own light would go dim for a few seconds, or whip around and flicker as though the storm wind was almost blowing them out. I was really scared to see that, really frightened that they *would* go out and leave me alone; but they always came back, bright as before. It just seemed to take a little longer each time.

The next-to-last time I fell, I tripped over one rock and turned my ankle, and my chin hit another one, or something that hard, and I didn't know where I was, or who, until I heard Tamsin saying my name. "Jenny, you must get up, Jenny, *please*," over and over, like Sally trying to rouse me for the school bus.

"Can't," I mumbled. "You go. Catch me anyway."

The Horsemen were coming on, still not making a sound themselves, but I could feel their beasts' hoofbeats, lying there. Beside me, Tamsin said, "*No*. No, they will *not* catch us, Jenny—not if you can only make one more effort. Only one more, Jenny." I didn't move. Tamsin said, "Jenny, please—I promise thee. One more."

It was the "thee" that did it, of course. She'd never called me that before. I got up with my ankle hurting and my head swimming worse than the one time Marta and Jake and I got stupid drunk on Jake's mother's Courvoisier. Tamsin was on one side of me, saying, "Oh, brave, my Jenny—only a little now," and Edric on the other. He still wasn't a bit happy about my entire existence, but he was practically polite when he growled into my ear, "Girl, for *her* sake." And I put my weight on that bad ankle, and I started on.

The one thing the storm hadn't had much of up to now was lightning and thunder. *That* all hit about the time the ground leveled off and the Wild Hunt really began gaining on us. Tamsin told me not to turn, but I twisted my head around once, and saw them in the flash, as though someone in heaven was taking pictures. The lightning made them look motionless, frozen in the moment, like the dead cherry trees, or the shrubby thicket coming up just ahead. Not Judge Jeffreys, though. He was dive-bombing us worse than ever, and he was screeching continually now. I couldn't make out all the words, but most of it was Jesus and God and the King, and Welsh traitors a stink in the nostrils of the Almighty. And Tamsin belonging to him through eternity—*that* one I got, I heard him right through the thunder. And all the while he kept smothering Tamsin and Edric's ghost-lights with his own, and every time they'd be slower coming back. Dimmer, too, now.

"Jenny, my Jenny—canst run only a little faster?" I didn't even have the breath to answer Tamsin, but I think I maybe got an extra RPM or two out of my legs. I like to think so, but probably not.

But it wasn't any good. The wind had switched around so it was blowing straight in my face, and between that and my ankle buckling with each step, we weren't even going to make that thicket before the Wild Hunt caught up with us—as though we could have hidden there for one minute. The Huntsmen had started baying at us again the moment the wind changed, which makes me think maybe they actually hunted by smell, not that it matters. They sounded different than they did in the sky: not as loud, not whooping maniacally, but *precise* now, united, calling to each other. Like the West Dorset Hounds blowing their dumb horns when the poor fox is in full sight and they're closing in.

And I couldn't run anymore. The last time I went down, it wasn't a question of getting me back on my feet, and Tamsin didn't ask me again. All she said was "Here," to Edric; and to give him credit, he didn't ever suggest that they drop me and head for the border. At least I didn't hear him say anything like that, because things were starting to slide away from me now, leaving me peaceful and sleepy, with my ankle hardly hurting at all. I did hear Tamsin say, "'Twas this place, *this*, exactly this. I am sure to my soul of it, Edric."

And Edric, with a sudden laugh that sounded very young, considering he can't have done *that* for three hundred years: "Well, dear one, you are *my* soul, so there's naught for me to do but bide with you." Miss Sophia Brown sat calmly down beside me, looked in my face and said "Prrp?" just like Mister Cat, only small and far-away. Edric was saying, "—there's no knowing or compounding her, nor there never was. She might as easily—"

Thunder and the wail of the Wild Hunt drowned the rest of it, just as Judge Jeffreys's last gobbling squall of triumph seemed to drown Edric and Tamsin's lights together. Far away as I was, numb as I was, I could *feel* them going out this time, as though a phone line between us had been cut. It hurt terribly—it hurt a lot more than my ankle—and I think I called for them. I know I tried to get up—or anyway I wanted to, but that line was down, too, and the Wild Hunt was on us. On *me*, their beasts rearing right over me on their spider legs, monkey legs, goats' hooves, hawks' claws . . . and the weird thing was that I didn't care one damn bit. Tamsin was gone, Tamsin and her Edric, and I didn't care what the hell happened to me now.

That was when I heard Mrs. Fallowfield.

Heard, not *saw*, because I was lying the wrong way, and I couldn't even raise my head, but I knew it was her. She was speaking in a slow, buzzing language that sounded like Old Dorset, but I couldn't separate any of the words from each other; and I hardly recognized her voice, the way it rang on the syllables like a hammer on a horseshoe. All around me the Huntsmen's beasts dropped down to all fours—or all eights, or whatever—and the Huntsmen got really quiet, a different quiet from the way they'd first been with Tamsin. Then they'd been puzzled, uncertain, practically embarrassed—now they were scared. Even in the state I was in, I could tell the difference.

There was another sound under Mrs. Fallowfield's voice, and it wasn't any of the Huntsmen. Or Judge Jeffreys, either—he was watching silently from one of the dead trees, wedged in the branches, a snagged kite now. The growl was so low it seemed to be coming out of the ground, and it was so cold and evil that the thunder just stopped, and the lightning shrank away, and the whole storm sort of sidled off, scuffing its feet, pretending it hadn't been doing anything. I got my elbows under me, and I dragged myself around to look at Mrs. Fallowfield.

She was something to see. No Russian hat; the long yellow-white hair she'd had bunched up under it was rippling down her back like something alive. No wool shirt, no Army boots—instead, a dark-green toga sort of thing, only with full sleeves, fitting close round her tough, skinny body. Her face was Mrs. Fallowfield's, feature for feature, but the woman wearing it wasn't Mrs. Fallowfield—not the one I knew. This face was the pale-golden color of the half-moon, and it was just as old: It looked as though it had been pounded and battered for billions of years by meteors, asteroids, I don't know what; the eyes weren't blue anymore, but black as Mister Cat, black to the bone. And even so, she was dreadfully beautiful, and she was taller than Mrs. Fallowfield, and she walked out of that thicket and toward the Wild Hunt the way queens are supposed to walk.

At her side was the thing that had growled. It was the size of the Black Dog, and it had staring red eyes like the Black Dog, but that was it for the resemblance. Nothing about it fit with a damn thing else about it: I saw long, pointed, leathery ears and a head like a huge bat, only with an alligator muzzle stuck onto it. The body was more like a big cat's body than a dog's, with the rear quarters higher than the front; but it had a sheep's woolly coat, coming away in dirty patches as though the thing were molting—and the skin underneath was pink! And I guess the moral of *that* story is, be nice to people's disgusting, yippy little dogs. You never know.

Mrs. Fallowfield—or whoever—didn't look at me. She pointed a long arm at the Wild Hunt, at each Huntsman in turn, moving on to the next only when that one lowered his eyes, until finally she was pointing straight at Judge Jeffreys. He looked right back at her—*he* didn't flinch for a minute. He had the courage of his awfulness, Judge Jeffreys had.

Mrs. Fallowfield said, "You. I know you." The Dorset sound was still there, but her whole voice was different—deep enough to be a man's voice, and with that metallic clang to it that I could feel all along my backbone. She said, "I remember."

Judge Jeffreys didn't give an inch. He answered her, gentle, almost apologetic, "I will have what is mine."

"The woman," Mrs. Fallowfield said. No expression—just those two flat words. Judge Jeffreys nodded. "The woman," Mrs. Fallowfield repeated, and this time there *was* something in the voice which would have made me a little nervous. She held her other arm away from her side, and Tamsin was standing beside her, and the first thing she did was to smile at me. And I couldn't breathe, no more than I could when we were running from the Wild Hunt.

"And the man," that voice said. Mrs. Fallowfield did something with her arm almost like something I've seen Tony do, dancing—and there was Edric Davies standing with Tamsin. As though she had somehow taken them into herself, and given them birth again—not that she could do *that*, I mean they were still ghosts . . . never mind. Maybe Meena can help me with that sentence, if I ever figure out what I was trying to say. All that mattered to me then was that Tamsin was smiling at me.

"The man belongs to *them*," Judge Jeffreys said, gesturing around at the Wild Hunt in his turn. "The woman to me." He might have been sharing out the dishes at a Chinese restaurant.

Mrs. Fallowfield's dog-bat-alligator-sheep thing growled at him, but stopped when she touched its horrid head. She looked at Judge Jeffreys for a long time, not saying anything. The night was clearing—I could see a few stars near the half-moon—but I was drenched and hurting, starting to shiver, starting to be aware of it. Tamsin saw. She started to come to me, but Mrs. Fallowfield shook her head. Edric moved closer to her, and there I was—cold *and* jealous. I'd have hugged that creature of Mrs. Fallowfield's just then, if I could have, for comfort as well as warmth. Hell, I'd have hugged a Huntsman.

Mrs. Fallowfield said to Judge Jeffreys, "I remember you. Blood and fire—soldiers in my woods. I remember."

"Ah, the great work," he answered, as proud as though he were pointing out those tarred chunks of bodies stuck up on trees, fences, steeples, housetops. "They'll not soon forget the schooling I gave them, the rabble of Dorset. I felt God's hand on my shoulder every day in that courtroom, and I knew they all deserved hanging, every last stinking, treacherous Jack Presbyter of them. And I'd have done it—aye, gladly, with my whole heart, I'd have rid King James of all of them but the one. All but *her*."

He never stopped looking at Tamsin, even though she wouldn't look back at him. Edric Davies did, though, and the hatred and horror in his face matched Judge Jeffreys's pride and maybe went it one better. Feelings like that don't die; memories like Tamsin's memory of Edric and her lost sister don't die. That's why you have ghosts.

Judge Jeffreys said, "For her I would have betrayed my post, my

King and my God—indeed, I did so in my heart, with never a second thought. That makes Tamsin Willoughby mine." I know it looks stupid, writing it down like that. But you didn't hear him, and I still do. He really would have done all that for her, you see, and done it believing he'd burn in hell forever for doing it. He *hadn't* done it, and it wouldn't have made her his anyway, but you see why he'd have figured it did. Or I saw it anyway, at the time. He was a maniac and a monster, but people don't love like that anymore. Or maybe it's only the maniacs and monsters who do. *I* don't know.

Edric Davies didn't say anything—he just moved in front of Tamsin, but she stepped past him and turned to face Mrs. Fallowfield. I remember everything she said, because they were the last words—but one—that I ever heard her speak.

"I am Tamsin Elspeth Catherine Maria Dubois Willoughby," she said. "I knew you when I was small. I was forever wandering and losing myself in your elder bushes, and your friend"—she nodded toward that patchy pink gargoyle—"would always find me."

Mrs. Fallowfield chuckled then, that coal-chute gargle I remembered from another world. "As *your* friend was aye rescuing *him*." She took her hand off the thing and gestured toward me, telling it, "Run see your deliverer, little 'un." The pink thing ignored her, thank God. I had enough troubles right then without alligator breath.

Tamsin said, "That one is my true and beloved sister. *He*"—and she smiled at Edric Davies in a way that squeezed my heart and roiled my stomach—"*he* is my love, and was delivered to the mercy of the Wild Hunt through my most grievous fault. Now I'd have him free of their torment, that I may have eternity to do penance. Of your great kindness, do for me what you may."

Word for word. I couldn't ever forget. I couldn't.

She started to say something else, but Judge Jeffreys's voice drowned her the way his ghost-light had done. "Nay, they're not yours to dispose of, those two! The Almighty rendered them both into my hands, and you dare not oppose His will!" As loudly as he spoke, he sounded practically *serene*—that's the only word I can think of. He was playing his ace, and he *knew* she couldn't match it, this old, old lady with her weird, nasty pet. Belief is really something.

Mrs. Fallowfield smiled at him. *That* was scary, because it was like the desert earth splitting into a deep dry canyon, or like seeing one of those fish that look like flat stones on the ocean bottom suddenly exploding out of the sand to gulp down a minnow and fall right back to being a stone. When she spoke, the Dorset was so thick in her voice I hardly understood a word. "Take good heed, zonny. We was here first."

I don't think Judge Jeffreys heard her much better than I did; or if he heard her right, he didn't take it in. He just gaped at her; but a sort of *whimper* came from the Wild Huntsmen, waiting where she'd ordered them to stay. Even in the darkness, I could see Mrs. Fallowfield's eyes: blacker than the Black Dog, black as deepest space. She said, "We was here when your Almighty woon't but a heap of rocks and a pool of water. We was here when woon't nothing but rocks and water. We was here when we was all there was." She smiled at Judge Jeffreys again, and that time I had to look away. I heard her say, "And you'll tell me who's to bide with me and who's to hand back? *You'll* tell *me?*"

And Judge Jeffreys lost it, lost it for good, and I'll tell you, I don't blame him. There's no way I'll ever again hear the kind of contempt—the *size* of the contempt—that was in those words. He went straight over the edge, shrieking at her, "You dare not defy, dare not challenge . . . You'll be as damned as they, hurled down with the rebel angels—hurled down, hurled down . . ." There was more, but that's all I want to write.

He was plain gibbering when he came for Tamsin and Edric Davies that last time, stooping at them like a hawk from tree-top height. I can't guess what was in his mind—he might have thought his rage would darken them, put them out, the way it had before, this time for good, before Mrs. Fallowfield could protect them. As much as I saw of him, as much as I feared him and hated him and tried to imagine him, finally I don't have any idea who he was— just *what* he was. It'll do.

Mrs. Fallowfield hardly moved. Judge Jeffreys was right over her before she raised her left hand slightly and made a sound like clearing her throat. And he . . . *froze* in the air. Or maybe he didn't freeze; maybe the air condensed or something, thickening around him so he couldn't move, ghost or no ghost. He stuck there, burning, like a firefly trapped in a spiderweb—although what he really reminded me of was the fruit that Sally cooks into lime-green Jell-O for big dinner desserts. It's always lime—I don't know why—and the bits of peaches and pears always look like tropical fish hanging motionless in the deep green sea. Except that the fish are silent, and Judge Jeffreys was still screaming his head off, though we couldn't hear him anymore.

Mrs. Fallowfield said, "I'm wearied of ye. Dudn't like ye then, wi' your soldiers—dun't like ye no better now. Off wi' ye, and dun't ye plague me and mine nivver no more. Hear."

I thought she was letting him go with a warning—not even a speeding ticket—and I was getting ready to mind, because it wasn't right, it wasn't justice, no matter who she was. But she hadn't been saying, "Hear," the way I heard it—what she really said was, *"Here."* The way you call your dog.

And the Wild Huntsmen came to her. Their monstrous beasts were actually trembling under them, actually having to be kicked and goaded toward Mrs. Fallowfield and that animal of hers, and even the most horrendous of the Huntsmen themselves were looking small and rained on. I still dream about them, like I said; but when I get awakened by the pounding of my heart, I can put myself back to sleep by remembering them then, as terrified of Mrs. Fallowfield as I was of them. And me not scared of her at all, but pissed because I thought she was going to let Judge Jeffreys off way too lightly. I can't believe it. I was really pissed at her.

Mrs. Fallowfield looked up at Judge Jeffreys for a long time without saying anything. He'd stopped his yelling and was watching her, poised helpless just above her in the flypaper night, his own ghost-light flickering like a bad bulb. I couldn't help wondering if he might be imagining what those people dragged up before him at the Bloody Assizes must have felt, waiting for him to sentence them . . . hoping, crying, praying—looking into that gentle, handsome face of his and *hoping.* Probably not. I don't think he had much imagination that way.

"Off wi' ye, then," Mrs. Fallowfield said again. "Till mebbe zomeone cares to come for ye."

She didn't seem to make any gesture this time, and I didn't hear her say anything else, but Judge Jeffreys was ready when the air turned him loose. He shot crazily backward like a toy balloon when you let go of the pinched end, growing so small so fast that it seemed as though we were racing in terror away from him. Maybe we were, in a way, Tamsin and Edric Davies and me. Not Mrs. Fallowfield.

She turned to the Wild Hunt, and she said one word. I heard it very clearly, and I'd forget it if I possibly could, but it'd be like forgetting my own name. *He* must have remembered it, too—however he learned it; he used it at least once, I'm sure of that. But I never, never, *never* will.

The Wild Hunt gave one great howl and went after Judge Jeffreys. They took off like helicopters, rising straight up into the night sky in a kind of windblown spiral; and in a weird way they made me think of children just let out of school, running and yelling for the pure unreasoning joy of making noise. But they weren't children: They were the Wild Hunt, the pitiless harriers of the dead, and they roared and wailed and laughed their skirling laughter, and blew their horns and spurred their dragony horses on, chasing that spark of desperation that had been Edric Davies for three hundred years, and was Judge Jeffreys now. It didn't matter to the Wild Hunt.

And it didn't matter to me. It should have—I know that—and it should matter now, on nights when I hear them again, the terrible Huntsmen in the wind, eternally hounding a human spirit whose only crime was being just as cruel as they. There'll never be a Tamsin Willoughby come to save Lord Chief Justice Jeffreys of Wem. Most times I go back to sleep.

Things get a little blurry here—not the things themselves, but the order they happened in. I can't remember when I finally made it up on my feet—maybe I could still hear the horns of the Wild Hunt, maybe not—but I know it was while Tamsin and Edric Davies were still there. Because it was time to say good-bye, had to be, and I didn't want to make a stupid scene. So I got up, all over mud and with my ankle giving me fits, and I limped toward them where they stood with Mrs. Fallowfield.

She was just Mrs. Fallowfield then: everything back in place, from the army boots to the cold, sharp blue eyes, to the little pink horror squirming in her coat pocket. No fur hat, though—that hair was still streaming away over her scraggy shoulders like the Milky Way. Her voice was strangely gentle when she spoke to me. She said, "Ye'll forget this, girl. Ye'll forget this all."

"No," I said. "No, don't make me—I have to remember. Please, I have to."

Mrs. Fallowfield shook her head. "And have ye meet me in the lane or the market tomorrow, and *know*? What I am—what we've seen this night, the two on us—"

"I *don't* know who you are," I practically yelled at her. "And I don't care, either!" I pointed at Tamsin, where she stood beside Edric Davies, so beautiful I could hardly stand to look at her. I said, "I don't want to forget her. I don't care about a damn thing else, but I have to remember Tamsin. Please. Whoever you are."

Mrs. Fallowfield smiled at me very slowly, showing her strong gray teeth; but when she spoke, it might have been to Tamsin, or maybe herself, but not me. "Aye, and here's first 'un, here's first on 'em. Aye, I knowed they'd be cooming along any day, the childern as wuddn't know Lady of the Elder Tree. Zo, there 'tis. No harm."

I remembered Tamsin saying—God, a hundred years ago— *"Even the Pooka steps aside when she moves."* I started in on some kind of dumb apology, but Mrs. Fallowfield had turned away and Tamsin and Edric Davies were coming to me. It was awkward with Edric—there's not a whole lot to say to someone who's been through what he'd been through, and who's now going away forever with the person who really did become your sister for a little while. I was happy she'd rescued him, and happy that her task was done, and that she wouldn't be stuck haunting the Manor anymore . . . but at the same time I hated him worse than I'd ever hated Judge Jeffreys, and that's the truth. There—I've got *that* down.

But he was all right. He said, "Tamsin has told me of all you did for us, and of what might have befallen her but for you. If I had the world to give you, we would never be quits." He smiled in a crooked, crinkly way that Tamsin must have loved at first sight— no, that sounds mean; it was a very nice smile, really. Edric Davies said, "But I have nothing, Mistress Jenny Gluckstein. I cannot promise that we will come to you at need, nor even that we will ever remember your kindness, because I do not know what waits beyond for us. I can only bless you now, with all my human heart. Nothing more."

And he was out of there. Just vanished, the way ghosts do.

Tamsin picked up Miss Sophia Brown. She came very close, and looking into my eyes, she said, "My Jenny," and then she bent her head and kissed me—here, on the left-hand corner of my mouth. And nobody knows better than I that I couldn't have felt anything, because Tamsin was a ghost—but nobody but me knows what I felt. And I'll always know.

Then she stepped back and was gone, and it was just me and Mrs. Fallowfield in the dark of the Alpine Meadow that seemed so much darker now. Me and the Old Lady of the Elder Tree, as though I gave a damn. Mrs. Fallowfield cupped my cheek in her calloused hand, and she said softly, "Forget, ye brave child. Forget."

And after that there's nothing but night—but thinning now, turning blue and silver, and I'm being carried somewhere, like a baby. First I think it's the Pooka come to get me, but it's way too bumpy a ride for the Pooka, and I can smell rubber, which I hate. When I open my eyes, it's Evan holding me, walking fast, with Sally on one side and Tony on the other, everybody shiny in rain slickers . . . or are we already in the old Jeep? If we're in the Jeep, then I'm lying with my head in Evan's lap while he drives us home, and my feet in Sally's lap. Tony keeps talking about the beating the fields have taken from the storm—he's really shocked, the way things have been battered down. Sally wants to hold me by herself, so Evan can drive more easily, but Evan says, "No, leave it, love, she's asleep," and I am.

Twenty-seven

But I didn't forget. I haven't forgotten a thing. I think that was Tamsin's doing, the reason she kissed me at the very last. I think she didn't want me to forget her, even if she doesn't remember me wherever she and Edric Davies have gone. How she did it, I won't ever know, but I'm pretty sure Mrs. Fallowfield knows she did it. I don't see much of Mrs. Fallowfield anymore; when we do meet, she's the same skinny, ageless lady in the duffel coat and the Russian hat, and she looks at me with those cold blue eyes as though she almost recognizes me from somewhere. As though she were the one who forgot.

He wasn't from Dorset, you see. Judge Jeffreys wasn't from Dorset, he didn't know about the Old Lady of the Elder Tree. Maybe things would have been different if he'd known. Maybe not.

Sally told me it was Evan who got anxious about me being out with weather coming on—he smelled it, and he was already cranking up the Jeep to start after me even before the storm hit. He wanted to go alone, because that clunker only has a canvas top, and it'll shake your teeth loose on pavement, let alone a dirt path. But Sally insisted on coming—and so did Tony, which surprises me in some kind of way even now. I asked him if he was afraid of losing his dance dummy, and he said that was exactly it. That's how you thank Tony.

Anyway, they racketed around the farm for hours, trying to figure logically where I might have gone. The Alpine Meadow was the last place they'd have thought to look; but the beasts of the Wild Hunt had left a track you couldn't miss, even in the darkness, and Evan followed it on an impulse, bucketing the Jeep up through that scrubby desolation as far as he could, until they had to get out and walk the rest of the way. Sally says they found me curled up like a baby, soaked through and sound asleep next to an elder thicket. I should have gotten pneumonia, but I didn't come down with so much as a sniffle, even though I can catch cold on e-mail. I *know* she's still wondering about that.

What's more amazing than me not catching cold, though, is how few questions anyone ever asked me about what the hell I was doing in the Alpine Meadows, and why I hadn't had the sense to come in out of the rain. I really expected Sally to put the screws to me, but she never did, and I'll always wonder if that was Evan's influence. I think Evan knows more than he wants to about the history of the Manor, and about what goes on around Stourhead Farm at night—wild geese or no. But he left it alone, and Sally pretty much did, too.

I had more trouble with Julian, who's got an incredible instinct for these things. He kept asking if I'd been with "that scary old woman," and why those prints in the dried mud and trampled cornstalks didn't really look like the Jeep's tire tracks. He stayed on the case for absolute weeks, until his hormones finally kicked in, and he abruptly discovered girls. Thank God for puberty, that's all I've got to say.

No, I've never seen Tamsin again. I really didn't expect to. What's odd is that when I dream of her—and I dream of her a lot—the dreams aren't exactly *about* Tamsin. She's *in* them, and I always know it's her, and sometimes we even talk, but she's not the *center* of the dream: That's more likely to be the Wild Hunt, or Judge Jeffreys, or even myself. And the dreams can be frightening, but they're never—I don't know . . . they're not *yearning* dreams, not dreams of loss. I'm just happy that she's there, and that's all.

I asked Meena, more than a year later, why she thought that was. Meena knows almost everything about the Alpine Meadow, except what happened to Judge Jeffreys. She'd feel bad for him; she wouldn't be able to help it. Meena doesn't need that.

Anyway, I asked her at school one day, and she answered me two days later, because that's how Meena is. "Maybe you don't have that kind of dream about Tamsin because you don't have to. Dreams are loose ends sometimes, dreams are unfinished business, but there is none of that between you and Tamsin. You are complete with her, I think—you *have* her, really, for always. You don't need to dream."

"Well, I don't *feel* like I have her," I said, "and I definitely don't feel complete. I feel like Mister Cat, still looking and looking everywhere for Miss Sophia Brown after a whole year. I feel like a whole damn *barrel* of loose ends, Meena."

"But you're not," Meena said, and she was right. I went on remembering Tamsin all the time, but not *missing* her, not always longing to be with her, the way I used to be when she was in the little secret room on the third floor of the east wing, and nobody knew but me. Mostly I've been happy thinking about her, these four years—almost five now—and pretty proud of myself, too, because she needed my help, and nobody else could have done it, and I actually didn't wimp out or screw up. And she told me I was beautiful, or anyway she said I had "all the makings of a proper beauty." I never told Meena about that, either.

The portrait of Tamsin and Judge Jeffreys is still hanging in the Restaurant, as far as I know—I don't go in there anymore. But I do go back to Tamsin's room every so often, me and Mister Cat. Once she was gone, I didn't keep it a secret, but nobody was ever much interested. Sally thinks it's cute—she calls it "Jenny's lair"—but the boys got bored, and I'm not sure Evan's been up at all. I sit in Tamsin's chair, and Mister Cat does his usual tour of the room, sniffing in corners and under the weird bedframe-trunk contrivance, because you never know. . . . But in a while he comes and jumps into my lap (a *little* stiffly now, but I don't notice it, for both our sakes), and we stay there for hours sometimes. Not doing anything, mostly not even thinking very much—we're just there, where they were for so long, even though nothing of them remains. Mister Cat's always the one who decides when it's time to go.

Stourhead Farm's doing fine. There were a couple of years, after Evan started using his no-till method, when the yield fell off a bit more than he'd expected and the Lovells started getting seriously skittish. But they picked up the third-year option anyway, and that was when things began turning around—you could probably grow pineapples and papayas in that soil now, except for one or two places where you somehow can't grow much of anything. The Lovells are so stoked on Evan that they want him to take over another dilapidated old property of theirs in Herefordshire. It's possible, I guess—Evan can get restless when he's not fixing something—but I don't think he'll do it. Sally likes it in Dorset.

And I don't know what musical Dorset would do without Sally, at this point. Dorchester and Yeovil, anyway: She's directing choirs in both places now, the last time I looked, teaching a class for accompanists at the university, still taking a few private students, and—for relaxation—playing with a *very* amateur jazz quartet now and then. She's branching out, too: This summer she's going to be handling the music for a Ben Jonson masque they're staging in Salisbury. I don't think you could get Sally out of Dorset with dynamite and a backhoe.

Like I said somewhere early on, Julian's the only one of us still home, with Tony mostly off dancing one place or another and me here at Cambridge, where Meena's *supposed* to be. Meena's back in India, for God's sake, working with a group that arranges loans for village women to start their own businesses. Mr. and Mrs. Chari are being good about it, but they're not a bit happy, and she's promised to come back sometime soon and go be a brain surgeon. I miss her a lot, in all the ways I don't really miss Tamsin. We send a lot of e-mail back and forth, when she can get to a computer, which isn't too often. I'm going to India to see her next Christmas.

I'm at Cambridge, reading English history, to absolutely everyone's surprise but my own. Because I was *part* of English history for a while, in a strange way, and it was part of me. It picked me up by the neck and shook me, and it scared the living hell out of me, but it kissed me, too. And afterward, after everything, I couldn't stop wanting to know more. About Tamsin's time first, of course; but then I started working backward, and my grades took off like the Wild Hunt, and here I am in Cambridge, biking to lectures, meeting with my tutor, sharing digs with a girl from Uganda named Patricia Mofolo, and feeling like somebody in an English novel. And there's a boy—or I think there's starting to be one—but that's my business. I get enough static from Julian as it is.

But I still feel like loose ends sometimes. Not a barrel, but close enough. It's not just remembering Tamsin—it's that world I got a glimpse of *because* of Tamsin: That night world where the Black Dog still walks the roads, and the billy-blind waits for someone to give advice to, and the Oakmen brood in the Hundred-Acre Wood over whatever it is Oakmen brood over. That world of moonlight and cold shadows where the Pooka is king and little creatures giggle under my bathtub. It's gone with Tamsin, completely, and I wish I had it back. I don't want *her* back, honestly—I know she's where she should be—but that other, that night place, yes. The Wild Hunt doesn't ever pass over Cambridge.

But you never know. I saw the Pooka the last time I went home. It was late spring, and I'd sneaked back to Dorset for the weekend to hear Sally's Sherborne choir, and to inspect Julian's newest girlfriend. He has terrible taste in women, but this one isn't too bad. Her name is Diana, but that's not her fault, and she obviously thinks Julian's the ultimate end of evolution, which he is *not,* and it's going to make him even more impossible than he already is. But he's my baby brother, and I like any idiot who treats him like the end result of evolution.

The night before I left was practically warm, and I went for a walk with Evan and Sally—just a slow stroll to nowhere special, talking about the farm and the choir and Cambridge, and a bit about Diana, and not at all about the boy I'm sort of seeing. Sally asked, "Did you ever think, back on West Eighty-third . . . ?" and Evan said, "I might try a few fruit trees in the Alpine Meadow next year," and I told them about the time Norris sang in Cambridge and hung around for a couple of days afterward. He took Patricia and me out to dinner at Midsummer House every night, made a mild pass at Patricia once, when I was in the loo, and whisked off to sing in Dublin. He was very good about not calling me Jennifer.

Evan and Sally went back to the Manor after a while, making their usual running joke of warning me to come in if it started storming. I stood watching them walk away with their arms lightly around each other's waists and Evan reassuring Sally that nobody noticed the soloist going flat during the Handel oratorio. When they were out of sight, I turned and wandered down the tractor path to check on Tamsin's row of ancient beech trees. I always do that when I'm home, even though I know Evan won't cut them until he really has to. I see Tamsin best there, for some reason, talking to them, dancing with them, laughing like a little girl. It's just something I do.

The trees hadn't changed. They're as huge and three-quarters dead as ever, and I'm not easy with them by myself. They tolerated me when I was with Tamsin; now they feel . . . not menacing, not like the Hundred-Acre Wood, but completely unwelcoming. But I can't not go there, even though I never stay long, because that's where I hear Tamsin's voice most clearly, saying, "Still holding to Stourhead earth, they and I." With her gone, I think they'll start to fall soon. She gave them permission.

I was turning away when my foot bumped against something,

and I glanced down to see a hedgehog. They're all over the place at Stourhead: grayish-brownish, with silver-tipped spines, about the size of a kazoo, and totally unafraid of people. This one looked up at me with angled yellow eyes and said, "Pick me up, Jenny Gluckstein."

"Fat chance," I said. "I'd be picking those fishhooks out of my hands for a week. I know you."

"Pick me up," the hedgehog repeated, and after a moment I did, because what the hell. The Pooka kept his spines down—they felt like rough silk tickling my skin—and studied me the way my tutor does when he's not quite sure I'm ever going to get a grip on the Corn Laws. He said, "You have grown, Jenny Gluckstein."

I blushed blotchy, sweaty hot, the way I hardly ever do anymore. "Well, I didn't have a lot of choice," I answered. "Hang around with ghosts and boggarts and the Wild Hunt—"

"And the Old Lady of the Elder Tree," the Pooka said. "You are fortunate beyond your imagining. She cares even less for humans than I, but she will take a fancy to this one or that betimes. Not all can endure her regard as you did." He curled up in my palm, the way hedgehogs will do. "And none see her truly, as you saw her, without growing greater or shrinking quite small. You have done well."

"I miss her," I said. "I miss you. I miss those nasty little monsters Mister Cat used to fight with at night. I don't mean *miss*, exactly, it doesn't keep me awake. . . . I mean, I wish there were pookas and Black Dogs and whatnot around Cambridge, that's what I wish. Or London, or New York, or wherever I'm going to wind up doing whatever I'm going to wind up doing. Somehow, I've developed some kind of nutsy taste for . . . for old weirdness, I guess you'd say. *That's* what I miss, and I don't think I'll ever meet up with it again. Unless I spend my life in Dorset, or someplace like that, where the nights are still different—still *dark*. But I can't do that, so I don't know. I just *miss*, that's all."

The Pooka didn't say anything. I started walking away from the beeches, back toward the Manor, but the Pooka didn't move in my hand. He didn't direct me to go this way or that, or to put him down, so I kept going along until I heard Sally playing the piano, singing "What Shall a Young Lassie Do with an Old Man?" and Evan singing with her. Then I stopped, and listened, and waited.

"Jenny Gluckstein," the Pooka said at last, "mystery belongs to mystery, not to Dorset or London. You are yourself as much a riddle as any you will ever encounter, and so you will always draw riddles to you, wherever you may be. If there should be a boggart in New York, he will find your house, I assure you, as any pooka in London will know your name. You will never be further from—what did you call it?—*old weirdness* than you are at this moment. And on that you may have my word."

"Thank you," I said. "*Thank* you," and I actually bent to kiss him, but his spines came up with a mean whisper, and I backed off. Then I said, "But a pooka's word isn't good for much. Pookas lie. Tamsin told me."

The Pooka kept his back spines up, but hedgehogs don't have any on their bellies, so my hand was all right. "True enough, Jenny Gluckstein. Pookas lie as humans lie, but not to hide the truth. Never that."

"No?" I said. "Silly me. I thought that was why everyone lied. Human or anything else."

"Of course not," the yellow-eyed little creature in my hand said. "Only humans would lie for so drab a reason. Pookas lie for pleasure, for the pure joy of deception, and so do all your other old weirdnesses—all those night friends you pine for now. Remember that in London."

"Yes," I said. I felt tears in my eyes, without knowing why. I said, "I'll remember."

"Yet sometimes we tell the truth," the Pooka added, "for very delight in confusion. Remember that, too. Set me down here."

We were near Evan's swing, which was stirring very slightly in the night breeze, like Mister Cat's sides when he sleeps. I stooped to put the hedgehog on the ground, but it rose through my hands in the form of a tall gray bird—some kind of heron, I think—and circled over me once before it flew off, away from the light. I thought I heard it say some last thing that ended with my name, but that's probably just because I wanted to hear it so. I stood there for a while, and then I walked the rest of the way to the Manor, because I had to finish packing and get moving early.